The Princely Quests
of
Sophie Wölf

BERNARD M LYONS

The Saga of Sophie Wölf: Book 2.
The Princely Quests Of Sophie Wölf
Copyright: © 2023 Bernard M Lyons.
All rights reserved.
Bernard M Lyons has asserted his rights under the Copyright, Designs
and Patents Act, 1988 to be identified as the owner of this work.
E Book ISBN: 978-0-6459435-2-8
Print ISBN: 978-0-6459435-3-5
First Published in 2023.
First Edition 2023.
Version 1:0.
Assassinus Publishing Pty Ltd
Developmental editor: Amy Allworden/ Proofreader: Belle
Manuel / Beta Readers: Eloise Lyons, Amber L, Jinx Moreland,
Kaylee Hayn, Jessica Posey, Stephanie H

Contact the author at BernardMLyons@gmail.com

For Eloise and Kaori

1. The Grand Magistry of European Mages

Sophie glanced at the face of the man standing out the front of the office building. Neat, clipped moustache, pressed white shirt and black tie, combined with an immaculate dark grey, fitted, pinstriped suit. His light complexion and dark hair, like Sophie's, though she sported a cobalt blue streak in her otherwise uniform jet-black bob.

"Sophie, old girl, good to see you!" Rupert smiled.

"Hi, Rupert." The fact that she had to work with her mama, who had abandoned her to go overseas and ignored her for years was *still* frustrating. It was the fact her mama both used the physical form of a British gentleman and spoke in the clipped mannerisms of the 1940s that she was still getting used to.

It was late at night; Sophie could see the haze of her breath in the chill. She adjusted the scarf, bringing it higher and tighter around her neck.

"You came by scooter? I'm staying nearby."

"Yes, my Vespa. There's a portal near here," Sophie replied.

They were in the office districts of Hannover, the Duchy of Lower Saxony. The glass doors of the building silently opened, closing behind them as they walked in to the impressive, shiny new office building together.

Rupert tucked his head in to Sophie's. "I'm warning you, there will be many good people here, but some of these mages would do anything to get the spell knowledge you have. Be careful."

Sophie felt compelled to nod, in response to the seriousness of the warning. They walked towards the lifts, past the concierge desk. Rupert nodded to a guard at the desk. They walked over to the lift doors; waiting as Rupert's fingers stabbed repeatedly at the illuminated red up arrow.

"You know, I wouldn't mind you reverting to your original form occasionally," Sophie said. They both got in the lift, and it rose silently through the building.

"Well, I suppose, old girl." Rupert slipped the *Ring of Gender* off his hand. There was a quick blue blur as the spell effect dissipated, and he reverted to the brown-haired, natural form of Anastasia Wolf, talented court mage and mother of Sophie.

"So… this big meeting, it sounds like the United Nations of Mages?" Sophie asked.

"Perhaps, more like a *European Union for Mages*. Well, before Brexit."

"And you're sure it's okay I'm here?"

Anastasia nodded. "Yes, I can have you on my table representing England. I want you here. You'll learn, and you may make some contacts. This is a big event, it's something that only select mages get to be part of."

"What will they talk about?" Sophie glanced up at her.

"They normally have various business to raise and discuss. But now, it's about the Hanseatic League, the Hansa. The Hansa of course hate mages, and they are incorporating more countries into the League, and when they do it's bad for mages. It's the current topic that has everyone on edge."

"Yeah, I know about the Hansa."

Anastasia/Rupert went to say something else, but pointed to the doors of the lift opening. She slipped the ring back on to her finger and returned to her male form once again. Sophie noticed the slight smile, relaxed posture. She was suspecting her mama was almost more comfortable looking like a man.

The door opened and a man in a suit with red hair and a dark beard, a late-night office worker, stepped into the lift. He glanced at Sophie quickly with tired glazed eyes. Sophie was surprised there were still people working this late.

"It's weird. You as an old British guy," Sophie said.

"But necessary for the good of the realm. It's method acting. I need to play a part. If I keep that form, I can do an Olivier level performance, with consistency."

"Olivia? Like that actor lady in Grease?"

Rupert looked surprised at the mix up. "Lord Olivier and Olivia Newton John…oh never mind."

"Sometimes I want a mama that looks like a mama."

"Sorry, old girl."

"You can pay for my therapy…"

The doors opened, and the office worker got out, turning about as he glanced over his shoulder at them, a harried look on his face. He scuttled away, not quite fast enough to break into a jog.

The lift doors closed once again, then re-opened at the fourth level, which the signs showed was a large conference room.

Coming out of the lift, there was a long corridor, red carpeted with scarlet walls ending in a purple door. Two barrel-chested burly men stood in front of it, solid as statues. Stony expressions, their jaws could have been carved from granite.

"Hello, my good fellow, we're here for the European mages meeting. Through here, is it?" Rupert pointed at the door. The men didn't react or budge, but simply remained in front of the door, blocking it.

"Oh, I forgot, here forgive me." Rupert took out a coin. The man on the left reached into his coat slowly and deliberately, all the while eyeing Sophie and Rupert. He took out some glasses, Sophie automatically recognised the ancient wooden frames with the bulky glass lenses. These were *glasses of true sight* the same as those possessed by her friend Harlan. The guard scanned Sophie, the bland look remaining on his face, and looked over at Rupert.

Sophie smiled; his expression quickly changed to surprise, as he looked Rupert up and down. The glasses could see people's true form and could detect if something were magic. He regained his staid look, still studying Rupert curiously, his enormous hands reached out and his big thick fingers engulfed the coin. He opened the door without a word.

Walking down another corridor past several more obvious security men, they continued until they came to two gigantic doors. She recognised a slight nervous flutter in her chest, tamed by a desire to see all the mages. It would be more mages than she had ever seen in her life, important, powerful mages from all over Europe.

Standing in front of them stood two women, casually chatting, both in pinstriped suits. A mid-50's lady with grey hair, neatly cut in a bob, and another younger lady with long blonde hair.

"Bonjour, Lord Rupert," the older lady greeted him. She looked inquisitively at Sophie. "I am Mathilde, from the Norman Druids. And you are?"

Rupert smiled and gave her a kiss on each cheek.

"This is Sophie, err, from Bamberg," Rupert quickly introduced her. The younger blonde lady leaned in to get an introduction, but he strategically kept moving. "Is the meeting this way?" he said, turning away from them, then leant towards Sophie. "Stick with me and be careful."

The doors parted to reveal a sight that Sophie had spent some time trying to imagine, but her efforts had not done it justice. She took a big breath, and bit down on her lip to avoid making an excited yelp.

Sophie was right, it did look like a United Nations meeting, like she had seen on the news. There were tables arranged in a circle, with four people sitting at each. In front of each person was the name of a country, and a flag. They had filled the tables with little name tags and flags. Sophie could see the German countries, the French-speaking countries were there as well as England, Scotland, and Wales. Oddly, there were tables missing for certain countries. Sophie frowned, trying to work out why, but then realised they were tables for states that are now part of the Hanseatic league, *The Hansa*. Of course, the Hansa hated mages. There were no mages left in any of those countries.

Rupert led Sophie over to a table with a nameplate which simply said *England* and four seats. Sophie knew her father was here representing England, as the Royal Court Mage; it surprised her to see someone else here, a man sitting by himself. He was a man in his sixties, balding, chubby, an aloof look on his face. She recognised him after a few seconds, and a shudder ran down her spine.

She tried to keep the look of disgust off her face.

It was Roderick Livingstone, the Grand Archmage of the London Illusionists. Sophie had previously encountered him in London when she and her friends had snuck into their headquarters. He'd tried to detain them, but they'd got away via a nearby portal. He was the pompous the old guard of the non-dreamscaping mages, those who had largely lost their abilities to do greater magic. Some of the traditional mages bristled at the sight of the mages like Sophie that had accessed magic through the Dreamscape technology. The technology enabled Sophie and the other dreamscaping mages, to meet their ancestors via their encoded memories in their DNA and study a large range of previously lost ancestral arts. Word had travelled like a contagious plague amongst the mages, about the child dreamscaping mages of Bamberg.

"You're that man that tried to lock us up in London. You tried your pathetic little card tricks on us. You were lucky I didn't fireball your butt."

Livingstone looked at Sophie. His eyes widened, shifting back in the seat, clearly unimpressed.

Sophie nudged Rupert, nodding towards Livingstone, and gave him a querying look.

"Why is he even here?" Sophie said.

Rupert was still smiling at the expression on Livingstone's face.

"Livingstone and I are both here representing England. Sometimes there's a druid as well."

Rupert took the seat at the table, a little cross of St George flag, evidently representing England, with Livingstone. As she sat down, another man came and sat down next to Livingstone. The man had blond hair and to Sophie was a lot more interesting than his fellow illusionist colleague. He was early twenties, quite beautiful, with thin features. His yellow-blond hair hung over his eyes, to the point she couldn't really see them. It was strange; his hair vaguely reminded her of an anime character.

"I am Zha," the blond man said, leaning over to introduce himself, "Archmage, London Illusionists."

"Sophie… errr… Bamberg."

Sophie felt odd sitting at a table for England, she looked around the room, and noticed there was a table for the Principality of Bavaria. If anywhere, she should be sitting there.

"My card. If you're ever in London, call me. Maybe we could swap notes on casting?" Zha handed his business card. He had a warm voice; Sophie immediately felt intrigued by him.

Rupert tried to intercept. "I wouldn't take that card."

Sophie slapped his hand away, taking it. "You lost the right to give me orders when you left. Papa and Hisako are my parents."

Rupert, for once, looked chagrined. He bit his lip, his hand retracting off the table to sit on his lap.

An older, thin, bald man in a suit came over and handed another card to Sophie, elegantly. The card said "Helga Graf, Illusionist". He pointed to a table, where a pretty lady with medium length boyish black hair and pale blue eyes smiled at her. She had a white matching suit, and patted a matching furry white cat in her arm, which matched.

"She's from the Munich Illusionists." Rupert leaned in, so Livingstone couldn't hear.

Sophie glanced at the card and smiled back at her.

As they waited, all sorts of people filled the room, chatting, some energetically. It was fascinating for Sophie; it was the first time she had seen so many of her own kind, even though they weren't dreamscapers. Grand robes adorned small clusters of mages chatting. Tall furry hats adorned others, some carried ornate, decorated staffs. Many of them dressed in smart suits, others wore T-shirts and trendy ripped jeans. Raised, frustrated voices in a large group, huddled together, indicated to Sophie that all was not right.

A woman at the centre of the table stood up, she waved her hand, at which the noise dropped off.

"Hello everyone. As most of you know, I'm Francoise Tormonaise, the new chair. I'd like to thank you all for coming to this extra special meeting. I can see we have all countries represented...well... except for those that have gone off to join the Hansa." Sophie noticed, when she said *Hansa,* there was disdain or perhaps sadness, in her voice. The crowd reacted with mutterings and a few loud words, some jeering. Not surprisingly, the *mage-hating* Hansa were not popular in this room.

Francoise. She held herself proud and spoke with authority. People's attention was transfixed on her. Sophie was impressed, hearing her speak to the room and the way people reacted. She imagined, one day in the far future, she would like to do that role.

The fact the dreamcasting mages' magic was strong might one day help them. They needed more representation here. Though she didn't know if there would be resistance to the more powerful dreamscaping mages getting involved from the envious old schoolers.

"Our first item is the new laws here in Lower Saxony."

A man in a red hoodie and torn blue jeans immediately stood up. "I'd like to know why this is the first item. The new laws haven't passed yet. They may never get made."

Francoise spoke. "Konrad, I have it on good authority the laws *will* be made and *will* make magic illegal in Lower Saxony. Mages that remain here will be jailed." She paused, seemingly to let the news sink in.

There was a slight uproar, though others in the room laughed, evidently scoffing at the idea. Murmurs, frightened voices, the odd curse. Sophie picked up an Italian swear word she had heard her Genoese friend Raffaella use.

It was the steady march of the Hansa Rupert had spoken about. They would use their powers to make mages illegal in a nation, normally as part of that country either joining the Hanseatic league or receiving trade benefits. She had read about the Hansa before. Careful negotiations would result in the banning of mages. The offering of money and subtle impositions, all as part of a neat subtly threatening package.

Unfortunately, the rights of mages were low down any country's list, compared to the advantages of being part of the Hanseatic League. The Hansa had a powerful trade block, and military.

"What are we going to do to stop it?" a mage from the Slovakian table called out.

Francoise spoke. "Nothing. It's too late for Lower Saxony. But you can stop it in your own countries."

"What about Dieter and Hans?" The Slovakian representative pointed to a table, with the Lower Saxony sign on it.

A blond man stood up at the table, his name badge identifying him as *Dieter Bruhommer.*

"It's too late for us, for Saxony. As Francoise said, the law is supposed to be debated in parliament before it goes up, but our sources tell us it's going through, seven days from now. Nothing will stop it. We are packing and going to the Rhine Palatinate."

"All…all the mages here are leaving?" an older, red-haired lady at the back of the room called out.

"All we can do… is get out. Otherwise, we'll end up in jail. Or worse, extradited to the Hansa."

There were some raised voices, and cries of surprise with the mention of "extradited to the Hansa."

Livingstone turned to Rupert. "This would never happen in England. It's inhumane. We would never join the Hansa."

Rupert nodded. "Let's hope so."

A bald man in a black suit rushed up and whispered into Francoise's ear. Sophie noticed a look of surprise flash across her face, for an instant.

"The police are here." Sophie noticed how firm her voice was, suppressing the desire for alarm. "They are coming up the elevator, and armed. We've not done anything illegal, but it's best to be cautious and get out of here now. Please remain calm and move to the stairwell, we need to get you back to your home countries."

There were instant raised voices, as various mages stood, grabbed their possessions, and made for the stairs, the thud of chairs hitting the carpet as people pushed them aside in the rush to get out.

"I'll help security; I can hold them off." Sophie called out.

"No old girl, you can't be doing that, you're coming with me." Rupert said, Sophie heard the protective tone in his voice.

"I'm not. And I told you, don't give me orders."

Rupert's face screwed up in exasperation, then he looked around. "Ok, I'll come with you."

People were running for the stairs; Sophie could hear Francoise yelling out to people not to panic. Sophie sprinted to the other door, where the security was. She knew she had to stall the police.

As they turned the corner, the security men were piling chairs and tables up against the doors. Sophie could feel the adrenaline pumping through her body. She took a deep breath and tried to remain calm.

She turned to Rupert, looking back at the fleeing crowd. The mass of mages was crowding into the stairwell. "What the? Why aren't they helping?"

"Sophie, none of the old mages know any powerful magic, they are all influential magic, court magic, cantrips, minor illusions. Your dreamscape mages know the older powerful magic."

"Yeah... I know... but... some of them may be able to do something. At least try."

Rupert looked at her and shook his head.

"Hey, we need help!" Sophie called out at the crowd. "We can hold them here in the doorway while the others get out."

"Yes, get back here, help you lot!" Rupert yelled at the top of his voice.

Sophie wasn't sure whose plea made the most impact, but about ten mages did run over and stood by them as a delaying force. One, a tall black man patted Sophie on the shoulder, his smile reassuring while his eyes betrayed concern, flicked left and right. Sophie felt frustrated at how few mages there were with her. The steady thud of the police smashing on the door was terrifying, but she knew she had to keep calm. She wasn't going to let them put her in jail simply for being a mage. She had family and friends to get back to in Bamberg.

She quickly ran the six spells, the cantrips and minor curses through her mind, thinking of her go to spells for combat like this.

The police were calling out something, but Sophie couldn't quite make out what they were saying from behind the barricaded doors. Cracks appeared in the wood; the police wrenched off the hinges. Sophie ducked and watched a chunk of wood spring off and shoot past her through the air, crashing onto the floor and skidding into a wall. All Sophie could think was that if she threw enough sleep spells and enough of Baldrick's Bolt of lightning at them, the police would back off and not come through the door.

She realised she needed to buy as much time for people to get out as she could.

The doors collapsed onto the chairs and a wall of police appeared. It was a mass of black uniforms, riot shields and helmets, truncheons waving above their heads wildly. They looked through the gap cautiously, then started clambering over the rough pile of broken doors, chairs, and tables. Sophie's heart sank. She certainly would not kill anyone or burn the building. However, had to stall them, get her and Rupert away, and delay for the others.

Her hands flicked through the air, drawing out the much-practiced glyph for *Arcturiouses Spell of Sleeping*. She could feel plenty of mana in her body, the essential energy needed for magic, as she hadn't casted for a couple of days. As she drew the glyph in front of her hand, the energy tingled in her forearms. The warm, vibrant energy then drifted down, filling her hands and fingers with a soft glowing feeling. The sleep glyph, three vertical lines and a horizontal was simple to do and she could get off three spells in quick succession. A trio of police crumpled to the ground.

She saw one of the police aim a chunky-looking gun and fired at their direction, with a loud bang. Sophie could see the projectile coming towards her, but with no time to react. The projectile stopped in front of her body, half a metre from her and hung suspended in air.

Rupert intercepted it with his one spell. Shield... *Forgen.*

The silver metal projectile sat suspended in the air for a second or two, smoke trailing behind it like a smoky wake in water, as though grabbed by an invisible hand in the air. It dissipated as the spell moved it from the front of her, to behind her body. It flew off and hit the wall. Luckily, there was no one in between.

It was a grenade, and gas was pouring out of it. Sophie, jumped over in an instant, picked it up and hurled it back at the police. She shook her hand; looking at her fingertips, they were slightly burnt from the hot metal. The police stepped back from it as it landed amongst them. They wore gas masks; but the smoke billowing out of it obscured the intertwined mess of police amongst the barricade of chairs and tables as they clambered over them.

The security men started throwing chairs at the police, one big guy laughing as he did. He turned to see the mages there and yelled at them in an English accent as he threw a table.

"Get out you lot, get to the bloody stairwell!"

It heartened Sophie that they had bravely stayed behind. Her hands flourished through the air, as she cast two more sleep spells.

"I think it's time we depart old girl." Rupert had her wrist, dragging on it, pulling her away. Sophie cast a final lightning bolt, which thudded into the mess of furniture and police, sending sparks and smoke into the air, and halting the police. Rupert and Sophie sprinted for the stairs. After a pause, the police clambered past the doorway, following.

When they got to the stairs, there was one mage waiting. His hands were in front of him, a glowing green glyph floating two centimetres off his hand. Sophie recognised the glyph; it was an earth elemental spell. They ran past him and didn't look back.

As they reached the bottom of the stairwell, they could see the crowd was all clogged in the bottom of the stairs, people shoving and pushing, all trying to get through. It was a mess.

Rupert nodded at the crowd. "There's a portal – an obelisk in the basement. They are all trying to get to it. It's going to take too long, quick this way." Sophie saw a fire extinguisher on the wall, she instantly thought of a scene from an action movie she had scene where someone had thrown it through a window to get out. She pulled it off the wall, moved some people away from the window, raised it above her head with two hands, and tossed it with all her strength. Glass smashed everywhere; the extinguisher flew through the air, tumbling into the dark. Rupert looked a bit surprised, then smiled, before looking out the now broken window.

Sophie looked back at the people crushed together in the stairwell. "There's no time, follow us!"

They jumped out of the window, dropping down the one floor, both rolling on the ground. Some of the other mages saw them, triggering a flurry of mages who flopped and tumbled out of the window in a clumsy fashion.

They started moving down the side of the building towards the front of the building, but Sophie could see the police were there. She followed Rupert, who had tucked into a wall of low shrubs that ran along the length of the office block, peering back she saw the other mages following do the same. They stopped when they ran out of hedge. Ahead of them was a parking lot, crowded with police and their vehicles, the lights on top flashing blue and red.

"Quick, over the fence!" Sophie called out. This side of the office block was next to a row of private houses. Rupert glanced at her and nodded. They both hopped over, landing in the backyard of someone's house. They sprinted through, going past a big pool and some children's swings. Some of the other mages followed.

"Quick, quick!" Rupert called, not even glancing back.

They ran through another backyard, and another.

They landed in a grassy backyard with a children's swing, and then in a laneway. Once in the laneway, Sophie could see Rupert spinning around, trying to get his bearings. They had collected five mages now, who were following them, clearly confused.

"Listen you lot, we are making for where I am staying tonight. It will be safe."

As soon as he spokes a police car turned the corner, flashing its lights.

"Over this fence, quick!" Rupert threw himself on the wooden fence, clambering over, leaving the laneway behind them.

As they hopped the fence and moved into a new backyard, the police car pulled up behind them. The bright white spot beams flashing through the wooden fence palings like the daylight through venetian blinds.

The police were scaling the fence behind them.

Rupert was scanning around, at the buildings; he was aiming for slightly larger two-story house. He called back over his shoulder. "The house there, with the flagpole. We're almost there, hurry."

They made it to a brick wall. It was substantially higher than the others they had scarpered across. Rupert cupping his hands, and starting to heave people over as they scrambled up. Sophie scaled the wall as the police arrived, and then tumbled into a rather ornate garden in the backyard of an impressive, two story, old red brick building.

She glanced up at the top of the brick wall, and a lone police officer's head and arms appeared at the top of the brick wall, just after them.

"Stop!" he called out.

She looked around her. The mages stood frozen, standing staring at him. She realised they could probably take a lone police officer, but seconds later, a second and a third officer appeared at the top of the fence. Rupert was standing still, facing to the police officer. She wasn't sure what to do.

The officer jumped down, into the backyard with them, scanning all of them, squinting.

"You're all Mages. You're all under arrest, under the new powers of the Magic Crimes act."

"It's not law yet," Rupert said.

The officer nodded. "It was passed through the Lower Saxony parliament today. It became law two hours ago. Any mage, or anyone consorting with mages, can be arrested."

Rupert shook his head slightly, scowling. "Damn sneaky fellow, aren't you? You moved it ahead so you could do mass arrests of the mages, you knew we'd be holding our council meeting here."

More clambered over the fence. There were six police officers there now, black uniforms, shiny badges reflecting the little light present in the backyard. They started to place themselves around Sophie, Rupert and the four other mages... Sophie noticed they had taken out their handcuffs but held them low, so they weren't obvious.

Rupert was looking up at the house, and the scowl lifted off his face, to be replaced by an odd, subtle smile.

"Officers, I'm afraid our presence here has got your hopes up, because while it's law in Lower Saxony, it's not law in England."

The officer looked confused. "How is that relevant?"

"Because, officer, you jumped the fence into English Sovereign territory." Rupert's hand spun in the air, a quick flourish, terminating with a gesture at a flagpole, flying a white flag with a red cross above the roof of the house. "You'll need to quickly go back over the fence. This is the English Embassy."

A look of confusion spread across the officer's face, he stared up at the white flag with the red cross, flying above the house.

He stared at the flag for what must have been thirty seconds. A long thirty seconds.

He then looked at the house, looked around, and then at the other officers. His face quickly turned into a sneer, and then anger. At that point, a door opened from the house, and a man appeared. He was older, long golden hair and a well-manicured beard, and a red nose perhaps Sophie thought, indicated he was a regular drinker. His eyes squinted, like he had just woken up.

"Rupert, what is going on here?"

Rupert smiled. "Oh, hello *Ambassador*." Sophie noticed he clearly was emphasizing the word for the sake of the police. "*Ambassador*, there are some police here, but they can't stay unfortunately."

The police looked at each other, with a combination of frustration and confusion, they filed out along the path to the front of the embassy where they left the property.

Sophie breathed a huge sigh of relief.

"Well, anyone for some tea? Or perhaps something stronger?" The ambassador looked at them and smiled.

***

The inside of the embassy was filled with traditional wooden furniture, and some nice royal blue velvet curtains framing some colourful stained-glass windows. There was a framed picture of the King of England with the ambassador, both drinking beer and smiling on the wall. Rupert sat with Sophie chatting to the ambassador, the other four mages sat chatting to themselves and drinking tea, seemingly happy to be away from the police and the fracas of the meeting.

Sophie pondered her circumstance. The whole banning of magic issue in Lower Saxony made her think only of getting back to the safety of Bamberg, and be with her papa, Hisako, Harlan, and her friends. She thought about the mages in Lower Saxony, how they would pack their bags to leave if they hadn't already gone, and what that must be like. She needed to get back to Bamberg, but with the police waiting around, she wasn't sure how that was going to happen.

It was a quick sandwich and Sophie declined the tea, having a hot chocolate instead.

The ambassador sat down and sighed.

"You know, the police are sitting out front. I'm not going to let you get arrested by these people simply because you're a mage. You could end up in some *Hansa Drudenhaus*...or worse. They can't come in here." He patted the wall of the building. "But... as soon as you step outside the embassy, they can arrest you. You can't leave."

"What? So...I can't leave... ever?" Sophie said. She started to think of her whole life, and what it would be like staying here for an extended time. Her papa was going to be angry. How long would she have to stay here? Was it going to be months?

"Brian, I have an idea.... The paper files room?" Rupert thumbed towards the office area of the embassy.

Brian, the ambassador tilted his head, gazed up at Rupert. "The paper files?"

He nodded and led them to a room which was filled with cardboard boxes and filing cabinets.

"I think it's time the embassy has to move its files to storage, don't you think?" Rupert remarked, peering at something in the corner.

"What? How is this going to help?" Sophie said. The room was musky, Sophie touched various paper files, her fingertips instantly turned dark grey from the dust.

Rupert pointed to a metal filing cabinet, about 1.5 metres high. Rupert began to toss out papers onto the floor, amidst Bryan's loud objections. Once the cabinet was completely empty, he put a hand out to measure the height, then matched his other hand at the top of Sophie's head.

It started to dawn on Sophie what was going on. Rupert was a bit eccentric, but if he was going to do what she thought, this was more like *dangerous crazy*.

***

Inside the filing cabinet was dark.

It seems a slightly short, skinny 16-year-old could fit in a large metal filing cabinet, but Sophie's tall friend Harlan would have had no chance. Rupert had added a few blankets to make it comfortable, a sandwich, and two water bottles, one full, and one empty. Just in case.

A tiny slit of light poked through one of the drawers of the cabinet, allowing her to see out. She kept her face away from it, worried that someone may see her. She was careful not to make any noise, the blankets helped by making her comfortable, but also muffling the sound.

The cabinet shifted from side to side, then a solid drop. The noise of squeaky wheels. *A trolley.* She was on a trolley. Looking through the gap she could see two men in front of her carrying boxes of files, and she could hear the ambassador was pushing the trolley. Wisely, Rupert and the other mages had decided not to come along, they wouldn't have fitted in the cabinet anyway. He said he would get the others and himself back to England, but it may take a while. Rupert had told Sophie to stay quiet until it was obvious, she was safe.

The door opened at the front of the house, and several police were standing around. As soon as they left the premises and stepped on the footpath outside the embassy, the police came over and started looking at the files.

"Hey, *Nein das ist verboten.* I'm sorry, you are *not* permitted to look at Embassy files. As the ambassador, I'm warning you, this is confidential information. You can see, it's all marked *diplomatic baggage.*" He emphasised the phrase, it clearly had important meaning. She noticed Brian spoke, in an official voice, different to the casual soft tone he had used with them. The police looked suspiciously at him, and spoke amongst themselves, but Brian didn't wait for their reply. The three men and Brian took the boxes and the filing cabinet quickly to a shiny black van and loaded them in.

Inside, Sophie remained quiet.

"You, okay?" she heard Brian say. She realised Brian was talking to her.

"Oh, Brian, yes. Lucky I'm not claustrophobic," Sophie said. She was nervous, but a bit relieved to be in the van.

She heard another voice, in the van, one of the other men. "The police are following. Some of them staying there, but some following."

Brian spoke, sounding calm. "Don't worry, drive to our destination. Sit tight Sophie, we'll have you home and safe soon."

The van drove silently, for about an hour. Sophie had a few sips of water but was careful not to have too much. The journey was mostly in silence, the men speaking only rarely, and in low tones. It seemed to go along a bumpy road. They stopped. She heard the door open, and her filing cabinet was wheeled out.

So much for the conference. She had been all geared up to see this amazing event, and it had turned into total chaos. She wondered if they could help some of the mages get from Lower Saxony to Bamberg, where they would be relatively safe. May be Rupert could help? Her instinct was to talk to her Papa about problems like this, but she couldn't talk to him about mages or magic.

Peering out though the slit, she could see she was in a forest.

The police car arrived, and they got out and looked at the cabinet and the files, but were not touching it.

Brian called out, "Oh, that rock, it must be an *obelisk.*"

He spoke very deliberately and loudly; she realised that was her cue. She had now been dropped at the obelisk portal.

She knew what to do.

Sophie started the spell, the blue aura emanating from her hands. The inside of the cabinet was now bright blue, almost too bright for her eyes. She squinted, enough to see, but kept the painful light out of her eyes. She saw Brian run back away from the cabinet and the two files. Through the tiny slit, she could see the police backing away, alarmed.

Sophie heard an angry policeman calling out something to Brian.

"We are just shifting our files to another embassy. It's very efficient," Brian lied, a cheeky lilt in his voice.

"See you all later..." she called out. She could see a police officer look angry when he heard her voice.

Inside the cabinet, she felt the usual feeling of a surge of magic, the sign the cabinet had appeared at the destination portal, in her beloved home town of Bamberg. She kicked open the doors of the cabinet, got out and stretched her legs. Opening the other files boxes, sitting next to the filing cabinet, she looked in an array of plastic folders. They were all filled with blank photocopier paper. They had bright yellow and black stickers over all of them, which said, very officially, *Diplomatic Baggage.*

Sophie chuckled to herself and began the long walk back to Bamberg from the forest.

2. Debriefing at the Electric Light Kafe

"SOPHIE WOLF!" Harlan stood up from the chair and ran over to Sophie, giving her an enormous bear hug. He lifted her off the ground, his tall and slender frame surprisingly strong. Sophie stiffened, preparing for the air to be squeezed out of her lungs. Harlan's hugs came with a price.

"Hey, Harls," she groaned through a tooth gnashing smile. "Good to see you guys."

"We have missed you." Tomoko wandered over, and touched her lightly on the shoulder, grinning.

"Hey, Bella," Raffaella said flatly. She came over from the table and gave Sophie a kiss on both cheeks, and a restrained, polite hug.

The *Electric Light Kafé*, commonly referred to as Jeff's, was their regular meet up choice, and their unofficial headquarters.

It had been a week since she had seen her crew, *Circle 66*. It was the longest she hadn't seen them for a while. She'd missed them. Her thoughts were still on the events at the Lower Saxony meeting, and the mess with the police. She had to put it past her and not dwell on it. Delivering the bad news would not be fun. She knew her, crew were expecting grand tales of exotic mages doing exotic things.

She thought about her crew and was looking forward to catching up. Recently they had been hanging in each other's pockets. Their circumstance and adventures over the last six months, in particular the final battle of the Faehome, had sculptured them into a tight little team.

"So, how did it go?" Harlan said.

"Not good." Sophie paused, glancing downwards, not sure how to meet the group collective anticipatory gaze and their expectations of fantastic stories. She tried to think of a way of delivering the news, so it wasn't too alarming. Being a fellow mage, it affected Tomoko the most, and she reacted the worst to bad news, anyway.

"Yes, so lots of mages from all countries in one room? Sagoi!" Tomoko said.

"I'm going to be straight with you. The police were there and arrested people. It was an ambush, I think. Lower Saxony passed the laws and made magic illegal *early*. They banned magic, I guess so they could get all the mages…" She considered. "…probably so they could get everyone that was at the meeting, in the one spot."

"Yeah? Dayum." Harlan shook his head, patting Sophie on the shoulder.

"What did they do to the mages?" Concern racked Tomoko's face.

"Most got away, I think. I don't know about the ones they got. Rupert got me out," Sophie said.

"I'm glad we are here in Bamberg. What the Hanseatic league does, mages get carted off and put in jail. Because they are mages." The usual cheery lilt in Tomoko's voice was gone.

"Seems there is only Thuringia between us and Lower Saxony. That law seems to be popular in the Northern European countries, moving down," Sophie said.

"It's something to do with the Hansa. It moves out of the Hansa countries," Tomoko added.

"Yeah, well, it's persecution. Being a mage is in your DNA. The whole idea of a league, ruling a group of countries through influence. And one guy in charge, who is basically a dictator," Harlan said. "I'm glad there is nothing like this in the States. Makes me realise we are lucky."

Sophie tried to be positive. "I mean before the police arrived; it was cool. The mages circle was cool. All the mages who have controlling influence in their country, were there, to discuss the law changes. It was amazing to see them all there. Just amazing. So many."

Harlan crossed his arms, looking under his furrowed brow at Sophie. The mood had turned decidedly glum.

"I've got Glyphs of Protection on all our houses, all our scooters, our workplaces, and the school. I think we're good. They will keep out anyone mage or otherwise, who want to do anything bad to us." Sophie forced confidence through her voice, though she wondered how much protection that could give them.

"Anyway, glad to hear you are okay. Kampai…a toast!" Tomoko raised her cup of coffee, clearly trying to sound positive. The rest raised their cups and smiled, all except for Raphael who was never good with emotion. She tried to smile, but made an expression that looked more like awkward, disguised pain.

Jeff, the café owner appeared at the stairs, and walked directly to their table. It was hard to see his face, so it was tricky to determine his age. He had shoulder length brown curly hair, a beard, and wore old fashioned aviator sunglasses all the time, even inside. He was a little but chubby, a testament to how good his own café food was. Ever since the spring of last year, the group had been using the upstairs of his café as their business meeting place. In the past, not being very discrete about magic had had them kicked out of several cafes. Jeff was the only person who had taken them in. Sophie tried to pay him back by buying a lot of cappuccinos. It was giving her a caffeine addiction, and she had started buying them and only half drinking them.

Jeff's accent remained solidly scouse, despite 20 years of living in Bavaria.

"So, the client sent you lot to retrieve all these things, but she…or he… gave you this back." He put a long object on the table, wrapped in slightly damaged purple velvet. "Here's your money for the job too, minus my commission. Right then?" He put a bag of goldmarks on the table, with a thud.

"Quest," Tomoko said.

"Hunh?" Jeff said.

"I prefer *quest* to *job*. Job makes it sound a little bit like a crime," Tomoko said.

"How about mission?" Harlan suggested.

Sophie glanced at him dourly and shook her head.

23

"Okay. I'll call them quests from now on. If I remember." Jeff nodded, half smiling.

Sophie considered, that while Jeff's main gig of course was running his café, he had an important side gig. Organising clients and jobs for crews with ancestral talents was unique…and profitable. Maybe the café acted like a sort of front business? The two of course were tied together, the café had traditionally been a tavern where mages met, so people still associated the two, and people occasionally raised it with Jeff as a point of interest. She knew he still had a few contacts from that world, but he didn't talk about them much.

Sophie had grown to like Jeff. He got little quests for their crew that paid well, and they tended to use all the skills of their little group, their fighter, their thief and their two mages. Lately, they had had to retrieve things, so their thief had been handy. They had in the past had to clear out a bunker of bandit Goatkin that had been harassing a farmer in the forest north of Bamberg. That had used mostly the mages and their fighter's talents. It had been more dangerous, but Jeff made sure it paid them well.

"I gave you lot a good one, n'all! You lot, yer know, can always wander down into the old undercity, clear out some bandits and whatever other bloody nasties are down there."

"Yeah, Dungeon crawling? Nah," Harlan said.

"Let's go to the dungeon now," Raffaella said, glancing down at her sword.

"We really need a healer in the party to do that," Tomoko muttered, glancing back at them. They all nodded, except for Raffaella, who maintained a long stare at her sword.

"Thanks Jeff, and can we all have another round of coffees?"

"No problem, Luv. I'm off at five, I'll see you all later. Oh, and nice work." Jeff turned and went back down the stairs.

Raffaella opened the velvet package. In it was the candlestick and one of the old swords they had retrieved from some thugs who stole the client's possessions. The client had kept the other things they had retrieved, but clearly had little need for the candlesticks and the sword. It was a minor paid job; they thought the thugs were goatkin, but they were stock standard humans.

Raffaella held the sword, balancing it on the back of her hand to get the point of balance, and then examining the sharp edge. "That sword…would come in handy."

The others glanced at each other. Sophie nodded. "It's yours. No use to us."

"I wonder why he, err … they didn't want these things back. I think maybe they should go to a museum," Harlan queried, picking up the candlestick. "Dang, they are old. Like seriously old."

Sophie grabbed Harlan by the shoulder, waving a finger at the objects, "The glasses, Harlan."

"Oh, yeah." Harlan patted his jacket pockets, and then pulled out a glasses case, opening it up to reveal the *glasses of true sight*, originally given to him by Rupert, last year.

"Dayum," he uttered. He picked up the sword, with his fingertips, examining it from all angles. "Yeah, the sword has a blue hue. It's only faint. The candlestick is bright blue, so it's strong magic."

Tomoko shook her head. "I don't know…what is the magical significance of a candlestick in the west?"

Sophie shrugged, her jacket collar momentarily coming up to her ears. "There isn't any, as far as I know."

"Oh, what's this then? a *toff*!" They heard Jeff's voice, addressing someone excitedly at the stairs. Rupert appeared at the top of the stairwell.

"Northerners!" Rupert hurled the comment back at Jeff, with feigned offence. Jeff laughed, trotted up the stairs again and gave Rupert a hug.

"Hang on old, boy, I'm a shaking hands sort of fellow, not your wife."

"I get confused, mate. I still can't give you a hug?"

"Oh…*Rupert*," Sophie said, sounding vaguely unimpressed.

"And yes, I got out of Hannover okay. Thanks for asking." He frowned, shaking his head.

"Err, uhm, so you got out of Hannover, okay?" Sophie asked.

"Yes, I waited a while, it cooled down, then got out with my diplomatic passport. The police eventually left after the English Embassy made a fuss." Rupert said, smiling.

Rupert pointed at Tomoko, "Have you told *her* the news."

"Magic being outlawed in Lower Saxony?" Sophie nodded. "I do feel a bit sorry for the Hannover illusionists, but it's in another country, it doesn't affect us directly."

"That's three German countries that have banned casting, and mages. And two of them joined the Hanseatic League," Rupert said, lowering his gaze.

Tomoko furrowed her brow. "What will they do?"

Sophie gave a little shrug. "Well, they can't stay there. Being an Illusionist is their life, and like all mages, it's in our DNA. Your country makes magic illegal... you leave. You got no choice."

Sophie started chewing her fingernail unconsciously. Harlan grabbed her hand and put it down on the table as he always did when she chewed her nails. She was distracted; she ignored him and did it again straight away and he pulled her hand down once more.

"The Fae are behind it," Raffaella added. Sophie gazed at Raffaella, always with the drama.

"Unfounded and highly unlikely," Tomoko responded, in a low tone.

Rupert crossed his arms. "It's fear. People fear magic because it's different. But mages have hurt no one for decades."

"Yeah...but they won't forget the Summoners." Jeff leaned into the table.

Every time she heard the word *summoner*, Sophie thought of the old black and white 1950's footage of the British civil war. She remembered seeing a huge demon attacking a town in England somewhere, people screaming and running past. In the footage, a summoner was there, in his black robes, surrounded by guards, smoking a cigarette, watching on nonchalantly as the demon wreaked havoc. The Summoner's callous disregard for violence, she would never forget. Seeing it, had burned the image into her mind.

"Shush!" Harlan was pointing to the TV on the wall. "You all need to listen to this."

Sophie could see a newsreader for the Bavarian News, talking about magic, being made illegal.

Harlan turned to her, his face blank. His German was terrible.

"Nothing new. They are talking about magic being made illegal in Hannover," she explained, flatly.

"You know, I have a job for you that you may want to take n' all," Jeff piped up.

Sophie shook her head. "Jeff, we… maybe not now, we are talking about magic being made illegal in Lower Saxony."

"Yes. That's why I want to give you this job," he said, a serious tone underlying his Liverpool accent. "The job concerns magic being made illegal *here*. In Bamberg."

3 The Prince Bishop of Bamberg

Sophie had heard of the Prince-Bishop. His ancestors had ruled over Bamberg as a *Bishopric* but now that it was part of the Kingdom of Bavaria, he wasn't a reigning prince. Or a Bishop. But he held the title anyway.

He *was,* however, the dean of history at the *Otto-Friedrich-Universität Bamberg,* the big University of Bamberg, and that's how Sophie had heard of him, from her father. He was the boss of her father's boss.

Sophie, Harlan, Tomoko and Raffaella meandered between the buildings, trying to follow the randomly placed, worn, ancient signs on the walls. White, yellow, red brick different buildings, each one beautiful, well kept, and old. They had been used for other purposes in the past, a warehouse, a barracks, a grand priory; all now used by the university. The ancient stone and wood buildings, ornate long thin wooden window frames allowing a glimpse of the offices inside, which held contradictory modern mundane desktop computers and office furniture.

Sophie heard a familiar voice.

"Sophie!"

She froze. It was her papa, Ernst. He worked at the University, so she could run into him, though being Sunday there was less. She hadn't thought it likely, which was a mistake.

"Sophie, what are you doing here?" He looked curious.

"Ahh, Papa, we were going to the University library. History project, need some books. Sorry running out of time, gotta rush, we are on our lunch break." Sophie always knew the best strategy of evading her papa's questions was to leave before he could ask any.

"But it's Sunday!" Ernst waved, his mouth half open, a question was clearly following…but they were gone. Sophie redirected Harlan, Tomoko and Raffaella to the library, until her papa was out of view, and they could circle back.

Some of the University buildings were outside the main University grounds sitting by themselves in the town. They realised to get to where they needed, they needed to go back along the river. The quaint boats, packed with brightly clothed, loud tourists sitting low in the water, passed slowly by. Sophie and the others made their way to the *Hochzeitshaus*, the 16ᵗʰ century building where history was taught. The stunning brown sandstone building standing out amongst the other ancient buildings around it with little white windows, sitting prettily on the edge of the left arm of the river Legnitz.

Sophie couldn't resist running her hands across the ancient crimson brick walls, as she walked along the corridors. The stone was cold with the damp moist air.

Ahead she saw two tall men standing out in front of an office, both in their 40s, one chubby, with shoulder length red hair and a moustache, the other with a dark goatee. The four froze momentarily when they saw them, not sure what to do. The men wore padded, green velvet gambesons, with a crest on the left breast. They wore baggy britches and hose with big black riding boots Even more curiously, they both held crossbows in front of them, resting the heads on the ground. Strange.

Sophie stood away from them, noting them silently for a while, before stepping forward, waving at them, and pointing at the door. "Can we…?"

The men's faces stared straight ahead, as if fixed into play by some invisible gadget, but their eyes lowered, regarding the four momentarily.

Sophie read the sign on the door. *The Dean – Sebastien Von Salzburg.*

Harlan studied the crossbowmen suspiciously. They ignored him, staring straight ahead. After a minute of contemplating them, he put his ear to the door, and listened. The men didn't react. Harlan nodded; a sign someone was in there. He went to knock.

Tomoko, who had been standing a few steps back from the crossbowmen, reached out and grabbed Harlan's hand. "No, Harlan, it is too early. We are *three minutes* too early."

Harlan glanced at her; eyebrow raised. Sophie realised given Harlan's general tardiness, he rarely had to deal with this problem.

Sophie ignored them both and knocked loudly on the door.

"Wilkommen – come in."

The four opened the door.

Behind a desk sat a man with floppy sandy hair, a long noble nose, and darker mutton chop sideburns. The sideburns gave him a vague Victorian look. A squeaking noise came from his chair, as he turned from his computer to face the four. The room had posters on the wall, pictures of the prince with students. It reminded Sophie of her father's office, crammed, busy and lots of books. He held himself high but smiled broadly and seemed somehow approachable.

"Oh, hello!" He glanced at each of them. "The people who are going to help me." He swished his hand at a cherry red Chesterfield leather sofa, and a big chair. Sophie Harlan and Raffaella took the sofa, Tomoko sat in the big chair, which immediately made her appear smaller than reality.

"So…" Sophie sensed the vaguest waiver in his voice. "Who are the *spell people?*" the prince asked, his hand, pointing, changing its target, alternatively at each of them awaiting confirmation.

Tomoko put her hand up. *"Spellcasters."* Any emotion of the correction tempered by her quiet voice.

"Mages. Sophie and Tomoko." Sophie thumbed her chest and pointed at Tomoko.

"Swordperson, Raffaella." Raffaella raised her hand.

He studied Harlan up and down, waiting for his role to be announced. Harlan was silent, a tiny shuffle of his feet the only response.

"He's, our thief," Sophie said.

Sophie noticed the prince's reaction, as he started speaking, he subtly moved his wallet, which had been sitting on his desk, into a drawer.

"So, are you a prince or what?" Sophie said. She caught Harlan's face, frowning at her bluntness. She knew it was part disapproval, part exasperation.

Harlan leant forward, pointing out the door. "And who are those guys?"

The prince moved back tilted his head, peered at the door and frowned. He stood up and walked over. Sophie could hear him talking to the Crossbowmen outside, politely, he seemed to be explaining something. She saw them both walk away. He came back shaking his head.

"Well, to answer such a delicately formed question…" I'm the inheritor of the title of the Prince Bishopric of Bamberg. Prince Bishop Sebastien Von Wittelsbach. Also, being the Dean, I'm officially… *Dean Prince Bishop Sebastien Von Wittelsbach.* Clearly, I'm not a Bishop. I mean, I go to church. Well, weddings mainly. Anyway, the Kingdom of Bavaria absorbed the Prince-Bishopric long ago, so it's all rather theoretical. So, call me Sebastien."

Sophie looked at him and fought the urge to talk over the top of him before he finished. She desperately wanted to find out about what Jeff had told them; magic being made illegal in Bamberg.

"So, the details of the job." He pulled out a bag of goldmarks and put it on the table. "Ten thousand." Harlan's hand extended across the table, but the prince's icy stare accompanied by a raised eyebrow forced him to retract it.

"You need to find out what the hell is going on. Every four years or so, they hold a referendum in Bavaria. People can vote on several things. The Royalists always put something in about a principality, the most it will get is 10%, it never passes and never will. I've learnt there will be three other things up for change this time around. Firstly, all taxis in Bavaria will be painted yellow. The installation of public toilets that play classical music, with heated toilet seats and doors that open automatically after three minutes. And the banning of magic in Bamberg."

Sophie looked at Tomoko, her eyes wide.

"Is this true?" Sophie said.

"Yes, its simply preposterous that anyone using a public toilet should be restricted to three minutes, I mean what if you…oh, the magic ban? Yes. I saw some leaked documents from the Bavarian Reichstadt Officeren."

"We'll take the job!" Harlan said. Sophie looked at him askance.

Sebastien ignored Harlan. "There are rumours and a few signs, that, someone has forced this on the referendum, and is trying to push through the votes. Not that the Bavarians like mages, but there has never been a local interest in changing the law. There are new people in town, outsiders, pushing for things, throwing money around, trying to gain influence in the vote. Unfortunately, that's all I know, it is someone from outside Bavaria. It's your job to find out who. I don't like outside forces dabbling in our little town."

He looked at them all earnestly.

"So, to make it clear, for the job, what do you want specifically?" Harlan asked.

"Well, indeed, good question. Three things, I want the names of the people behind this, details of what they are doing, where they are from and what their motivation is."

"Ungh, yeah, that's four things. Not that we have three as a limit. Four is fine." Harlan said.

"Oh, well, four then. And give the information to me, not to the police. I don't trust them." The prince shook his head as emphasis.

"And before you ask, I personally don't want magic banned. There's traditionally been an association with mages and nobility, via the court mages and as a prince, it's my duty to look after *all* the people in Bamberg. All the different communities. It's not like we are a horrific Hanseatic league country where they toss certain people from some communities into prison. Or chase them out of the country, or worse. Besides, I think mages can be useful. And…I certainly assume *you* don't want magic banned."

***

They walked five metres or so until they were out of earshot before a polite chuckle from Harlan broke the silence.

"He was a little peculiar. I liked how he talked. Very formal," Tomoko said, a lilt in her voice Sophie mostly heard when she was entertained.

"He probably thinks we are peculiar. Yeah, well, he pays well," Harlan observed.

"He seemed honest enough. I mean, he is both a prince and a dean," Sophie said.

"…and a Bishop," Tomoko added.

They all looked at each other. No one seemed sure about the bishop part.

"Yeah, well, he's going to pay us money for something we need to be investigating anyway," Harlan added.

They chuckled at the slight awkwardness of the meeting and glanced at the others. They all smiled back, and Tomoko responded with her high pitched unusually loud laugh that Harlan,

Sophie and Raffaella agreed was strange.

4 The Hatmaker

Raffaella's Vespa sped along the cobblestoned streets of Bamberg's old quarter, as it took her home from the prince at the Hochzeitshaus. She glanced off to her right, she could see the *Brückenrathaus*, Bamberg's famous rose garden, off in the distance. The chilly wind penetrated the gaps of her visor, biting her skin.

The vibration of the gear change clunked up through her left hand, and she felt the bumps of the ancient cobble streets. *Must think about getting upgraded suspension.* The off-road tyres, each with big square treads designed to grip both mud and snow, were slower than normal tyres, but did grip better.

Her mind considered recent events. The magic ban didn't affect her personally in the slightest, but if the mages in Bamberg all had to leave. Well, that would be bad. The money she got from the jobs working for circle 66 would probably go; clients needed mages for a lot of their jobs.

Raffaella realised working in Circle 66 was a good way of improving her sword skills. She worked well in the team, liked Harlan, trusted Tomoko and was confident of Sophie as a leader. She knew Harlan would be upset if Sophie had to leave. It was possible her and Harlan could continue without them as a team, which would be good. She considered, that if Sophie went, Harlan may leave as well. This troubled her. As she ordered, her thoughts drifted to recent sword techniques she had learnt. The thought of the techniques warmed her heart, as she suspected they would fit quite well with her normal repertoire. There was little as exciting as the thought of learning techniques that would hone her skills and give her any edge against an opponent.

She switched her thoughts to her riding, looking at the shops and old buildings. As the Vespa flew along the street, as she listened to the engine noise. It was perfect, almost like music; the new engine and new carburettor were both working well together.

Arriving home her mother was in the loungeroom, watching TV, her father in the garage, tinkering.

"Papa, Mama," she called out, as she put her helmet down and peered into the workshop/garage.

"Hey, Bella. You eaten?" her mother, Anna called out. Always the food. Spending lots of time on food preparation was a family trait that Raffaella didn't have. The time could be better used in sword practice or pulling an engine apart.

"You going in your room to listen to music again? That's what you mostly do these days. Why don't you sit down and eat something with your mama and your papa?" Anna called out.

Raffaella grabbed a bowl of fettuccine to appease her mother and fled to her room. Her mother had seen the dreamscape headset and had assumed it was headphones, without commenting on the visor. Raffaella considered it was lucky they looked like that; her parents didn't ask about them too much on the rare occasion she didn't have it hidden.

Having a few quick bites of fettuccine Raffaella closed the door, plopped her phone into the Hi-Fi dock. She selected some metal tunes as covering music, and then sat down with her back against the bed.

She opened the box and pulled out the new headset, the most recent headset Marcus had given her before he disappeared. Examining it once again; she had looked at it many times but not yet put it on. It was exactly the same as the old headset, except it had the phrase *Hutter 8:1501* typed on a white label stuck on the side. Raphaella, and the others, had no idea what it meant.

Raffaella had been using her old headset to visit her swordmaster in renaissance Italy, her long ago ancestor, from 15 generations ago. They attuned the headset to her vestigial DNA memory chain. The new headset she had got from Marcus, who had run the dreamcast sessions until he fled, would connect her to the memories of a different talented ancestor.

Her recent real-life encounters, some months back, had tested her fighting abilities. So, it was finally time to try the new headset and learn something new.

She picked up the medieval fighting manuals strewn across the blanket on her bed and put them on the floor, so she could lay down. She put a pillow behind her head, got comfortable, and the headset slid over her ears. The lights flashed on the inside of the visor of the headset, she felt herself tugged into the comfort of a light REM sleep.

And suddenly…. A medieval town.

Raffaella looked around. It wasn't Italy, it was a German town, all the signs were in German. It had to be; her ancestor was German. Then she remembered, her *father* had some German ancestors, not that far back. It must be an ancestor on her father's side.

She thought of what someone wrote on the side of the headset… *1501,* the year… *Hutter? Was that a name?*

Hutter. Hutter, Huttmaker? Hats?

What if he wasn't a sword master, but was going to teach her to make hats? She knew many of the people in the original dreamcast sessions, had met Talented Ancestors who taught them artisan crafts. It was only the minority that learned the sorts of talents that were useful in crews. And Mages were the rarest.

What if he was a hat maker? She shivered at the thought. Disgusting.

She wandered around, looking at the 15th century town. Whatever she was supposed to do here, or wherever her ancestor was, the town was interesting. There were shops in little alleyways, selling all sorts of trinkets, food, and clothes. The angles of the buildings were mismatched, not quite perpendicular to each other, but close. Little glass windows, most of which were framed by open wooden shutters. The buildings were white plaster with brown timber supports, but others painted colourful yellows, blues, oranges. The shops had colourful, illustrated signs that hung out the front. Shopkeepers greeted potential customers with wide smiles, their hands waving in the air to suggest a purchase of their wares. The people wandered about, but everyone seemed happy, or at least, not unhappy. It was a living postcard from the 15th century,

The dreamscape, because it used your mind, did tend to make things happier than reality. Raffaella wandered about, her hands impatiently trying to slip into jean pockets that weren't there.

She was here to learn, and that's what she wanted to do.

She found one shop, coming to a dead stop out the front, and stared at a sign. It was a profile of a hat, hanging from a wooden fixture. It was black and had painted on it some text in an ornate font.

Hutter.

This was the shop she needed to enter.

The room was dark, the glass glazed, so it cut down the light. The buildings around it were artisan shops that had people bustling in and around. She looked at their faces, they were either delighted, or shocked at the prices.

Raffaella opened the wooden door and walked into the shop, looking around as her heavy leather boots stomped the hard packed dirt floor. It was full of 15th century styled hats. Huge floppy things, smaller ones in piles. Clearly a mix of cheaper, more simple ones. She recognised a chaperone she had seen in other dreamscapes; a circle of material, with a floppy hanging part and then a long tube sort of thing that hung down to your knees. Some practical, but mostly it was elaborate ones, using more expensive materials. Brightly coloured cottons, more sturdy looking woollen hats for winter, and some sumptuous velvets.

Raffaella looked around, and suddenly felt the need to wear a hat. There was nothing in black. *Disappointing.*

"May I interest you in any of zees? You wear no hat. You should wear one. It will add to your whole appearance."

The shopkeeper was a flamboyantly dressed man, all waving hands and head adjustments; he was here to sell something. He was pale white, with brown eyes, and shoulder length almost black hair. He had a strong aquiline nose and thin lips. There was barely a line in his face, which made it hard to judge his character or age.

"These hats. Wonderful." Raffaella looked at the man, trying to gauge if he was her talented ancestor. "This shop, she is yours?"

"Yes, I am Jörg *Wilhalm* Hutter, a hat maker of some small reputation."

Raffaella's brain pinged. Yes, his surname Hutter, in German meant Hatter... maker of Hats.

Who cares about stupid hats. Does this guy teach sword? She felt her fingers clench into a fist. She wanted to find out what was going on.

"I have some exquisite hats here, some very popular." Jörg bowed slightly and swished his hand in a flourish. Raffaella noticed he was looking her up and down as he spoke.

The dreamcast would put you in the clothes for the period and give you an appropriate haircut and makeup if needed. In this case, she was wearing a long velvet scarlet dress. It cut in tight at the waist, and then contrastingly billowed out from below the hips, falling voluminously to the floor. In addition, she had tall black boots, no makeup, and was hatless.

Raffaella heard a loud noise reverberating down the stairwell from upstairs, not something she expected to hear in a hat shop. It was instantly recognisable, the sound of a body hitting the floor, followed by a groan. She glanced at Jörg; eyebrow raised.

"... that noise?" Raffaella enquired.

"Oh that. Nothing to interest you," he said, batting the concern away, then moving over to some nice velvet hats.

Okay, maybe there is some training happening here.

"Here, have a look at these. You have big beautiful brown eyes, pale skin, and the long black hair. Purple will go perfectly, with... all zees." His hand flourished through the air again.

"I'm not here about hats. I am here to talk about swords," Raffaella said, her voice betraying her waning interest in haberdashery. She knew in the dreamcast, you could be more straight to the point than you could in reality. These weren't real people; they couldn't hurt your body and you couldn't hurt anyone. You *could* offend them and then they could be difficult to get help from, which made the session long and painful.

"Ah!" He pointed upstairs. You want to join in what's going on up there, then?" He frowned, and he stepped back so he could examine her full length.

"Where... what is zer accent?" The fathoming frown was still on his face.

"I am from the Duchy. Savoy."

"Ah, Savoyard. You're a girl...and even worse, you are Italian. Why don't you try the style of your country? What I teach here is a German style, from Bremen."

"I have done Italian style, the Dardi school. I need to learn something different."

"Ah," he said, nodding.

"Plus, I have heard many people speak well of you as an instructor. As for being a girl, that should not matter either way. Men aren't good with a sword because they are a man. Plenty of them aren't."

"Zis is true enough." His eyes flicked up and down, assessing her "What is your name?

"I am Raffaella Cuppertino, student of Master Marozzo."

"Good, Raffaella. Good. Let's take you upstairs and see what you can show us." Raffaella noticed his demeanour changed. He had dropped some of the flamboyant nature of his speech and was now a bit more straightforward. Clearly, he was now talking to a different clientele, not someone here to buy hats. He was now smiling, and his posture seemed more relaxed.

Raffaella felt relief that she had found the master. A flurry of excitement filled her chest.

Jörg took Raffaella to a stairwell, out the back. She noticed the front half of the house was quite ornate, but the back half was more rudimentary. Raffaella carefully walked up the stairs; they moved around more than they should under her feet. Drifting down the stairs were the sounds of grunting, the odd cry, and the crunching of what she recognised as wooden swords cracking on a human body. Hearing the noises, her body automatically tensed up, even though she knew it was only training.

She reminded herself that it was the dreamscape. They couldn't hurt her.

As she got to the top of the stairs, she stepped through the doorway Three fencers, all in black padded jackets, were having at each other. Raffaella recognised the similarities of their strikes. The stances were the same as her Italian style sword training, but there were also aspects that were different. *Interestingly different.*

One person was instructing, a fair skinned man, slightly skinny, with a long red ponytail. Not the build of a warrior. As soon as they saw Jörg, they stopped and moved back, waiting.

Raffaella scanned the room quickly. One freshly painted white plaster wall was covered with a rack of swords and various other weapons. Poleaxes, staffs, small buckler shields. A cupboard was on the other wall, with a bunch of arming jackets and big padded gambesons.

"And who's this?" The tall skinny man with the red ponytail peered at Raffaella with a big smile.

Great. Why do these fighters smile? This dreamscape is all floppy velvet hats and smiling happy puppies.

"I'm Raffaella Cuppertino."

"From the Italian states?" A few of them asked, in unison.

She nodded. "Savoyard."

"Wilkommen, Fraulein." They spoke in unison, a few of them bowing slightly.

The tall skinny trainer stepped forward.

"I'm Gregory Van Helsof, a student of Master Jörg. Are you a customer from downstairs? The hats are beautiful, I have several myself."

"Not here for hats."

The three men shifted on their feet, curious expressions appearing on their faces.

"But you're a girl." Two of them said.

"And err… Italian!" Gregory added.

Jörg crossed his arms. "That's exactly what *I* said."

Raffaella figured the best way to stop the conversation about her being a girl *and* from Savoy was to pick up a sword and show them. Sometimes showing was more effective than telling.

"I need jacket and sword" She grabbed a jacket from a table, without waiting for the response. She put it on herself, and then took a longsword she had been given. She hefted it in her hand to test the weight, then did a few practice cuts in the air. It was a practice sword, with a dull blade so you couldn't cut someone with it. It was not too heavy, which she preferred because it favoured speed over the ability to do heavy hewing cuts.

She studied the men. They were looking at her curiously. She realised they may never have seen a woman ever pick up a sword before.

Raffaella stood in an Italian guard, *posta de lonzo*, with the sword pointing down at the floor.

The three men stared at Raffaella for slightly longer than was polite, and then turned back to the master. He nodded to them, and Gregory, stepped towards her quickly, almost skipping, his long red ponytail swishing on his back. Raphaella, instead of attacking, stood waiting, as he came forward. She flung the sword up from the floor pushing it to the ceiling, however, as he adjusted to bring it back at her, she had already stepped to the side. She then moved in close to him, putting her knee in the side of his. He lost his balance and toppled over; as he did, she stepped back in her guard, perfectly composed.

The other two men went silent.

Raffaella, glanced back at the master. She caught the faintest hint of a smile surface on his face, quickly replaced by nonchalance.

Another one peered up at Master Jörg, who once again nodded, and he attacked. Once again, Raffaella stood waiting until he attacked, and when he did, she stepped to the left, bringing up a hanging guard to block his sword. However, she then bought the hilt down and caught his sword on his hilt, pushing the sword to the ground. His face expressed confusion momentarily, but before he could react, she quickly smacked him lightly on the head with the pommel.

His brow furrowed, and a flash of anger flickered across his face for a second or two. Holding his head, he then scanned the room, slapped his cheek dramatically as if to knock himself back into his senses, and smiled at her.

Lastly, a tall German with long, blond, curly hair approached, introducing himself as Gunnric. The swordsman moved in quick, not even asking permission. A flurry of blows was aimed at her, going low then high, then left then right, moving fast so it was hard to see where they would land.

Raffaella backed up, receiving the blows. She then blocked, holding the sword with a vertical, tip pointing to the ground. Before he had time to throw another blow, she turned the tip and smacked him in the knee, then pivoted away from him. Gunnric held his knee as he went down. He grimaced but smiled at being bested.

They all stood back, catching their breath, looking at their master. Jörg crossed his arms, put his head down, and then almost reluctantly, took off his brilliant purple velvet jacket, and put on a dark green gambeson that had been hanging on a rack, next to several swords.

"Italian style, Ja?" He adjusted the jacket arm, moving his shoulder into it to get a good fit. "Let's see how *we* go."

Master Jörg immediately started circling around Raphaella. She noticed this was different, his students had come straight on and been predictable. Jörg was circling one way, but then would change his stance and circle the other. He was also subtly changing his guard, going from a high-guard to a mid-guard. Raffaella changed guards, matching his.

Then mid guard, incredibly quick, he sniped at her hand, a flash, she barely saw it before she felt the pain. She involuntarily had to let go of the sword, but still held it up with the other hand. She shook her hand momentarily, then gripped it. For a master, hand sniping was a basic technique, but he was *so fast*.

He then swung the sword over, so it hit the floor, bounced up, and then laterally threw continuous blows at her, left and right. He made her go to a high guard to block, and then, amazing sunk to one knee and was completely under her guard. He hooked his sword under hers, pulled her forward, and disarmed her.

Dramatically, her sword flew across the room, the swordsman watching ducked as it sailed over their heads, hitting the wall. She stood there, simply looking at her empty hands.

It impressed Raffaella. The master was excellent, and clearly knew things she didn't. She could learn a lot here.

"Raphaella, you are waiting to attack too much, and then responding. This is no good. You must attack more, being so defensive will always put you at an advantage."

"It worked on these three." Raffaella said.

"Ja, but not on me, my child," Jörg responded.

"But you are a master," Raphaella said, her voice low to show deference.

He looked at her. "If you are only here to defeat zeh easy students, with no intention of defeating the more difficult challenges, then you should give up swordplay."

Raffaella thought for a second, realizing he was right. "Of course, this is true, thank you Master Jörg."

"For an Italian, your work is not too bad. Bellissimo!" Gunnric's Italian had a distinct German accent. He came and went to give her a hug.

"No hugs." She held her hands palms out at shoulder height, stopping him in his tracks. She then turned to the rest of the room. "Thank you for the bouts."

"Master, do you think we may have room in the *Fechtschule* for another student?" Gregory asked, with a wry smile.

"Yes, can we keep the Italian?" Gunnric said, pulling his long black hair out of his face.

"I think she may learn from me, but perhaps may be able to teach you three something at the same time. Ja?" Jörg said, as he was taking off the green gambeson.

Raffaella bowed to the students, and bowed deeply to the master, who nodded in return, smiling.

"Please come again, ve have the training again tomorrow."

***

5 First Day Back

It was Monday morning, first day back to school after the holidays. The holidays had gone by fast. Over the break they had done two jobs (or *quests* as Tomoko rather romantically referred to them). The four of them, with their different skills made up quite a good team, they could deal with some pretty challenging situations. Both jobs had been easy. And, unexpectedly, they had made some pretty good money.

Sophie pulled her scooter up and spotted three scooters there already: Tomoko's Japanese scooter, Harlan's old red classic and Raphaella's *highly-modified-extra-add-on-bits-sticking-out- almost-steampunk-speedy-mint-green Vespa*.

The scooters were all decorated with the magic glyphs she had painted on their sides, looking like they should be the centrepieces of some great arcane magic scooter ritual. Her talented ancestor Johannes had shown Sophie how to put glyphs on the side of houses to protect them. He never could have imagined them being used to protect the rider of a scooter from damage. In fact, he could probably never imagine a scooter.

She spotted Harlan's tall frame standing on the footpath and then noticed the less obvious Tomoko next to him. They were both staring at the wall.

As she went up, she noticed there was an enormous poster, freshly put up, loudly addressing the upcoming vote. With big red block letters, it attacked the mages:

Magier in Bayern Vernieten! ...

"Ban Mages in Bavaria! Wow," she uttered. Her hand unconsciously reached up to cover her mouth. Harlan stared at her, peered back at the poster, and shook his head.

Tomoko squinted at it, then crossed her arms, an expression of concern across her face. "This is not catastrophic, but personally, moderately frightening."

"It's horrific." Sophie felt a hollow feeling in her chest. It had been one thing talking about it, but now, seeing an actual poster in real life was hard. Her mind raced through imagined images of her future, and what options she had if they banned magic. Confess to her papa she was a mage. Stop doing magic. Leave Bamberg and her wonderful friends and go somewhere you could still do magic.

It was all bad. She shook her head, trying to shake the thoughts out of her mind.

Sophie glanced down the street, and could see a fair way down, someone putting up another poster. She pointed, grunted her disapproval, and ran down to him. The others followed.

He was a boy of about their age, a backpack full of posters. He turned, eyeing them suspiciously, holding his wet paint brush between them. It was covered in glue, Sophie stepped back a little.

Harlan pointed at the poster. "Yeah, err, what company do you work for?"

The boy shook his head. "I'm not going to tell you."

"Yeah, okay, how much do you earn in a week?" Harlan said.

"Harlan, no you should not…" Tomoko said.

"50 Goldmarks," the boy said, eyeing Harlan up and down.

"Here's 500—what's the name of the company you work for?"

He nodded. "Okay, the company behind these is Schleisburg advertising and Promotions—here's their number and address."

"Thank you," Harlan chirped. Sophie quickly checked the information on her phone. It matched up. "See, Tomoko? Sometimes paying is easier." Harlan smiled, clearly happy about his negotiation.

Tomoko pointed to the bottom of the billboard. In writing, it had the same company, the phone number contact and website details.

The boy stood there still staring at them.

"Oh, dayum. What are you looking at, go away."

The boy shrugged and left, whistling a catchy pop tune.

"Harlan, you are my best friend, you have some impressive thief skills, and you have glorious hair, but sometimes *you are dumb.*" Sophie noted.

They walked silently to maths class. During the class, Sophie and Tomoko were unusually quiet while copying down perplexing formulae off the board.

The second class was Mr Freidrickson's, their history teacher, which made them chattier.

"Hey, Soph, get your butt over here. I saved you a seat." Harlan's hand made a slapping sound on the chair.

"Thanks, Harls." Sophie whacked him shoulder.

"Sophie, please no weird dreamscape questions," Tomoko said.

"They're not weird questions, they are research. Tomoko, you would probably be asking them too, but Freidrickson knows nothing about Japan." Sophie retorted.

Mr Freidrickson entered the classroom and threw a casual glance at the class. He walked around in front of the table, and sat on it, closer to the students. He was an Australian teacher, and his casual nature and groundedness made him an interesting comparison to some of the stuffier teaching staff. It also made him a favourite of the students. Freidrickson had an eyepatch, and a prosthetic arm, matched with slightly long hair not quite reaching his shoulders, and a bushy beard that looked like it hadn't been shaven in many years. Sophie stared at his arm, then quickly realised she was and looked up at his face. He caught her staring, noted her momentarily, and then looked around the room.

"Good morning, sir." Sophie realised the seating she would get now at the start of the year, would last her for the semester, so was happy to sit next to Harlan. Raffaella appeared, scanned the room, and narrowly beat a skinny red-haired boy to the chair next to Tomoko. The skinny boy looked disappointed and stared momentarily at Tomoko before sitting down behind her.

Freidrickson was shuffling papers.

"Okay, everyone, come on you *tin lids*, calm down. History for this semester, we are talking about the British civil war." His broad Australian accent belied the seriousness of any conversation.

They were still yet to find out how he had lost his eye and his arm, but despite the initial interest when he started two years before, the students now had stopped talking about it.

"So, who can tell me how the war started?"

A slight blonde girl, up the back, shot her hand up into the air energetically. It waved frenetically, begging to answer.

"Oh, g'day, Heloisa. Yes?" Freidrickson noticed her.

"Oh, g'day, sir. It was the end of WW2, and the British ran away from the Germans to Britain."

Freidrickson frowned slightly. "The British had *withdrawn* back to Britain."

"Sir, that's where we get our fear of the magic from, isn't it? My dad says mages are dangerous and should all be jailed." A boy with long blond hair, sitting next to Heloise asked.

"Hans, your dad says a lot of things, particularly as he's always drunk." Sophie responded sharply. The room went immediately quiet, except for a nervous chuckle from the back row. Harlan looked at her, shaking his head.

The boy looked at Sophie, and was about to respond when Freidrickson stood up, still looking a bit perturbed. He shook his head.

"Well Hans, let's not say such things please about mages little matey." He paused, his head swivelling slowly as he scanned this year's new class. "Our fear of the summoners. It was 1951, when both sides resorted to using Summoners to summon demons and they destroyed whole towns. You've probably seen pictures of them." He looked at his laptop. "Here, look at this."

Pictures of summoners flashed up on the large projector screen on the wall.

The students immediately went quiet.

There were photos of cities that had been destroyed by demons, and one hazy picture of a demon. The demon had a long head, finishing in a sharp, pointy jaw and jagged teeth. It had evil long claws, as long as swords, and sharp talons on strong muscular legs that looked like they peel apart steel like it was an orange. It had a tail that as long again as its body, muscular, finishing in a barb that looked like it was made of steel. Some kids in the class gasped, Freidrickson noticed this and hurried past the actual picture of the demon, instead showing images of rubble, smoke and flame. Sophie realised he had carefully chosen the pictures for the class, so as not to alarm, because she'd seen a lot worse. Her father, being a history professor, had books lying around that she would peek into.

"Now remember. Summoners did all these things. Not all the mages."

Heinrich, a boy with long black hair, tied back in a ponytail, put his hand up to ask a question.

"Magic was just made illegal over in Hannover, sir."

Sophie and Harlan glanced at each other at the comment.

"Yes, it was matey." Freidrickson nodded. "But that's nothing to do with this class. I'd like to move on. Please everyone, open your books to chapter two, page 45."

After the class, the four of them headed for the canteen. Students seemed happy to be back at school, the trill of student's voices raised, laughing at the telling of tales from the break.

"Hans." Harlan shook his head. "Yeah, guys, don't let it get to you." He ruffled Sophie's hair.

"I'm thinking of all the curses I could use on him. *Two heads. The bulbous nose of the long-time ale drinker*," Sophie muttered.

"Sophie, that is both extreme and largely irresponsible," Tomoko said.

Sophie glanced over at Tomoko and smiled.

"Before I met you two… I was like them," Raffaela said, briefly assessing them all.

"Like them?" Tomoko said.

"Scared of Magic. But now, in combat…magic is handy. Even Harlan is."

As per usual, it was hard to tell if she was being sarcastic, or serious. Harlan shot her a curious glance with a touch of scowl. There was an awkward quiet for a second, followed by a duet of Sophie and Tomoko chuckling.

As they headed to the canteen, Sophie checked her bag, realising she was missing her lunch. "I just need to grab my lunch from my locker."

"Okay, Soph. See you at the canteen. Spaghetti and meatballs today," Harlan said, heading straight to the canteen. Never one to delay eating food.

Sophie went to her locker and had to double check. Her locker was open. She thought carefully, surely, she had closed it, but the padlock was open.

Everything in her locker, checking the money she had in there, her books, smelly gym shoes. *Everything is there. Nothing is missing. What's going on?*

Sophie took the money and her lunch out of the locker, shut it, and made a mental note to buy a new lock. She then ran back to the others but noticed Raphaella's seat was empty.

Harlan had a concerned note in his voice. "Soph. Raff's gone, someone's taken her bag. She's trying to find it."

"Well, what is going on? Someone broke into my locker. I think. Unless I left it open."

Raffaella and Tomoko appeared. "Got bag back. Nothing missing."

She started pulling out daggers, swords, a fencing mask, putting an array of weapons on the table in the middle of the cafeteria. A few students walking past slowed down, looked at the weapons on the table, and quickly sped up. Raffaella ignored them.

"Yeah, erh. No idea what's going on here." Harlan scratched his head. "People never steal stuff in this school."

Raffaella put the last sword back in her back. "They stole nothing."

"Back to Adeline." Raffaella said, darkly. Sophie realised they had been talking about her before she turned up. "We need to deal with her. Finally."

The way Raffaella said *finally* sounded ominous.

Tomoko, as always, was cautious. "She has done nothing lately."

"I think we should leave her alone. I am content."

"If we haven't heard of her, that means she is planning to do something, but not yet to act. The fact we attacked her little dungeon isn't going to help," Sophie noted.

One of their recent jobs had ended up being a raid on a goatkin lair, and they were loyal to Adeline. However, she wasn't there, and they learnt nothing about her from it.

Sophie sat down and the table was quiet. They hadn't seen much of her since they had the stand-off at the Fae village. "We don't know that Adeline is behind this. We can't assume."

Tomoko looked serious. "Maybe we shouldn't have gone to that lair, maybe it is, that we have provoked her."

***

The four of them complained to the principal, who was at a loss to explain it, and when they said nothing was missing, Sophie detected a hint of scepticism in her voice…. The school was a fairly small school, with many students from the tight-knit international community in Bamberg. Theft was rare.

Sophie spent the rest of the day thinking about the incident. There were few possibilities, but she tried to put it out of her mind. Maybe she could ask Johannes what he thought about it all on her next dreamscape. Could she describe the situation to him, in broad terms, and ask him for a solution? She wasn't sure if the dreamscape worked like that.

After school they decided to visit the company that had put up the posters to see what they could find out about them. Harlan left, mentioning to all he was going to the portal to see his kindred Fae at the Faehome. Sophie wished she could leave her problems behind and duck off to the Fae homeland. The Fae always sounded so friendly, though it no doubt sounded that way when he described it, because they were friendly to Harlan. He was half Fae.

Harlan's white scooter split off from the three as they continued down the main road past the ornate 16th century wattle and daub building in the old town of Bamberg.

They eventually found the company that the poster boy had been working for. The building was a big white oblong box shape, in the small part of Bamberg where the buildings were very new.

The scooters parked neatly in one car spot, and they went inside. It was only at the counter, Sophie realised they hadn't really planned what they were going to say. A big man, with a white business shirt, bald with grey mutton chop sideburns, stood looking at them, curiously.

"Hello, we'd like to find out about the anti-mage posters."

The smile, sitting so obviously on the face of the man at the counter, disappeared. Sophie's heart sank. She hadn't thought this through, and now the man was on his guard.

"Ah, yes. We agree with them. We love the posters and want to buy a couple for our house and our friends." Tomoko said, nodding to reinforce her eagerness.

Sophie looked quickly at Tomoko, impressed by her quick thinking.

The man raised an eyebrow, quickly scanned all of them, and gave them a slight nod.

"You're anti mage?"

"Of course," Sophie added.

"I hate mages. Kill them, kill them all till there are none left! Scum!" Raffaella said.

"Hey!" Tomoko said, then bit her lip, looking away.

Sophie looked at the man. He was nodding slightly, in silent agreement with Raphaella.

"Okay." He scribbled something down on a piece of paper. "These guys are looking for new members. Go along, you sound like the right sort of people." He looked around, the bench, went over to a table, and retrieved some poster roll, briefly opening them so they could see they were the same posters. "Normally charge for these. You can have them for free. "He scribbled down something on a piece of paper and gave it to Sophie.

They thanked the man, and Sophie got out of there as quickly as possible, without running.

"What is the address?" Tomoko said.

"It says Die Nieu Nation, in English, *The New Nation*. That's who we are dealing with. It's a political party," Sophie responded.

Tomoko sounded serious as she spoke. "Was the killing the mage stuff necessary?"

"Improvising," Raffaella said and shrugged.

Sophie shook her head, smiling.

6. Hisako

At home Sophie had been trying to finish *Sense and Sensibility*, her favourite Austen novel. She kept thinking instead of her current problems, which made concentrating on it impossible. The banning of magic had weighed heavy on Sophie. The fact her father didn't know she was a mage had always bothered her. She was close to her father, so keeping something so major from him always plagued her. It was always there, a constant niggling source of guilt.

Was now the time to tell him? With all that was going on, it would be one thing she could get off her chest.

Being honest with her father seemed like a good idea.If they banned magic, mages would be as well. She'd have to move, her father needed to know. It would allow them to prepare. It was a very strong possibility that the vote would come in, and that their lives would change. Tomoko would have to leave Bavaria also.

Harlan and Raffaella wouldn't be forced to leave. She didn't know about the Fae, or the Cervitaurs

The previous problems with Adeline and Mabuse, seemed simple in comparison to this. This could disrupt her entire life. She had spent most of her childhood moving from country to country, making new friends, new houses, with her father's work. Now she had settled in the one place, made friends and was at a good school. The dreamcasting had given her abilities that were useful, could help people.

Now all this was going to be tossed in the bin.

She felt her nails pushing into her palms, she was squeezing them that tight. Pure frustration.

Finally, she made up her mind. It was time to tell her Papa. The bedroom door opened, and she listened to where he was in the house. She heard noise in the kitchen, and went to see, but instead it was Hisako, sitting on a chair, eating some complex looking dish.

"Sophie san, hello! Would you like some. Meatballs, very nice."

"Oh, Hey Hisako. No, not hungry at the moment. Is Papa here?"

"He's not, he left to go to work early" Her expression changed to a frown. "Is everything okay?"

Sophie realised how stressed she was, and worried, was clearly showing.

"Actually, no." Hisako was someone she trusted. Her need to talk about it was so great, she felt the conversation flow like water breaking through a dam. She felt a weight lift her shoulders with each word she spoke.

"You know I'm a mage. Well, there is going to be vote on banning magic in the next referendum," Sophie said.

Hisako sat back in the chair. She put the plate of food down, and her hand involuntarily went up to her mouth.

"Sophie san...I had heard a bit about it in the news but didn't know a ban was included."

"It was only recently announced. If it goes through..."

"That's going to really affect us," Hisako finished off the sentence. She sat there looking straight ahead, clearly contemplating what was going on.

"I need to tell Papa. He may have to prepare for us to leave. He may have to quit his job."

"NO," Hisako said very loudly.

Sophie sat back, a bit surprised.

"Sorry, no. You can't tell him. You don't know how much Ernst takes issue with mages. He hates mages even more than the average Bavarian. Or fears them, or both, I'm not sure. If he found out you were one, I don't know what would happen."

"I mean, I saw him get angry that once..." Sophie remembered when her papa absolutely lost control, getting incredibly angry about it. He later apologised, but it had really surprised her.

"No. I've spoken to him. You don't want to raise this with him," Hisako said, dramatically shaking her head.

"It's only that, I have so much on my mind, this would be something to get off my chest, and we can prepare…"

"Trust me, telling your Papa this, will be the end. It will be bad. Let's wait and see what happens with the vote, then we can deal with your papa," Hisako said, nodding her head reassuringly. "If need be, we will talk to him together."

Hisako was in a relationship with her father and had been their nanny/cook for many years. She really knew him well. Sophie trusted her, and realised, yes maybe they should wait.

"Ok, thanks Hisako. We'll wait and see what happens with the vote."

"Good, trust me, it's the right thing to do," Hisako said, nodding. "Your papa's anger, when he finds out you're a mage…Well… let's not deal with it unless we need to!"

7. A Texan in Count Aegwir's court

Harlan left school early, planning a quick trip to the Faehome before he went home to his host family, the Hochmaier's.

The Fae didn't seem to mind Harlan turning up in their little town. Word had got round that there was a half Fae, half human visiting. Harlan was still getting used to his recent discovery he was half something, half something else. It was only recently he had got together the guts to understand his Fae side.

So far, he found the Fae to be generally stand offish with humans, except for the ones that travelled and lived in human society, who were friendly with them. They were interested in human technology, and used and adapted a lot of it, but had a lot of their own traditions they followed. They used a lot of magic to keep their world separate, and of course, they were very much in touch with the forest and trees in particular.

In any case, Harlan was fine with them. He was half Fae, and they were now friendly with Sophie, Raffaella and Tomoko, for the part they had played in helping defend the Faehome against Adeline, Mabuse and the Goatkin. So that was good.

He was enjoying being a novelty, walking around in the Faehome he got consistent curious looks. A few of the Fae had even been coming up to ask him questions about life with the humans, and he didn't mind the attention.

Harlan crossed his arms, pressing them tight against his chest squash out the butterflies. It was still a culture shock, coming here, by himself. Coming here gave him the same sort of buzz he got when he travelled overseas for the first time. And there was the curiosity of finding his mother. He had run the scenario of the meeting through his head. What would he say to her? Would she like him? Would they get on? Could she teach him some cool Fae ability?

Presently, he had to use Sophie to get him there via the portal. He'd limited the trips as he didn't want to be bothering her all the time.

Harlan had mastered the art of using the glyph tattooed on his left breast, just above his heart. Despite not being a mage, Akshay had arranged for the spell to be permanently cast on his body, and he could turn it on and off.

His ability to change in appearance from Fae to human initially shocked him. He remembered standing in his bathroom, looking at the mirror, turning it on and off, repeatedly for almost an hour. One moment he was the son of a rancher from Texas, tall, lanky, speaking with his drawl, and used to riding motorbikes to round up cattle. Then, instantly, he was pale white, with pointy ears and light blue eyes. Fae. He had put down his abilities to track and hide in the forest as a natural gift, or maybe it was somehow connected to his thieves training, but of course he now knew it was a Fae trait, so that was why he was good at it.

That aside, he got used to the appearance, and after a while, instead of thinking of human Harlan as normal, and Fae Harlan as odd… he now realised he had two identities, though the line between them was blurred. And that blurry line, was him.

Moreover, was his identity as a thief. That at least he was good at, and he understood pretty well. He could learn to be a thief in the dreamscape, and no harm could ever come to him while he was there (though it was still traumatic at times). Discovering he was half Fae, trying to learn about their culture, trying to make friends, becoming part of their society, was difficult.

He looked at the little hand-drawn map that would take him to Aegwir's house. Aegwir had asked him to stay in his house while he was here, which at least gave him a comfortable place to stay and people he could talk to. What made life easy so far was he had been taken on board by Aegwir who's house he stayed in the Fae town. Also, being connected to Aegwir, who was an important Fae, got him respect through association.

Harlan thought about his father. This was the secret his father had been keeping from him, that his mother was Fae. He had been annoyed with his father, but then he put himself in his father's shoes. How do you tell your son that your actual mother is a white-haired mythical creature from Germany? Difficult.

The forest was quiet around him, but he knew there were Fae hidden in the forest watching the general portal area. Following Adeline's attack on the peaceful Fae, they were wisely on guard. Harlan stopped, looked generally around, and waved at where he guessed they could be hiding, hoping not to get shot. Waving at a forest, not getting a response, made him feel stupid.

Aegwir's house was in the north part of the Fae Town. He noticed it wasn't as nice as the central part where the nobility seemed to live, but the houses here were still pretty, and big. He looked at certain features, taller buildings, a big tree, all things he'd learnt in the dreamscape to navigate. Useful when you didn't have time to look at a map or read streets signs, or you didn't have a mobile phone.

Like all Fae houses, Aegwir's house was walled in living tree trunks, with stone and wood filling in the gaps. He'd been friendly to Aegwir and his wife Inusthen, since they had met, and they liked him in return. Aegwir had almost adopted him as a sort of Fae version of his father.

Aegwir's wife, Inusthen appeared at the door before he had even knocked on the door, or worked out what the Fae equivalent was, at least.

"Ah…. Harlan, my friend come in, Aegwir is expecting you."

Aegwir instantly appeared. "Ahh, my friend, how is it humans greet?" Aegwir gave him a hug, his arms strangely too high. Inusthen then did as well, hugging him too low around the hips. Harlan sniggered.

"Yeah, it's good to see you, good to be back. Coming here is so peaceful," Harlan said. It was true. The Fae were peaceful, reserved, and polite. It was a great place to come and escape, where you could detach yourself from the worries of the outside world.

"But first, I've heard about the vote in Bamberg. To Ban Magic," Aegwir said. He said it quickly; it was clearly bothering him.

"Yes. You know Tomoko and Sophie are both mages… if the vote passes, they may have to leave."

"Who is behind it?" There was heartfelt concern in Aegwir's voice.

"Yeah, errh, that's what we need to find out," Harlan said.

Aegwir's look changed, Harlan thought he wanted to move on to a happier subject. "Harlan, this is where we will eat."

"Yeah, this house is awesome, I mean…just great, and thank you for your kind hospitality."

Aegwir motioned for Harlan to follow him to the kitchen, which had a low table in it but no chairs. Harlan sat down. Everyone was sitting cross-legged on the floor. Harlan crossed his legs but knew he could only do it for about five minutes before the circulation stopped, it clearly wasn't a genetic skill.

As Inusthen poured tea, Harlan finally broached the topic he had been hoping to bring up for some time.

"Aegwir, sorry to be upfront about it, but, well, yeah, I want to ask about my mother… and I'd like to meet her." Harlan glanced over at Aegwir and sipped on a red tea in an ornate glass cup.

"Harlan, of course, we know a bit about her."

"Oh. Well, er…. What do you know about her?" Harlan raised an eyebrow. "I don't suppose she is a princess?"

"No." Aegwir stared at Harlan straight faced.

"She's like Nobility?" Harlan asked again.

"No. Not that either." Aegwir responded.

"Well, what does she do?" Harlan asked.

"She's a *ropemaker*." Aegwir responded.

"Oh…well ok, is that a term for a mage or something?" Harlan

"No. She makes rope." Aegwir responded.

"Magic rope?" Harlan said.

"Normal rope, from hemp we grow."

"So, she is like an artist?" Harlan said. Hopeful.

"Not really. A ropemaker. But it's important, we need rope here, and the rope made by the Fae is very strong."

"Sooo… where is she?" Harlan said, trying to sound patient.

"We are still trying to find her. She is one of the great *Eanigswir*, or…travellers… but I guess you would know that. She travels to live with the humans, to learn about them, investigate what they do and to gain insight."

"When...she isn't making rope," Harlan said.

"Yes."

Harlan shook his head slightly. Finding his mother was tricky.

"Harlan, tell us, with the ban on mages, is it something that could affect us?"

Harlan knew the Fae lived in their hidden world, protected by magic. The Portal was the only way in. He figured they would already know somethings from the Fae that visited Bamberg disguised as humans.

"Well, the big thing is. The referendum... err... a vote about the banning of magic."

"Do you think Adeline is behind it?" Harlan could hear the emotion in Aegwir's voice. She and Mabuse had tried to take the Fae's home, and many had died on both sides before she was defeated. Clearly, they still have hatred for her, and Harlan didn't blame them.

"Yeah, well, we're not sure," Harlan said. Aegwir nodded, looking serious.

Harlan heard voices coming from the front of the house. They spoke in the Fae language, but from the tone, sounded like... *visitors perhaps?*... announcing their presence.

There was a knock on the door, and Harlan heard footsteps coming through the front door. A man and a woman Fae both appeared. Both young, around Harlan's age.

"Aenithur!" Aegwir looked at the Fae Girl. He grabbed her on the arms. "Wurthir!" It's good to see you.

"Father." Aenithur was tall, with long white hair, and wore a crown made of flowers on her head. She was not pretty, but elegant. Wurthir was also tall, and skinny, like many of the Fae men. He had piercing blue eyes and seemed proud the way he kept himself.

"It is fortuitous that you both come at this time. This is Harlan. Harlan, this is my daughter and her friend."

"Hey..." He waved, then he held out his hand as a handshake. They book looked at it and slowly held out theirs, copying his. However, they didn't actually grasp his hand, as if the holding of the hand in the air was the custom itself. Some of the Fae knew about human customs, and some had no idea.

"Well, it is nice to meet you, Harlan. Are you here to learn of our customs?" Aenithur said.

Harlan looked at Aenithur and had to force himself not to stare. She was stunningly beautiful, her long white hair almost glowed, her big pale eyes almost hypnotic.

"Hello, are you half Fae?" Wurthir asked. His tone was very business-like.

"Errh, yes I am." He was quiet for a second, not sure what to say next. "I'm only here for two days." Harlan decided not to mention he was largely here to find out about his mother.

"Aenithur, Harlan has some issues with what is happening in Bamberg. I thought perhaps, one of the travellers could help? Wurthir?"

"I have not travelled much," Wurthir said.

"I'll take him to someone who has been travelling for a while." Aenithur reached out and grabbed Harlan's hand, as she waved goodbye, almost excitedly. Wurthir turned and followed, having barely entered the house. Aenithur seemed full of energy. "I know what we need to do."

Aenithur and Wurthir took him quickly through the streets, and down to the lakeside, where numerous Fae were sitting around, chatting, and enjoying the sunshine and moderate weather.

"So, I hear you are friends with Sophie Wolf. We have much to thank her for, when she helped to defend the Fae home," Wurthir said.

"Yeah, Soph's my bud. Very talented. I'll tell her you said that."

"How is her training? Is she an accomplished mage now?" Wurthir asked.

"Yeah, she is damn good. I wouldn't want to make her angry, now, no good would come of that."

"Do you know what level she is?"

For a second, Harlan thought it was a strange question, but Wurthir was Fae, and here with the others. The Fae came across as a bit blunter than humans. Sophie, who was super blunt to the point of being rude, would have felt home here.

Harlan shook his head. "Oh, I don't know about levels and such. Sophie doesn't talk about that."

Harlan noticed Wurthir was about to ask another question, when Aenithur pointed at a Fae girl, sitting down by the lake.

"Oh, good she is here. Harlan this is Tylltyr."

She had turned to face them as they came, an eyebrow raised. She smiled, but Harlan could see she seemed a bit surprised. Harlan looked at her, she was tall, skinny, and her pointy ears stuck out of either side of her long blonde hair, and big almond-shaped hazel eyes. With of course, the standard pale Fae complexion.

"Oh, hello, I am Tylltyr. You're... you're the half human!"

"Well, dang, yes. Please don't hold that against me," Harlan quipped.

"Hmm, how exotic." She looked him up and down, with a wry smile.

Harlan felt himself blushing.

"Hey nothing wrong with you humans. You gave us electricity, chess, hydroponics, light planes, Seinfeld.... Sheep shearing technology. Many things." She was holding a laptop, presumably another thing acquired from human society. "I venture into Bamberg a lot. I've heard of recent events... the voting on the magic ban."

"Do you know anything about it? Who's behind it?" Harlan perked up. He hadn't expected to find out about the issues in Bamberg here with the Fae, it certainly wasn't why he was here.

She was quiet, and looked at the three of them, judging them before she said anything. After twenty or so seconds of silence, she spoke.

"It's people who have come in from outside Bamberg. They are a threat to mages. May be the Cerviaturs, all the horned peoples, the *allegitemae*. They may be a threat to us. The way the ban on magic is slowly moving through the German nations, now down to Bavaria."

They all sat down, Tylltyr smiled, changing the conversation. She started chatting about Fae culture, almost like she felt she needed to teach Harlan about his newfound background. Harlan asked as much as he could. Aenithur and Tylltyr answered his questions about history and etiquette, and where things were in the town. Wurthir remained quiet, but Harlan noticed he was listening intently, only asking the odd question about Sophie and Tomoko, he seemed interested in magic.

Tylltyr rapidly hit him with questions about Bamberg and human nature, though it was clear she knew a lot about human society already. Harlan answered her questions, then when he sensed she was satisfied, fired back his own in retaliation. The more he knew about his Fae culture, the more conflict he felt. He was human, he was Fae, but should he adopt one culture and dump the other completely? Could he move into the Faehome and live here forever?

8. Interlopers

Sophie realised she needed to catch up with the other members of Circle 66 so they could work out how to deal with the prince-Bishop's mission. The magic ban in Bamberg had kept her awake through the night, and she knew Tomoko was worried as well. She arranged to meet them at Jeff's Kafe.

It was chilly, Sophie had put on her scarf and extra thick gloves to ride her scooter over to Jeff's. She could feel the wind chill cut right through her jacket, almost like it wasn't even there. The jumper underneath kept her warm. She stopped her scooter to adjust her scarf which had unravelled and was flying behind her like a flag.

Parking out the front, she noticed Raphaella's scooter there as well. It was one of her *unglyphed* ones, it was plain red, one of the few Raffaella hadn't modified to make go faster.

Jeff welcomed them. Jeff was all hair, brown curly hair, curly beard, and aviator glasses, worn at all times. As it was hard to actually see his face, none of her crew had been able to work out his age, with guesses ranging from 40 to 60. He was making some coffees for the people downstairs. *The Beatles* played in the background. Jeff was from Liverpool, same as the Beatles, which he had pointed out to them far more times than necessary.

They recently found out that Jeff had also been in a band in the British Isles but was forced to leave because he had a close relative who was a mage, even though Jeff had nothing to do with magic himself. England was harsh with mages. Jeff still toured with his band around Germany every so often.

Sophie trotted up the stairs to the "dreamcaster room."

"Where's Harlan?" Sophie asked. Tomoko and Raffaella were both sitting at the table, talking, quietly. Sophie realised she hadn't seen them talking together much and wondered what they were talking about. They glanced at her, and both shook their heads.

"Fae town," Raffaella said simply.

"Ah. He's trying to find out about his mother, and he said he was doing a *deep dive* into his culture."

"Enculturation." Tomoko giggled awkwardly. "I wonder if he would take me along?"

Sophie waved at Jeff, who was coming up the stairs. "Café au lait, and a chocolate muffin please Jeff."

"Sure Soph." He went back down the stairs again.

Just at that moment, they heard someone coming up the stairs. However, it wasn't Jeff.

It was another group of people.

They all peered at each other in surprise. Sophie noticed Raphaella's hand reach down into her bag. It was her long bag, and there would be a sword in there. Probably. Jeff limited upstairs to adventuring parties, and mages. Jeff roped off the stairs, so no one came up. Though occasionally, people came up by accident, or if downstairs was full, they would wander up trying to find for a table.

The three glanced at each other, then at the top of the stairs.

Four young people appeared at the top of the stairwell and entered the room. They were led by a Chinee girl, Sophie recognised her as Ying, from school. Then to her surprise, she recognised two others from her history class, Heloise and Hans. A chubby guy followed them who she didn't recognise; he was about the same age and ate some chocolate as he pulled it delicately out of its wrapping.

They stopped momentarily at the top of the table when they saw circle 66, seemingly not expecting anyone else to be there. They then entered the room.

Tomoko lowered her voice. "The one with the long blond hair, is Hans... the guy in history class. He was the one who said his dad says all mages should be killed."

Sophie gave Hans a foul stare. What he had said in class was straight up prejudice, but the townspeople didn't see it that way.

Raffaella lowered her voice. "Why would they come up here?"

They strode into the room, glancing over at Sophie, Tomoko, and Raphaella. They glanced curiously at Circle 66 as well, clearly not expecting the three to be here in the room. Ying walked over to a table, and sat down, the others followed. They walked across the room with a sense of pride, Sophie imagined them walking with their own theme music. Tomoko and Sophie nodded curtly at them, while Raffaella stared at them blankly. They nodded back.

"This is somewhat confusing, and I think potentially challenging. I thought Jeff said we were the only ones that were to come here? He wanted to keep talk of magic away from the other customers. This is our safe place from the Bambergians?" Tomoko said.

"Well, let's keep chatting about non magic stuff," Sophie muttered, her voice low.

Raffaella raised her voice so the room could hear. "I rebuilt my 30mm Piezo Carburettor the other day. Put in new jets to get better fuel flow."

"I do not understand what you said." Tomoko furrowed her brow.

Unable to talk about magic, and their work, they sat there quiet for a while. Sophie noticed the other group was talking with muffled voices.

After a while Jeff came up, to ask if they wanted any more food. The sound of a vinyl record playing some 70s music drifted up the stairwell.

Sophie grabbed Jeff by the sleeve." Jeff, I thought you generally kept people away from us, up here because of us two." She pointed at Tomoko and her. "being mages."

He glanced at them both, and then over at the newly arrived others. "That's why they're here. They're mages as well."

Sophie and Tomoko stared at each other, and then at the table.

"More muffins?" Jeff asked.

9. Three Bells Incorporated

Sophie and Tomoko both peered on eyes wide. Raffaella stared at them blankly.

"That's Three Bells Incorporated. Ying and Hans are both Mages. Heloisa, is a dancer... or something, and the big guy is Oskar."

Sophie realised Hans had played her.

"Hans... you're a jerk. You were rubbishing mages in Freidrickson's class!" Sophie said.

She realised that perhaps, Hans must have been denigrating mages in the history class, to throw off the fact *he was one himself.* He smiled at her.

Sneaky. Marcus, who had headed the dreamscape program, had told her before there were more dreamscape mages, from the numbers he mentioned, in this room there may be nearly half of them.

"Heloisa is a dancer?" Tomoko glanced over askance at the thin girl.

"The big geezer, Oskar." Jeff nodded in his direction. "He likes my muffins. He's a healer. Slept on my neck the wrong way one night and he proper sorted it. Allright then, what sort of muffins did you want?"

Sophie looked taken aback. "A healer!"

Raphael glanced Oskar up and down. Oskar was a bit chubby, dark skin, and had shoulder length dreadlocks. "We need one."

"Jeff, I thought this was our space?" Sophie said.

Jeff looked at each of them. "Guys, I want to help your mages out by keeping you out of trouble with the locals, but I only have two rooms here, upstairs and downstairs. Every separate crew that comes in here doing magic...well I don't have enough space to give you separate rooms. This is the level for you crews... the dreamscapers. Downstairs is for the everyday Bambergians."

Sophie lowered her gaze slightly. "Okay."

"Plus, I pass on any jobs, anytime anyone needs a party of people to do anything, to both."

Tomoko pointed at Jeff, then back at them. "So, you get jobs for them as well?"

"Of course. Okay, muffins." He scampered off, Sophie tried but failed to catch some of his final words, as he muttered to himself and trotted down the stairs.

They sat there quietly for a while, contemplating this latest development. Sophie peered over. Three of them sat at the table chatting, while Heloise, who apparently contained more energy than allowed her to sit stationary, would lean in to chat to them intermittently, interspersed with a variety of dance moves.

Sophie momentarily wondered how this would go down if Harlan was here.

She stood up abruptly. "Let's go talk to them."

Tomoko shrank down in her chair. "What. NO!"

Raffaella stood up and started wandering over to the table, Sophie leapt out of her chair and took three long quick strides, getting to the table first.

"Hi, guys, we know most of you from school. Heloise, Hans, Ying." Sophie nodded at each.

The healer glanced up from his coffee. "I'm Oskar. Ve gaits."

Ying spoke up. "We're *Three Bells Incorporated.*" Her hand traced through the air, pointing to each of her party as a way of introduction. "There were three of us at first. We have bells..." She stuck her boot out from under the table and shook it, there was a tiny bell, making a slightly dull bell ringing sound. "...and before you ask, yes, there's five of us, but we'd already bought the domain name."

"You have a website?" Tomoko asked.

Sophie noticed they all had a bell tied to their boots in various ways. *Interesting.*

"We hear you're... in the same business," Ying said.

"Our crew's name is Circle 66." Sophie pointed to the three of them. "Well one of us isn't here. Our...spy."

"You mean Harlan, your thief," Hans said, with a wry smile.

She wondered how they knew what Harlan did. "How did you learn magic?"

"YouTube," Hans said, with a little grin.

"Same as you." Ying ignored him, frowning. "We are two of the 12 mages, from Professor Marcus's dreamscape sessions."

When Ying mentioned 12 it immediately reminded her that Marcus had said there were other mages around. *Who or where were the others? Had they been abducted? Were they a threat?*

Sophie stared at Ying and Hans. "What path mage are you?" Sophie actually wondered if it was rude to ask. Tomoko shook her head. *Too late.*

Hans, who Sophie thought gave off a hippie sort of vibe, shook his head, "It's *cool and the gang.* Magic is about sharing. I'm a Druid. German druid."

Tomoko, Sophie and Raffaella stared at each other. Sophie had never heard of German Druids, and from the expressions on Raph and Tomoko's faces they hadn't either. They had heard about Druids in Britain. Being half German, Sophie thought her people seemed to be too industrial and efficient to be mystical druids.

Hans looked at them. "Oh, you're surprised, yes, we are rare as hen's teeth. Dreamscaping, there's only a few, and in real life even fewer, there is a small community left in the Rhine Palatinate."

Ying asked. "What levels are you at?"

Tomoko raised an eyebrow at the bold question.

"I'm a journeyman level for Druid. It's the third level of progression," Hans quickly answered, he seemed proud of the fact.

Sophie sensed the body language in the group. Ying asking people what levels they were at, and she herself asking about their path...they were questions you don't normally ask.

Sophie fessed up anyway. "I haven't been studying for long, My Master says...I'm only an adept. Some mages in the dreamscape told me she thought I was an illusionist. Not that I have ever created an illusion," Sophie said simply. She didn't know what "level" she was. Johannes had never mentioned levels. It sounded a bit like Karate belts.

Ying raised an eyebrow, then nodded, looking impressed. "An adept? Oh. Respect to you. That's the fifth level of progression in Dubrovnick's rating."

"Fifth?" Sophie uttered out aloud. "Oh." Sophie had been working hard, and Johannes had been telling her she had been doing well. But fifth sounded unexpectedly good.

Ying hesitated, looking between them. "Well, if we are sharing, I'm a lesser sorceress. It's the third level of the progression."

"What do you people do for jobs?" Tomoko said quickly, Sophie suspected she was changing the topic.

"We just come here; Jeff gets us jobs. We go do them. We earn money. We've been earning good money," Ying said. "Jeff seems to get work for both groups."

"What sort of work do you get?" Raffaella asked.

"Same as you, I guess? Though we aren't as picky. We do it for the goldmarks. Nothing *very* illegal."

"We do nothing illegal either... Unless we have to," Sophie quickly added, and Tomoko shook her head supportively. Fact was, as a thief, Harlan broke into places to get information, but it was always as part of a mission against dubious people, like Adeline, or to get something back that had been stolen from its rightful owner.

Hans spoke up. "Yeah, because we are going to be able to do this forever?" He rolled his eyes. "We got to do all this while we can, there is limited time. You know, mine it before the gold is gone."

Three Bells Inc were clearly cautious with what they were saying, but the common bonds of their similar experiences gave them obvious notes to compare, and things to chat about. Sophie realised that these guys, were their professional rivals.

They chatted for a while, and eventually Three Bells got up and left.

"An interesting development. Another crew." Sophie said, laconically.

Tomoko leaned in, "Well they are our rivals, but there are few dreamcasters around, and even less who are mages. Plenty of quests for us both."

"Jobs," Harlan corrected, with a half-smile.

Sophie thought for a second. "True. And there is probably going to be even more work."

"We may even learn things from them, we could show them things, if they show us," Tomoko said.

"Can't train them in spells, unless they are from our path," Sophie said.

"I like their bells," Raffaella commented.

Sophie realised these guys were different to them, Sophie could see it in their attitude, and it made her cautious, but overwhelmingly knowing two new mages in Bamberg made her feel happy. Made her feel a bit more normal.

***

Sophie hopped off the tram, the high pitch of the squeaky wheels slowly disappearing off down the old, wet cobbled street. It was raining lightly; she brushed the droplets of rain, not yet soaked into the fabric, off her shoulder. Home for dinner, she let the warmth of the family apartment soak into her skin. Her father was in the kitchen once again, humming to himself. Hisako was puttering around. Sophie was glad to have her around. She wondered if Hisako would eventually move in or not.

"Papa, I'm home."

"Sophie! I keep missing you. Where have you been?"

"Just out with Harlan, Tomoko, and Raph," she replied. Sophie gave her father a kiss on the cheek and glanced down at the sandwiches he was putting together. Her papa didn't really cook... *he assembled*. She was in a rush, so grabbed a tasty sandwich, thanked him, and went into her room to do some dreamscaping.

She noticed the window was open, which was odd. However, when she went to grab the box that had her dreamscape headsets in it... they were both missing.

Sophie started to panic.

Without the headset she was ruined. No contact with Johannes. No dreamcasting. No new spells. Her face was red, the heat rising up her neck. She checked everywhere but couldn't see them.

"Papa, has someone been in my room?" she called out, she could hear the exasperation in her own voice, "The window is open and my…headphones are missing."

Hisako came out of the kitchen. "Oh, Sophie. I put the window up to let in some fresh air. I put those headphones on the hi fi system in the loungeroom."

Sophie rushed to the Hi fi; the headsets were both there. The heat was residing on her neck, and she started to calm. She was upset but found it hard to get angry with Hisako. She took a second or two before she spoke.

"Hisako…ahh, okay." She was pleased with herself that she had fought off the urge to say something blunt. It wasn't Hisako's fault.

Her Papa appeared out of the kitchen with a blank look. "Beruhige dich! Sophie… why do you spend all your time listening to music in your room?"

"Papa. I don't want people in my room."

He squinted, then frowned.

"Sophie, give me those headphones." He grabbed them out of her hand, she clutched at the air, failing to snatch them back, as he took them and held them away from her.

"All you do is sit in your room and listen to music." He waved his hand in the air, and then pointed at her room rather dramatically. He looked at the headset, a curious look on his face. At a quick glance, they looked like normal headphones. The fact they had a thin visor that went over the eyes meant they obviously weren't, but with the visor flipped up, it wasn't so obvious.

She thought quickly. She didn't want her father looking at them. Desperate she pulled her emergency strategy.

The complete and utter raging meltdown.

"Papa. You never listen to me, you're always working! If you cared for me, I wouldn't have to be in the room listening to music." She ran into her room and slammed the door.

She could hear her Papa and Hisako talking. Then, a quiet knock.

"Ok, Ich bitte Sie, Sophie. Sophie. I'm sorry, I have been spending a lot of time at work lately. Here mein liebe, open the door."

Sophie cracked the door open slightly, pretending to cry, she kept her head down and her hair over her eyes.

"Take these. Listen to your music. It's ok, we'll talk about this later." He handed over the headsets.

A pang of guilt struck Sophie, realising in her panic she manipulated her papa and Hisako, but the headsets were incredibly valuable. She glanced up at the top of the cupboard, top shelf where she could hide them in future.

The room was cold from the window being open, and splatters of rain had started coming in.

Sophie pulled the window down, sat on the floor and put on the headsets.

Her father and Hisako were outside, talking.

She lay down, the flickering of the lights in the visor bringing on the quick REM sleep.

***

Medieval towns in summer were noisy and hot, and the dreamscape served up noise and heat perfectly well, an historic dish for the senses. Sophie figured that if it were technology based, it would have been nice to have a heat control for the place you are going. A moderate 21 degrees would be nice. She then remembered; the temperature was coming from her *ancestor's memory of the heat*. The memory came from his ancient DNA, intertwined, buried like biological lost treasure, in her own. The dreamcast probably tied the heat to his memory of the town, or his house.

The headset took her once more to 15th century Europe, to meet her most *talented ancestor*.

She appeared in the old wooden house, the bedroom once more, as she always did.

Changing quickly into the woollen tights, some knee-high leather riding boots, and a white linen shirt. She picked up a hat, the circular one with the floppy bits that hung down. Flashy, over the top, but it kept her head warm and the sun out of her eyes. She had googled it at home. A *chaperone*.

This time, as she stepped out on to the street from the house, a long procession of men in armour, accompanied by their retinue, were going past.

The man who lived next door had chatted to her on occasion. Heinreich was a fruit seller, and he stood, watching the procession, his eyes darting from one glistening armoured knight to another. Sophie wondered if he dreamt of being one, instead of selling apples and pears.

Others came out of their house to watch as well. The men in armour, many of them knights she guessed from their colourful banners, coats of arms, and expensive harness, rode past her. The pace of the men riding was slowed by the men following on foot, the retinue who traipsed behind the knights, carrying weapons, and leading pack mules.

"Heinreich, good day to you…errr…who are these people?"

"Another tournament." He spoke. She looked at him as he ate an apple. No. It was a turnip. *Yuck.*

"Hah! People seem to love Tournaments in this town. Why is watching people bash other people so popular here, eh?" He looked at her straight-faced, laughed, and then looked back at the procession.

"Because it's the nobility hurting the nobility." Sophie said.

He looked at her a bit shocked, looked around, and then smiled cheekily.

The wandering stream of men, polished armour beaming in the sun, were meandering off down a road to the nearby larger town where the tournament would take place. Bamberg was too small for such a thing.

Sophie avoided the procession and took the left fork. Once again towards Johannes's house.

As she approached, she called out to her sardonic talented ancestor. She couldn't see him, which generally made her apprehensive. He was just as likely to play some ridiculous trick on her, which he would then explain was part of a lesson.

"Johanness? Where are you?"

The farmhouse was as it always was. A lamb wandered around, grazed some grass, with the occasional excited buck. Some ducks pecking at the ground, a noisy goose.

As she wandered around, she spotted Johannes sitting in the back of the house, talking to two other men. She had the feeling they were mages as well, though she wasn't sure. A tall man, with a long brown cloak, and long black hair looked up at her, his face looked tired and serious.

A shorter man, but balding, bearded and fat also sat next to them.

"Ah, Sophie. Just in time. It's time for your test."

"Test?" Sophie said.

"You need to progress. I've taught you a great deal."

Sophie got nervous. "Who are these men? Are they mages?"

"They could be. Or maybe not."

Sophie quickly cast *Heinreich's detection of magic*. It was used to find if there were magic items in the area, or people themselves were magic. The men's rings on their fingers started glowing a bright blue hue. One of them had a dagger, which also glowed.

"They are," Sophie said.

"Okay, we will do a test of these, a run through. If you do well enough, we will do the test once more, for real. If you do badly, you come back 6 months from now and try again."

Sophie mulled over his comment. She knew Johannes in the dreamcast would make her wait an actual real six months. That seemed a huge gap. She had no idea why it was so long.

The men stood up and moved out into the paddock. They shuffled out through the grass, checking each other's distance, forming into a triangle.

"Hey what are your names? I'm Sophie."

The men said nothing and continued walking into the field. They positioned themselves, into a large triangle, about 20 metres each side.

Suddenly, the man with the long cape used a spell to lift a wooden wheel off a wagon that had been lying obscured in the long grass. He hurled it through the air. Sophie started to cast a shield spell, realised it was coming too fast, and tumbled out of the way as the wheel flew past her. She landed on her feet.

The short balding man cast another spell, and the earth started moving. She realised he wasn't an illusionist, he was an elemental, like Adeline. The earth elemental started forming, but it would take a minute or two.

As it was forming, she feigned casting a spell at the caped man, but instead just as she had almost prepared to cast it, rolled on the ground and threw it at the bald man. She caught him off guard, he moved his hands from controlling the elemental to casting a shield spell. The sleep spell caught him, but it only seemed to freeze him momentarily.

She casted another spell, and then with all her energy, staring deep into his eyes, she cast a third. He stumbled forward, and crashed to the ground. The elemental froze, half developed, mid-cast.

Sophie knew this was her chance, she ran around behind the half-formed elemental, and cast *Leopolda's bolt of lightning*. It struck the remaining mage with the cape in the leg. He winced and ran limping towards the house. As he ran Sophie noticed an enormous barrel in the garden moving from side to side, erratically, like some invisible people were moving it.

She now couldn't see where the caped man had gone. She realised he was trying to levitate the barrel to throw it at her, but fortunately for her it was stuck to the ground by plants that had grown around it. The delay gave her the five seconds she needed.

She used another Leopolda's lightning bolt on the barrel, splitting it in half, showering splinters all over the grass.

In the past, she had been afraid of casting the lightning bolts, the big noise, the power, but she realised now she was comfortable with them.

The caped man had disappeared into the dark, so she ran into the house. Johannes was in there, playing chess with himself.

"Come back and tell me when it's over. And go back out there, my dear."

Instead of going out the back door again, she went out the front door and sprinted around the side of the house. She crept through the bushes and could see the back of the man, as he hid down behind a haystack. He was watching the house, expecting her to come out the back door.

"HEY!" His face turned to her, caught in surprise. Her hand flicked through the air, drawing the glyph for *Adelfried's Spell of Immediate Sleep,* three quick lines vertically, and a line through the middle.

He was hit by the sleep spell but stood his ground and shook his head. He turned to her and went to cast a spell, but she threw an apple she had picked up from Johannes table straight at his face; he flinched, ruining the spell. He cursed, turned his back, and began to run. Another sleep spell caught him and the momentum of him running propelled his body, tumbling forward into the grass. She walked over to check on him, his face was an expression of bliss, and he started to snore.

Sophie looked at the carnage in the backyard. Broken things here and there, a half-formed elemental, the smell of burning...something... still hung in the air from the lighting spell.

This was only the practice run, she thought.

Johannes was still inside, playing chess with himself.

"You passed," he said simply. "I was watching out the window."

"The practice run?"

"That was the test." He moved another piece around, then removed a piece from the board.

"Sooo... What happens now?"

"Welcome to world of the Initiate mage. You are now a full initiate, the sixth level of achievement in our order."

Sophie wasn't sure of the significance of all this, but it sounded like she had achieved something important. She remembered Hans and Ying had said they were third level. She was six, *twice* as much as them!... if her path level achievements were the same as their paths. She immediately thought of asking Rupert what all this meant. If she asked Johannes, it was the sort of question he would tell her something that made little sense. Or he would make up something odd.

Both the bald man and the caped man came inside. Sophie immediately felt sorry for them and helped them, but they seemed perfectly happy. They both smiled, bowed to her, and congratulated her on her new status. She felt excellent for a moment, and her spirits lifted, but then remembered the trouble they were facing back at Bamberg in the real world. It immediately brought her back to earth.

"Johannes, have people here ever tried to ban magic?'

His head jutted back, giving himself an extra chin. He looked at her askew.

"Why…would they do that? Everyone knows mages help people, magic helps people. I mean, you can suffer from magic, but people benefit from it too. You can't get rid of it, it's nature."

Sophie realised that ultimately, they misused magic in a terrifying deadly fashion, and that was enough to ban it. But that was 600 years after Johannes.

"If someone was to try to get rid of it, who could it be?" Sophie asked him.

"Hmm..." He poured the two testers some mulled wine, she could see the steam coming off it. She looked for a cup for herself and handed it to him.

"Well, the Church of the Sun wouldn't, they use magic themselves. The Half beasts wouldn't, they also use magic, and they keep to themselves. A path that wants to monopolise magic, or someone that really hates all magic. But there's no one like that I know of."

Not yet there isn't, she thought.

Sophie sat and pondered his comments. Johannes cast some healing on the caped man's leg. She felt a little guilty, but he smiled, and they all seemed genuinely happy at her passing the test.

10. Akshay's Greek Cypriot Monarchist Café

"Soph, so there's something I want to show you," Harlan said. Rare for him to be dramatic and mysterious, Sophie thought.

It was Tuesday night, and Akshay had summoned them to the Greek Cypriot Monarchist Café, which was a front for the hidden Cervitaur community in Bamberg, the half dear, half man people that lived a clandestine life dwelling in human society. But apparently, Harlan had something to show on the way.

The pair walked along the narrow-cobbled streets of Bamberg, in the old market quarter... which they had started calling the Cervitaur quarter, as this is where most of them lived.

"Harls, what is it you are showing me?" Soph asked. She wasn't used to surprises.

Harlan glanced across at her. "Yeah, another two blocks, but hey I wanted to ask. How you are holding up, yer know?"

"Not sure to be honest." She was quiet for a few seconds, thinking exactly what she felt. She felt comfortable with Harlan, it wasn't like she didn't want to hold back her feelings, but she didn't want to stress him out with her worries.

After some thought, Sophie continued, "I'm a bit scared. I know if it goes all wrong, I'll have to tell papa I'm a mage. We'll have to move. Poor Tomoko will have to move, and she loves it here, but I think she will go back to Japan, and I'd miss her."

"Dang. You two are both friggin' awesome, but not sure what I'd do if you left Soph. We've been friends for so long," Harlan said. Sophie picked up genuine sadness in the timbre of his voice. He wasn't just being polite.

He suddenly looked troubled. "Also, not sure how this affects the Fae."

"Don't worry, Harls, we have two of the best mages in Bamberg, probably all of Bavaria. And you and Raphaella, Three Bells may help, and Rupert is helping. We'll beat whoever's behind this, we have a good chance against Adeline and Mabuse." Sophie felt the need at that moment to be positive. There was a lot of truth in it, but she knew if there was a vote on banning magic, it was up to the people of Bamberg and Bavaria. They would vote how they wanted, and most of them feared mages. She thought about telling her Papa, but... that was a nightmare scenario.

"Yeah, true," Harlan responded, honestly it seemed.

"How did it go with the Fae? Any info on your mama?" Sophie studied Harlan's face, eager to see his reaction.

"Nah, I learned she is a ropemaker."

"A Ropemaker?" Sophie scanned his face, trying to read his expression.

"Yeah. And before you ask, it's not a fancy title. She makes actual rope. Good rope though," Harlan said, overexplaining.

"You okay about it?" Sophie peered at him; he didn't seem worried.

"Yeah, I got time. I'm probably more focused on learning my culture. I met this Fae girl Tylltyr who is helping me."

"Oh, helping you?" Sophie elbowed him and smiled.

"Nothing like that, though...she is sort of cute."

"Well, I'm sure she can teach you all about your culture." Sophie chuckled. She enjoyed nothing more than ribbing Harlan.

"Dang, cheeky! Oh, we are almost here. Check this out." Harlan pointed at a white shop as they turned the corner.

There was a short queue of people out the front. The sign on the front said *Oskars*.

"What is this?" Sophie stood back, trying to take it all in.

"Oskar from Three Bells. Their healer. He got his uncle to set up a shop, and he runs a business from it, using his spells to heal people."

Sophie eyes grew wide as she looked between the shop and Harlan. "But the people... he's a mage, how can he do that? Magic...in public?"

"Makes little sense to me. We know how the people in Bavaria are about Mages. But when it comes to healing sickness, I guess people want to be healed, and are happy with the results and to pay the price."

"He's making money out of this?" Of course, he was part of Three Bells, who were more than a little focussed on making money from their ancestral arts.

"Actually, look, he's pretty cheap." Harlan pointed to the prices on the window. Sophie read off a few items. Healing a minor cut, a cold and a sprained ankle were all treated for 1 silver. Broken bones were five silvers. It seemed very reasonable.

"Yeah, dang, I mean, apparently, he wants to help. But he also said, this may help us with the vote. People can see mages doing healing as good. Think of Frenssen's rule *Not a thief until you are caught.*"

Sophie wasted a second trying to work out how Harlan's rule was ever vaguely relevant, before peering at the window. The business was very professional. She noticed he had a domain name, social media links, and there was also a link to a website for Three Bells Inc.

"Damn, we need a website and some work on our brand," Harlan said, gazing at the window.

Sophie peered in the window, and she could see Oskar using a healing spell on someone's arm. At that point he glanced up, saw both, smiled and gave them a thumbs up. He spoke quickly to his patient, who flashed him a scowl, which he ignored and ran out to them.

"Well, you two, what do you think of my shop?"

"Well done." She shook her head; a mage operating so publicly wasn't safe. "What do three Bells think of this?

He shrugged, "Don't know. Don't care. I've left Three Bells."

Harlan and Sophie gazed at each other in surprise. They had only just been introduced to him as part of the crew.

"You wha... why?" Sophie started to realise Oskar wasn't your average dreamscaper.

"It's...well... I want to use my mage abilities to help. Don't care about the money. Hearing that you guys aren't all about the money, sort of inspired me. I've been with them for six months, that's long enough. Anyway, I gotta run, catch up with you both for a coffee sometime?"

"Yeah, fer sure," Harlan replied, as Oskar ran back in to deal with a grumpy looking patient. The people waiting in the small queue stared at them, frowning.

"Dang." Harlan scratched the back of his neck. "Yeah, err, that's a new one for the books."

"Think we inspired him to leave them?" Sophie said.

They both waved and Sophie gave him a thumbs up. He was a decent guy, in all this mess, he wanted to help people.

"Oh, and your comment about their social media."

"Hunh, oh yeah." Harlan glanced over.

"No, not for us. I can't have my papa finding out." Sophie kept calm, not raising her voice.

"Oh, yeah, I forgot. Dayum, yeah. He goes ballistic at the mentioning of mages. Sorry." Harlan nodded.

They left Oskar's and continued to the Greek Cypriot Monarchist Club to see the Cervitaurs, it was surprisingly close, and Sophie wondered if Oskar had chosen it for that reason.

Walking into the Greek Cypriot Monarchists club, a tall lady behind the desk, looked up from her phone and regarded them curiously. She was tall and well built; Sophie was pretty sure she was a Cervitaur in human form.

"Sorry members only," she said, then said something to them in a language Sophie didn't understand, she guessed it was Greek, but wasn't sure.

"We know Akshay, he said we are welcome," Sophie said.

The woman looked at them both for a space and put her phone down on the tabletop.

"Yeah? Well, a lot of people know Akshay."

Harlan at that point stepped away from the doorway, flicked his hand across his chest, and quickly morphed into his natural form, that of a Fae. Sophie watched intently, it was always interesting to watch him change, if not a little disturbing. His eyes lightened, his skin went a silver blue, white. He flicked it back again to his normal form.

"Oh. Wow. You're handsome now." The lady behind the desk said. She was genuinely surprised and stared at him for a few seconds longer than was normally polite.

"Yeah, thanks, wait, what was I before?" Harlan looked offended.

She then picked up the phone, spoke quickly into it, and motioned for them to come through. They went through two doors, and then into a large space, which had about 20 people all playing cards at a curious variety of antique tables.

Akshay ran up to them, from behind the serving counter. He was in his cervitaur form, tall his strong stag features belaying his noble charismatic self. He bent over to give Sophie a hug, and she winced, hoping not to get stuck by his huge antlers.

"Hey watch the antlers!"

"Oh, sorry, hugging me can be dangerous." He smiled and gave Harlan a fist bump.

"Here you are, lord among your people," Sophie said.

Sophie, seeing him here with his people, realised even though he was the leader of the Cervitaur community, he still made time for her. Despite some early conflicts, they had had out their differences and he was now not only a good ally, but a good friend.

"Hello, come in, come in. Have a seat." He poked two fingers in the air, and a waiter snapped to attention and headed in their direction.

He was all smiles.

"Akshay, I always wondered, this club is a front for the Cervitaur community. You guys all hide your form with the Jajunks spell. What if a human came in that *actually was* a Greek Cypriot Monarchist?"

"Sophie, there aren't any Greek Cypriot Monarchists in Bamberg. I don't even know if there are any in Cyprus. Anyway, this is solidly in the Cervitaur quarter."

"So how many Cervitaurs are in the quarter?"

"Ah... about 20% of Bamberg," Akshay responded.

"So, it should be the *Cervitaur one fifth*?" Harlan smiled to himself.

Akshay looked at him pokerfaced, and continued, "I'm glad I got you here, I wanted to find out where you are. I mean things don't sound great; the magic ban is awful. It also makes me feel unsure about us. Not that we are mages. But...you know."

Sophie ordered a Café Au Lait and Harlan ordered an English Breakfast tea, and the waiter nodded and shuffled off.

"So, what's happening? How can I be involved? You helped us with that trouble with Adeline, the least we Cervitaurs can do is help you back."

"Well, so far, we know someone is behind the vote to ban mages. The prince has asked us to investigate. Also, there is a second group of dreamscapers now, operating out of Jeff's. Who sort of may help." Sophie said.

"*The* prince... Prince-Bishop Sebastian? You met him?" Akshay looked surprised.

"Nice guy. A bit weird. We are doing a job for him. Has his own squad of crossbow guards which you don't see every day. Seemed friendly to us, even though we are mages." Sophie said.

"Impressive. He may be able to help. He has connections in some quarters," Akshay noted.

Sophie shrugged.

"If we pay them enough," Harlan added.

At that point, a strange human girl, skinny, with long brown hair ran across the room, giving Harlan a huge hug.

"Harlan! HARLAN! What are you doing here?"

Harlan pushed the girl back, with a distressed look on his face. Sophie smirked at the look of near horror on his face at being hugged by the girl but was perplexed as to why a human girl would be here, and how she knew Harlan.

"Ah... you don't know who I am." She beamed from ear to ear, seemingly pleased at having him at a dis-advantage. Here, I'm in traveller mode." She ran her hand over where her form changing glyph tattoo was, on her chest. Her formed changed into a skinny Fae, the usual bright features, pale skin, and pink eyes.

"Tylltyr!" Harlan called out.

"Yes, I hang out here sometimes when I'm doing my travels." She put her arm in his and pushed her way into the chairs around the table. Akshay had a half smile on his face, as he looked at Harlan shuffling uncomfortably in his seat. Sophie caught his amused look and they both smiled at each other. For Sophie, seeing her friend in naturally occurring awkward situations was even better than when she could cause him to be in one. Despite that, there were few people of whom she was fonder.

Harlan introduced them all, Tylltyr seemed very happy to meet them, and moved her chair as close to Harlan's as she physically could.

"Walking around, learning about Human culture must be interesting," Harlan said.

"Yes, Harls, it's like, I guess, for you, visiting those big centres where people go to see things and learn about stuff."

"Oh, like going to University, or a... museum?"

"No, I mean, what's it called?" She frowned, thinking, "Oh, yes, a Zoo."

"Oh. Okay," Harlan said, scratching his head.

The waiter bought over their drinks. The Café Au Lait was in a huge bowl but tasted superb.

"Oh, you said another crew of dreamcasters, like yours? We know about Oskar, he's in one?" Akshay said.

"Well, he *was* with them. Three Bells," Sophie added, emphasizing the past tense with a wry smile.

"They have good corporate branding; their social media presence is hitting some of their major markets," Akshay noted, sounding vaguely impressed.

"Yeah. That's what I said," Harlan said.

"Also, we found out a new political party has formed. The New Nation. They are behind all the anti-mage posters going up around the place," Sophie said.

The New Nation," Akshay said. Are they connected to anyone?

"Not sure," Sophie said, wondering as she spoke. "They could be people that don't like mages. There are plenty of them in Bavaria."

"Yes, the prince said it was people from outside, pushing their influence around, paying people off with money," Sophie noted.

Akshay nodded. "Okay, well I'm not sure what we can do to help, but if we hear anything, we'll let you know."

"Cool," Harlan said.

Sophie quickly downed the Café Au Lait.

Akshay left the table, and the crew continued chatting.

"I was hoping Akshay would have some information, something to help us. We need more information about these guys if we are to stop the magic ban."

The three sat there quietly for a few seconds.

"Dayum, you know something has been bugging me. It may or may not be a lead, but I'm going to follow it up. Tylltyr?"

"Of course, handsome." She smiled broadly. "What are we doing?"

"We're going to check out someone who I think maybe a... *rat*."

Bernard M Lyons

11. Wurthir

"So why do you humans say they are going to the bathroom, when they are really using the toilet?" Tylltyr asked Harlan. They were together in the Faehome, walking towards the portal, after leaving the Greek Cypriot Monarchist café.

"Dang Tylltyr you ask a lot of questions. I don't know," Harlan said.

"Are they *pretending* to take a bath, but actually using the toilet?"

"No. They are actually using the toilet."

"So… they say they are going to the Bathroom, if they are having a bath?"

"Hmm, not exactly."

"So, restroom, is a room where you have a rest?"

"Hmm. Actually, that is a toilet, as well."

"Humans and their bathroom visiting ways. It's confusing."

"Yes. Look, anyway. What time did you say Wurthir was using the portal?"

A few things had been bugging Harlan about Wurthir, nearly as much as Tylltyr was bugging him. Though he trusted her.

Tylltyr mentioned Wurthir had only started a recent relationship with Aenithur. He was one of the few travellers, and he regularly went out. The travellers generally have an aspect of human society they dwelt in. Wurthir's was supposed to be shipping, and the dockyards, but after pummelling Tylltyr with questions about him, he'd worked out that Wuther worked there, but had little interest in the area. Harlan wondered why he had chosen that field, and how it would be useful to the forest dwelling Fae anyway.

Tylltyr and Harlan had both concluded he was worth checking into. They would follow him when he left the Faehome and see where he would go. Sophie had thought it was a waste of time, but as Harlan had argued, they didn't have many leads, so it was worth checking out.

They got to the portal, and Tylltyr took Harlan into some bushes.

There was a Fae guard standing there with his weapon drawn, aimed loosely at the portal. He looked at her for a second, and then his head flicked back to peer at the portal. It seemed to be a little defensive position, there were trenches dug and sandbags piled up high around them. The little set-up appeared to be used to observe people coming through the portal. Harlan noticed there were two more Fae soldiers there, who were quite well camouflaged, sitting down in their trenches dug well into the earth. Freshly sodden earth had been dug out and formed low protective hills in front of them. Harlan realised Mabuse and Adeline's attack on the Faehome had obviously shaken the Fae, and they weren't taking any chances.

"Hey!" A Fae soldier, dressed in camouflage, with machine gun in his hand, a sword over his back, and a longbow and arrows sitting in a rack next to him shouted at them.

"We are approved. I checked in with Wynscrim." Tylltyr said.

"Yeah, err, when does he go out?"

"Soon, Wynscrim is in charge of the portal defence, he told me Wurthir' s travelling times. I let him know we are following him."

One Fae appeared in the normal glowing blue aura of the portal. Harlan had used it a few times, but it still looked amazingly beautiful to him. Another couple went out. Wurthir hadn't been out yet, and he apparently went out every day.

"So, your mother. You're interested in her?"

"My mom? She's ok, she's in Texas. Oh, you mean my *bio Fae mom?*"

"Yes."

"MY mom is my real mom, but yes, I want to find my Fae mom. Plus, everyone seems to want me to, in particular my dad. I think he feels guilty or something. No reason for him to be." Harlan was aware people kept bringing up his mother. It was a little bit tiresome to discuss, and he himself wasn't even sure how he felt about it.

"She makes good rope."

"So, I'm told." Harlan wondered why the Fae didn't buy rope from the Bavarian hardware stores.

"Oh, look!" Tylltyr said, she grabbed Harlan by the arm. He noticed she did that a lot. More than she needed to.

"Hey, I need to ask you one other thing, before Wurthir comes. I don't understand it, I think it's important," Tylltyr said.

"Sure, what is it," Harlan said.

"Can you explain human character alignments to me?" she said.

"Uhm, character alignments... uhm. Yeah, I think so. They are in games, like roleplaying games. I think Tomoko could probably answer this better."

"So, what is Chaotic good?"

"Well, I always see myself as Chaotic good. Don't follow rules but try to do good. Stupid rules can get in the way," Harlan said. "Sophie probably is too."

"What is Lawful good?"

"Yeah, Errhh that's Tomoko. She doesn't like breaking rules."

"What about Chaotic Evil?"

"Yeah, breaks rules with evil motivations. I guess that would be Mabuse. Hmm, yeah, I reckon."

"True neutral."

"Yeah, err, that one Uhm, the psychopath that does anything they want."

"Would that be Raffaella?"

"Hah, yeah, err, may be, but best you don't tell her that Tylltyr."

"Shhh," the Fae soldier growled at them.

Wurthir appeared, walking along the path from the town. He nodded to the invisible occupants of the bushes generally, stepped into the circle, and cast the spell.

As he did, Tylltyr stepped forward, concentrating.

The blue blur, the pulse of light, and even a little distance from the portal, Harlan could feel the heat.

"Bamberg," Tylltyr said. "That spell was for Bamberg." She looked over to the guard for confirmation. He nodded back.

"Okay, give him five minutes, otherwise he'll hear the portal behind him. I can track him in the forest."

When they got out of the Portal at the other end, they tracked him to the road. He was waiting at the bus stop.

"Damn, we can't get on the bus with him. We'll lose him," Tylltyr said.

Harlan sent a message to Tomoko and Sophie, then turned back to Tylltyr.

"Don't worry, I had some transport on standby."

They waited a couple of minutes, and the engine noise of the two scooters coming their way was all too obvious.

"Harls!" Sophie pulled over. Tomoko pulled over just behind, smiling at both.

Tylltyr stared at the scooters, squinting. "Oh. These are old. Are they safe?"

"Of course, we wouldn't ride them if they weren't. I've magicked the hell out of them. That's what the glyphs are." Harlan noticed Sophie had snapped a little bit. He gave her a frown; she flashed him a guilty pout. She had no idea she was being blunt to people most of the time. Hopeless.

The bus flew by them, and they could see it up ahead. It stopped to pick up Wurthir and continued on into Bamberg. They had to follow it at a distance.

***

Sophie throttled down her accelerator, she had to judge her distance to keep her scooter behind the bus, but also not get too close to it in case Wurthir saw them. In any case, he would only see them if he were sitting in the back seat. Probably.

She really wasn't sure about all this. There were lots of Fae going out of the Faehome. Harlan seemed to think Wurthir was acting unusually. Though, Harlan did have good thieves' instincts. She'd seen it before. He could see things, behaviour in people that she or the other crew couldn't see. Part of his training, part just… Harlan.

She alternated keeping a visual on the bus, and peering at the map on her phone, sitting on an attachment on her handlebars, she had recently got off the Internet. It came in handy.

"Whoa there," Harlan said to Sophie, raising his voice so she could hear him with the helmet on.

The bus had stopped, and Wurthir had got out. The good thing about the scooters was they could leave them anywhere on the footpath. They quickly parked on their stands and ran with their helmets in hand towards Wurthir. He was walking on the footpath ahead of them and turned a corner.

"Where is he going? Sophie muttered, glancing at the others.

Tomoko and Harlan both shook their heads. The area was a mix of offices blocks, and houses. Harlan Sophie didn't know where he was going, and she didn't think anyone else did either. Sophie realised carrying their helmets made them conspicuous, but they couldn't leave them behind. They continued following Wurthir at a distance, and he finally stopped out the front of a big modern office building and went inside.

What's this place? Tylltyr asked, looking at it slightly confused.

Sophie didn't know, she could only see a number on the front. It looked like a fairly standard office block. Tomoko and Harlan both shrugged, and they went in.

"Damn, where is he?" Sophie said. He wasn't anywhere to be seen.

They walked into the foyer area, and then over to the lifts.

"The lights on the lift show they are not going up. He must have taken the stairs." Tomoko said. Made sense, Sophie thought.

They cautiously went to the stairwell, and they could hear Wurthir go up. Sophie felt instant relief they hadn't lost him, after following him for so long. Following the noise of him leaving the stairwell out on to the floor, the first thing they saw was a classroom, full of people sitting down, with someone providing instruction.

Carefully, they peaked over the top of wall though the window. Luckily, there were posters stuck on the window, and they could see between the gaps. They could see inside without being too obvious.

"Oh, there's Wurthir." Tylltyr pointed. Wurthir had come in and joined the class which had already started.

"Sophie. That's your papa," Harlan said. Sophie looked over, and strangely, there sat her papa, sitting peering back at the man giving instructions. *What the hell is Papa doing here?*

"Oh...no. That's..." Sophie looked at Tomoko, who was pointing at the man giving the instructions.

Sophie stared at the man standing up in front of the class, it took a few seconds for her brain to reconcile what she was looking at.

Standing in front of the class, giving instructions, and pointing to some diagrams on the whiteboard, was a familiar man with a slick backed grey ponytail and dark glasses.

It was Mabuse.

12. The Classroom.

Sophie ducked down in fright. Mabuse and Adeline had caused a lot of trouble for them, and his powers of control were not something anyone understood. Sophie had all seen the power of hypnotism and persuasion on the Internet, but she had seen no one misuse them as Mabuse did. His powerful charisma and masterful control over people were both evident by the continuous presence of a small entourage of people, who seemed enthralled by him. Most of all, they had witnessed him control Adeline. He had used her like a real life, tiny lethal puppet, to attack her own mother. He was a seriously powerful individual, and now, with no warning, he had her dad with him.

Tomoko's eyes were wide, Harlan had his hand over his mouth, supressing an audible reaction. Tylltyr, looked at them all taking in their reaction, confused, she of course had no idea who he was.

She looked over at Harlan, there was a look of concern on his face. She knew he would be worried about her, with her papa here in this room.

So, Harlan's hunch was right, Wurthir is somehow connected to Mabuse. But her papa? What was he doing here?

She peaked back over the into the classroom through the window again.

He then left the stage and walked among the people in the classroom, he started picking people and sending them to the stage. Sophie could feel herself get hot, sweat started forming on her brow, but she ignored it and watched what direction he was walking. He walked over to her father and picked him. Sophie's hand raised to her mouth, supressing the urge to cry out.

He whispered something in each of their ears, their eyes glazed over, and their heads nodded forward on their chests, each of the five, including Sophie's father, standing still as statues.

Then two of them turned to face each other, a man and a woman, both with short brown hair. Mabuse flicked his fingers, and the woman slapped the man in the face. Then the man slapped the woman in the face. Both then turned, robotically, slowly to the crowd, and smiled.

The whole thing was eery and disturbing. Sophie wasn't sure what it was supposed to prove if anything? Was Mabuse doing it because he enjoyed doing it, or did it prove something to the audience. The audience clapped at the show, and Sophie noticed the red marks on both their faces.

Mabuse sent them all back to their seats and was now pointing to some diagrams that were on the whiteboard at the front of the class. He seemed to be giving instructions on speaking in public, conveying a message, communication. But there was something odd about it. Tomoko shuffled over to Sophie and whispered to her. "Listen to him, there's something odd. He is emphasizing certain words. It is… he is trying to push some other message through, with certain words."

It was unsettling seeing him do it.

Sophie looked at Mabuse, trying to listen to his words. Trying to pick out the words he was emphasising. She glanced at her papa, poor papa! She went back to listening to the words. What was he trying to do?

"You should go inside," Harlan said.

"Yes, go inside. You can hear the message better," Tylltyr said.

"No. I'm not. I want to help my papa. I'm not going in there."

Tomoko leaned in. "Yes go in. You'll hear the words."

The last thing she remembered was Tomoko's face.

Then things went blank.

***

Sophie woke up in the stairwell. Harlan was carrying her over his shoulder, the others with looks of concern were running down the stairs.

They ran out of the building, as Sophie looked around, trying to work out what was going on.

"She is awake. Kawaisou!" Tomoko said.

Harlan put Sophie on her feet, grabbed her hand, and they kept running. Sophie was still foggy but running away from the building seemed like a good thing to do.

They finally got back to the scooters, before they stopped, trying to get their breath.

"You started going into the classroom," Tomoko said.

"What? Yeah, last thing I remember you three were telling me to go in? Sophie said.

"We what?" Harlan, Raphaella, Tylltyr, and all said in unison.

"You were going in the classroom. I had to sleep spell you," Tomoko said, a quaver in her voice.

"None of us told you to go inside. Why would we do that?" Harlan said.

"I... don't know. I remember you turning to me and telling me to go inside. But it was sort of blurry. But I was listening to Mabuse, concentrating on his words." She shook her head. It was like she was in a fog."

Harlan, Raphaella, Tylltyr and Tomoko looked at each other, concerned.

"I think...uhm... that was Mabuse making you think we were telling you to go in," Tomoko said, "and also, you look drunk."

"Hang on Tomoko, You what? You sleep spelled me!" Sophie said.

"Yeah, errh, she did. I grabbed you and pulled you down. Are you okay?" Harlan's face was frowning and worried, concerned.

"I'm groggy. I think I need to go home." Sophie shook her head again.

Sophie noticed the expressions on their faces. Harlan and Tomoko and even Tylltyr looked very worried. She tried to keep a normal expression, so as to not concern them, but she was worried about apparently had been her under the effect of Mabuse's power, not to mention the fact her father was in some room with their very dangerous foe...

Harlan rode her scooter, back to her place, and she went inside and went to sleep.

13. The Convenient skillsets of Mr. M

Harlan and Sophie had both met at a park, to run through what they knew so far. Her scooter was still warm, so she stood, leaning on it to keep off a bit of the chill.

"Soph, you okay there, bud?" The look of concern on his face was heart-warming.

"Really, I'm fine. But thanks. It's my papa I need to worry about now."

Harlan nodded, a serious look on his face. Mabuse was always a concern to the crew. Having people's family involved was worrying business indeed.

Harlan had explained Tylltyr to them, and what he had learned from her about the Fae. In turn, Sophie had told everyone Johannes's insights. But out of it all, the ropemaker story seemed to get Johannes's interest. It was a trait of the people in the dreamcast, they didn't always behave like real people.

They then started discussing the magic ban, and the prince's job they had to do. All they had so far was that a new political party had formed, New Nation, and it was involved in the ban. It wasn't much to go on.

"Oh, dayum." Harlan was looking at his phone. He showed it to Sophie.

Sophie looked at his phone, there was a newspaper article, with   big   letters.

It's official. Anti-Mage ban to be included in Referendum

She read a bit more of the article. It was official. The day of the vote for the referendum had been planned for Sunday 14th, and the magic ban was to be one of the items. It was about two and a half weeks away.

"Yeah, dayum," Harlan said again.

"We have two and a half weeks left. We have to convince people not to vote for it, or to reveal the people behind the vote and expose them to the public so people don't vote for them. If there are outside people interfering secretly in our politics, it will look bad." She paused. "Somehow." Her voice sounded less than confident.

They both sat in silence.

"Hmm… well. Let's keep thinking about what we can do," Harlan said.

***

Tomoko had rung ahead to meet their information gathering consultant, Mr. M, while Raphaella said she was practicing some sword work. They generally had to meet him at a Starbucks. Out of all the quirky old world coffee places in the modern medieval setting of Bamberg, Mr. M insisted on a big US chain café for coffee.

Sophie wondered momentarily what Mr. M's background was. Why was a Chinese Businessman in Germany? How did he become an investigator? Was there some international element to his work here?

They walked in, Sophie scanned the room for Mr. M, she initially hadn't spotted him, but then saw him quite close to her, and he swished his hand through the air slowly at her to get her attention. He had a man with him, a colleague with glasses and a short dark beard, long blond hair, and a beanie. Mr. M himself wore a suit, a black flat cap, and round slightly shaded glasses. As always, a bit unusual, but it was a busy place, and he wasn't the only person walking around wearing sunglasses in the room. Sophie gazed at the man with the blond hair but couldn't actually tell his ethnicity. She guessed he may be Asian as well.

"Mr. M." Sophie nodded.

"Ah, hello, Sophie, Harlan, Tomoko san. So nice to see you. What is the pleasure for which you have contacted me?"

"Nice to see you too." Sophie peered at the odd man sitting next to Mr. M. His long blond hair, its nature betrayed by obvious black roots, fell over his sunglasses and his face.

Harlan leaned over, putting out his hand to the mysterious man. "Hi. I'm Harlan."

The man ignored him.

Mr. M smiled. "Oh, don't worry about my friend. He's very shy. Please ignore him."

Sophie shuffled her feet; the situation was awkward. Sophie noticed Tomoko gazing at the man, rather oddly. She seemed to be studying him intently. At this point, the man stood up and walked off. Mr. M ignored his departure.

"So, I would assume you have a job for me?" He drank from a ridiculously big sized ceramic mug with the usual oversized green logo on the side.

"We do," Harlan said.

Sophie leaned into the group, and lowered her voice. "We heard about the movement to make magic illegal in Bavaria. Obviously, as mages for us, this is really, bad."

"I do not want to leave here; I don't want to see the Cervitaur's forced out," Tomoko added.

"This would make life very difficult for us. I mean, some of us haven't even told our families we are mages." Sophie glanced over at Harlan, every time the topic of her being forced to leave Bamberg, she noticed he appeared upset. She turned away from him, before he noticed her staring and continued. "But we know that after the Government banned the mages in Lower Saxony, it could happen in the Rhine Palatinate, then if the Bavarian Principality banned it here in Bavaria, it could run out of control. We heard rumours about some people being behind it. Controlling the vote."

"Ah, yes… I have heard something about that. Why people would want to make magic illegal. It has hurt anyone. Well, *recently,*" Mr. M said. Sophie gathered he was trying to be sympathetic.

"Any information you could get us...would be good. Apparently, the Party that is trying to push through the new laws to make it illegal is called The New Nation. It's a party..."

"...to protect the people and make Bavaria safe for Bavarians," Mr. M said. "I know a little bit about them. Most...interesting." He sipped his coffee, looking down at the table before looking up again.

"Harlan, what about the Fae?" Tomoko looked over at him.

"Fae use magic, but the Faehome is protected from human society as you can only access it via the portal. The Fae travellers come into human society and use limited magic. But if the vote gets through and forces the Mages out, and the Cervitaurs left, I don't know what the Fae would do. Maybe they would relocate, though that would be hard. Maybe they would close off the portal and stop contact with humans."

Sophie was a bit shocked to hear him say it. She hadn't really thought about how it affected the Fae.

Mr. M finally spoke, breaking the silence. "Okay...and I think there is something else we need to discuss."

Sophie looked at him blankly.

"Our fee. 2000 Gold marks."

Harlan coughed. "1500!"

"Just pay him, Harlan." Sophie knew they needed the information. They were getting 10,000 from the prince. Overall, they were way still in front.

Harlan pulled out two bags from his backpack and gave them to Mr. M.

"Yeah, are you going to count them?"

"Ah, no. I trust my young friends." Mr. M took the bags of coins, nodded to each of them, and left. She noticed that when he was outside on the street, his mysterious blonde friend joined him, and they walked off together in what seemed like a serious discussion.

Harlan was still mildly shocked. "Ouch. That hurt our bank balance."

Tomoko stared at them both as they walked off. "Odd."

"Yeah, but he's one odd guy that may help you guys keep out of Witch Prison," Harlan said.

Sophie gazed at Harlan expecting him to be smiling. He wasn't.

Harlan's phone rang and he picked it up, an expression of surprise and a smile came across his face. "Tylltyr? You have a phone?"

The smile disappeared, and he dropped the phone to the table.

"Tylltyr just rang. She said we need to meet her. Something about your papa and Mabuse."

14. The Old Palace of the Prince Bishop

"Hello Gorgeous, aren't I lucky to see you again so soon!" Tylltyr Hugged Harlan, who politely hugged her back, then peeling her off him, and shrugging at the others.

Raphaella, Sophie, and Tomoko had all agreed to meet her, urgently considering the circumstances.

"What this about my father?" Sophie said.

The smile disappeared off Tylltyr's face. "Sorry, I think its worrisome news, for you. I had to call you right away. Wurthir contacted me.

"Wurthir?" Tomoko said.

"Yes," Tylltyr responded.

"We can't trust him!" Sophie said, her voice raising.

"Well, he says your father is with Mabuse, and you should come   and   see   him."
Sophie's eyes widened. She picked up her phone and rang Hisako, normally around this time, her papa would be home. However, Hisako said he wasn't there. She rang her papa.

"He's not at home, and he's not answering. Where is Wurthir?" Sophie said.

"He wants us to meet him at the Old Palace, The old Prince Bishop's palace."

"Yeah, Erhh do we trust him?" Harlan said.

"No," Tomoko said, shaking her head violently, "He is untrustworthy and at least moderately compromised."

They all looked at each other blankly, silently.

Sophie nodded. "Okay, we need to see him. We don't have any choice. However, I'm going to call in some help. Akshay owes me a favour or two."

***

They got on their scooters, Tylltyr hopping on the back of Harlan's. The trip to the Old Palace was not a pleasant one for Sophie. She felt her heart beating in her chest. All she could think of was her papa. And she was very worried.

They got off their scooters and could see a lone figure standing in front of the Old Palace.

"That's him over there," Tylltyr said. "Traitor!"

"Raphaella, are you armed?" Sophie said, staring at him.

Raffaella nodded and pointed at her earrings. It was a magic item, a tiny sword they had got from Johannes's buried chest. It was tiny, and could be worn as an earring, but upon command expanded to a full-size two-handed sword.

"I think this is more subtle," she said.

They walked over to the old palace, and there standing, blankly out the front of the palace, was Wurthir. He was calm, his hands clasped in front of him.

"Hello, Tylltyr. Hello again, Harlan." He nodded at the others. "Hello, we have not met. I am Wurthir."

"Yes, we know. What are you going to tell us about my father? Where is he?" Sophie could hear her voice raising. She tried to calm herself, but the familiar heat rising up her neck, the creeping feeling of anxiety was coming on. She tried to control her breathing. She needed to concentrate.

"This way," he said simply. He remained calm, not reacting an iota to Sophie anger. He then spun on his heels and started walking briskly. They followed him, and he kept walking down by the river Legnitz, and then into the older merchant quarter of the town, filled with a hodge podge of older buildings.

"Hey, yeah, err, where are we going?" Harlan called out.

He ignored them.

Tomoko furrowed her brow and crossed her arms. Sophie could only think about her papa.

Finally, they came to a laneway. It was dark, a thin laneway between old buildings. At the end was a small door. He knocked on it, in a complicated series of knocks. The door opened, and he led them into a house, and then into a big room.

Sophie peered into the room. There was her father, standing, with a blank expression, and also the diminutive mage, Adeline.

Between them, at a table, sat their enemy, Doktor Mabuse.

15. Doktor Mabuse Der Spiegel

"This is Doktor Mabuse, Der Spiegel." Wurthir said.

There sat Mabuse at a table, a pack of cards in front of him. He had his usual dark glasses on so you could not make out his eyes behind them. He had grey hair, slicked back in a tight ponytail, he was pale, but thin. He had black gloves and wore a high white starched collar. To his left sat her father, and to his right stood Adeline, a hood over her face, the lower part of her face and her blonde hair hanging down.

There were three men behind him, two large bald men, both wearing black T shirts and jeans, who looked only similar, except that one had a beard, another had a silver chain and cross around his neck. Sophie wondered if they were human, but suspected Mabuse could have transmuted goatkin. He had used the half goat creatures as hired muscle in the past; they were easy for him to control. With them was a slighter man, with a beard, a cap. He wore glasses and a black medical mask over the bottom part of his face, and he stood behind everyone.

Her father face expressed only nothing.

"Give me back my papa you Bastard!" Sophie screamed. She felt a hand on her shoulder. It was Harlan.

"Sophie. Stay calm. Focus," Harlan said, in his calming voice.

"Come in, sit down. Do you like to gamble?" Mabuse said, dramatic cheer in his voice. His hand motioned to the chair at the table, opposite him.

"I'm not gambling with you," Sophie said, trying to keep from screaming at him.

"Sit!"

She felt oddly compelled to sit. She sat down. Mabuse got out a deck of cards and started shuffling the cards as he spoke.

"So, I wanted you to come here and gamble with him, what type of game should we play?"

"I'm not gambling with you I said!"

"You are. You need to offer me a prize, what stakes do you have? This is mine." He motioned at Sophie's father with a card in hard, "Win him back."

He paused, flipping the cards.

"What do you want from us?" Harlan said.

"Don't forget, Mage. We haven't forgotten you. We haven't finished with you yet!" Tylltyr said.

Sophie had forgotten that Mabuse had previously organised an attack on the Faehome. She was surprised at the anger in Tylltyr's voice. Tylltyr had until now seemed quite happy and lightweight.

"Oh, I'm not a mage. I can't do magic. But I can control people who do. I have one, but… I think I need more. Probably a lot. The Hanseatic league do what they do with mages, but…" He shook his head. "wasteful…mages are very useful tools, and not to be discarded."

He pointed at Sophie and then pointed behind him. "Come over here."

There was something in his voice. Sophie felt compelled to stand up and join him on his side of the table.

She felt Harlan grab her on the shoulder. Then Tomoko and Tylltyr stood in front of her, between them. She saw in her peripheral vision, Raffaella moving towards the edge of the room, circling to the right. Mabuse's people were eyeing her. Things seemed to slow

At that point they heard a crashing sound behind them. Sophie quickly turned.

It was Akshay, stepping through a doorway, the broken door partially off the wall, a lock dangling off the door frame. *Just in time,* she thought, and felt a weight lift off her shoulders, her mind cleared. Sophie had asked him to follow them. She looked back, and he stood there, filling the broken door frame, his big presence supported by two other large Cervitaurs behind him.

Mabuse just smiled. There was a flash of light as Adeline's hands traced two shield spells, the glyphs appearing in each hand. Then to the right, Sophie could see a huge split appear in the door, breaking it down the middle. Two mud golems were behind it, smashing their way through, bits of wood flying. They pushed through to defend their creator. Of course, Adeline was an earth elemental, Sophie realised she should have expected it.

Sophie shook her head, regained her thoughts. "Tomoko!"

They both cast lightning bolts at Adeline, who easily deflected them with the shield spell, its violet haze hanging in the air, the energy from the spells dissipating on the ground.

Mabuse stepped back behind Adeline, his henchmen stepping in front of him, shielding him.

Then, Adeline drew another glyph in the air, and cast it at the stone wall behind them. Akshay and his cervitaurs started clashing with the Golems, but they Sophie feared for them, the golems were huge, and crouching in the house.

The stone wall behind them disappeared, the stone looking like it was melting, a vast hole appeared in it.

"Papa!" Sophie called out. He seemed to be in a daze.

Mabuse simply left through the hole, with Wurthir, his henchmen and Adeline. Sophie moved forward and grabbed her papa's hand and dragged him to her.

The golems moved forward aggressively, stepping in front of them, barring anyone from following. Sophie could see the ducking and weaving of Raffaella, as she pummelled them with sword blows. They stood there, taking the damage, as she hewed at them. Akshay smashed at them with the chairs.

"We need to go!" Akshay yelled.

They left out the front of the house, Sophie overwhelmingly relieved.

As they left, walking back to their scooters parked back at the old palace, she looked at her father. He seemed to be in a daze.

"Is your father going to be All right, do you think?"

"I hope so. I know who to ask. In any case, I'm glad we have him back. I have to keep him away from all that now."

"Tylltyr, thank you so much."

"That's okay, happy to help out a nice human." She turned to Harlan. "But he owes me a coffee."

"By the way… you know," Harlan said, sounding unsure. "I don't think that was Mabuse."

"What?" Raphaella said.

"I'm not sure, but that guy was dressed as Mabuse. I mean he looked like him, but I could see the seamline for that wig." Harlan traced the line above his own brow. "And he had makeup on. It was incredibly well done, but it's part of my training to spot it."

"Do you think the guy behind…?" Tomoko said.

"Yeah, errh, yeah. I think Mabuse was the guy behind him, with the glasses and the face mask covering his mouth. He could speak to use his power of suggestion, and yeah, the mask, well we couldn't see him," Harlan said.

"Yes, another thing, Wurthir made a very obvious introduction for Mabuse. There was no need really, but it was part of the set up," Tomoko said.

"Sneaky. I will kill him next time I see him," Raphaella said, crossing her arms.

They said their goodbyes, and Sophie finally felt the adrenaline leaving her body. Her papa grabbed her around the waist as the rode home. She thought about the night, what it all meant. But overwhelmingly, she felt relieved to have her father back.

16. History 101 and Mr Freidrickson

It was Thursday morning before school, and as Sophie came out of her bedroom, she bumped into her father coming out of the bathroom. As soon as she saw him, it triggered her concern.

"Hey, Papa."

"Oh, Guten Morgen," Ernst said. Despite everything, he seemed perfectly normal.

"Err, do you remember last night?"

"Yes, of course," he said, without adding any further detail.

"Err, I mean, what did you do?" she asked. It was odd. He seemed perfectly normal.

"I went to the confidence building course, presentation skills."

"Did you do anything after that?"

He frowned momentarily, and then just shrugged, and shook his head.

"Yes, Hisako mentioned you are going to confidence building/presentation skills workshops?"

As yes, I am. Just to help me with my lecture presentations. They are done by a man called Konrad Böckstiegel. He's very charismatic, he has the whole class glued to every word he says."

I bet he does, Sophie thought. Not surprisingly, Mabuse was using a fake name.

Ernst considered something momentarily. "You know, you would get benefit from it, you should come along."

Like hell, she thought. "Hmm, not sure papa, when is the next one?

"Ah, about two weeks," he said, focussing on making a coffee. *Good, he doesn't remember anything. At least that allows for some time to stop him from going again* Sophie thought.

***

Back at school, Harlan was on an upper-level veranda, looking down below. Sophie walked up to him, and noticed he was looking at the girl students.

"How is your papa?" Harlan said.

"He seems normal, though I haven't seen him much, I spoke to him. I'm relieved now."

"Relieved?"

"I have a plan, using Oskar. So much more relieved. Sooo much."

"You know, Sophie, if you left here, and Tomoko left, I don't know what I'd do. We are a great little group. You're such a good friend. I wanted to tell you that. I was thinking about it, but thought too often yeah, you know, we think of things but don't say it."

Sophie was taken aback. She knew they had gone through a lot together, and Circle 66 was a tight little group. She reached up and gave him a hug. Momentarily thinking about leaving, her eyes started to moisten. She kept hugging him so he couldn't see.

"Don't worry, we will fight it. Plus, If I leave, I will bring you with me," Sophie said. She knew it wasn't that simple, there were his ties to the Fae to consider.

Sophie decided it was a good idea to change the topic, she pointed down at the girls he had been admiring. "Got your eye on anyone in particular?"

"Aww…yeah… only for you Soph." He whacked her playfully in the arm. She rubbed it, frowning. He then seemed slightly serious, like he was considering something.

"Actually, you know, well yeah, there is…" Sophie's suck in her breath involuntarily, *was Harlan actually going to talk about a love interest?*

Exactly at that point, Tomoko appeared, turning the corner. Harlan saw her, and he stopped mid-sentence. *Damn.* Sophie made a mental note to follow up later. Harlan never talked about girls.

"I have been looking for you two. See this?" Tomoko waved some bit of paper in her hand. "I keep getting letters in my bag from boys. It is annoying. I think I get these letters because I am the only Japanese in the school, it is like I am some rare exotic jungle creature."

"Ye-ah...I dunno. I mean, isn't that a good thing?" Harlan said.

Tomoko pulled out some letters, gave them to him, and shook her head. "Far, too many. You can go out with them."

Raffaella exited a doorway, her head swivelling quickly until she caught sight of them and strutted over. Sophie noticed Harlan straightened up when he saw her and smiled.

"Mr Freidrickson's class. I am excited." Raffaella said "excited" without even the barest hint of excitement in her voice.

Sophie smirked.

They made their way into the classroom, dumping their bags on the floor and pulling out their books. Freidrickson's class was starting, however, this time they realised that "Three Bells Incorporated" were not around. The Three Bells student members would usually sit over near the wall, slightly in front of Sophie, but their three chairs sat very obviously empty. Sophie noticed a few students staring at the empty chairs, presumably surprised. It would have been the first time they had seen them in class after discovering they were a group of dreamcasters as well. Tomoko and Sophie both gazed at each other.

"You thinking what I'm thinking?" Sophie said.

"They aren't here...mmm... so they are doing a job?" Harlan gazed back at her.

"Hey, you three." Freidrickson pointed at them. "Class is starting no chatter please. Please open your textbooks to page 53."

Sophie tried to stay focussed on Freidrickson's less than interesting class on the invention of the three teeth shearing comb in Australia and its effect on the wool industry. Glancing over at the three empty chairs, she could only feel envy.

17. The Boyfriend

Sophie had timed things right. When Oskar arrived at her house, only Hisako was there.

She spoke to him outside before they went in. "So, the plan is. You're my boyfriend."

"I'm your WHAT?"

"I need a reason to introduce you to my papa. So... he will sit and talk to you. Otherwise, he will be running around and, on his computer, marking student's papers.

"Oh okay." He smiled. "My *love.*"

She shook her head, with a curt smile. It was stressful, but she wanted to make sure her papa was okay.

As they went up the stairs, she saw Hisako.

"Oh, Hisako, quick before Papa comes home. What do you know about the course papa is doing?"

"Oh. It's supposed to be good. It's about personal confidence in public speaking. He's doing it to make his university lectures more exciting."

"It's not. It's bad. There's a bad mage involved in it. You need to trust me. Do whatever you can to stop him from going."

Hisako stood staring at them silently for a good ten seconds, then finally spoke.

"This is a joke, right?"

"It's not. It's serious. I'm here to break a spell type effect," Oskar said.

"Who are you?" Hisako said, and Sophie realised she hadn't even introduced Oskar.

"I'm a healer."

Hisako went quiet for another ten seconds. She flicked her hands through the air, in a vague replication of a mage making a glyph. "One of those sorts of healers?"

He nodded.

Hisako studied their faces. Apparently, their solemnity convinced her.

"Okay. I'll get him to stop going. Don't worry, I have my ways. You just make sure he's okay."

Sophie heard the keys in the door. It was her papa.

"Quick!" They went and sat down on the Sofa. Sophie shifted the coffee table closer to the sofa, and put her hand under it, to see how it appeared.

As Ernst walked past, he glanced over at Sophie. "Hello, Sophie, hello…err."

"…Oskar. Nice to meet you."

"Nice to mee you." Her papa kept walking. Sophie knew she had to get him back.

"Papa, I thought I would introduce you to Oskar. My boyfriend."

Ernst stopped dead. Sophie peeked over and noticed Hisako cover her face, trying to hide her smile.

He immediately turned around and sat down with them.

"Oh. Her boyfriend. Oh. Uhm, oh, Sophie's first boyfriend." Sophie realised her papa was a bit stunned, but now was her chance. She gave Oskar the look, and he moved forward, with his hands under the table. He cast it, she could sense the magic spell go off, as it did, she stood up and coughed, to distract her father who glanced over at her.

Oskar cast the spell again quickly, which made Sophie cough again, very loud, and dramatically through her hands in the air.

"Are you okay?" her papa said.

"Yes, fine. Anyway, Oskar has to go now," Sophie said.

"Oskar must go. I haven't spoken to him."

"I have to go? Oh, yes, I have…err…. training. Nice to meet you both."

As they left, Oskar went to give Sophie a kiss, she strategically turned her check,

"Bye, love!" he spoke.

Cheeky, Sophie thought. She whispered to him, "Thanks so much. I owe you."

"No, you don't. I'm happy to help. That was *Vanderveldts Dispellation.* It will take off any magical effect and will remove any mind controls."

He is a genuine nice guy. "Thank you so much. Oh, also why did you cast it on him twice?"

"Oh, I didn't the second one was on you. Harlan told me to in case *you* were still affected." With that, he left. Smiling. Quickly.

Harlan! she thought.

18. Muffins and The Electric Light Kafe

They were all at Jeffs. Once again, there was another round of Muffin purchases, and multiple coffees. It was the obligatory over-purchase of food and coffee to thank Jeff.

Raffaella stared down at all the food in front of her. "I can't eat it all." She took out some silver marks and went to hand it to Jeff.

"No. We can't give him the money. It's a lot better us purchasing things from him. Plus, it always appears good to the other customers if we are here buying things and eating everything." Sophie said.

"You buy it. I'll eat it." Harlan raised an eyebrow, trying to pick which muffin looked the biggest. "The only issue though is, it's hardly good advertising. We are mostly hidden upstairs."

"This is troubling for me. I am going to need a bigger engine on my scooter if I keep eating all these western foods." Tomoko put her hand on her stomach and looked at the pile of muffins. She picked the smallest muffin on the plate and gingerly nibbled on it.

At precisely five p.m. on the dot, Three Bells Incorporated came up the stairs, led by Ying, who seemed annoyed, possibly because of Oskar leaving them.

Oskar was not with them, but now they were joined by a new member. He was an Asian man, he had a bowl haircut, jet black glossy hair and big round dark eyes. *Is he a healer, to replace Oskar?*

Hans introduced him as they walk past. "This is David Chan." They all nodded and introduced themselves briefly. Chan nodded, at all of them, without saying anything.

Sophie examined him up and down. She vaguely recognised him from their school, but he wasn't someone she had spoken to, nor was in any of their classes. She glanced at the others; Tomoko shrugged. They didn't seem to recognise him either.

The Three Bells members walked, always exactly together, on time, giving off an element of pride. The faint clinking of the bells tied to their boots followed them to their table. They all sat down.

"They need theme music. May be to go with the bells," Harlan whispered.

"I want bells." Tomoko muttered.

"Drums." Raphaella said.

Hans looked over to Sophie. "Did you want to speak to us?"

It was awkward, and Sophie thought a bit of a powerplay. Clearly, they would not come to Sophie, so Sophie and the other Circle 66 members went over to them.

"Mind if we join you for a minute?"

"Please." Hans waved his hand at the empty chairs.

Sophie sat down. "Thanks for the warning, we wanted to know what magic you used?"

"Ah. Trade secret," Hans said, straight faced.

Sophie Harlan and Tomoko laughed, then realised Hans was probably serious.

"We've heard some bad news. Something that affects both our parties." Sophie said.

She was hoping this would get them on side and build a bit of trust. So far, it seems to be them doing all the building.

"Yes? What is it?" Hans said. It had been a minute and Heloisa was already standing up, and doing some dance sort of moves, while smiling to herself, and mouthing some words to a song.

"We're trying to stop Magic being made illegal in Bavaria. We could do with your help."

Ying, and Hans's expressions were suddenly dour. Heloise kept dancing, half listening, till she realised the serious tone of the room and halted to join the conversation.

Hans leant in. Sophie noticed his arrogant attitude disappeared. It was satisfying.

"We don't want to live in a place where magic is illegal. I've done it," Hans said. His expression was cold.

"What do you mean?" Sophie said.

"I lived in Vilnius. In the Hanseatic League. When Latvia joined the Hanseatic League, all the mages left. Stupidly my parents didn't. We weren't practicing mages, but we were of mage lineage. We got tossed in an "education camp" with thousands of other mages. It was called an education camp, but it was a prison. There was a big insurrection, a breakout, we got away. Lots died." Hans said, Sophie cold see him gritting his teeth, he looked down at the tabletop as he spoke.

Everyone was quiet. You could have heard a pin drop.

Hans crossed his arms and glanced at each of them in turn. "Take it from me, magic is banned, and not long after, the Hansa moves in. They ban art they don't like; they burn books. They control the internet. It's worse for mages, but eventually everyone suffers."

"Yeah, wow. Not good," Harlan said.

"How do you think you can stop it?" Hans said, he peered at all of them, his gaze stopping at Sophie.

"We are gathering information on who is behind it. Maybe it's directly the Hansa, maybe not. After that we will expose them to the public and use that to try to discredit their campaign. Hopefully, that will swing the numbers," Sophie said, even impressing herself as to how dramatic she could make it sound.

"Mabuse…and the Hanseatic league, have a fragrant disregard for mage rights," Harlan said.

"Flagrant." Tomoko muttered below her breath.

"Harlan… you just said the Hansa have a *sweet-smelling disregard for mage rights*." Sophie shot him a smile.

"Oh," Harlan said.

"Yes. Why would anyone have a sweet-smelling disregard for mage rights?" Tomoko said, staring at Harland, grinning.

"Okay, I think there are more important things to talk about than English usage," Sophie said.

Hans stared at them, scowled slightly. He stood up abruptly and left.

The rest of the Three Bells Mages watched him go, with blank expressions. They didn't seem happy about it. Ying met their gaze, and then said rather formally. "Well, this is something we need to address, we'll consider it and get back to you."

With that, they left the room. There was still a professional if not personal rift between the groups. Sophie wasn't sure if it would get better.

After they had left the three sat around, trying to finish off the remainder of the muffins.

"Well, at least they are good muffins. Monday they were like rocks," Harlan said, his voice muffled as he started putting another in his mouth.

Sophie sat, ruminating.

"I still think we need a healer. They had one. Or a doctor," Raffaella said.

"I think it is both a deficiency and a medium gap in our team." Tomoko nodded.

"There could be a death," Raffaella added.

"Yeah, well a doctor won't help that," Harlan added.

"A doctor in Circle 66? That sounds expensive. Plus, much of the time I don't think they would be doing much. We would need a doctor/mage multiclass, or a doctor/warrior. They'd get bored otherwise," Tomoko said.

"Healer makes sense," Raphaella said.

"Yes. A doctor for us would be both majorly expensive and probably inappropriate. The doctor could be elsewhere, helping the sick," Tomoko agreed.

"Well, we wouldn't have them walking around in their white coats and stethoscope. Yeah, that would just be weird," Harlan added.

Sophie had sat there quietly thinking to herself while the doctor conversation was ongoing.

"Okay. I have an idea. Tomoko and I went to a meeting with all the Illusionists before with Rupert. There were the illusionists from Bavaria there. They have a lot to lose from this. Maybe we can get their help?"

Tomoko nodded. "Okay, that makes sense. They may know what to do."

Just as they got through the plate of muffins, Jeff came up the stairs. Sophie was on edge that he would offer them more and they would have to say yes, but he came over to the table and sat down with a huge dramatic sigh. He had a purple and red backpack draped over his shoulder.

"All right then? Three Bells 'ave gone, yeah?"

Sophie nodded.

"Okay, so I need to bring this to your attention. I have another job for you. I know you have a lot on your plate 'n all, but this is a special job."

"Jeff. No, we are concentrating on all that's going on. We don't have time…"

"How much does it pay?" Harlan asked instantly.

"It's a quick job. And it pays 3000 goldmarks."

A big smile came across his face. Tomoko seemed impressed. Raffaella glanced at it and said simply, "Cool."

Sophie realised 3000 would cover their fees to Mr. M, with some left over. That was a good fee for a quick job.

"Guys, I'm told it's *easy peasey*. You must put something in a room."

Sophie appeared blank for a second. "Something in a room? We must put a glyph in a room for a spell to work. Or some sort of artefact?"

Harlan glanced at Jeff. "Generally, I'm used to taking things *from* rooms."

"No. You need to put THIS in the room." Jeff emphasised *this*.

"Okay, so what is this?" Sophie said.

Jeff didn't say anything, He had a bag draping over his shoulder. He unzipped it and pulled out an old, smudged, smoke alarm, the flat round cylindrical type that go on the ceiling. Sophie recognised it, she always had to reset the one at home with a broom handle when her dad set it off by burning the sausages… before he gave up on cooking.

"This." He put it on the table in front of them.

Harlan gazed at it, stroking his chin. "Yeah, well, so we err, have to install a smoke alarm in a room?"

Sophie smiled. "*You* have to install a smoke alarm in a room."

Jeff stared at them all. "Well, sorta. You got to replace the one that is there with this. It looks the same. Bring the other one back to me, don't lose it. It's very important, apparently. A'right?"

"Why is it very important?" Harlan asked.

Jeff shrugged his shoulders. "No bloody idea. These are the instructions for the job. I just let people know. One thing though.

a.m."

"Tonight!" all three said.

Jeff nodded. "That's why they are paying so much."

Harlan scanned each of their faces. "Jeff, before we accept this job, we normally only take jobs we are comfortable with. I only ever breaking into someone's house for a good reason, and if the risk is low. Where is this thing going?"

Jeff gave them a bit of paper with the details.

"You've been there before. It's the headquarters of the London Illusionists."

"I do not like London Illusionists, too much ego," Tomoko said, laughed, then stopped when she noticed no one else was. Then sneered.

Harlan smiled, Sophie nodded at them all, smiled and held out her hand to Jeff. "Job accepted!"

Bernard M Lyons

19. The Standing Stones of London

The London illusionists of course, had an ancient obelisk in the basement, the building having been built around it in the late 1700s. But since Circle 66 had used it before and been found out, it was likely now guarded, or booby trapped. The illusionists themselves didn't know the spells to use it, however, they could easily stop it from being used by others.

For Sophie, it was another Thursday night of study at Tomoko's. Her father didn't seem to mind, Sophie thought it was because he always regarded Tomoko as being the sensible, straightforward one of the groups. After Oskar's work, he seemed to be back to normal, but Sophie felt reassured Hisako was keeping tabs on him.

After much discussion, with a boisterous Harlan pushing his thoughts on the matter, they found there was a large standing stone outside London that was on the list of place names they could use. They would take their scooters and passports; someone may stop them.

The scooters of Circle 66 rode out to the standing stone in the forest. It was getting cold, and the *dak dak* sound of the engines sounded unnervingly loud in the relative quiet of the chilled night-time forest. Harlan rode first, looking around, left, and right like he was more worried than usual about things. Sophie knew there was no issue *now*. The issue would be… when they got there.

They lined up the four in front of the big stone, in the space that Sophie knew the spell would concentrate on, so that they would leave no one behind.

"It's over to you now Sophie. Spell us up, Scottie!" Harlan said, giving a thumbs up and a big grin to Sophie.

Sophie smiled, though a little confused about who Scottie was. It certainly wasn't the first time she didn't understand a Harlan reference.

She cast the spell anyway.

The usual blue blur dropped all about them, like glowing blue snowflakes. Energy filled the air. Sophie could feel it on her skin, bright and warm, always reassuring that the spell was working. She felt the shimmering energy, the prickling sensation. It was only the second time they had taken the scooters with them using the portal, and they had to be careful to squash them together. Sophie still didn't understand if the portal would cut off half a scooter if it weren't close enough to the Obelisk. Like much of her spellcasting, she only ever understood 90% of how it all worked.

In what was probably only seconds, the scooters and riders appeared in a *circle* of large stones. Tomoko had found them on Google maps, these were the Avebury stones. The grass was a bright green, the area well-kept and touristy.

England... Sophie thought. She took in a deep breath of cold English air. Despite her mother being from here, she had spent little time here and didn't feel overly English. But being here felt good, and a twitch of excitement tingled in her chest.

Still cold, and a slight drizzle, but not as cold as the mountains in Bamberg

"England again!" Tomoko said excitedly.

Raffaella glanced about her. She had decided not to bring a large sword with her but was wearing one of the tiny magic swords as an earring, just in case. It was a relic she could activate on a command word to turn into a full-size sword. Sophie knew she kept it on her in case she got into trouble and didn't have a normal sword with her. *Handy.*

Sophie looked at her watch. "About two hours to get to the London Illusionists HQ. Let's go."

They stayed on the back roads, avoiding the main freeways, with Tomoko's scooter leading. She had the best GPS and was the one that had spent the most amount of time in the UK before.

Within an hour, their scooters had rolled into the busy and slightly scary streets of London. All of them except for Tomoko were nervous of driving in a big city, Sophie reassured herself with the fact that the headquarters wasn't in the busiest part of town. Sophie felt the heat coming up her neck, the familiar feeling she had when she was nervous, but there was a thrilling feeling in her chest. There was the challenge of driving on the other side of the road, when they drove in Tokyo, she had to drive on the left-hand side of the road, the same as London, so at least she was used to that.

Finally, getting to the headquarters for the Illusionists, they parked their scooters in a nearby park as planned this part of the park wasn't well lit. Teenagers on scooters were common enough in London, they didn't look unusual.

***

There was a clump of trees, where they had positioned themselves, away from the park lighting. There was a more open part of the park, which connected to the headquarters, a grand old 1940s building, white columns out the front that stated out loud, the importance of the structure.

The area out the front of the building was a little car park, enough for five cars.

They stood around, waiting for the designated time. Harlan, as with the others, had seen the inside of the building when they visited previously. He now felt a lot more confident about breaking in.

Harlan glanced over at Tomoko and her scooter.

"Hey Tomoko, why haven't I seen you shooting your longbow, like doing your Japanese archery thing?" Harlan looked over at Tomoko.

"I stopped doing archery, my neighbour got angry." She shook her head, frowning.

"Why, did you accidentally shoot him in the head?" Harlan asked, with a wry smile.

"No, the leg," Tomoko replied.

"Oh," Harlan responded. His smile quickly disappeared.

"Well, err, yeah, I thought doing archery in your backyard is illegal?" Harlan asked.

"No. Only if you kill someone," Raphaella said. "Practice with a weapon -it's important where you do it, and what you are wearing."

"What do you mean?" Tomoko asked.

"I do sword practice in my own backyard, wearing a mask and safety gear. I have no problem." Raffaella said.

"Ahh…whereas if you were waving your sword around down at the local park, wearing shorts and underpants on your head you'd be in trouble?" Sophie added.

"Yes. Exactly," Raphaella said.

"Yeah, I reckon that's normal in Florida," Harlan said. He glanced down at his watch.

"Oh, it's time. Two a.m.," he said.

He walked over, and round to the side of the building, where there was no light. He shimmied up the drainpipe and hopped on to the roof. He then hung from the guttering, dropped on to a ledge, and opened the window with a small crowbar. He had done this in the dreamscape and, many times, and he could do it quickly and quietly. It was relatively easy with older places like this.

Slowly easing up the window, he slid in through the window frame and into someone's office. It was just 2:00 a.m. He was early… but decided to go in anyway.

Harlan tip toed quietly through the office and listened at the door to the outside corridor. He couldn't hear anything. He tried it, it wasn't locked, it opened, and he peered out into the corridor. There was no one there, and the whole building was dark from outside, so there *should* be no one inside. Harlan hoped.

Harlan moved down the corridor, the lifts would make noise, so he took the old stairs. The building was old, and there was no modern security, or cameras he could see, but in case he pulled a balaclava down over his eyes, leaving the bottom part of his face exposed.

He moved down to the room where he had to complete the goal of the mission, switching the smoke detector device. Force of habit, any building he went into he would look at the alarm systems subtly. Half through curiosity, but always handy information if he ever had to... *come back later.* In preparation, he'd found the old plans for the building in the planning records database for London and committed them to his excellent memory.

A sudden thought struck him, his *Glasses of True Sight.* He could use the glasses to see if there was anything odd about the place. He pulled the balaclava up, quickly peering through the glasses, he scanned the room, but nothing glowed or changed shape to indicate anything unusual.

He moved past a corridor. He recognised the two suits of armour, standing as silent sentries, from their previous visit. He examined them with his glasses and immediately had to catch himself from yelling out in excitement. There was a faint glimmer from a suit of armour. A vibrant hue – the sign of the presence of magic, covered the breastplate with a subtle blue glowing sheen. He moved down the corridor and used a little mirror to look around the corner.

Nothing.

He went back to the suit of armour and removed the breastplate, initially trying to undo the strapping but it was too noisy, so he pulled out a knife and cut the straps. He squashed the breastplate and backplate into his carry bag and put it back on. He wasn't a big fan of these people, for what they had done to Sophie, when they had previously detained them and treated them so poorly. Apart from that, they were arrogant old guys that seemed to think the world owed them respect. Taking this was a bit of revenge for how they had been treated before. Plus, it would be a nice thing to give to Raphaella.

He continued to the room where he was supposed to change the smoke detector. It was the office of Roderick Livingstone, the Grand Illusionist. Harlan snarled thinking of him, the guy was a jerk. He had met him when they came here before, he had tried to detain them and was particularly arrogant. Harlan chuckled to himself, thinking of how pathetic his magic had been, and how dumbfounded he had been when Sophie had cast a few basic spells.

He approached the office. All was dark and quiet. Being inside quiet dark strange places like this would generally scare people, but Harlan was so used to it, it almost didn't bother him. Harlan got to the door and checked under it. It was dark.

Then for a moment, he thought he heard something inside. He listened again carefully... but now nothing.

What noise would there be inside an empty office at 2.20 in the morning? Why would there be anyone in there at this time? Could someone be sleeping in there?

It was another 5 minutes, listening all the time, before decided to slowly open the door a crack and use his hand-held mirror to peek around the corner.

There was no one there he could see. All the lights were turned off, and everything was quiet. Glancing around, he spotted the fire alarm. He though if he moved the table, put a chair on it, he could reach it. He eased the table into the right spot, slowly to avoid it making any noise. He reached into his bag and whipped out a piece of felt he had brought with him, put it on the table, and then put the chair on it. This gave him enough height to reach the ceiling.

Reaching up, he pulled the fire alarm off, and took the backs off the adhesive strips on the new one. It fitted back into place nicely. and then put it on. He studied them, they were both old with scuff marks and some scratches. Someone had aged the new one, scuffed it up to look exactly like the old one. It was purposely detailed with dirt and scratches, for it to look exactly the same.

A huge sense of relief washed over him. The hard part was done, he hadn't noticed it before, but now he could feel the adrenaline in his body and took some deep breaths to calm himself.

Just as Harlan took the chair off the table and put the felt cloth back in his backpack, he heard a noise.

Footsteps downstairs.

Someone had arrived in the building.

Harlan padded his way to the door to get out, but then heard the footsteps coming up the stairwell. It was too late.

Hide.

He looked around the room, there was one other door. He quickly moved to it, his feet padding softening the noise of his steps. Silently he opened the door and slid into the little room, carefully easing the door closed behind him. It was a photocopy room, with old things stored in, some shelves of old files.

He hopped down behind the shelves furthest from the door.

There hiding already, was David Chan.

He looked at Harlan confused.

He was holding, in his hands another smoke detector… the same as Harlan's.

20. David Chan – mid level thief

"What the hell are you doing here?" David said, in a hoarse whisper.

Harlan grabbed David by the arm, trying to calm, steady him. He put his finger to his mouth and pointed to the room next door. He had no idea why David was there in a cupboard on a job *he* was supposed to be doing, but right now Harlan was more worried about the people outside that had just arrived.

David moved towards the door to try to hear what was going on outside. Harlan blocked him with his body, quickly put his eye at the keyhole before David could. He could make out part of the room, including the desk. It was Roderick Livingstone (the current archmage of the London Illusionists) and his brother. They were talking to someone.

"You may wonder why we are having a meeting at this time. It's important that no one is around while we discuss these things, and you need to know exactly what is going on." The voice was familiar. A deep-toned voice, and a pretentious, confident tone. It was Roderick Livingstone.

"Yes, you have been loyal to us. You know the Livingstone's are the most powerful faction." Roderick said.

"We wish to do the best for the society. Even if that means pushing some of the other factions to the side."

Damn There was a third voice, it was coming from the left side, out of view of the keyhole.

"Why, of course. I've recognised the Livingstone faction has the honest interests of the society at hand."

Livingstone's seem to have their own interest at hand Harlan thought.

Suddenly the man moved closer to the desk. They were all looking at a laptop.

Another voice spoke. "So, the meeting is called here. The three factions attend the meeting. Its's a secret meeting, so it's away from the Headquarters, and it will be called near Strasbourg because that's where the standing stones are, so while it's convenient for travel, it also gets the factions in the one spot."

"…They are done. We fill the power vacuum. Just us." Harlan recognised the voice. Anton Livingstone.

"It's a good plan. You have my support." It was Roderick Livingstone again.

Harlan looked; the third man came into view. It was a man with blond hair, bright blue eyes, tall, and he had a black mask over the bottom of his face. Harlan couldn't see him very well.

David started jostling, trying to see out of the keyhole. Harlan smacked him in the forehead and peered back through the keyhole again.

Roderick pointed to the laptop a bit more, then handed them both a piece of paper each. They took it, nodded, turned off the lights. They were gone.

"Well, dang, apart from the application of *Böckstiegel law: Sometimes something is too heavy to steal. Get some friends to help*… What the hell are you doing here?"

David started to get up from behind the shelves. "I was going to ask you the same question. Also, that's Wankel's rule. But what are you doing with the smoke detector?"

They looked at each other in silence. "I'm here doing a job," Harlan said.

"To switch the smoke detectors?" David said.

"Yes. Well…except I was told to do it after 2:30, but I came early," Harlan said.

David seemed a bit sheepish. "I was a bit late. The flight was late from Heathrow."

Harlan rolled his eyes. "You flew here? How 1950s. You didn't come here via the standing stones?"

"The standing… *what*?" David looked confused.

Harlan patted his shoulder, almost sympathetically. Apparently, Three Bells knew nothing about the portals. "Never mind. Let's get out of here David. We can chat more outside."

They snuck out of the door, carefully listening for voices or footsteps. Harlan used a small mirror to peek out the window. He could see the blond man and the Livingstone brothers out the front of the building, apparently a final discussion before they left.

He felt his phone buzz, there was a message on it from Raffaella. "People in the front of the building. Watch out." *Thanks, but a bit late* he thought.

"So why am I putting in a smoke alarm and then retrieving someone else's smoke alarm, which has just been put in?"

"Do you have to retrieve yours? And give it back to someone?" David said.

"Well, yeah. We need to give it back to Jeff, as part of the job," Harlan responded.

David squinted, thinking for a second. "Well… that sort of makes sense. Most of our jobs come from Jeff, but we get some of them from another place we hang out occasionally, Ruprecht's Kafe."

"Ruprecht's?" Harlan asked.

"Yes. It's in North Bamberg. Coffee is better than Jeffs, but the music is a bit loud. Anyway, Ruprecht asked us to do this job."

"When?" Harlan asked.

"Monday."

"That was before ours." Harlan tried to work out the timeline.

As they climbed out of the window, David grabbed Harlan on the shoulder. "Be careful there, bro, window edge is a bit rough. Thieves Guild insurance doesn't cover minor damage to clothing."

Harlan stared at him, "Thieves guild… insurance?"

David glanced back, his head askew, a quick eyebrow raise. "You don't know about Thieves Guild insurance? Bro, you're living in the 1950s."

Harlan bid David an awkward farewell, David fist bumping in an apparent sign of Thieve-ish solidarity. He slunk back to the group sticking to the shadows. They were still in the park sitting on their scooters. Tomoko was asleep, He could see Raffaella standing there, watching the building intently. He noticed as soon as she saw him, she put her hands in her pockets and relaxed. Sophie was glad to see him as well.

"Yeah." He rubbed the back of his neck. "All good. Job done. I got the smoke detector. Well, one of the smoke detectors."

Sophie peered at him. "What do you mean, *one* of the smoke detectors?"

"Long story. Yeah, uhm, I'll tell y'all when we are back." He glanced at the others. "Have you all heard about Thieves Guild Insurance?"

"Thieves…what?" Tomoko said.

"Never mind." Harlan shook his head, sighing.

"Okay, let's get back to the standing stones. It's a 2-hour drive back to Avesbury and then Bamberg," Sophie said, tossing Harlan his helmet. They all put on their gloves and helmets and the scooters pulled out and rode down the street.

***

Raffaella was tired after the trip to England. She wondered why everyone was so excited by it.

It didn't have anywhere like the history of the Italian states, it rained all the time and the coffee tasted like mud. England had lost its own sword arts, and used Italian or German, so there was nothing going for it there. The huge ugly cityscapes, monstrous grey buildings, were nothing compared to medieval Genoa, or even Bamberg.

That said, the English loved Italian food, coffee, they loved their football and Vespas and Lambrettas. They had good taste.

Raffaella wondered about the mystery of David Chan doing the same job as they had been given. They had discussed it, and no one understood why. One thing Raffaella didn't understand about Three Bells, they had no fighters in their group.

A mistake. They would probably get killed. Every crew needs at least one fighter. Mages can be helpful, but in a crunch, the fighters were backbone of any crew.

"Raffaella, bella, where are you? Do you want a coffee? I'm making a latte," her father was calling out.

"Papa, I'm in my room, doing the studies. I'm okay."

"Okay, Raffie. Okay."

Raffaella was trying to catch up the regular hours she had assigned herself for sword training. She had stuck a roughly drawn table on the door, which indicated she had to do an hour in the morning, and two hours at night, as well as the time at the club. But there had been so many meetings and now actual trips and jobs with Sophie and the others, her schedule had gone off track.

She looked at her phone. Harlan had sent through a meme on the Circle 66 message chat to all the members. She had no idea what it meant. Harlan's memes were generally pop culture references, so she knew he was trying to be charming or funny, but many of them she didn't get, and she deleted them.

She lay on the bed, her head pushing into the pillow, bringing on a relaxing feeling over her body. It was important to be comfortable when doing a dreamcast session.

Switching the headset on, it immediately flashed the lights that would send you into REM phase, where the dreamcasting work is best.

There was a bright flash of light, and then she appeared in a 16th century German market street once again. There were more people buzzing this time, going here and there. Raffaella stood there, squinting, momentarily stumped, before she got her bearings and moved off down Hannover Street to Jörg Hutter's hat shop. Well, it was a hat shop filled with bustling energetic sword wielding folk. nominally, but inside was the practice.

After meeting Jörg initially, Raffaella had looked around for more information about him, something she thought could establish background about the sword master. There was almost nothing.

It was known what time he lived. He made Hats (thus the name, Hutter). He was a sword master, and he wrote some books on medieval fencing. These books covered not just sword work, but also poleaxe, fighting in armour, spears, dagger... a few other things.

Apart from that, little was known of him. His books still existed, and people in the real world would faithfully study them, endeavouring to work out the truth of the man through his books. He wrote about combat with various unusual weapons.

Scythes, garden hoes, four section studded flails. *A man who liked variety in his weapon choice* she thought.

Just from looking at the books, many people started clubs that could teach his style.

"Jörg... Jörg. Master Jörg?" Raffaella looking into the shop, peering through the shuttered windows.

No one inside, he was not about. Raffaella looked down at her costume. Not costume, clothes. The dreamscape had put her in a long glowing black velvet gown, with white lace at the neck, white undershirt, and long black sleeves.

Completely impractical for the longsword, but she would get changed once training began. If she could get into the building.

She looked around the street. People were bustling about, wares from their shopping in hand. Some had cloth linen bags to put food items in, others she noted had servants who carried things in wicker baskets. Some purchased, some for sales. There was a continuous barrage of voices of people calling out to sell things. Raffaella considered most people would have found it all very charming, but she specifically wanted to do training.

She stood outside and called up at the top floor. The sound of clashing swords, someone was up there.

Eventually Gunther the red-haired student appeared. He was tall and athletic; in ways he reminded her of Harlan. Though, not as good looking.

"Oh, hello Miss Raffaella. Please wait, I will come down now."

It wasn't long before he appeared at the door and let her in.

It had only been a few days that he found her quite amusing and was very dubious about why a girl would be doing longsword, but now he was chatty and friendly, treating her like all the others. Raffaella understood someone like her was quite rare and put it down to the weirdness of the dreamcast.

The nature of the group changed after she showed what she could do.

He opened the door, and he walked her up. Master Jörg was there watching two of the men fight it out. They were both okay, she thought, and probably better than some of her pupils at school. But they were being trained directly by a real-life period sword master.

"Raffaella!" He held out his hands, as a gesture of welcome.

"Hello, Master, Jörg." She took off her hat in greeting, bowing slightly.

"Please, don your fighting garments." He was direct about training. "Here is a gambeson that was washed recently."

"I washed it for you," Gunther said. If it were real life and not the dreamcast, it would have been a bit creepy.

After about five minutes, Raffaella had her gear on. Jörg had put on his as well.

"I don't normally put on this for the others, but for you, I will," he spoke. It sounded a bit like a compliment, though Raffaella was always missing compliments.

As soon as they contacted swords, he said to her. "Close your eyes."

Raffaella did as told.

"Raffaella, keep contact with my blade don't let it get away. Keep your eyes closed."

She kept her eyes squeezed tight and kept the blade on his. She moved it up so that the thicker part of the blade touched his, and exerted pressure on it. Occasionally he would lift it off, but never far away, so that she could always move her blade slightly to find his.

"This is the *fullen*. If you do this, you will feel for the blade, without having to look at where it is. Your head should work independently to the body, so that some senses are working almost without thinking."

He moved his sword up to the tip of hers, and then down and took a step so he came close to her, with the hilts interlocking. His hand then quickly left the sword grip and touched her wrist, and he went to tip her over. She countered by moving her wrist away, stepped to her side, and made a lunge at the side of his head. He saw this and repositioned himself, to block it.

"Good. Good. The Italian's style teaches a lot about gripping and using hands."

"Now, open your eyes, we will do a proper bout." Jörg stepped back, presented his sword up to his face, swung it down and to the side as a salute. The bout would begin.

Raffaella repeated the same salute, with a bit of a flourish at the end, she liked the Genoese flourish, a little bit of style the Germans didn't have.

Master Jörg immediately went into a high guard, circling around her. The other students moved back to the walls of the room, away from the two fighters. Their faces bore expectant, as they flashed looks to each other. Raffaella was in a better mindset now. She had seen Jörg fight a few times, and new a bit more about what to expect.

He alternated between the high guard, and the low guard, then attacked, using a German specific technique, winden. Attacking at the head, left side, right side, left, alternating. She kept blocking either way, stopping the attacks. Raffaella was shorter, so she went to her knees and after a block, tried to get shot in under his arm. He raised a single eyebrow, a vague expression of surprise. He stepped back.

Jörg quickly regained composure, he went in high again, and then kicked out her leg. It was a feint. She looked down and moved her leg back to avoid the kick at it, but it was the vital two seconds she spent doing that that he needed. He deftly stepped to the other side and put the pommel in her face, clearly indicating he could have hit her if he wanted to.

Raffaella bowed and acknowledged the pulled blow. He could have struck her fair square in the face, probably knocking her out if he wanted to. Jörg was good, at least as good as her old master. It was an honour to fight him.

"Now Hans and Leiders will fight…" Jörg said, motioning for them to step forward.

They nodded and stepped forward, facing off against each other.

"…they will fight Raphaella." Jörg said, dramatically finishing off his sentence.

They peered at each other and smiled, and then faced up against Raffaella. She looked at her opponents. Hans was beaming, but Leiders seems to be a bit awkward. Raffaella gathered it was some sort of ego issue from Leiders, having to fight a girl. She didn't care.

Raffaella knew she had to take the initiative. She took a long lunge, leaping across the room, fell to one knee and cut up under

Leiders' guard hitting him square on the arm. He yelled out and dropped his sword, looked around, and then stepped back out of the combat, nodding deferentially at Raphaella.

Raffaella quickly got up off the knee, and shepherded around Leiders, keeping him between Hans. She sniped at his arm, but he easily retracted it.

He then lunged at her. She stepped left, blocked his downward cut with the hanging guard, and then spun out on the one foot and cut down at his back as he went past her. It would have been a big cut to his back in real life.

He stopped, frozen knowing she had won the bout, and gave her the broadest smile.

"A pleasure bouting with you Frau Raffaella." he bowed to her, his right hand flicking a flourish through the air as he did.

The was a little clapping from the remaining 6 students, all smiling at her.

Raffaella was enjoying the sessions.

Jörg now took off his padded jacket, put it on a table to air out, and motioned to Raphaella.

"Get changed my dear. Let us go for a walk. I want to discuss…things."

Quickly getting changed, he was waiting for her in his resplendent robes when she came out.

***

They went downstairs, and walked along the cobbled lane, glancing at the busy shops.

"Raffaella, why do you want to learn to fight with the sword?"

Raffaella thought for a second, considering if this was some sort of important test she answers strategically, or truthfully. In the end, she went for truthfully.

"Because it's fun. I enjoy it, I get a lot from it. I am pretty good at it. Lastly not everyone has the opportunity to learn from a great swordmaster as yourself. I do. So, I should take advantage of a situation many would like to be in. Some people would give a lot to be doing all this."

Jörg stopped and studied her. "Raphaella, for a young woman of your age that answer shows a lot of maturity," he continued, talking as he strode. "The reason I have asked you to come, and chat is actually a bit serious. I've been asked to duel a visiting sword master. This is business I have much distaste for, but without any convenient way of avoiding it, I must accept the duel. It's a matter for sword masters that we do this."

To Raffaella Jörg spoke of it like unpleasant business, almost like doing taxes… but if he had any fear of dying, she couldn't see it.

"Master Jörg, are you worried?" Raphaella asked.

"No, we can be killed or die at any point, which is why I live my life to the fullest." He stopped to peer into a shop window, full of candies and fruit. "However, those who challenge a master are generally themselves only doing it because they need to prove something. And if they feel the need to prove something, I have found in most cases… they are in fact not that good."

"Ah," Raffaella said.

"That said, it is a duel out of town, and I will not have friends or family close by. Which is why I wanted to ask you to accompany me.'

Raffaella frowned momentarily, looking over at him inquisitively. "Why do you want me?"

"You are a new student to me, but even so, I can see you are very talented. Come and accompany me on the bout, make sure nothing unfair or untoward happens. I will explain the etiquette before the bout occurs."

"Of course." Raffaella tried to think of the appropriate thing to say, it wasn't every day she was asked to be someone's witness in a duel. "It would be an honour."

"Good. Very good," Jörg said simply and smiled.

21. Dubious Wisdom and Apples

Friday night. It was time to go home. Sophie's body was aching, and she felt tired to the core. They had been doing so much lately physically, and she wasn't tired from the magic and from riding scooters. Everything sapped her mind, the thoughts and considerations constantly running through her head. It was like, when she thought she was on top of one issue, a new problem would appear.

She locked her scooter up in the little garage and walked up the stairs. At the door, she could hear her father and Hisako laughing and chatting.

Her papa seemed genuinely happy when Hisako was around. His mood always picked up... *he came to life*. She was so good for him. Sophie realised there were three major good things that had happened to her in the last year. Discovering her magic and Johannes, the three buddies forming Circle 66, and Hisako becoming family.

"Sophie, it's sort of late. Or early!" her papa said, his voice stern. "How is your boyfriend?" She heard her papa's voice out of the kitchen.

"Oh, sorry, Papa. I was studying algebra with Tomoko. What boyfriend?"

"You don't have a boyfriend?"

Suddenly Sophie remembered. Oskar... "the boyfriend."

"Oh... uhm...we split up."

Her papa came out of the kitchen, a bit stunned. "What? But you only started going..."

mush and sometimes people put wooden planks down to walk on.

"So, what are we doing in the town?" Sophie said.

"Apples," he said, simply.

"We're selling apples?" Sophie crossed her arms. What was she going to learn from that? She realised that there had been times when she had to spend too long learning a particular technique. But each time she visited Johannes, she did learn something. She had assumed that was how the dreamcaster worked. It gave you a lesson each time if you were seeking it.

Walking up to the stalls, Johannes walked up to a stall with fruit and some vegetables fronted by a man with long brown curly hair underneath an orange knitted floppy hat. Johannes opened the bag. "Apples," he said, simply.

The man picked one out and studied it in his hand. They were big apples; Johannes was semi famous for them.

The man nodded. "Arll… arll give yer three silver for 'em."

"Three silver it is… very generous." Johannes smiled.

The man jerked his head back at the immediate acceptance. Glancing at Johannes, his blank expression disguising the true reaction of someone well trained in the art of the merchant's haggle. He then smiled momentarily, scratching his head under his hat.

Johannes went to the other stall. It was a travelling tinker's cart, in town for a week before it moved on to the next town. The tinker had covered it in pots and pans, and… metal candlesticks, Sophie noticed.

"Hello, you would be a tinker," Johannes said, waving his hand at the wagon, and the pots hanging off on little metal S hooks, or tied with twine.

The chubby, rather scruffy tinker looked at Johannes. "Errhh…well, you're an observant one," he said, a dry sarcastic tone in his voice.

"I think I have something you may want." He opened the bag. The man peered in and smiled.

"Errhh." He rubbed his beard. "How much do you want for them, my observant friend?"

"I have no idea; they traded these with me for some furs. You make candlesticks, would you know what these are worth?"

The man, still rubbing his beard, looked at them. "Candles are low quality. I'll give you two silver marks and four tins."

Sophie could see the candles were fine. The man was obviously lying about the candles to get a better price.

Johannes studied him earnestly. "Is that a good price?"

The tinker nodded. He picked up the candles and crushed them in his hand. It cracked and fell to pieces, as any candle would.

"Ahh." Johannes handed over the bag and took the silver marks. "Thank you so much for your generosity. I owe you much."

They left the town, and on the way back Johannes purchased a couple of apples he had sold with a silver piece.

Sophie was quiet until they left the town. "Johannes. I have no idea what that was all about. I assume you didn't make any money out of that. Both those men seemed to be taking advantage, the tinker will be able to re-sell those candles for ten times what he gave you."

"Well, yes. And that my good gentle girl, is the point."

"What?"

"I have lots of money, it needs to be distributed. There's lots of stock back at my house... but they don't know how much I have. It can't be given away for free; it will destroy the relationship. So, I sell it to them cheap, play naïve and make them think they bargained a good deal. They then make money from re-selling it."

Sophie thought about it. She wasn't 100% sure of the relationship he was building but it made some sort of sense. He wanted to keep the villagers happy, by being generous. But perhaps, if he constantly gave them something, then maybe they would always be asking for more. He had to give them things, so they knew he was an important part of the town. They would respect him. He wanted it to look natural.

They kept walking. Sophie looked around. "Are we going back to the house?

"Why yes."

"Magic lessons?" Sophie said, looking at him, and becoming edgy that there may be none.

"Lessons." he said taking a bite out of an apple and tossing it to Sophie.

Sophie crossed her arms again, a little bit annoyed. Johannes glanced at her, realising she was.

"The lesson here is… the value of something is not in how much you have. But in how much an opponent thinks you have. Same with apples. Same with spells." He took another bite, then chewed on it enough so he could talk, and she could understand him. Surprisingly, he didn't choke.

"That advice may save your life one day." He paused. "Spells are like apples. Their value is in how big they are, how good they are, how many you have… but most importantly, not letting your opponent know exactly how many you have available. Do you fathom, the meaning, here?"

Sophie tried to think of the moral of the story, but it only roughly made sense. Apples were spells. Their power related to how much your opponent knew you had. She frowned, thinking. *Don't let your opponents know how many spells you have, nor how powerful they are.*

She shook her head. He could have told her that. They'd spent probably an hour wandering about talking to villagers.

Always with the drama. Then again, Johannes was one of the great archmages in the history of magic. So, whatever he was doing, worked for him in the end. She smiled, thinking she'd like to be as accomplished as Johannes was. Sometime in the long future ahead.

***

It was Friday Morning. Sophie left her room bleary eyed, lightly slapping her cheek to wake up. The dreamcast always rested as you were sleeping, but she had tossed and turned after she had taken the headset off and gone to sleep properly. Her Papa was up getting ready for work.

Skipping breakfast, with her dad calling out goodbye, she ran down to her scooter and drove it to school.

Another day, but a chance to catch up with the other members of Circle 66. As it was Friday, the weekend was coming up. Always good.

They met up before history started, quickly chatting to swap information. Most of the developments were from Harlan. It was the first time they had seen him since he had snuck into the London Illusionists and seen David there as well.

Harlan mentioned how they had heard about a meeting, of various factions. Sophie agreed, he needed to go to watch what was going on, getting evidence of some sort of plot to push the anti-magic vote was something they desperately needed, particularly if they could identify some bad involvement, something they public would find suspect.

It was on Tuesday, so Harlan had time to plan it at least.

History class again, this time, the ancient Greek vegetable trade routes. A lot of Romans ate Greek carrots, apparently. Also, the ancients. Not very exciting stuff.

Sophie looked down at her phone in the middle of history class. It was a text from Rupert.

Call me when you get a chance. Urgent
Okay Rupert. In a class, just starting at the moment.

Harlan, Tomoko and Raffaella all appeared, walking through the door together.

Sophie was getting good at the quick text in class. Freidrickson didn't mind the odd text but doing anything complicated on your phone would get you a quick sarcastic comment, and confiscation of your phone for the class. Sophie wondered about Rupert. His contact with them seemed to be more frequent than before. He was eternally busy with looking after "Royal Mage Business" as he liked to call it.

Sophie noticed Harlan looked a bit annoyed. Raffaella had been making taunting remarks lately about the role of a thief in the party. Harlan had taken objection to it.

Freidrickson switched topics and started talking about the Siege of Constantinople, which was a lot more exciting than the previous topic, *The ballooning prices of cucumbers in the 4th century BC due to the ravaging of Etruscan pirates.* Freidrickson started detailing a huge siege of Constantinople by Turkish forces in Medieval Times. So, the Turkish forces surrounded the city, with a huge army. However, the walls of the city were thick. The Byzantines, who lived in the city didn't have a lot of troops but did have money and were cunning.

"Sir, so you would say, that in this case, that intelligence kept the Turkish fighters at bay."

"Well, yes…" Freidrickson looked at Harlan dubiously, rubbing his beard. Freidrickson always seemed wary of Harlan's questions, like if he couldn't tell if they were real or part of some joke.

"So being a dumb fighter will not win. Sometimes you must use intelligence."

Raffaella put her hand up. "But in the end didn't the Turkish fighters overwhelm Constantinople and kill everyone?"

Freidrickson nodded, "Well yes." Harlan slunk back in his chair. Tomoko looked at Sophia and smiled. Freidrickson went on about the siege in probably too much detail. Sophie's thoughts wandered off.

After the class, the four grouped together outside the door, occasionally stepping to the side as students bustled pass them.

Sophie called Rupert, his voice answering, sounding unusually serious.

"Hello old girl. Have you had a look at the news? Not good at all really."

"What do you mean? No, I haven't." Sophie looked at Harlan, his expression questioning. She shrugged back at him.

"You need to get down to the town hall straight away. Tell me what the damage is like firsthand. About half an hour ago, someone used magic on it, and it was caught on various cameras."

"Rupert…what…are you serious?" Sophie's heart stopped. This is bad. She turned quickly to the others. "Someone used magic on the town hall, made a big mess of it."

Tomoko raised her eyebrows, Harlan crossed his arms, shaking his head.

"Why would someone do that? Any mage doing such a thing knows it's going to be bad for mages."

Sophie shook her head, a little bewildered. "I don't know." A sense of fear was sinking in. The Bamberg people, and just about all the German nations people, put up with magic, because it had largely died out and was no longer a threat. That was the main reason they had got by unbothered by people, and by largely keeping quiet.

"Let's skip class and go and see," Tomoko said.

Sophie thought she would never hear Tomoko ever say she was going to skip class. Rule breaking was not something she did easily.

***

Sophie knew her dad would be unimpressed if he knew she left school, and of course the school itself would as well, but this was a desperate situation. Plus, the fact that Tomoko was going meant she had no choice.

They grabbed their helmets, hopped on their scooters, and raced down to the town hall. They hard to park on the street to get to the courtyard.

There were already people standing around, staring, talking. The old town hall was one of the most beloved buildings in Bamberg, and was a focal point for the tourists, who Sophie always saw standing out the front posing, or getting selfies.

There were police cars around, ambulances, and a fire engine squashed into a little street.

The sight transfixed Sophie, she looked on silently. The rest of Circle 66 stood there, staring.

The front of the town hall had its doors smashed in and the windows smashed. But what was most disturbing was the twin statues. One had its head removed, the other was snapped in half. They stood there looking at the devastation, in silence.

"Well, they hurt no one, at least." Sophie said.

"When did it happen?" Tomoko asked.

"Oh…" The actual footage of it happening was now online. "Damn," Sophie said.

She glanced at her phone, and the others crowded around to watch. The video showed a massive demon type creature, at least 2 and a half metres tall, attacking the front of the building. People were screaming, tourists running everywhere.

The demon kicked in the front doors and the windows. It used some sort of magic to destroy the statues. It held its palm on the statues and they came apart.

"Demons. Cool." Raffaella said.

Harlan shook his head. "Not cool. At all. If it's a demon… that means people will think a summoner has created, it."

Everyone went quiet. Some people standing next to them looked immediately at Harlan when he said *summoner*. Their faces went white, and they immediately stepped away from him. Harlan looked at the ground, shuffling his feet. Sophie scowled at him. They didn't need undue attention.

"Is it a demon? Can demon's come from somewhere else?" Tomoko looked at Sophie.

Sophie tilted her head, lowering her voice. "Only a summoner can bring forth a demon. But there's no summoners left? They all went with the war in England."

"There is the one in the *Drudenhaus*," Raffaella said. Trust her to think of that.

"The Drudenhaus?" Tomoko said, raising an eyebrow.

"The witches' prison. It was used to imprison witched back hundreds of years ago. Then it was used for summoners in the last…Erhh, eighty years. Now it has the last summoner left alive in it. She's the only person locked up in it, all by herself. But she couldn't be bringing forth demons, she would need to be near where they are appearing," Sophie said. She looked at Tomoko, who was frowning at all this news.

"Yeah, errr, this is very bad," Harlan said.

Sophie was thinking of all the worst things that could now happen because of this. The way the Bambergians and probably even all the Bavarians, would think of Mages was now going to be worse than ever before. Without a doubt, people would support the laws and magic would be forbidden, even the good magic.

"Maybe we aren't even safe anymore. What if the people started getting angry with mages on the street?"

Tomoko fidgeted, spinning her scooter keys on a ring, around her finger. "Let's go to Jeff's after school. Maybe he'll know what to do."

They hopped on their scooters. Back at school, it was lunchtime, and because of the hubbub from the attack on the town hall, no one noticed them missing. For Sophie, the rest of the day was a waste; she spent most of the time thinking about the incident.

Sophie didn't wait around at school. She went straight home. Her father was already home.

As soon as she came through the door, he was there, and he had an expression of concern on his face.

"Sophie, are you okay? I have been calling you. I was worried!"

Sophie glanced down at her phone, she had a bunch of missed messages, from various people.

"Sorry, Dad. I was in class."

Hisako walked in, wearing a Japanese band T-shirt, and jeans.

"Hi, Sophie." She went off into the loungeroom. Sophie's dad gave Hisako a hug, and a kiss on the head.

"Did you see the footage from today?"

"The demon? At the town hall?" She decided not to tell him they had gone to the town hall to see it live. "Yes, I saw it. It was scary, Papa."

"Demon. No. I don't think it was a demon."

Sophie frowned. It was obviously a demon. She'd seen pictures of them.

"What do you mean, Papa? It was a demon we saw it…on the video."

"No, I immediately got out some old photos from the English civil war. There are quite a few black and white photos in the University's History department archives. Probably twice as many as what are online. I had a look at the pictures of it and compared it to the photos." He shook his head as he spoke, in the determined voice that Sophie often thought he was reassuring himself as well as the person he was talking to.

"How do you know it's not a demon?"

"Well, according to the primary sources, Demons only ever appeared at dusk. I think that's what the spell says."

Sophie remembered an old nursery rhyme about demons.

In turn comes the demon, with horns, tooth, and tusk.
From darkness is birthed, at the advent of dusk.

"Like the nursery rhyme?" Sophie asked.

"Yes. The nursery rhyme matches up with the primary sources."

"The other thing is. It's too short," her dad said. "Well, the historical descriptions I could find describe it as a bit taller, and the photos look taller. This one is short."

Sophie squinted at the pictures; this was confusing. "Well, if it's not a real demon what is it?"

Her dad shook his head. "I don't know, and I don't know how dangerous it is. I expect we can't bring on those anti magic laws soon enough."

Sophie bit down on her lip. Anything defending magic could trigger her papa. She felt her eyes tearing up a little, hearing her own father say that. It had been an eventful day. She went to her room to do some homework and fell asleep after finishing trigonometry.

22. The New Nation

The weekend passed and everyone caught up on some dreamscapeing by Monday Morning. Sophie couldn't risk going out with the crew, she had not been around home much, and her papa would be unhappy. She put in an obvious effort of doing lots of homework in front of her papa. He smiled and muttered his approval when he caught sight of it.

Things were bad… and getting more complicated all the time. Sophie felt the tightness on her brow and tried to relax. Threats, issues, and problems crowded her mind, all competing for her attention. She realised she was taking the load of the decision making and perhaps the stress of it all on by herself. She again, there was that unnerving feeling she started getting when anxiety would take its grip on her, that uncomfortable feeling in her stomach.

Sophie sat on her computer, watching a New Nation political party press conference. It was the second one she had seen that day. They were interviewing "Various concerned members of the public" and had them speaking about "the evil mages were doing." If she went to the school, she would see an advert on the wall. She went to the shops, and it was in the newspaper, or a poster adorned a lamppost. They were drumming up a mania about summoners coming back and doing bad things.

Bamberg was completely turning against mages. The TV channels were doing surveys of what people would vote, both in the principality of Bavaria, and in Bamberg, it was looking like most people were supporting the magic ban.

Sophie endured Monday morning's English class, Tomoko and Sophie were both quiet. Harlan made a few witty comments, trying to cheer them up, but Sophie sat glumly, ignoring him.

After school, they huddled together and sat down in some garden chairs in the courtyard of the school, discussing where things were. The demon sighting at the Town Hall was on everyone's mind. It had triggered an even worse wave of anti-mage mania. There were polls on the referendum that showed that it was now worse, about 70% of people were going to vote for the magic ban, 30% against.

"We need some marketing," Tomoko said.

"Well, yeah, marketing is good, but what do you mean?" Sophie said, she instantly perked up "My papa! My papa told me he was sure the demon wasn't a demon. What if he's right? We need a way to prove this wasn't a demon attack. Maybe Mr. M can figure it out?"

"Yeah? uh, well if that's really the case, we need to get some spin out about the demon, let people know it wasn't real. So, it looks like people are trying to frame us…and people are less threatened by magic and magical creatures, which they blame on us mages." Tomoko said.

"How… do we do that?" Sophie replied.

They were quiet for a while, all staring at their shoes. Sophie realised how grubby hers were.

"Sophie had a good idea. Why don't we ask Mr. M?" Tomoko said.

"OH! Yeah, err, no. That is going to cost us!" Harlan said, coming to life.

"Harlan, sometimes we need to spend money. Think of it as an investment," Tomoko said.

"I'll ask Mr. M if there is anything he can do." Sophie smiled at Tomoko.

Sophie's phone buzzed in her hand; she looked down at it.

"Oh, the prince sent me a message!" Still a bit distracted, Sophie held up her phone to read it out. "I never thought I would have princes texting me."

"Dang Soph, Royalty has you on their smartphone contacts," Harlan said, smiling.

"Shut up you!" She looked at the smartphone. "And your hair is a mess, I'm going to put in plats for you later."

"Good. You do the best plats. Anyway, forget my hair, what does the prince say?"

"He sent an address in the Bamberg Old Town district. He said to meet him there in half an hour."

"Well, I guess, when a Prince-Bishop wants you somewhere, you go."

***

Harlan, Tomoko, Sophie, and Raphaella found the address of the place the prince had sent to them. It was in a small alleyway. The building was an old church.

However, when they got there, Rupert was there instead.

"Rupert, what are you doing here?"

"The prince told me to come. Okay, you four, let's all talk all this through, before the prince comes along."

Sophie and Harlan poured forth the details of the demon at the town hall, Sophie interjecting Harlan's version with extra detail and observations. Rupert sat, a taut look on his face, his silence occasionally broken with a question. "What did the break in the statue look like? Was it smooth? How tall exactly?"

"Rupert, we've told you what we know. Sorry, if you want to know more, you'll have to talk to the demon. I don't have his number or his email on me." Sophie felt a bit of pride in herself, being able to get a rare sarcastic comment in on her mother. It was getting frustrating.

"Okay, I need as much information, so we can make some informed decisions, all par for the course."

"Rupert, there is something I want to bring up," Sophie said. She wasn't sure if this was going to sound ridiculous, but her father had raised it, and it was his area of specialty. It was history, and he was an associate professor.

"What's that Sophie old girl?" Rupert looked up, picking up the awkward tone in her voice.

"Papa… well… he said that it wasn't actually a demon."

Rupert raised an eyebrow and stopped writing his notes. "What? Ernst said it's not a demon?"

"Yes, well Papa said it looked like one, but there were a few reasons why it wasn't." Sophie said.

"Ah, Ernst," Rupert said, shaking his head. "Well, that's damn peculiar I must say. Sophie old girl, why in the dickens would it look like a demon, but not be a demon." Rupert looked confused.

"Well…. I don't know that. Papa didn't talk about the *why*. I guess… he talked about… *what*. He had photos of demons from the University archives. Lots of photos that aren't generally available and on the web. So, he could do a better comparison. He said it was like someone was probably trying to make a demon but hadn't quite got it right." Sophie said.

"I thought it was an excellent demon. Could have been bigger. More horns. Longer claws." Raffaella nodded her head in approval.

"Yeah, well then it would have looked like Heavy Metal music cover art." Harlan said, with a vague eyeroll.

Raffaella nodded again.

"Well, I guess your father's expertise *is* history, and examining primary resources. I don't think there is anyone alive who has seen one up close." Rupert stroked his moustache, gazing down at the table, before snapping out of his pensive moment dramatically.

As they waited, a black taxi turned up. Sophie wondered why the prince would travel in a Taxi, but then was surprised to see Tylltyr hop out.

"Oh, I texted her," Harlan said.

"Why?" Raffaella said.

"Thought she may have some good insight," Harlan said.

Raffaella muttered something in Italian Sophie didn't understand and put her hands in her pockets.

"Hey, everyone. Hey, Harls."

"*Harls* is my nickname for him!" Sophie said.

"Oh, mine too!" Tylltyr said.

There was an abrupt silence, so Sophie made conversation, plus she was curious about the Fae.

"So, Tylltyr, tell us about the Fae powers? I've heard a little bit… I mean, does Harlan have skills or abilities? What are you guys good at?" Sophie asked.

"I get my tracking ability from being Fae, and I can blend in with nature, good for hiding. I didn't really understand why I could do it naturally. Now I know. I sort of feel good in the forest, like it's re-charging my batteries, you know?"

"Yes, and we can talk to trees." Tylltyr went over to a tree, and put her hand on it, closing her eyes. "We get a feeling for what trees feel, what they can sense through the earth, the people around them."

"YOU!" She pointed to Tomoko dramatically. "Intelligent, cautious, knowledgeable, formidable."

Tomoko's head jerked back, then smiled and looked at the others, a look of surprise on her face.

"You!" She pointed at Harlan. "Caring, strong, tall, formidable. Down to earth. Attractive." Harlan crossed his arms, a broad smile covering his face.

"The leader. Proactive. Short." She pointed at Sophie.

Sophie raised an eyebrow, glanding around at the others.

"This one." She pointed at Raphaella, closing her eyes. "Dangerous psychopath." Raphaella crossed her arms, her head tilted, studying Tylltyr.

Harland smirked, then rolled his eyes. "You know she's just joshing you, right?"

"Heh heh." Tylltyr chuckled to herself and sat down. "We can't really talk to trees. Pretty sure they wouldn't have much to say. Animals though, they have all sorts of opinions on things, particularly pets. *Why do the humans buy the cheap pet food? Why do I have to wear this leash. Why do the humans pick up my poo and put it in a bag when they take me walking?*" She shook her head. "Always full of questions. A bit annoying."

"Wait, what?... we can talk to Animals?" Harlan said, his voice raised.

"Sorta. I'll show you later, Gorgeous," she said quickly glancing at him and smiling.

The prince said he would meet them there on the hour, and with five seconds to go, he arrived in a low to the ground, sports, shiny black car. A blue van with blacked-out windows, somewhat ominously, pulled up behind it.

"Hello, Prince-Bishop Sebastian," Harlan said, sounding awkward. They all repeated it. Tomoko did a curtsey.

"You all can call me Prince Sebastian." No need for formalities. Here, you devils. One must partake of good fortune, when it arises, and I had word that there were items in this place that may be of interest."

Sophie peered inside, through the ornate arched wooden door, Sophie smiled to herself as Harlan had to duck to get in. It was an old church, remodelled as some sort of shop, with some stained-glass windows still in place, the flicker of a light inside playing of the red and green glass that was part of a window portraying the famous patron saint of Bamberg, Saint Otto.

Sophie followed the prince and Harlan inside. The man working there instantly smiled. A man in his 50s, bald on top, brown hair circling the side of his head, staring at them over his glasses.

"Hello, Prince, so glad to see you," the man said, smiling when he saw the prince.

"Of course, you are Berthold. Because every time I come in here, I spend a bucketload of money."

"Well why else would I want to see you?" Berthold said.

"500 years ago, my ancestors would have had you executed for that comment," the prince said.

"500 years ago, my ancestors would have risen up in an ugly mob and had the royal's heads on pikes," Berthold said back.

They engaged each other with serious expressions, quietly staring at each other for a moment... then both laughed, and Berthold gave the prince a hug. The prince, who was taller, smiled and grasped the man on the shoulders affectionately.

"Berthold is a good friend; he has been supplying artifacts for quite some time to the house of Wittelsbach... that's my family," the prince said.

"Ah," Tomoko said. She then laughed nervously, and rather loud. The prince studied her, his eyebrow raised.

"So lo, gaze upon the wondrous things! Not many know of this place, and Berthold is choosey about who he lets in here. One can never be too trusting, of course." The prince flamboyantly waved his hand around the shop.

Sophie looked around the shop. The place was truly amazing. There were medieval lanterns on the walls, swords, maces, shields.

A cabinet held a row of helms, and breastplates. 5 full suits of armour stood up on a well.

There was a clashing of metal and Sophie looked around to see Harlan and Tomoko had taken swords off the wall and were trying to hit each other.

"Take that evil sorcerous Tomoko," Harlan said, feigning a big blow.

Tomoko hesitated, before coming up with a suitable line. "I am a strong fighter... I will kill you for... what you have done to the babies!" she shouted, clumsily making a slow high strike at his head.

"Guys! Stop that," Sophie yelled.

"Excuse me don't play with those," Berthold said, an expression of horror on his face.

The prince stood there, half smiling.

As they put them back in the display case, Sophie scanned the room, the display cases, items on the wall. The place was a treasure trove of weapons, and what seemed like ancient adventurers' equipment. Sophie was a bit bewildered by it all. The prince had wandered over to Berthold and were have a friendly chat. Evidently, the prince leaving them to make up their minds about any potential purchases.

There was a lot to take in. Raffaella at least was approaching things scientifically. She had selected three swords from a cabinet and was balancing the blades on the back of her hand, apparently checking the midpoint of the weight, or something. She then used her phone to magnify them and was examining the finer detail.

Something struck Sophie. *Harlans' glasses of true sight could pick out things of value.*

"Harlan," she whispered. "Glasses."

He frowned, then his expression changed. Padding his pockets, he pulled out the metal glasses case he kept them in. He put them on and scanned the room.

"Glowing blue," he said. He pointed at a lantern, a shield, a sword and then a goblet. "Magic items."

Harlan walked over to Raffaella and whispered in her ear, "Glowing blue." Then he pointed.

Raffaella immediately went over to the sword. Unlike the other items under glass, it was stuck on a wall. Raffaella shrieked. "That's not medieval. It's 19ᵗʰ century."

"Harlan, how much money do we have?" Raffaella said. She had lowered her voice, but Sophie could still hear. She went over to examine the sword.

"300 gold."

"Give it to me." Raffaella held out her hand.

Harlan shrugged, pulling out the coin. Raffaella took the money from Harlan and handed over the 300. "This is what we are paying for this sword."

"Err, no. The price is 30." The man studied her, under his furrowed brow, apparently waiting for a reaction. There was none, so he shrugged, and took the 300 anyway. He gave her a receipt, and the sword.

"So, you think it's worth 300?" Berthold said, smiling, as he put the money in a drawer.

"No, its worth about 10,000. But all we have is 300 and you were selling it for 30" Raffaella said. Sophie realised it was rare she spoke so much. She must be happy.

"You are supposed to be a merchant here, but a 16-year-old is telling you what your swords are worth. Ridiculous!" Sophie snapped at him, then saw Harlan's face as she spoke, and wished she could have pulled the words back into her mouth.

"Oh, but..." His expression changed to confusion, he glanced at Sophie, and then the sword.

"I think we should probably leave," Tomoko said.

"Bye Berthold!" the prince said, smiling.

Berthold put his hand up to say something, but he simply closed his mouth and watched them leave, silently, a vaguely troubled expression on his face.

On the outside, the prince walked over to Raffaella, he pointed at her recent purchase.

"What made you pick this sword?" he spoke.

"It's a medieval longsword. The hilt. 15ᵗʰ century. And Harlan said it glows blue, so it's got some magick property."

Harlan pulled out his smartphone, typing something, then smiled. "Worth between 10,000 and 12,000."

"You're welcome," the prince said.

"Goodbye my happy little mages. Dealing with the middle class has never been such fun." He squashed down into the car, it pulled off accelerating down the street, the van noisily taking off, in an effort to catch up.

"Prince Seb." Tomoko turned to him.

"Don't call me that." He glanced down at her, with a raised eyebrow.

"Err, why did you call us here?" Tomoko asked.

"I need to protect Bamberg's mages. I think you are up against it. And if there was something in there that helped you, then it helps you to find what I need," he said.

They bid their goodbyes, each hopping on their respective scooters, and headed off in various directions.

As she drove home, through the old narrow streets, it started to drizzle, so Sophie stopped by the side of an old Tavern and pulled a plastic jacked out of her little glovebox on her scooter and put it on.

She rang Mr. M and asked him if he could do something to expose the demon. She expected him to say it was impossible or ask her questions about how it could be done or name a price they couldn't afford.

He didn't. He simply said yes, and named a price that seemed a bit high, but manageable.

Not a bad idea. She realised, for Tomoko's odd ways and quirks, she often came up with ideas that could be seen as either genius or crazy, simply by the fates of how things turned out. She learnt spells fast and was clearly smart. A great asset to the crew, and a good friend.

"While we are talking, Sophie. I have some information. However, there is a fee," Mr. M said. Sophie looked at Rupert, who nodded reassuringly.

"A fee...How much?" She never really cared about the money side of things. But Harlan would.

He ignored her question. "It's big news. I think. The big parade, with the monsters."

"The monsters. You mean the Krampuslauf? The Krampus parade?"

The Krampus parade was a Bavarian tradition going back 400 years. People got dressed up in monster outfits and scared little children. It sounded odd whenever she tried to explain it (normally to international students at school) but it was a cool parade.

"Yes. The Krampus parade. You need to attend and be on the lookout for the demon to reappear."

"How do you know?" Sophie asked.

"The usual sources. Thank you." He closed off, short and sweet.

Sophie realised she needed to prepare her little group. It seemed they had a demon to fight.

24. The Krampuslauf

It was Tuesday early morning, and Sophie had decided to meet Tomoko to do some magic practice before school. The flurry of events had forced Sophie to think of extra time in the week to prepare. Sophie was *not* a morning person, but she needed to be prepared for whatever was coming. Sophie knew she couldn't teach her spells to Tomoko, but she could learn a few general casting techniques, and spell dodging tricks from her.

After they discovered the previous training ground, a spot in the forest near a mountain road up near an old abandoned alpine house in the mountain, was being monitored by a newly installed traffic camera, they had planned to go to a different spot, out near the obelisk. It was a bright day for a change, and Sophie tilted up her helmet visor to feel the sun on her face.

The scooters travelled down the road, with Sophie racing Tomoko, mostly neck and neck. On the way there they passed Adeline's old house. Adeline had moved out of course and it was empty.

The German Mountain house they had been using for practice appeared around the bend, jutting out off the road into the forest. The owners have abandoned it for 10 years or so; no one around, so it was perfect. It was white with the old style rendered white plaster, contrasting dark brown wooden beams, and wooden shutters. The old parking spot next to it enabled the scooters to be parked where no one could see them. They walked into the forest into a little clearing.

"I meant to ask you, are we definitely going to the Krampus parade on Friday?" Tomoko asked.

"Mr. M said we need to. And I had to pay him to tell me that. So yep!" Sophie said. She could see Tomoko frowning. She thought briefly about Mr. M as they walked into the forest. He had been expensive the last couple of months, though he seemed to be reliable and have volunteered a few things for free. The main thing was Rupert trusted him, and Sophie got the idea that Rupert was actually having Mr. M look out for them.

"Okay, a bit of a practice duel?" Tomoko said.

"Sure. We need the practice," Sophie said. "I have a few new spells…"

Tomoko laughed, the maniacal edge in her voice ever so slightly alarming Sophie. "Oh, so do I," she said, dramatically waving her hand.

Sophie shook out her shoulders, and stretched out her legs against a tree, while Tomoko twirled her wrists and flexed her arms over her head and down her back.

"Ready?" Sophie asked.

"Yes," Tomoko replied. Tomoko bowed politely, while Sophie gave a little flourish with her hand to indicate she was going to start the duel.

She started walking around Sophie, circling to get a good position.

The area they were in was a patch of cleared grass between the old house and the forest. It was ideally secluded as they could hear any cars coming from miles around.

Sophie walked slowly on the grass, intermittently sprinkled with pine needles from the forest trees.

Tomoko struck first. Her hands flashed through a succession of shapes in front of her. She impressed Sophie with quickly she could now hand cast. Sophie started moving to the left in anticipation, her hands flicking through the air, the glyph for shield appearing centimetres in front of her fingers.

Tomoko's sleep spell bounced off and Sophie sensed the energy soak into the ground. She grinned. She flung back a sleep spell in return, which Tomoko easily bounced off with her own shield spell. Tomoko allowed herself a momentary giggle, then a look of concentration quickly returned to her face.

Sophie saw Tomoko prepare another spell and cast it, Sophie got off her own spell, and sent it towards her opponent.

The surge of magical energy was a lightning bolt. Tomoko flashed a shield spell which easily blocked it, and it dissipated into the grass, bright shards of lightning and sparks flickering around. Tomoko's reactions were excellent.

Tomoko threw her body onto the ground and rolled. Sophie ran to the side to present a moving target.

As Tomoko rolled Sophie saw her hands quickly moving. Another lightning bolt, but Sophie caught it with the shield, and it dissipated.

They stood there, circling each other. The quick cast shield spell was easy, but Johannes had always told her that simply casting shield spells against everything was predictable.

Sophie went for broke. She knew two new spells; solid higher-level illusionist spells that Tomoko didn't know.

Sophie cast *shadow duplicate.*

In an instant there were two Sophies, facing off against Tomoko.

Tomoko gracefully lifted off the ground, landing on the roof of the house. Sophie was surprised how precise she had become with her landings, and Tomoko then leapt out of view. Sophie looked at her duplicate, which looked rather blankly back at her, and circled around the house after Tomoko.

She suddenly heard a noise from behind, and she immediately knew Tomoko had her. She quickly turned anyway, to cast a shield spell, but was too late.

Tomoko had cast glue, and her feet were stuck. Sophie's duplicate uselessly ran at Tomoko, who threw a sleep spell at it. It dissipated into thin air.

Her feet wriggling in frustration, Sophie put her hands up in the air, as a sign of submission.

"Ok, brilliant work. I do need practice. I wish I could levitate."

"You know I can't teach you." Tomoko said. Sophie noticed real regret in her voice. "Same as you can't teach me yours."

Tomoko cast a dissipate spell on the glue spell. Sophie spun her ankles to get the circulation back in them. Tomoko's work was getting impressive, but Sophie knew she had more illusionist spells she hadn't used.

"The practice is excellent, but I wonder how it's going to prepare us for the real thing."

"I think the real thing is going to be a lot worse. A lot, lot worse."

"Johannes says, the only thing that can prepare you for the real thing, is the real thing."

"Sounds like something my Sensei would say. Do they get all their wise sayings from some book of wizard's wise sayings?" Tomoko smiled.

Sophie stamped down a few sparks settling into the ground from the lightning magicks, before they lit a fire in the dry pine needles that covered the ground. They both picked up their helmets and walked back to the scooters.

Tomoko gave a side eyed glance at Sophie, as she put her gloves into her helmet and carried it against her side with her arm. "Sophie, can I ask you something?"

Sophie peered back at her. "Sure."

"Do you have feelings for Harlan?" Tomoko said. She spoke the words quickly, with a touch of awkward.

The question surprised Sophie. While she had known Harlan for a long time, she hadn't known Tomoko and Raffaella for that long. She had chatted with them about things… but it was never really that deep or personal.

"We're good buddies. I mean." She scratched her head, switching her helmet to the other hand as she scrambled up past the side of the house to the road. "…we are close. But would I want him as a boyfriend?" Sophie had to think how she felt about him. "I don't really think that's what our relationship is."

Tomoko nodded; a subtle smile appeared on her face. "Okay, good."

Sophie froze, unsure of how to respond, then spoke. "Are you… interested in Harlan?"

Tomoko just smiled. "Never mind." She put her gloves and helmet on, and they both pulled off from the house and drove back. Sophie spent the rest of the drive wondering why Tomoko had asked. Did Tomoko like him? She hadn't seen any other signs of it. She only saw Harlan as a friend, a sort of goofy brother. She had no idea who Harlan liked, they were close, but it never seemed

to come up.

***

The week passed quickly; the only major event had resulted from an arrangement she had forgotten about.

On Thursday morning, Tomoko showed them a newspaper article *all about people pretending to be a fake demon.*

Mr. M had come through.

They all read the article on their phones, fascinated and a bit shocked that they had been responsible for it.

Mr. M had evidently got someone to speedily make a demon suit, which appeared pretty much like the demon in the video. He had shot some rough stills of people putting the suit on and sent them to the newspaper.

The newspaper and the public lapped it up. It seemed a lot more interesting to people, and believable, that someone would be faking a demon, than that there actually was one. And Sophie's father didn't think it was for his own reasons.

There had been a poll run after they made the photos public, and people were now voting 60% for the anti-magic ban, 40% against. It seemed the fake demon photos had brought the anti-mage vote numbers down.

***

Friday soon came, and it was finally time for the famous Bamberg *Krampuslauf* or *Krampus Run,* the street parade where people dressed as the traditional Krampus demons. Tomoko was excited to see it, as it was new to her, and Harlan and Raphaella. Sophie, being German, had been going to the Krampus festival since she was a young child, and found it a bit wearisome.

The Krampus monster outfits had their roots in Norse Mythology and German Paganism. In most of the world, Santa Klaus gave obedient children presents. However, in Germany, there was also the Krampus, who came and put the *bad* kids in a sack and took them away. It had always seemed a bit cruel to Sophie… but somehow very German. Just one of many German traditions.

People were gathering about for the parade to start. Sophie could see the kids bouncing around, looking down the street eagerly for the head of the procession to appear. There were families, groups of younger people… and lots of tourists. There was a general procession that the Parade would take place, and the different clubs that the monsters would get dressed up from would attend.

Everyone else was excited, except for Sophie herself. She wasn't getting the buzz from the thrill of a new "exotic" event that the others were getting. They clumped together; Harlan had his original sweets. Raffaella had a bag over her back that looked sort of like a longer than usual sports bag, but Sophie knew there was a sword in there.

Harlan pointed to a small group of people amongst the crowd with signs, they seemed to be protesters.

Squinting, it dismayed her to see they were anti-magers. One of the white signs was scribbled on with black marker. "Mages Verbotten! Owt."

"Great. They are magic ban supporters." Sophie looked down, suddenly feeling bleak.

"There are only 30 of them," Tomoko said.

"Well, yeah. Yeah, that is a good thing," Sophie said.

"Yes. There are only 30. But there are probably thousands that hate mages, but do not want to be seen with stupid signs," Tomoko said.

"Yeah, uhm, hey the guys in the tracksuits. Standing behind them, back row."

Sophie glanced over. There were five or so taller men standing behind the protesters. All wearing the same sort of tracksuits, matching tops and bottoms, with white stripes down the sleeves and legs. The tracksuits were different colours, but otherwise the same.

"Hey, short hair, long fringe at the front, and at the back. They all have the same," Tomoko said.

"Hansa!" Sophie said. They were Hanseatic League people. She knew them from the Hansa version of the mullet.

Harlan motioned for them to clump together for a chat. They grouped closely, stepping out of earshot from a family all wearing matching beanies next to them. Sophie noticed Raffaella had her eyes glued on the procession.

"Okay, ignore those guys," Harlan said, scanning the crowd as he spoke. "What sort of plan do we have?"

Everyone went quiet and looked at Sophie. Sophie was dreading this moment. She had got everyone here, arranged things so far. But really had no idea what to do. The only thing she knew was that they should be here, prepared to help if a demon appeared, but otherwise...

Sophie stared back at their expectant faces. "To be honest, I haven't thought about this one, I don't know what to expect."

Tomoko's face instantly appeared stressed. She raised her voice slightly. "You mean we don't have a plan?"

Raffaella spoke. "I have my sword. I have some sweets and good mulled wine. I'm fine."

The little medieval buildings were all around, and they were on the main street where most of the procession took place. Sophie guessed if anything were going to happen, it would be here. In any case, they would hear anything that was going to happen and could run to it, if necessary. Sophie waited. The crowd seemed happy.

Harlan continued scanning the crowd. "Yeah, well, here's hoping nothing happens and we just see a bunch of people in great outfits."

"Mr. M has not been wrong so far." Tomoko had a serious expression on her face.

Raffaella seemed generally happy. Or maybe content was a better word. Her natural expression, at all times, was a perfect poker face that any card player would appreciate. Sophie noticed there was a murmur down the lines of the crowd, and around the corner, came two dancing Krampuses. They were leading the procession.

The first ones were short and could have been children in costumes. They were skinny, with their long grey hair and red eyes. They had little horns.

After that, a group of more people dressed in Krampus outfits walked in.

"Dayum. They are amazing. Check out their outfits. Yeah, I'd love to have this at home, but if we wore those in Texas, we'd die of heat exhaustion." Sophie agreed. They wore an abundance of long fur, of a variety of colours.

"Sagoi." Tomoko stared at them, her face like that of an awed six-year-old.

There was a clump of eight of them, walking together. They would run over to the crowd, and tease some of the children pretending to try to steal them. The children would instantly hide behind their parents, who would laugh. The Krampuses, would then run away, to tease another child.

Another bunch of Krampuses appeared, these ones had wicker baskets on their backs. They had huge ornate horns, sticking up in the air. Despite how evil it all looked; it was a traditional family outing for Bavarians.

More groups of Krampuses came by. Some were taller, probably on stilts under their fur. One was breathing fire. One pulled an ornate cage on wheels, with children inside. Despite the fact they were captured by monsters who were apparently going to punish them, the children in the cage smiled and waved at the crowd.

"There is no honour in capturing children. The children should rise up against the Krampuses. Some could sacrifice themselves, while the others escape," Raffaella said, pointing at potential infant child heroes.

Next came the main platform. It was a truck with a big platform on it, and on the top was a Santa Klaus, waving to the crowd. He had Krampuses dancing all about him.

"Santa doesn't seem too bothered by all the Krampuses." Harlan laughed.

"I think the plural is Krampi." Tomoko said.

Sophie grabbed Harlan on the shoulder. "Yeah, I mean if you are Santa, and you dealt with an entire world of brats wanting presents... dealing with horned demons would be a nice little break."

Tomoko laughed. "See...that one." It was a particularly tall Krampus on stilts.

"HARLAN!" Sophie heard a loud voice call out his name. She spun around to see who it was.

Tylltyr, in her human form, appeared out of the crowd, a broad smile on her face. Tomoko beamed at her appearance, Raffaella crossed her arms, and Harlan smiled.

"OH, fancy running into you here, Harlan! It's almost like I'm stalking you."

"Err…are you?" Harlan asked, his expression instantly changing to concern.

"Probably." She shrugged and beamed at him.

Sophie glanced over at Tylltyr, studying her, still trying to work her out.

Harlan peered down at her. "You know Tylltyr, Lamprecht's law *A running thief gathers many purses*. You should think about it."

"How is that relevant to her?" Sophie glanced at him. He didn't answer. She suspected Harlan wanted to sound like he was wise by quoting his thief rules, sometimes randomly.

Tylltyr then seemed to belatedly notice everyone else, glancing at them askance. "Oh, hello, Circle 66 humans."

"Yeah, you know… we… we are actually… we are here on work," Harlan said.

She nodded sagely. "Ah. A mission." She touched her nose. "Your uncle's the word."

"Mum's the word…I think is the expression," Harlan said.

"Bob's your mum?" Tylltyr frowned.

"Bob's your uncle. Mum's the word." Sophie said, both expressions Rupert used.

They all stared at the particularly impressive platform as it came past, with some angels. This seemed to be a group of angelic floats. Then more Krampuses. The crowd cheered and clapped.

Sophie noticed Tylltyr chatting to Harlan and Tomoko, while pointing at the procession.

"Ice cream is so awesome. It is one of the best things you humans have made. I don't know why you don't eat it all the time," Tylltyr observed.

"Some people do eat it all the time," Harlan said.

"I've never seen anyone do that." Tylltyr glanced over at him.

"That is because they are dead. Malnutrition," Raphaella said.

"Raphaella." Harlan glanced over at her. "That was sort of funny. Yeah, like dark...but funny. You should do that more often."

"Please do not," Tomoko muttered.

Sophie picked up something unusual in the people watching. There were a group of Krampuses *in the crowd.* They were big, but their horns were a bit different, they had huge stag horns. They had bulkier physiques than normal and wore strange plastic masks.

"Guys. Do those Krampuses in the crowd look odd to you?" Sophie whispered to the others, trying not to appear too obvious.

Harlan had been observing the procession and switched his gaze to the crowd.

"Harlan don't make it obvious," Tomoko said.

Raffaella pulled her hoodie over her head, using the movement to sneak a peek at them. "They look cool, but they are different."

Harlan's struggled to not look at them while staring straight ahead, he whispered to Sophie, "Are the Krampuses supposed to be in the crowd? Shouldn't they be over there?" He pointed at the procession.

Sophie shook her head. "I don't think...hmmm... maybe they are people with their own outfits."

The Krampuses wandered around the crowd. People laughed at them, and they pretended to scare the children, but Sophie noticed that while they engaged the crowd, they were looking at the procession, and were scanning the crowd.

"Something is up with these. There's about 12 of them."

Sophie noticed one of them was very deliberately coming towards her. Her anxiety levels rose, her hands shaking, the familiar awful feeling of heat rising up her neck. There were people everywhere.

She stepped back to do a spell.

25. The Procession

As she stepped back to prepare the spell, she saw a quick flash of movement to her right as Raffaella went for her bag.

Harlan grabbed her on the arm. "Sophie, NO!"

Sophie noticed Raffaella staring at Harlan and hesitating, the sword was mostly out her bag, her hand gripped tight, and her body poised.

"Hey...their horns," Harlan said, pointing and leaning into Sophie's   ear.

Sophie peered at their horns. *Real* deer horns.

The closest "Krampus" leaned over towards her and lifted his mask.

It was Akshay. He was in his natural half man/half stag form but had put on a cheap Krampus mask to disguise himself, his real horns sticking out the top.

"Sophie, darling, it's me Akshay. Don't lightning bolt me!" A playful tone in his voice, he waved his hands dramatically in mock fear.

"Akshay, you idiot. I could have zapped you into barbequed Cervitaur," Sophie growled.

She noticed Tomoko had a glyph glowing in her hand, down low. Sophie threw her a glance, and Tomoko shook her wrist, so it flashed out, energy dissipating and falling down her dress, tiny sparks bouncing off the dirt. Tylltyr, Raffaella and Tomoko stepped over closer and greeted Akshay.

"So, what are you doing here at the parade?" Sophie asked.

"We've been alarmed at the New Nation Party, and their moves to ban magic. You know…we use magic to switch form. It may affect us. Oh, hello Tylltyr darling, good to see you hanging around this lot. You can learn from them." His comment to Tylltyr was light-hearted, but there was still concern in his voice.

"But the Cervitaurs aren't out. No one knows you exist," Sophie said.

He lifted his mask so he could talk, wiping the sweat off his brow. Evidently, the mask was hot. "We may come out one day. I mean, people don't know about our community. We've kept living here secret for hundreds of years." He paused, contemplating. "But all this mess may bring us out."

Sophie nodded, she noticed the concern on Tomoko's face, who was unconsciously shaking her head, and muttering something in Japanese under her breath. Tomoko was close to the Japanese cervitaurs, clearly, she was concerned.

"But what are you doing here… I mean… specifically?" Harlan said.

"We think that demon may show its face here. The attention it is getting is no good for any of us."

Sophie felt an instant lift in her spirits. Sometimes it seemed like all the responsibility of this huge, awful situation was on her shoulders. Finally, someone was going to help, and Akshay was a good man to have on your side. Well… a good *Cervitaur* to have on your side.

"Yes, that's what we heard as well." She grabbed him on the shoulder and had to reach up to do so. "Glad to have you with us."

Harlan smiled. "Dang, Akshay buddy, great to have you on the team. We don't exactly know what we are doing. This one's a bit out of our normal work."

Akshay scanned the crowd. "I think we must be here, and if it appears, try to deal with it. The least we can do is stop it from causing damage. Try not to use any magic if people are looking."

Sophie glanced over her shoulder, at the parade. It was of course, the perfect place and time to make a fuss and get attention. With so many innocent people in one spot, it was also the perfect time to hurt people a lot of people as well, if that was the   intention.

***

The Krampus procession was trailing off, with the end of the procession followed up by small bands of Krampuses teasing the crowd. Sophie had been tense, expecting something to happen, but now relaxed and was admiring the costumes, and the energy and enthusiasm of the people in the procession. The energy of the crowd rubbed off on her, they loved it.

The Pro Magic ban Protesters were still off to the side in her peripheral vision, but it was good to be in a festive atmosphere. People were happy, there were lots of kids smiling. Sophie looked over at Akshay, who scanned he crowd, taking it all in. He looked at her and smiled it was good to see him out in public, enjoying himself.

Then suddenly Sophie heard a loud cheer and talking and clapping.

A huge demon was standing in the crowd. She had to look twice to make sure it was real, and no idea where it came from. She had just been looking there a second ago, and it wasn't there then.

It was various shades of grey, with great horns and long claws. It scanned the crowd around it, opening its enormous maws and letting loose a deafening scream. It towered over everyone around it. But what was disturbing was, the crowd wasn't panicked. They were turning to look at it, most of them seemed in awe, many were smiling.

Tomoko pointed. "Look." Sophie turned to the others. Raffaella was already gone, her sword in hand, springing towards it, as she zig-zagged through the crowd.

Horrifically, instead of running away or screaming, people were running *towards* it. A sickening feeling hit Sophie in the stomach. The people must think *it's part of the parade.*

Some people were clapping and laughing. Tomoko yelled out, exasperated. "Those people think it's part of the festival."

"Quick, get between it and the people." Sophie called out, running straight towards it.

Sophie looked around. Raffaella had disappeared into the crowd already. Sophie ran towards where she saw her last, she glanced around, and saw Akshay running right behind her, as did a clump of his cervitaur buddies.

"We're with you." He yelled to Sophie, before turning to his cervitaur friends. "Let's get to it quick."

A ripple of clapping came from the crowd when they saw it, accompanied by applause from the Krampus costumed people trailing at the end of the procession.

The demon was in the middle of the road, it's head swivelling, scanning around it. It lifted its fist into the air, and then pounded it into the ground. Sophie watched as its fist pummelled the concrete road, which cracked with the force of its strength. It then turned its attention to a stone building and smacked that with its fist. The bricks cracked, bits of stonework were pulverized and dissolved, bits of stone and dust flew into the crowd.

The demon was at least seven feet tall, dark grey/mottled dark purple, huge horns, cloven feet and a huge broad head. Sophie stopped, fear gripping her body. Her legs momentarily were frozen, it was like her body wouldn't move. She had to wilfully push herself forward.

There was now general confusion in the crowd. The cheering turned to muttering, and conversation. More people were pointing, and the odd scream could be heard here and there.

Tomoko seemed confused. "What are we going to do? If we use magic on it, we will be outed. Everyone will know we are mages." Sophie realised that was the end of them if that happened. Her father, her school. Everyone.

"Let's lure it away from here. Get it away from the crowd, quick. Make it chase *us*," Sophie screamed.

More people had started screaming now, moving away from it. Others were still moving towards it to peer at it, while others stood around, stunned, confused.

Akshay's friends moved around it, and all pulled out swords, waving them about. It put its head back and roared. A Cervitaur ran towards it, but it smacked her aside. She flew about ten metres back onto the cobbled street.

Raffaella screamed and ran at it. Her sword struck out, like lighting, stabbing at its arm. It lashed out at her with its leg, which she dodged.

Raffaella stepped in again, raining blows on it, left and right. It blocked the blows with its claws, then stepped back. Its long gait meant that Raffaella had to run to catch up to it, as it moved from side to side.

The cervitaurs attacked it from various sides, Sophie could see they were calling out to each other working in unison, trying to flank it, getting between it and the crowd. She realised, to the people the cervitaurs appeared to be just people in Krampus costumes. To the onlookers, perhaps this seemed like a mob of Krampuses attacking and driving away some demon.

Suddenly, it stepped past, out of the ring the cervitaurs were creating, and headed straight for Harlan.

It slashed at Harlan with one claw, which he deftly ducked, smiling.

But then, in an unexpected quick move, it hit him with his other claw, and he was tossed to the ground. Sophie stared in horror as it jumped three metres in the air, landing on top of him.

She flicked a spell in her hand, but had trouble tracking the demon when it jumped, it moved too fast. It was over the top of Harlan, and just as he got to his feet, it used the claw on its foot to pin his leg to the ground. It raised its left claw above his head.

Just as she went to cast, she felt a sharp pain on her shoulder. She turned to see one of the pro magic ban supporters, an older woman in her 60s, wearing a crudely printed T-Short calling for the jailing of mages, and a purple cardigan, hitting her with her protest sign.

"Out of the way, can't you see I'm fighting a demon?" Sophie called out.

"Well, you, you." She paused, gathering her strength, then shouted, "You brought this demon here, it's your fault!"

At that point, two of the Hansa men, in the tracksuits came over. Sophie didn't have time to even glance at them, she peered back in time to see a sleep spell hit it the demon from Tomoko, however, only distracting it for a second. Sophie traced the glyph for a lightning bolt, but it was going to be too late.

As its claw came down, it didn't make contact with Harlan. There was a steel clashing sound, claw against metal, and Raffaella was there. She had thrown her body on top of Harlan's, sword up, and was bracing against its claw, protecting him.

The demon raised its right claw above its head, and in a flash, Raffaella flipped up onto her feet and started raining blows again at it. Left, right, high low. Lightning fast, the blows flowed landing all over.

It stepped back, once again, its big legs and long gait meant it could move easily away.

Quickly moving away from Raphaella, it lashed out and hit another Cervitaur, while another attacked it with a sword.

Sophie knew she had to act. She was wearing a black hoodie; she pulled the goggles she normally wore on her scooter out of her bag and put them on to disguise herself. She also pulled her Hoodie over her head. She ran out onto the street, directing her voice at the demon. "LEAVE US!!!"

The Demon's long arm touched its clawed hand on the ground. As soon as it did, cracks started appearing, spidering out in different directions, with a large one moving towards Sophie.

Enough was enough. With no one in the way, she had a clear shot. Sophie started the handcasting, and a lightning bolt flew out from her hand and hit the Demon square in the chest. It looked shocked. It lifted its hand from the ground, and the cracks stopped appearing. It roared and moved off into a side street, evidently it had had enough.

"C'mon. We need to chase it. Get it away from the people." Sophie screamed out. She looked at Raphaella, who was picking herself up from the ground. Akshay and the other Cervitaurs started screaming at it, moving in and out of its range as it swirled around. Tomoko and Harlan were there, waving their arms at it.

Sophie gave chase, as it moved off. It had long legs, and it was fast. It bellowed and screamed, moving off quickly down the little laneways. Sophie was now sprinting to catch it, and it moved off into smaller laneways.

Sophie looked around, she was now the first of the group after the demon, chasing it on foot. It was ahead of her, and now it was out of sight.

She saw it ahead, leap, bound and turn into a laneway up ahead. She sprinted with all her might, she could hear the cervitaurs and Harlan calling out something behind her but didn't turn to look, focussing on the demon. She felt her heartbeat in her chest, felt her lungs in her chest. The scooters were parked too far away.

They sprinted out of the busier area, along a grey street with businesses, a cobbler, a travel agent, a café. They people looked out at them surprised, at the demon, and then at them, as they sprinted past. Oddly, Sophie noticed some of them smiled. She assumed they must have thought it was entertainment, was part of the festival. Others looked confused, trying to make sense of it all. Some shoppers jumped out of their way, hugging the plaster walls of the older daub and wattle buildings as they screamed past.

She turned the corner and came into a small alleyway. Cobbled stone streets, the street was lined with white walled terrace apartments, the white walls interspersed with older wooden doors, blocky steps leading up to them, and narrow windows.

But there was no sign of the demon.

There was a large, tall man with dark hair, and a boy, standing in front of their doorway, the man with a key about to open the door. They looked shocked to see Sophie, and then suddenly Akshay, his seven Krampus-cervitaurs friends, Harlan, Tomoko and Raffaella as they bounded into view, almost knocking over Sophie as they appeared around the corner. Tylltyr appeared last.

Sophie was stunned. She couldn't see where it had gone, how it could have disappeared?

"You didn't see a…a… demon looking thing go past here, did you?" Sophie blurted out. She instantly felt like it was a dumb thing to say.

The man looked at her with a raised eyebrow. "You mean like them?" He pointed at Akshay's and his cervitaur comrades.

"No…I mean…did a huge man…thing…run past here before I did?" Sophie blurted out, exasperated, and trying to catch her breath.

Harlan stepped in. "Did you see anyone at all run past here?"

The man pushed his child behind him, "No. Could you all please leave? you are scaring my son."

Tomoko and Akshay both said sorry at the same time, and they all quickly left.

26. The Prince Bishop at the Hochzeitshaus

After the drama of the demon appearing at the Krampuslauf, Sophie got a call from the Prince Bishop. They hadn't updated him for a while, so it was only natural he wanted to know where they were with everything.

It was Saturday morning, so they didn't have to worry about fitting his visit around school. The prince always seemed to be at work in his office, even on the weekends.

Raffaella had left, telling everyone she needed to do a dreamscape session. Sophie, Tomoko, and Harlan made their way to his office at the University, riding their scooters on the roads next to the bank of the river Legnitz. It was the Little Venice part of Bamberg, where canals and bridges were prominent. There were a few places in Bamberg that compared themselves to Italian states.

They arrived at the Prince Bishop's office in the old grand faculty building, the *Hochzeitshaus*, and parked their scooters.

Once again, they made their way to his office Sophie nervous that she may see her Papa at the university, as it was his workplace. However, it was a large university and they managed to get to the office of the Prince-Bishop-Dean. Sophie tried to remember what order his title was but couldn't remember. Luckily, she didn't have to go through the formalities, he was just Sebastian.

There were now ten men, the crossbow guard, all out the front of his office, resplendent in their green velvet uniforms, big puffy sleeves. They looked straight ahead, eyes staring under the brims of large floppy hats. Despite apparently being there to guard the prince, they said nothing to Sophie and Circle 66 as they politely knocked on the door.

They had planned to be exactly punctual for their meeting and got there dead-on time.

"Come in, come in. Have you brought your assignment? If there are grammatical errors again, I will remain unimpressed."

"Oh, hello? Prince Sebastian?"

He looked up and was a bit surprised. "Oh, my apologies. I thought you were a student. The Crossbow guard have taken it upon themselves to increase their numbers when they guard my office, but it doesn't stop the students from coming." He lowered his voice and smiled. "Unfortunately."

Sophie wasn't sure if he was joking or not, so chose not to comment.

"Oh, you wanted us to come by, so we can give you a report," Sophie said. The four of them shuffled in.

He offered some glasses to them, then a drink from a bottle.

"Yes, of course. Would you like some Ginger Schnapps?"

They all stared at each other curiously, rounded off with a nervous giggle from Tomoko.

"No. We are all underage, and Schnapps is alcoholic."

"Is it?" He raised an eyebrow, and then held the bottle up to the light, reading the label. "Well, so it is. That explains a lot."

"Well." Sophie stared around, and as per usual it seemed to be up to her to speak. "So far, we can see the New Nation Party is the group that is pushing the Ban on magic. I mean a few parties are, but they are going around and putting up posters."

The prince nodded. "Ah, okay, what else."

"The polls are bad for the magic ban. We got our contact to spin the demon as fake, which brought the numbers down," Sophie said.

Sophie noticed the prince raised an eyebrow at that news.

"Ahhh…well we found out so far someone is pretending to be a demon. Possibly to cause trouble. That was the disturbance at the Krampuslauf," Sophie added.

"That was real? I heard it was part of the Festival?" Sebastian said.

"It was real. And…" She tried to think of anything else important but couldn't. "That's all we've got." Sophie shrugged.

"Okay, thank you, m'dears. Let me know what else you find as soon as you do." Sebastian seemed thoughtful staring at the desk on the left, his head snapping up to bid them goodbye only as they stepped out the door.

Sophie felt vaguely guilty about not being able to tell him much, for the money he was paying. He'd be a good person to have on side if they could make him happy. She steeled herself to follow
up the clues they had and make more progress.

27. The Duel

After it was clear the Demon was gone, Raffaella left the group at the Krampus run, and headed back to her scooter which was parked in a little car park, away from the tourist areas. Oddly, the people were calm about the appearance of a huge demon. Passing by a few people talking about it, they even seemed impressed. Coincidentally, it had appeared at the end of the procession, some people assuming it was a *grand finale.*

On the way home, she encountered three people in Krampus outfits, waving huge birch branches. They stood in front of her, waving the branches, but quickly stood aside when they saw her scooter wasn't stopping.

Fighting the Demon had been interesting. She ran the events through her head, and the actual combat sequence, thinking of the techniques she used. What techniques would have worked better? What advantages did she have? Did she rely on them? What did she learn from the experience?

The others were going to see the prince, but Raffaella had a strict training routine she had to stick to, and that involved dreamscape lessons with Master Hutter.

Ideally, she would have asked Jörg about fighting a demon, but she doubted he had any experience or insight on the matter, or indeed how he would react to her asking about them, as the average German renaissance person would not be encountering them. She would have to think of some other way of asking him.

***

"Raphaella, you went to the Krampus festival, si?" Her dad greeted her, as she hoisted up her scooter in the garage and pulled out the keys.

"Yes."

"Ahhh." Davide smiled. "Did you see the business about this fake demon publicity event?"

"Err, no papa. I heard about it on the news."

He looked at her and smiled. "Anyway, I am glad you went. I like that group of people. Good friends, eh? They don't do the swordplay."

Raffaella could see where her papa was going with his questions. She knew her father was angling for her to do normal things, and not spend so much time on her swordwork. He seemed happier when he knew she was hanging out with her non sword friends, Sophie, Harlan, and Tomoko, who he thought were normal…and safe.

If only he knew.

Fact was, her papa didn't know how much time she spent in the dreamcasting, and she was making social contact with people on there. The people in the dreamcast weren't real, but they felt real. They were real memories, and you could even form friendships in the dreamcast. Though ultimately, in the back of your mind, you knew you would never physically meet them in the real world.

However, meeting and discussing various arts with what Professor Marcus had referred to as their *talented ancestors*; her original mentor, Salvador Digrassi, and now Jörg Hutter, you spent so much time with them you did form a bond. The fact you were related to them, may have made the bond closer, but she was so distant from them, they weren't similar to her in any way like her close family were.

Generally, Raffaella didn't have a lot of time for friends and a social life. She had her scooters, her sword arts, and her schoolwork. Apart from that, there was little time left for anything else.

She thought about the group for a second. They spent a lot of time laughing and smiling, which was strange. They also tended to talk about their private lives and personal issues more than Raffaella did. However, they were a nice bunch, and respectful of her skills. Most importantly, being part of it gave her excellent opportunities to try out sword techniques.

Raffaella went into the house, grabbed an orange juice, and almost dodged a plate of leftover reheated fettucine that was shoved in her hand by her mother. She manoeuvred left and right to avoid more questions from her parents and got to the safety of her bedroom. Taking a few mouthfuls of her mother's excellent pasta, she laid down on the bed, got comfortable, and then turned on the Dreamcast headset.

She appeared this time, out the front of Jörg's Hat shop.

There wasn't the usual noise of battle coming from the upstairs room. Jörg was downstairs, resplendent in a purple velvet doublet, with red laces, brass tips off the lacing. A billowing white shirt was underneath. It was all very carefully acquired and arranged and looked amazing... but not very practical. Raffaella stared at it and was impressed, but her heart sank as she realized it meant they were not fighting any time soon.

"Raffaella darling, Ve Gaits!" he said. He seemed a little bit more serious than usual but welcomed her. "Today, is a day of vindication. All the work, my thoughts, and my training, will they make me the better man?"

Raffaella looked at him askew. "What are we doing?"

"Today is the day, I take you as my second for a duel."

She remembered when Master Hutter had spoken of the duel before, asking her to be a witness... or a *second*. The dreamscape queued events, as they were memories, and it queued the duel for her for the next time she dreamscaped. It tied into her subconscious, which sometimes swayed the lessons depending on what her needs were. She made a mental note to discuss it with Harlan, or perhaps Sophie, as she didn't completely understand it, though she suspected he didn't either.

A duel? A real duel? She listened for fear or emotion in his voice, concern on his face. Overall, he seemed in good spirits, but Raffaella picked up a hint of seriousness in his tone.

They strode through the streets, leaving the shopping district, and walked out of the town proper, and into the surrounding area outside the town walls, which was basically countryside. Jörg found a stables and bartered for the use of two horses and saddles. He haggled, getting the ostler, a large bald old man with an ancient straw hat, down to two silver marks per day for their use. Jörg was well known in the town as a fencing master, which seemed to help.

Raffaella looked at her white mare and looked at her saddle. It was strange, it seemed different to Jörg's, sort of awkward.

"Hop on, oh do you need some help getting up? So rude of me, and I've asked you to assist me as well."

He came over and gave her a leg up, and she tried to sit on it with a leg on either side.

"Raphaella, my dear, have you not ridden a horse before?" he asked, appearing slightly bemused.

"Well, yes, a few times. I can ride okay, but the saddle…" she said, examining it.

"You can't ride it like a man. You're a lady. It's side saddle. You need to ride with both legs on the left of course."

Side saddle. Raffaella now remembered. Historically, women rode this way, because it was improper for a woman in her dress to ride with a leg on each side of the horse. *Ridiculous.*

"Errh, can I have a normal saddle?" she asked, glancing between the ostler who was handling the horses, and Jörg.

The ostler came over to her. "Well, young lady, I'm scratchin' mar head here. It's an odd request yer make of me. Yer sayin' yer learnt to ride on a man's saddle, but not a lady's?" His expression was confusion, he threw a questioning glare at Jörg, who just shrugged.

"Well, it's the same price, so rightly, I don't mind. I'm of a mind to keep the town's Fencing Master happy, 'course, I might need lessons one day, for me'self."

He bent down, groaned a bit, started undoing saddle straps and switched it all over. The two horses then proceeded down a well-travelled dirt road, bordered with fig trees, out of the town.

The things, the sights, the world you saw in the dreamscape, it struck Raffaella just how visually incredible the world was.

The horses trotted along, and soon they came to the next little village.

"We have another couple of hours ride, and then we meet Master Boris." Jörg adjusted the saddle strap, and pulled a water skin out of the saddle, offering to Raffaella before drinking it himself.

"And when I say Master, I'm using the term rather loosely. In any case, a duel is a duel, and not to be taken lightly."

As they rode, Jörg explained the story of how the duel came about in more detail. Jörg had to visit Bremen for business with an expert swordsmith, and he had to see some merchants about cloth for his hat making business.

Bremen, however, was home to Master Boris, who was one of two of the main fencing masters in town. Apparently, Boris bumped into Jörg on the street, and immediately issued a very loud and arrogant public offer of a duel to Jörg. Jörg was required to fight the duel, otherwise it would make him seem weak.

Jörg said he found duels stupid; however, he needed to continue to go to Bremen and couldn't avoid Boris, so the duel would have to be fought.

He had offered Boris a reasonable time and place to meet, hoping it was inconvenient for Boris and he would back down. Boris accepted straight away.

Boris had all to gain from winning the duel. Jörg was confident in his ability and gained little from such things.

They came to the outskirts of Bremen, where Jörg stopped to water the horses.

"Well, m'dear, we need to find the apple orchard. Boris will meet us there. There is an old round tower, he said to meet us there."

They asked some locals about the apple orchard, and eventually found it. Wandering around the tower, three men sat at the base of the tower.

Raffaella had a sinking feeling in the pit of her stomach. She knew if she were killed in the dreamcast, she would simply come back, but could Jörg be killed? What if this was how he was killed in his real life? Would the dreamcasting with him then stop? She had only had about 10 lessons from him, she had learnt much, but nowhere near as much as her other dreamcast master, the Italian Master Sergio Guardia.

Raffaella could see a slightly older man in a white shirt. He was accompanied by another man in his twenties, wearing long leg leather leggings and a black leather doublet, as well as a teenager wearing a woollen cowl over a leather tunic.

Raffaella looked at the two younger ones and sensed their arrogance. The flaw of so many sword people, arrogance got you killed. They each wore a longsword at their belt, and Raffaella realized she was at a disadvantage, wearing a dress. She asked Jörg to wait a minute, and then rode off behind the trees, quickly getting changed, all the while wondering what was going to happen. She put on a white tunic, which had freely flowing arms, and some leather hose, and quickly rode back up to the scene.

Jörg looked at her and nodded approval of her decision to change. It also gave her a chance to put her sword belt on, which now swung from her hip, without obviously arming herself in front of the three.

"Raphaella, this is Master Boris of Bremen, and this is…" He paused for a second, pointing to the older man first. "Dietmar." Then pointed to the younger teenager. "Dietriech." They are both here as witnesses and Boris's second."

Master Boris tipped his head to Jörg, then frowned, a look of vague confusion on his face.

"Jörg, this is your second?"

"Yes. She has taught many of my better students a few lessons already," Jörg said.

"Well…" Boris started swinging his arm about, stretching it. "…Shall we?"

"Of course." Jörg hopped off his horse, drank some water, and then took in some big breaths of fresh air. He crossed himself, took out his sword inverted it, and kissed it on the hilt.

He stood facing directly against Boris and saluted him with a hand flourish.

Boris looked at him directly. "Well, today, we will see whose school has the master with the most skills."

Jörg said nothing for ten seconds, focusing on the situation, his eyes moving up and down his opponent, judging his stance, demeanour, and his weapon. He then simply said, "Good luck to you, Master Boris of Bremen." He raised his sword to a high stance.

Boris put his sword low, then charged in. Jörg side stepped, smashing down on top of Boris's sword, as Boris tried to come up underneath him.

Boris turned to face Jörg straight on again, and Jörg adjusted his stance. He lowered his stance so that his sword was now on the ground.

Jörg started circling. As he circled, he switched guards, between low and high guards. He continued to circle, stepping carefully, all the while focussed on Boris. Each time, Jörg moved his sword, he always moved it through an arc so that it was between himself and Boris.

Raffaella considered what she should be doing and switched her focus to Boris's two seconds. They were sitting on a well, that was next to the two bouting masters. They were about ten metres away from them, a respectable distance, and about the same distance she was. She wondered why there was only one of her and two of them, and quickly put the thought out of her mind. She had to concentrate on what was happening, worrying about what could have been done was something for tomorrow.

Jörg circled around, and then Boris charged in. Boris went to strike at Jörg's leg. He quickly blocked it, and in lightning speed swung the sword around and hit Boris's own leg.

Boris went down to the ground.

Jörg recovered in his stance, and held his sword pointed at Boris, but respectfully back.

There was a sharp intake of breath from Boris's seconds, and also from Raphaella. It had all happened so quick, and it looked like Boris was now out with a big leg wound. There was a lot of blood, and from the force and the angle, Jörg would have done some serious damage. The man shouldn't have been able to stand up.

The man moved about on the ground and did an odd thing. He adjusted the way he was half sitting and placed the hilt of his sword on the wounded leg but adjust his body so that neither Jörg nor Raffaella could see it.

"Do you yield Master Boris? I will not strike down a lame man. If you get yourself to an apothecary, or a butcher, there may be some help for your leg. You won't be continuing the fight this day." Jörg spoke confidently, but still had his sword poised over his shoulder, ready to strike or block if need be.

Boris stood up.

Everyone was a bit shocked, including Boris's own seconds.

Jörg looked surprised, and was trying to look at the wound, while keeping his guard. Clearly the wound wasn't as bad as it seemed, Boris was now circling Jörg again.

Jörg in turn, with a slight shake of his head, started circling Boris in turn, switching guards.

Boris feinted at Jörg's head, then lunged forward at his chest. Jörg, caught it, stepped slightly to the side, and then with the same parry, thrust down into Boris's chest.

Boris held his chest, frozen for five seconds and then crumpled to the ground. He lay on the ground motionless.

Jörg still stood on his guard, over Boris. Raffaella could see he was wary that Boris may still get up. However, Boris was not moving. He was apparently dead.

At that point, Raffaella saw a red blur, it was Boris's second, Dietmar, charging at Jörg.

"JÖRG!" Raffaella just had time to scream. The warning was enough. Jörg turned and blocked a wild downward strike from the Dietmar. Jörg rained blows on him repeatedly, from the left and the right, pushed at him and got in close, and then hit him in the head with the pommel. The man went down.

There was a scream from the remaining second, who moved towards Jörg with a sword, but instead of charging with it, shifted its weight and balance into his hand, so he held it horizontally, with his hand under the hilt, in a deft blur of movement, and then threw the sword as hard as he could.

The sword moved through the air, but slow compared to an arrow or bullet, Jörg parried it, and it flung off into the grass. The teenager glanced at them both, and then ran.

Raffaella surveyed the scene. Two men lying on the ground. Jörg stooped to check Boris. He was indeed dead, his second was unconscious.

Jörg shook his head. "Such a waste. He could have remained a good fencing master in Bremen, and me in Stuttgart. But he wanted to be the master of both cities. For no reason, except for his own pride."

Raffaella peered at Jörg. "Master Jörg, are you okay? Wounded?"

"No. With good fortune. And thank you for the warning. I should have expected such a thing. I have done duels with no seconds, when I was caught travelling without companions and no friends or family nearby. As you can see, they can save one's life. Excellent work in saving your master's life, M'dear," Jörg said staring directly at her. He nodded, genuinely thankful.

He then bent down and stared at the sword. He then examined Boris's body.

"Gods Hooks. I could have sworn I gave him a substantial wound on his leg. I was deliberately aiming to put him out of action, without killing him. His hose is cut, there is blood there, but…" He got close to the leg to study it. "No wound at all."

Raffaella thought about the wound. It surprised her when he got up, because the way he went down initially indicated that it *was* a serious wound.

Jörg picked up both swords, put them on the saddle. He mumbled a quick prayer, then picked up Boris's unconscious second and put him on the saddle.

"Master Jorg, can I please see that sword?" Raffaella examined it and it struck a chord in her memory. It was familiar to her but seemed out of place She had seen many swords in her dreamcasting, and her fencing club at school. So, it was hard to think where she had seen it. It was an odd, slightly uncomfortable feeling, nagging at her that she had seen it, but couldn't remember where.

Then she realised, the pommel shape, the blade, even the purple leather binding on the handgrip, was almost the same as the one she had purchased from Bertholt. She knew that sword had magic properties as it glowed blue. Was this her subconscious intervening in the dreamscape to tell her something about the sword? On rare occasions, it would intervene in the dreamscape, changing the DNA stored memory if it needed to tell you something important.

"We'll drop this man back to the priest. He can sort him out, and deal with poor unfortunate Boris."

Raffaella helped him put the young man's unconscious body up on the horse, and then hopped up on her own horse, now a lot more comfortable wearing woollen hose, rather than a dress.

"Well, the good thing about this is, it will certainly discourage people from requesting duels with you."

Jorg looked at her in earnest, tilting his head down and looking back at Boris's body.

"Unfortunately winning this duel my dear… it's going to encourage *more* invitations."

They rode back to the town along the dirt trail, passing merchant's wagons plodding unsteadily and noisily on their way to market. Its suddenly struck Raphaella, that she could ask Jörg about their current situation.

"Jörg, can I ask you a sort of strange question?"

"Most certainly, m'dear."

"What do you know about demons?"

Jörg stopped his horse, and studied her, raising an eyebrow. He then kept riding slowly, looking forward, apparently thinking, before finally turning back to her to respond.

"An old monk once told me, if you see a demon in our world, it's not the demon you need to consider. You need to think about the reason why it's there, and indeed who put it there." He said nothing else, and they kept riding, Raffaella thinking about how it applied to their Bamberg demon problem.

28. Villagers and Mages

Sophie had not had a chance to see Johannes for a week or so, and it was starting to nag her. Saying goodbye to the others, she got home and said hi to her papa.

"Sophie! I heard about the parade," her Papa said, raising from the sofa, laptop in hand.

"Oh no. News is out already." Sophie had been hoping to stealth past her dad without his interrogations. "What did you hear papa? I really liked it this year."

Her only chance was to play dumb about it in case he hadn't heard everything that happened. She could see how much he knew. She hadn't had a chance to check the news.

"It was on YouTube. And the news. The fake demon," he said, pointing to his phone, which still had the footage running.

"It looked real, but yes it was fake," Sophie responded. She wasn't entirely listening to her papa's thoughts on the demon.

"YOU SAW IT?" His head snapped around to look at her, alarmingly fast.

The level of tension in her dad's voice forced Sophie to take a step backwards.

"Well, yes, it was from far away. I thought it was part of the show. Can I?" Sophie grabbed her dad's phone to read the articles on it. The photos Mr. M had planted were there, but the articles seemed a bit confused. Some articles were talking about evil magic and fighting between mages. There was politics involved, and the New Nation party was pushing this as a reason to make mages illegal. Some of the public seemed to have been convinced it was fake, but some thought it real.

Interestingly, some noted that there were mages fighting against the Demon. Sophie felt a bit of pride that they and the Cervitaurs fighting the demon had been recognised by people, in what was now a confusing situation. The articles also noted that the demon was driven away, by these mages, and that no one was hurt.

However, some of the articles were saying it was all a performance put on using pre-arranged explosions, pyrotechnics, and people in costumes.

It was a spectacular event, and certainly some of the things that happened, could be explained either by special effects, or magic. Fortunately, people tended to fill in gaps about things they didn't understand, with what they did.

"Was it real?" her papa asked, glancing at the footage. "It seems…pretty impressive."

"Well, papa, you yourself said you thought it was fake. I guessed it was some sort of performance." Sophie peered at the photos. Circle 66 had been wise enough to cover their faces, but there were photos of Akshay and his friends, dressed as Krampuses, fighting it.

In some photos, it was clear they were cervitaurs, but fortunately the articles seemed to assume they were people in elaborate masks. Sophie thought about it, it made sense; people normally explained the unexplainable by using the closest most obvious explanation for something.

According to the articles, the demon damaged some buildings, but Sophie was glad to read that fortunately no one was seriously hurt.

Her papa nodded. "I agree, you think of the context. It's a big event that brings in a lot of money for Bamberg. These days, everyone wants to promote their events, through any means necessary. No subtlety in it."

Sophie leaned on the fridge, thinking. "It's very smart, Papa." She left her papa with the thought. He'd caught himself on the hook. Sophie smiled, then felt a sense of relief her papa hadn't caught wise to her.

Sophie decided to get to her bedroom before he asked any more questions. She grabbed some fruit and a plate of oatmeal muesli from the kitchen, and headed into her room, locking the door. Four gulps of oatmeal and two bites of apple later, she laid down on the bed and drifted off to sleep.

***

Sunday morning, she woke up with the headset in her hand, realising she had slept with all her clothes on, and had fallen asleep before she had dreamscaped. She felt tired. Things were taking a toll and she wasn't getting the sleep she needed, but at least this was a sleep in.

She put the headset on and headed off to see Johannes and 15th century Europe.

***

As Sophie approached Johannes's house, she could see some dark figures. They were people in cloaks, which was not unusual, except that they were all black, and the cloaks all nearly identical. She knew black material in the 15th century was rare, it was hard to die the materials (or so her Papa told her). Auspiciously, big cowls covered their heads, under which she could see the light on their chins, the lower part of their faces. Sophie noticed, strangely, they all looked tall. One of them was standing with his hands on his hips, preparing to call inside. She counted eight of them.

Sophie stood back from Johannes's house watching the hooded figures as they milled around outside it, leaning in to talk to each other. So far, they hadn't looked at her, they either hadn't seen her, or paid her no heed.

An excited feeling course through her body, excitement, mixed with fear; they were here to do harm to Johannes. She had to get to inside the house, warn him. The wet grass squelched under her leather shoes, the leather giving her no grip as she ran. As she sprinted around to the back door, she abruptly came to a halt; there were several of them on that side as well, it looked like six in total.

Damn. What did they want? Johannes, could be, probably was, asleep inside for all she knew. Sophie could never tell exactly what the time was in the dreamscape. Clocks were rare in this time.

The group looking like a motley bunch of cowled monks, walked closed to Johannes's house. "Johannes Van Meditteran. Come out, come out. We want to deal with you. Speak of what you have done."

Speak of what you have done? She recognised one man from the village. They seemed to be here to judge him, or harm him in some way. Johannes was generally careful; this seemed a bit out of character for the generally docile village people. Sophie wondered if there were some outside influences involved.

The man at the front started calling out, more passionately, "Come Out!!!!! JOHANNES!" They exaggerated his name, daring him to appear.

Sophie moved back into some bushes, now more wary of the group. It was dusk, and cold, but still enough light to see.

Sophie thought quickly.

This was bad.

She didn't know where Johannes was, the people looked angry. She could see part of their clothes under their robes. As the main leader talked, she vaguely recognized him.

She began to think*, may be these weren't people from the village? Other people. She could go back to the village and get some of the villagers to help.*

As she stood and watched, the main cowled figure, the one that had been calling out the most, bent over and opened a satchel on the ground. He unrolled a bag. She could see he was doing something, striking something.

Sophie peered at him, squinting, trying to see. A *click click* sound accompanied his sharp motions. He was striking a flint, to get a spark.

The brand he was holding lit up in a whoosh.

Sophie took a step back and inhaled. They were going to attack his house.

Johannes was either quiet inside or not at home.

What the hell could she do?

The men were now spreading out, so that they covered all around the house. There was no escape for Johannes now. He was a competent Mage, could he fight his way out?

Then it started. The men passed a fiery brand. Each of them had   an   unlit   torch   in   their   hands.

The fiery brand went around the circle, and as it did, it lit up each man's torch. Now the whole house was surrounded by men, the flames flickering illuminating the house, with an orange dancing light.

"Come out Johannes. We'll burn it, and you in it."

"WAIT," Sophie stepped out of her spot in the bushes. "You don't want to do this! Johannes has been good to you all, why do you want to hurt him."

"He is a mage. He casts spells, he is evil and must be destroyed by the purification of fire." The main man said.

"He is a witch! He steals our babies!" Another man said.

"He has a cow with two heads, in his yard. It speaks evil. The two heads speak to each other in the tongue of man."

Sophie thought the villagers seemed a bit unhinged, she wasn't sure trying to talk to them would help but had to try something. So far, they didn't seem aggressive to her at least.

"Have you seen all these things? Are you sure?" Sophie said.

"YES… and much worse," Another man called out.

"Please, can I go in and take him away? I will take him to another place, where he will not bother you anymore."

One of the men, a taller one spoke. "You should be gone, lass. You should not be here. This is not a good sight for gentle folk to see. TONIGHT, WE BURN A MAGE!!!"

Sophie couldn't think of anything else to do. She was going to have to take them on. If Johannes were inside, which he could be, hopefully he would wake up, come out and help or run off. She knew it was only a dreamscape, so she couldn't get hurt, though she didn't know how this affected Johannes.

"Okay, I will leave." She turned and headed into the bushes out of their sight, then quickly circled around to a spot where she could see them better. The bushes were thick, and she could easily hide in them. She waited a couple of minutes. They looked around, assuming she was gone.

The leader, a woman with long red hair, moved towards the house and started waving her fiery brand. Sophie's reactions cut in, almost before she had finished thinking of it, her hands were a flurry of movement. She cast the spell, she knew she had limited range, but it looked like it did the job.

A sleep spell, the woman fell to the floor, her long red hair flopping about her head.

The rest of them went crazy. "A spell! Johannes has used his evil magic and killed the maiden, Birgit."

"Watch out," another man said.

"The two headed cow may come. It will use the magic of the demon cow."

"Let's burn the mage. He owes me money."

Sophie realized, knocking one of them down, she had made them even more angry now. Fortunately, they hadn't seen her, they assumed the spell came from within the house. They were moving about, ducking down, if that would stop them from being a target of the spell.

Sophie needed to work fast. She decided she would put as many to sleep as possible, targeting any of them that got too close to the house.

"Burn devil mage! I thought you were ugly the first time I saw you. May the fire make you prettier!" Another man said. He moved closer to the house, and Sophie used sleep to put him down. He flopped to the ground, and the rest of the group once again, became agitated, crouching down, looking around, trying to see where the spells were coming from.

They continuously kept the cowls over their faces, to hide their identity. Sophie assumed Johannes would know their voices. She knew Johannes would normally be in there at this time of the night on this day of the week. Maybe he was waiting strategically to run out?

Sophie built up her mana, feeling the energy throb slightly in her body, her arms, flickering down into her fingers. Each time she cast a spell; it disappeared a little. She traced a glyph, then cast one more spell. Another one collapsed.

They screamed out strange obscenities, and pulled back from the house, still assuming that Johannes was casting the spells from inside.

"We attack all at once. Brave villagers will not be scared by mages," One man called out, moving forward.

"I am a brave blacksmith." One of them said.

"I am the bravest of cobblers, who makes solid footwear for other brave men." Another said.

205

They seemed to have mustered renewed confidence, and all moved in together.

Sophie had to act now. She started quickly doing sleep spells one after the other, then cast two lightning bolts over their heads, being careful not to hurt them.

Two of them fell on the ground, rolling around, and flailing their arms, even though they had not been hit.

But three had put their fiery torches to the house. She looked on as flames appeared on it, and it started to catch fire.

There was nothing she could do. It was too late. She could put more of them to sleep, but she couldn't stop the fire. It was a wooden house, and there was no modern fire equipment.

"Burn evil mage, may your ugly face not be seen here again!"

There were too many, she couldn't stop them all. She froze, only hoping that Johannes was not inside.

"Sophie." from behind her, someone called her voice.

It was Johannes. He had been standing quietly behind her. He had a big smile on his face.

Then she heard a snigger. A chuckle. Then a roar of laughter.

All the men were laughing. Not polite laughter, but hunched over, almost losing control, some were on the ground.

Sophie looked at the house. The fire was gone.

Manfred Von Brunswick's Fire illusion spell?

She turned to Johannes. "Wha…?"

"Good work, Sophie. You have done well. I'm sorry to put you through that. But mostly… I'm sorry *I* had to sit through all these folk and their ridiculous overacting." He rolled his eyes, shaking his head slightly.

"I don't understand…"

"This was your ultimate test. For the rank of Sorcerer. From now on, you are no longer a novice journeyman. But a sorcerer, a full mage."

Sophie was still looking at the *pretend* lynch mob, who now came over and were patting her on the back.

"They aren't angry villagers?"

"No. These men…they aren't even villagers. They are my mages friends from various parts. You haven't worked it out yet?" He sniggered. "They came here to help with the test."

With the light on their face, she recognized two men from her previous test. "THE TWO-HEADED COW." He started laughing, as did they all.

"May the fire make you prettier!"

"I am the bravest of cobblers!"

They all started repeating their lines. Each time they did, they all burst out laughing.

Sophie looked at them, she felt the hot flush up her neck of embarrassment. "Yes, very funny. Morons." She turned to Johannes. "I thought you may be inside. I was worried!"

"I was worried that I was going to start laughing at the ridiculous dialogue. Really Sophie, the bit about the two headed cow, the two heads talking to each other?" Johannes said, shaking his head.

As soon as he said two headed cows, the men started laughing even more, some of them rolling on the ground.

"I don't know the sorts of things villagers talk about. A two headed cow might…"

As soon as she said two headed cow, they all started laughing again.

"I give up." She sat down on the ground, as the men, came forward, patting her on the back, and shaking her hand. One of them had a wine skin, and was drinking generously from it, and started passing it around.

"Good job, Sophie. This was a test of your magic ability, but also a test of what is going on up here." He pointed to her head. "That's as important as the type of spells you know."

"The thing is, if I was inside, and there were 'villagers' attacking me, you did exactly what I would have hoped someone would do. You could have probably hurt a lot of them, but you didn't really need to because you weren't sure I was in there. So, it was just my house." He looked directly at her. "Is it worth using magic to hurt a whole lot of people, over a house?"

"Well, a nice house, maybe. Not yours." She smirked.

He ignored the comment. "I'm very proud of you Sophie, good job. A mage of my age, who has seen five apprentices, always gets to a point where he can calmly say he has lost an apprentice and made a mage. You are now, a mage."

29. Breakfast at Jeff's

It was a rare chance for a coffee before they went to school. Jeff's was open early Monday morning, and as always, to thank him, they bought all the donuts he had.

"Hey, I got a chance to dreamscape last night. I passed my apprenticeship. I'm a proper mage now!"

"Oh, sagoi!" Tomoko beamed. "I am so proud of you!" Sophie felt almost embarrassed how happy Tomoko seemed. Raffaella gave her curt congratulations, and of course Harlan gave her a huge hug, almost as happy as Tomoko was.

"Oi, happy Monday, who's a clever geezer then? Congrats 'n all." Jeff appeared, overhearing the excited re-telling of the story of the test. He ran off and came back with some donuts. Raffaella had two donuts, Sophie had one, Tomoko one (but left half of it on her plate) and Harlan had five.

Sophie shook her head, still slightly abuzz from the congratulatory fuss, "Harlan, how can you eat so much?"

"Yer know, I'm tall, and growing. My body needs nourishment. I can't help it, yeah…it's natural." he spoke, in a brief gap where he didn't have a mouth full of donut.

"I do not know how you can not be chubby from eating," Tomoko said.

"You know growing up on a farm…." Sophie started.

"Yep." Harlan replied.

"Did… your papa have to buy a farm so he could feed you?" Sophie said, with a slight smile.

"Yeah, no, it was in the family before I was bor…. Oh, Sophie, you're pulling mah leg, aren't you?" He picked Sophie up, and put her over his shoulder, and spun her around twice. Sophie smiled as he spun her around like a rag doll. For a thief, he probably had the strength and build of a fighter.

"Look at all the things you can see from up here. No wonder you keep hitting your head on things when we go to Japan." Sophie called out, smiling.

Jeff cleared his voice. "Oi, no playing silly buggers then, you lot."

Harlan dropped her down, quickly at first, but catching her at the last minute.

"Tall. He'd make a good fighter. Long arms, long reach." Raffaella glanced up at him, then down at her café latte.

They were downstairs, unusually, but there was no one around. Tomoko referred to going downstairs as "Visiting the spell deprived," always saying it in front of Raffaella and Harlan, who of course also didn't do spells.

This was the first time they had been back to Jeff's since the police were there. They had messaged Jeff first, and he had let them know that there was no one there.

Sophie thought for a second of the time before the troubles and challenges that they currently had to deal with. She thought briefly of her life before meeting Professor Marcus and using the dreamscape. She had been a fairly normal 15-year-old, Bavarian/English girl, got relatively good marks, who worked part time in a restaurant and like to buy books.

Now, she was a mildly accomplished mage, leading a party of various skilled adventurers, doing jobs for money, and trying to investigate who was trying to make magic illegal in Bavaria. Thinking about the changes that had happened in a year… left her breathless.

"Okay, let's try and think through where we are," Sophie said.

"We need to work out when that demon will appear next. So far, the damage has been contained. Many people seemed to think it was part of the celebrations. Luckily, the Government didn't comment. They probably don't want to frighten people by saying it was a real demon," Tomoko said.

"It was formidable. I was honoured to fight it," Raffaella said.

"It was a monster. It knocked you down and tossed one of Akshay's buddies across the street," Harlan said, an element of surprise in his voice, looking at Raffaella as he picked up donut number six.

"We need to find more information about this demon," Sophie said.

"How do we do that?" Tomoko said, looking around the table. They met her question with an extended silence before Harlan answered.

"So…yeah, okay, so it comes out at certain times. Makes a big scene." Harlan put the remainder of his donut down, finally at his capacity. "Why is it doing that?"

Sophie shook her head to clear her thoughts. "It's trying to make negative attention, right? It's obviously trying to drum up all this fuss to support the political parties for the anti-magic legislation. Like so people vote to ban magic."

"Makes sense. That's what it was doing when it wrecked the town hall." Harlan glanced around.

"Yes, it is both stealthy and annoyingly formidable." Tomoko nodded.

They sat staring at each other for a while.

"What do we think Mabuse's involvement is?" Sophie asked.

"Involved in pushing the anti-magic campaign. Possibly involved in the demon business. We know he captures mages to use them… somehow related to that?" Harlan said, "Maybe we can find out something from the political party…errh… Die Neue Nation, The New Nation. They are pushing for the anti-magic law*s."* Sophie said, really trying to think of any idea that made sense.

"Well… I could… Investigate their offices. We still have that lead on the Strassbourg meeting that David and I heard about at the London Illusionists," Harlan said, rather slowly. Sophie thought he almost was waiting for someone to tell him not to.

"You can't do that Harlan. That could be dangerous," Tomoko said, obliging. Harlan suppressed a look of relief.

"Soph, when you went to see the Magistry thing with Rupert, there was a group in Munich right?" Harlan leaned in.

"Yes."

"Well, maybe they have something to do with this? Well, we could go and talk to them?"

Sophie nodded. "Hmmm, I guess we could. They seemed friendly, well friendlier than the London illusionists. Like you said, they seemed different to the London Illusionists."

Tomoko affirmed, "I would support we talk to them at least, rather than send in Harlan to get their help."

"Okay…" Sophie said, thinking out aloud. "We need to get in contact with them."

Harlan broke in. "We can ask Rupert or Mr. M to try and make contact."

"Well…Mama…Erhh, Rupert would be cheaper." Sophie knew Rupert was always keen to help. She still felt bad about everything she had done, and Sophie was aware she was always trying to make amends. Sophie still didn't feel inclined to forgive her.

Glancing past Harlan, over his shoulder, Sophie noticed a man she didn't recognise appear. She wondered why he was here *He appears to be looking for something, may be the bathroom?*

He had long black hair, parted down the middle, and glasses, partly glazed so you couldn't see his eyes that well.

He came over to the table, Sophie stopped mid-sentence and smiled at him politely.

"Excuse me…" he addressed the four of them at the table. "Could you help me? I'm lost and looking for a way to get out of here. But it's cold outside, and my body is almost frozen."

Sophie noticed the way he said *frozen* when he stared at them all. Sophie went to point him back downstairs, but he spoke again.

"Yes, my body is almost *frozen*."

When he spoke the word *frozen,* he slammed his hand down on the desk.

Sophie felt an odd calm come over her.

Her body seemed like all the energy had gone.

She went to move, and point him to the stairs, but realised… something was wrong. She couldn't move her hand. Or her arm.

She desperately tried to move her fingers, hand, or her arm, or any part of her body. None of it was budging, not a centimetre. She felt an immediate sense of panic.

She looked at the others, none of them were moving. They were moving their eyes, looking around, their faces were locked in the same black expression. A feeling of horror started to overcome her.

She then looked at the man who was standing at the table, he looked at each of them, seemingly confirming that they actually couldn't move. She looked at his face, weirdly, it was unsettling. *Parts of it* were familiar. Not the hair, or the nose, they were different, but she recognised his cheeks, his brow, and especially, his eyes.

It was Dr Mabuse.

And they were unable to move a muscle.

Mabuse stood there for a minute, without saying anything, looking at them suspiciously ensuring everyone couldn't move. Then smiled. There was a noise of people coming up the stairs. Sophie hoped this was someone to help. But it was four men she didn't know, all wearing black tracksuits with double white stripes down the arms, and black joggers. All the men wore big bulky black jackets. They were Hansa. They looked around the room, seemingly checking all was ok, then two went over guard the top of the stairwell.

Mabuse leaned over and put his hand on Sophie's shoulder. He whispered in her ear.

"Time to go. You will walk behind me. You will follow me. Your hands are like heavy steel. Too heavy. They will stay by your side, you cannot lift them to do any magic, or anything at all." He leant over and whispered into Tomoko's ear. Sophie could just make out what he was saying, and he was saying the exact same thing. He stood up and walked to the stairwell to go down to the main level of Jeff's.

Incredibly Sophie found her body rising from the chair, against her will. She felt like a remote-control dummy. She tried to stay fixed to the chair, to resist her legs lifting her body up, but couldn't. Every ounce of her will, her arms, legs, body wanted to follow him. She filed in behind him, walking slowly. She could hear the scrape of the wooden chair on the floor as Tomoko stood up, and then her footsteps.

The power of Mabuse was frightening. She thought quickly of when she had seen Mabuse control Adeline. No wonder he could control her so easily. She thought quickly of her options, how she could get out of this. Sophie thought of all he had done to

Adeline, how he had controlled her to do anything he wanted. She had no power to resist him, even forcing her to kill her own mother. Sophie felt sweat break across her brow and actual physical pain in her arms as she tried to resist. He had an iron strong grip, it was like invisible hands gripping, moving each arm and leg against her will.

Sophie continued down the steps. Jeff was sitting down at a table eerily staring straight ahead. Jeff's two kitchen hands were sitting there with him. They all stared, none of their bodies moved except their eyes moving around, trying to see what was going on. It was early, and there were no other customers there. Mabuse continued down the stairs and was leading them to the door, his pace was slow, so they followed behind.

Rather suddenly, someone came through the door. Sophie recognised him. It was the man that had been sitting with Mr. M, the mysterious blond man that was never introduced. He came into the room, took his hat and his glasses of, he had Asian features, his shoulder-length blond hair tumbled down in front of his face. He turned to face Mabuse. Mr. M himself came through the door after him.

There was a flash of movement, as one of the Hansa men tried to touch him, but Mr. M's arm, flicked out, deftly grabbing his arm, and using some sort of Judo throw, tossed the man onto a table. There was a crunching sound, as the table gave way and broke. The man rolled off the table, onto the ground, stunned.

Mabuse approached the blond man. "Wait! There's something wrong with your legs isn't there?" The blond man looked confused. "They are like steel columns stuck to the floor. Your whole body is heavy like concrete. You can't move."

Sophie watched as the man's eyes grew wide. Like Sophie, his body was locked in place. Mr. M leaned forward, and moved the blond man's arm, but his body stayed in place, resisting even Mr. M's movements. Mabuse stayed still for a second, looking at him to make sure he was frozen in place.

But despite Mabuse's command, there was movement. Sophie noticed his hand move. Just his hand. Then the other hand. Mabuse saw this, his eyes widened, and he stepped back. He spoke again, this time more forcefully. "Your body is like *rock*, you *cannot move*. Moving is like trying to push a huge block of steel, an immovable force," Mabuse spoke, forcefully, almost chanted.

The blond man now moved his whole arm, his other arm then his whole body. Finally, he cricked his neck, and smiled at Mabuse. Mabuse looked dumbfounded, clearly, he didn't expect this.

"Who… who are you?" Mabuse said, taking a step away from him, staring.

"I have seen the shogun's armies clash in great battles, thousands of black armoured Samurai clash in deadly battles that decided the fate of states. I have seen tall ships sail into Tokyo harbour and change my land. I have witnessed the burning of great castles, towns and villages destroyed. I have witnessed the flames of an atomic weapon, laying low a once great city." As he spoke, his hands started moving, his face grimaced, slightly to shake off Mabuse's unseen grip on his body. "I have seen the demise of a Shogun, and Emperors fall from the status of divinity to that of man. I am Kentaro, the talented ancestor of Tomoko. *Let.Her.Go.*"

With that, Mabuse stepped back further, a slightly confused look on his face. "…a talented ancestor…?" Sophie heard him say it, questioning, as if he were trying to understand how there could be one here in the room.

He then screamed, "His hands!" The two Hansa stepped forward and tried to grab the Kentaro's hands to stop him from casting. He deftly ducked to the left of them, his hand quickly reaching out and in one swift movement, grabbed a chair and flung it at the men.

Mabuse stepped back, shocked. "*You are frozen. Your hands are lead. They cannot be moved,*" he spoke quickly, there was power in his voice. It was commanding, powerful, more powerful than when he commanded them before.

Kentaro's hands locked again, but his face was contorted in concentration, his brow covered in sweat. He was challenging the command, and his hands were started to move already, slowly.

Mr. M meanwhile grabbed one of the Hansa men, and in a brisk throw, threw him over a table. He and moved to another, stalking him. The Hansa man backed away.

215

Mabuse hurriedly scuttled out of the café, his remaining men threw chairs at Mr. M, and then ran after their boss. Mr. M blocked the chairs deftly with his hands, knocking them to either side. A car immediately pulled up out the front, and they scrambled into it, the two hansa men bundling their dazed colleague, into the vehicle.

As they were getting in the car, Kentaro snapped out of the effect of Mabuse's control, spun around, and rushed out to the street.

Kentaro swished his fingers through the air and cast a spell at the car as it accelerated quickly down the street. Mr. M had a horrified look on his face and pulled him back inside the café.

"I thought you were going to fireball that car!"

"No, that would attract too much attention here. Police swarming all over here. It was a glyph."

Mr. M ran after him and grabbed his arm, pulling it down by his side. "No, Kentaro. Not here, not now."

Sensei stopped and nodded to Mr. M, staring at the car as it disappeared out of view. Silently he headed back inside.

Sophie could see them, but still couldn't move. At that point she heard someone come into the room walking behind them but couldn't see who it was until he came into her limited view.

It was Oskar.

He stood still in shock, taking in the mess around him, then shook his head and went from person to person, casting some of his healing magic. His hands glowed, a warm yellow/orange. He only needed to do it briefly, just a matter of seconds, to each person, and they immediately came out of the effect, though he sat down after it, and took a breath, evidently tired.

As soon as Tomoko was free, she ran over to her Talented Ancestor.

"Kentaro Sensei, thank you so much!" She gave him a deep bow. He politely bowed back, with a quick smile.

Harlan shook his head. "Yeah, wow. I don't want to go through that again."

Raffaella ran her hands through her hair, then looked at them, almost like they belonged to someone else. "He is only going to get away with that... *once*." Her tone was dark.

Kentaro sat down at a table and reached down to a bag he had brought with him and pulled out a laptop. He pulled out a little round metal square plate, about the size of someone's palm, and attached it to the side of the computer.

The computer started to power up, and as it did, he cast a spell into the plate. The red Glyph for the spell sat glowing, on top of the plate.

Sophie watched on, transfixed. She had never seen anything like this before.

"This is from Marcus. *ZauberMaschine*... machine magic. It's an interface between magic and electronic. Marcus and his wife have put some of these together. Those two working together are brilliant."

Tomoko visibly recoiled from it. "It connects magic and electronics. ...What?"

Don't be surprised, you all have this tech," Kentaro said.

"What? We all have devices that connect electronics and magic?" Sophie said.

"Yes. The headsets! It's a spell interfaced with some electronic device. I mostly work on magic. Didn't you wonder why you never need to change batteries?"

"Ah..." Harlan said, scratching the back of his neck.

Kentaro glanced down at the screen. "Good, it's working. I wasn't sure if I got the glyph on."

Sophie peered down at the screen. It was a map of Bamberg, and it showed where the car with Marcus was going, as it blipped away from the Electric Light Kafe, towards the main street of Bamberg.

"Hey, those Hansa men, Mabuse, I think they were waiting in a black car, parked opposite the café," Sophie said. Strangely, the effects of Mabuse's powers were completely gone. Almost like they were turned off with a light.

"That was us," The Sensei said. "We had been watching Tomoko, trying to learn about her dreamscaping with Kentaro. It was lucky we had."

Tomoko seemed dumbfounded, her eyes squinting, trying to grasp it at all. "You are my sensei... but how are you still alive?"

He held up his hand, pointing to a ring on his right-hand ring finger. "Ring of longevity. It stops ageing for the user for 200 years."

Tomoko froze for a second, her lips moving but no sound came out, before she realised and spoke. "Oh, sensei, thank you. Thank you for all you have taught me. I am indebted to your kindness."

"Well." He scratched the back of his head. "No need to thank me. It's not me, it's my memory. I heard you had been using a memory version of me in Doctor Marcus's technology. That's why I came to see what you were like."

It dawned on Sophie that in this case, Sensei was the Talented Ancestor, and so Tomoko was learning off a version of him. Sophie realised how this might seem weird from the Sensei's point of view. Almost like being trained by a version of yourself, and without your permission. However, he didn't seem too unhappy about it. It was weird.

"So, I realise she has been an apprentice, and I want to ask her to stop using the dreamcast headset."

Sophie was horrified. She looked at Tomoko who looked shocked, her eyes wide.

"Because I want her to come to Japan with me... to become my apprentice here, in *real life*."

30. Surprising Offers of Mage Apprenticeships

Tomoko looked surprised. Sensei motioned for her and pointed at another table.

They both sat down. Tomoko looked at his hands, and the ring of longevity. It surprised her to notice neat scars that ran around his fingers, at the knuckles. She remembered historically that some mages had their fingers cut off so they couldn't do magic. Someone had cut Sensei's off, but it seemed sewn back on. A shudder went down her spine, and she put the thought out of her mind.

"Japanese?" she said.

"No, English. Or German. I need the practice."

"So do I," Tomoko admitted.

So, you have been learning magic from me, training?

"Err, yes, Sensei. Through the dreamcast."

He looked perplexed. "I'm not sure how to feel about this. I mean it feels like you are learning from me, without my permission."

"Well, it's your memories, in my DNA. You are my great great great great grandfather."

"Yes, I know. If it wasn't for that…" He seemed serious for a second, but then smiled a little.

He shrugged. "Well in ways, I have gained an apprentice without having to do any work. Let me make you an offer. There may be something I can do."

***

Sophie watched Tomoko and her sensei walk over, and the thoughts and fear of what happened with Mabuse, quickly disappeared as she processed the idea that Tomoko had received an offer to leave them. The thought of Tomoko leaving left a hollow feeling in her stomach.

She had grown attached to Tomoko. She didn't want her to go.

Mr. M waved his hand at Sophie to get her attention. She realised she was vague. He put his hand on her shoulder to steady her. In the background, she could hear Oskar helping Jeff and the kitchen staff, who were now back to normal. Jeff's voice in the background was a bit traumatised by it all, it sounded like Oskar was calming him.

Mr. M sat down next to Sophie, looking at her directly. "Okay, I know you are all in a bit of shock, but I need you all to focus. This is important. "He reached into his pocket.

"I was sent a job, by a client in England. I was going to decline it, it's not my thing. But then, I realised, you need to know about it and it's a job you can do."

Harlan spoke, "Yeah, so what is the job?"

"You need to get to this New Nation meeting near Strasbourg and take a photo of everyone at this meeting, at this place."

"Send the photo to this address." He gave them an email. It was an email, but a series of numbers.

"Hang on. Hang on. Dayum. Is this tomorrow night?"

Mr. M seemed surprised and nodded.

"I already know about this meeting. I was already going to go," Harlan said.

Sophie looked at him. "oh…the meeting you heard about in London at the illusionists' HQ."

"Yeah, the Illusionists were talking about this meeting at London. Someone was talking to Livingstone, it's a meet up of three factions. Or so he said."

Mr. M stood back; his brow raised in complete surprise.

"You were already going to this meeting? Who said this?"

"Yes, to gather more information. We were following up to see who works together. It was someone talking to Livingstone, I couldn't really see him."

Mr. M nodded. "Well, seems like you have another reason to go now."

"Are you going to pull out a yellow envelope of photos now?" Sophie said, smiling.

Mr. M studied her seriously. "No, it's brown. I was sent this about the meeting, but I think you will be interested."

Mr. M pulled out a yellowish-brown envelope, and then some photos. She thought these days, spying would be all digital.

"Do you know this man?"

They all peered down at the photo and shook their heads. A slightly tatty tall skinny man with reddish brown hair, three-day growth, and a sharp suit.

"This is Deitrich Marcarian. He is the leader of the New Nation. He is the one pushing for magic to be made illegal."

"He doesn't appear as evil as I thought." Harlan's head tilted appraising the photo.

"Hmmm. Three-day growth." Raffaella nodded at the picture.

Both Tomoko and Sophie crossed their arms. "So, this is the guy that's been causing us so much grief?" Sophie said.

"This Marcarian person. Mabuse must be behind him?" Tomoko frowned.

"Yeah, well its possible he is against magic? People do bad things when they are scared. But we have never hurt anyone. Magic is our tradition, it's in our blood," Tomoko said. Sophie noted there was a quaver in her voice. Sophie felt she would have said it herself if Tomoko hadn't.

"Completely agree." Sophie nodded. "This is us. Being a mage isn't a job, it is what we *are*."

Harlan nodded. "Yeah, it's something they can't take from you. It is you."

"It is like being Genoese. You can't make this illegal," Raffaella said.

Mr. M sat there patiently listening. "This is the man you need to deal with. Maybe talk to him, make him see sense. Maybe talk to the other members of his party."

Mr. M pulled out more photos, his fingers flicked through them nimbly, and stopped at one, his index finger pushing it across the table at Sophie. It showed several men, all sitting around a table.

"This is a photo of a previous meeting they had last night. This is Marcarian, this man is the secretary, George Silver. He is English but has lived in Germany for many years. This man here is a businessman, who visits them a lot. He seems to donate a lot of money to the company. I found out his name is Anton Livingstone. He keeps a very low profile."

Sophie studied the photo of Anton Livingston. She looked at the others.

"Could this guy be…" Harlan began.

"Related to the Livingstone's from the London Illusionists?" Tomoko finished his sentence.

Raffaella uttered, below her breath. "*He is a mage.*"

Sophie thought of their encounters with Roderick Livingstone. Would he be involved in this? Would mages want to do this to their own kind?

"So, this political party is talking about making magic illegal, and blaming it on safety, when the mages are behind it and helping to make it illegal? Why would they do this to us? Like…we are also mages…" Sophie stopped herself from ranting further.

They all stared at each other, quietly for a minute.

"Well…" Harlan broke the silence, almost awkwardly. "What's our next step?" He glanced at each of the group, but no suggestions were forthcoming.

Sophie ran through the options in her head. "We're running out of time. The only answer here is, we need to get evidence of what is going on. Evidence of the connection. People expect to see politicians be honourable and act correct and legally. We need a photo, or video, or something."

"Have they done anything illegal?" Tomoko asked.

"Well, no, but what they have done is not important. It is about perception. How people perceive what they are doing… that is what can destroy a person. You need to shape that perception." Sophie said.

"*Control the narrative.* I have heard that phrase. That describes it, I think." Tomoko said.

"Yeah, ok, I know from what I overheard there seems to be a big meeting at the New Nations headquarters. I'll go there and

see what I can see. May be there will be evidence I can get."
Harlan looked doubtful.

"Yes Harls, that's the only thing we got going for us. That
information you have. If you can get photos or video, some
incriminating evidence of something happening at the New
Nation Headquarters, then we can publicise it in the media
before the vote. That will make people see through the
campaign."

The group nodded; it seemed this part was up to Harlan.
Sophie felt confident in him. He hadn't let them down so far.

Mr. M glanced at her and nodded. He pulled out a notepad
and wrote on it. "Here is the address of their headquarters in
Strasbourg,

The four thanked Mr. M for his help, he snapped off a polite
bow, backed away, and left. Sophie realised he was expensive, but
the information he provided was invaluable.

As Mr. M wandered off, Sophie patted Tomoko on the
shoulder. "How do you feel about the offer of being an
apprentice. Like Kentaro's real life apprentice."

"Yeah, it's like you'll be dreamscaping, with no headset. Dang,
that's weird," Harlan said.

"And how do you feel about going to Japan?"

They were all quiet. Sophie knew they would all be unhappy
about Tomoko leaving. It was an odd feeling. At a time when
mages may be banned, and forced to leave the German countries,
an invitation to study magic with a mage in Japan was a timely
godsend. Sophie was happy for her, sad about the situation, and
angry that their enemies had put them in this awful situation in
the first place.

"Yes, well it is a great opportunity," Tomoko said. Her eyes
darted in either direction, her hands clasped together awkwardly.

"Well, if things go bad here, you at least have somewhere to
go."

Sophie glanced at Tomoko. She could see the sentence hit her
hard. She tilted her fringe down, gazing silently at the floor.

No one spoke as they left the café.

***

The day at school went slowly, as they made plans to go to the headquarters that night. Freidrickson's class was most interesting. Ying and Hans were both in the class and had switched seats and were now sitting closer to Circle 66, behind Tomoko and Raphaella.

After class they had their lunchbreak, hanging out at the table they often sat at. Tomoko glumly looking up from her phone, a serious expression on her face.

"The news on my phone. Tomorrow. Bavarian Parliament decides if the anti-magic laws go ahead." She was pale and was quiet after saying it. It seemed unfair that they had tackled the problem with the Minotaur man, but now the Government would make magic illegal.

"Tomoko, at least you live by yourself. If my papa finds out I am doing magic, he will kill me, I think you remember me telling when last time I started talking to him about it? He went crazy. He's always hated it, more than the average person. To be honest, I don't know why." She was silent, thinking about her papa and the way he reacted.

As Harlan tucked into a second plate of pasta, Sophie felt her phone buzz in her pocket.

She gazed down at the name.

Rupert.

She took a deep breath before answering.

"Rupert. Oh, did you hear about the attack?"

"Yes, are you okay, old girl? I hope you've glyphed up that café and, thrown a few around various places you stay as well."

"Yes, we're all okay. Don't worry the café is properly glyphed up, we're keeping an eye out for them."

"Good, good, listen up, Parliament votes soon. I've been trying to pull some strings. I'm awfully afraid, it looks like it's going to go through. You don't have much time left before the polls open for the voting. Pull your finger out old chap!"

"I know. We have a plan sort of. We're trying to expose the New Nation, leak something about them that destroys them, and brings down public opinion, so the public vote down the ban." She looked at Tomoko, Harlan, and Raphaella, all of whom gave her blank looks. "Rupert, any other ideas?"

"Like I said, I've been trying to pull some strings. I've been talking to the various communities in Bamberg that have a stake in the referendum and getting them to vote against the magic ban." Sophie realised this was, of course Rupert's area. He dealt with diplomacy in a royal court setting, making deals between factions and opposing parties. Most of his spells worked on influence and communication….which was why he was so hopeless in combat. He paused, considering. "I think your plan, trying to incriminate the New Nation… it's worth a shot. If you can swing the public vote in your favour."

He paused; she could hear him breathing quietly down the phone.

"Being an official employee of Her Majesty, I would *never* suggest something like that of course. But we are a tad desperate. We need information, and you do have a rather spiffy thief at your disposal."

"Thanks, Rupert." Sophie felt a touch of relief for the support; there was still a lot to do.

"Sophie, old girl, as I've mentioned before, this is all dreadfully damn important. See you."

Rupert went and Sophie sat there pouting for a minute. Why did things seem to end up on her shoulders? Sometimes she just wanted to time out from the world…go into her bedroom, lock the door and read some of the Bronte Sisters .. for a week. She fantasised about it, then put it aside, and started thinking of their current predicament.

"Everyone, are we up to this? It's going to be an all-night-time ride to Strasbourg? Harlan?"

"I've had plenty of practice at stealthy activity in the dreamcasts. I've trained over and over for a situation like this. Now it's finally time to do it for real." Despite the danger he felt excited.

School finally finished. Mr. M had sent them some photos of the building, and Harlan had used them to look at the windows and doors.

The four met at Raphaella's house, Sophie telling her father she was sleeping over there. Harlan lived with a host family who didn't mind him staying over.

They had taken to hanging about in Raphaella's workshop, which was in the family garage. She had multiple Vespa's there, lying around in parts. Big racks of shelves lined the walls, and cardboard boxes sat in them, filled with engine parts, headlights, and various other odd looking things Sophie didn't recognise… or want to. Harlan did, however, as Raffaella had taken him on as her Vespa mechanic apprentice and had scheduled him to take lessons. As all of them rode scooters, having a full scooter mechanic and her trainee in your party was handy.

Raffaella was there with Sophie and Tomoko. Raphaella's mum came out and offered them some cake, and coffee.

As they sat, Sophie turned to see Harlan's scooter drive into the garage. It was a peculiar sight. It seemed like ALL his possessions were on it. He had things tied to the front, side and back Sophie glanced over at him, perplexed. "Harlan is this all your possessions, on your scooter?" "Well, yeah. I'm also wearing four shirts and four pairs of jeans.

Sophie was incredulous. "Okay, but why?"

He frowned. "I got kicked out, I had nowhere to go, so came over here." Raffaella stared down at him, given her usual lack of emotion, Sophie guessed it may have been pity. "Why did you get kicked out?"

"The Hochmaiers were sent photos of me doing thief things, while just wearing my black thieving gear. Sent anonymously. They look like they're from a CCTV camera, the ones we've seen being put up around Bamberg."

Sophie remembered seeing the odd camera being installed here and there. At the time, she hadn't thought much of it.

"Kicked out because they said I was a criminal." Harlan said, looking at the ground.

"You are a criminal," Raffaella said.

"Well, yeah, err, but I'm a *good* criminal."

"You can stay here," Raffaella said. She pointed to a shelf. "It's big, we'll make space on this shelf."

Harlan stared at the shelf, then looked at her to see if she was joking. It was impossible to tell.

"Hey, could I stay here too? It would save me a lot in rent," Tomoko said.

"No." Raffaella snapped.

They helped Harlan unload a million things impossibly packed all over this scooter. Tomoko opened a glove box to discover some underwear, squealed, and jumped back two feet. Raffaella went in to discuss him staying in her workshop with her parents. They then sat around talking about their next plan, that being to go to the headquarters, try to see any files, and get any evidence of the New Nation's connection to Roderick Livingston, and get a photo of the people at the meeting.

Sophie had suggested a few things, possibly trying to see if any computers were still turned on and read the files, find any important paperwork. They chatted about ideas, but Sophie realised, they were a little over their head. They were getting to be good mages. Harlan was an excellent thief, Raffaella was a great swordswoman. Detective work however, they were not good at.

Considering how cold it was, they rugged up in big jackets and hopped on their scooters to drive to where the New Nation's headquarters building was. Mr. M had told them the New Nation had a beautiful and sophisticated headquarters in the flashier part of Strasbourg, which was just a respectable front. New Nation actually got together to devise their plots and plans in a more suitably archaic 19th century building, in the run-down part of Bamberg.

It took them about three hours to get to the location, and about 30 minutes to find it, thanks to Harlan getting them lost. The cold, night wind cut through clothing easily, and it was a long journey. Sophie reminded herself she needed to stop putting off getting a car licence so she could drive her papa's little old 1960's Fiat 500. It was tiny, and not even as fast as the scooters, but it had a nice heater.

Strasbourg was a big city, for the German nations, and the older part was a maze of old streets. There wasn't a lot of the old part of the city left, after the war, but what was there was confusing. They eventually drove past the headquarters, Harlan waved to indicate that it was the building, they kept driving around a corner. They had all looked at a map already, and worked out the best place to park and wait while Harlan went in.

"So, the plan is Harlan goes in, eavesdrop on the meeting, get a recording or video if you can. Anything incriminating," Sophie said, directing her instructions at Harlan.

"Yeah, well, what do you guys do?" Harlan said with a raised eyebrow.

"We wait here." Sophie smiled. She whacked him on the shoulder for good luck.

***

The four of them left their scooters in a park. It was as quiet as midnight in a church cemetery.

Harlan checked the building, it sat in silence, and the carpark was empty. The big meeting he needed to take a photo of either wasn't happening or was, but later.

He pulled off his big jacket, big riding gloves, scarf and hopped over the fence at the back of the building. Sophie watched him disappear and felt a pang of worry for him. He never seemed bothered by it.

Harlan practically leapt over the fence in one bound. He sat down in the backyard and quickly attached the climbing spikes to his shoes. His climbing gloves slipped over his hands, and he flexed his fingers in them. They had been modified with glue and grit powder so his grip on brick, tile and metal was excellent for climbing.

He had already identified the drainpipe for climbing. From Mr. M's photos, it had looked secure enough to climb. He went over and shook it vigorously, but quietly, making sure it didn't come off the wall.

It was time.

He put one hand around the base, and the other hand on a part that was most secure where it was affixed to the wall. The drainpipe held solid, his foot gripped on a secure point, and he started climbing up. His adrenaline was pumping now, and he felt a smile on his face. It was about 12:30 a.m., and it seemed like no one else was awake but him.

Harlan was quickly on the roof. There was a little window, leading into a small office built in the attic of the building. It was an old window latch and being this high up, it didn't have a good lock. He jimmied the window open easily, and eased himself slowly through the window, his padded feet gently touching the ground.

229

Scanning around the office, he wasn't sure what he was looking for. He checked the room, trying to identify something important, something that may give them some information. A laptop sat on the table, Harlan walked around to stand in front, and flicked the screen up and turned it on. A blank white box appeared, asking for a password to be supplied. He tried the ten common standard passwords that thieves used – the ten that people who used basic passwords used, but none of them worked. He couldn't do anything with it here, he tucked it under his arm. It could be cracked it later.

Before he had been excited, but now there he was getting a touch nervous. It wasn't particularly logical. There appeared to be no one in the building, but it was there anyway.

He opened the door slowly, and stepped gingerly into the foyer, then moving down, looking into rooms, offices. He searched on people's desks but was careful not to disturb anything else that would indicate he'd been here. He peered into more rooms, rummaging through drawers, checked computers, but could see nothing that could help.

Harlan's heart was now thumping, and while adrenaline and the excitement initially had been dominant in his thoughts, cold hard logic was starting to overtake his mind.

He had no idea of how to find what they needed. *Something incriminating.* He had done lots of training as a thief, but this was more like sophisticated industrial espionage. He put the laptop in his backpack and would pull the hard drive back at home. That was all he could really think of. Plus, the people would think someone stealing a laptop were normal thieves. He thought quickly of Kriechbaum's rule: *Stealing as revenge also gives you something useful.*

His feet padded softly on the stairs, barely making a noise as he went down the next level. He stopped regularly to listen for footsteps. He needed to find where people were having a meeting, he couldn't hear anything. The one advantage that put him at ease; his hearing was excellent. He would hear anyone else before they heard him.

Down another flight of stairs, to the ground floor. Harlan then noticed the stairs continued, there was a level below that, a basement level. It could well be where files were kept… but was probably cleaning equipment and computer servers.

The door was locked. Harlan decided to look at it later, after he checked out the room on the ground level.

Before he could go in the room, Harlan heard noise coming down the corridor.

There was someone else here, in the building.

He padded his way down the corridor, modern functional purple carpet, and generic inoffensive scenery photos adorned the walls, regularly spaced. Wooden doors to offices on either side, mostly with the doors open. His heart was beating loudly. He took a deep breath and continued. There was an odd room at the end of the corridor, a faint flashing light came out of it, reflecting off the rood. He could hear the rolling sound of office chairs with wheels on the bottom, perhaps moving around on a flat floor. One or two.

The little mirror peaked around the corner of the door frame, giving him vision of what was in the room without exposing himself.

It was a bizarre sight.

At first, he didn't recognise the man from that angle, and from behind, but it was clearly him. The long grey hair, from the back, he could make out that arms of glasses over his ears, and his black gloves.

It was Mabuse. He was sitting in a chair, looking at a wall full of monitors.

Another man stood with him. He pointed at a screen and Mabuse adjusted the camera, focussing it.

Then Harlan almost gasped, he checked one monitor, then another and another to make sure.

It was Bamberg.

Mabuse somehow had access to the surveillance cameras in Bamberg. He was monitoring the whole of the city.

Harlan realised the risk he was taking, he could easily be discovered if either Mabuse or the other man simply got up and walked to the door, though it seemed they were the only two in the building. He quickly retraced his steps, going back up the stairs to the ground floor.

The main room on the ground floor level was a large meeting room. The floor was a polished black marble. It seemed to be a meeting room, with a big table, but they also used it for storage.

***

Sophie sat with the others, her legs twitched nervously, thinking about Harlan in the building. There didn't seem to be any reason to nervous, he was alone in it.

At that point, her phone buzzed… *an unknown number.* She cancelled the call; it wasn't time to be talking to some random person.

It called again.

Suddenly it clicked… *what if the call was something to do with what was going on?*

She answered the phone, looking around her.

"Hi. This is Hans. Harlan needs to hide now. Tell him to get behind the big wooden table near the door."

"What?" Sophie recognised Hans's Bavarian accent, but she couldn't work out what he was talking about.

"Someone is coming into the room. Tell Harlan to hide. QUICK…NOW!"

Sophie quickly rang Harlan, who answered.

"Harlan, someone is coming in the room, get behind the big wooden table near the door."

"What? There's only two people here Sophie, it's Mabuse and someone, but he's on another level."

"Don't argue! Just do it *quickly* Harlan," Sophie said, worry and fear rising in her voice.

"Okay." Harlan closed off the call.

She looked at the phone. Hans had gone. *What the hell was going on?*

***

Harlan sat down behind the table, wondering why he was, and feeling stupid. There were no cars out the front. Every instinct in his body told him, except for Mabuse and the other man, there was no one in this part of the building. Anyway, it made sense to wait a bit and see. Just in case Sophie was right.

Then he heard the door opening.

There *was* someone else here.

He heard the creak of what the door to the basement must be. From under the desk, he could peer out and see the room. The door opened and out walked a few men and women, all in dark-coloured business suits. They were speaking in German, something about the company and profit. He could make out part of what they were saying, something about "making magic illegal." He thought guiltily about being in Germany for all this time, and still not knowing better German. Harlan craned his neck forward and peered at them, trying to see their faces, carefully not exposing himself.

He suddenly realised the timing of the situation. Sophie warned him in time to get under the table. *But how did she know?*

Dietrich Marcarian, the man that Mr. M had warned them about, was here. As per usual, Mr. M was reliably informed. Marcarian seemed to be leading the discussion.

Harlan scanned the people with him, checking the faces. He instantly recognised one. Roderick Livingstone was here. It was definitely him. Next to him was Anton Livingstone, as Mr. M had shown them in the photos. Harlan waited for them to file in, and then poked his tiny surveillance camera over the top of the table, took a few silent photos, then retracted it out of sight.

Frustratingly, between the fact he couldn't quite hear them, and his bad German... he couldn't quite understand what Roderick he was saying.

Harlan heard the odd crackle of some overhead announcement system. The static crackle of it turning on.

"BLACK." One word came out over the PA. *What the hell?*

Harlan felt the power of the word, like it was telling him to do something, trying to take control of his body. He shook his head, and he felt the influence of the word slip from his body. He looked at the others in the room, they continued unaffected, didn't seem to notice it.

Strange.

Then the door opened. Harlan's heart jumped into his throat. He felt himself involuntarily move back. It was Mabuse standing at the door. He moved in silently, and leaned back on a chair, to watch the meeting.

The strange thing was no one greeted him. No one even looked at him. It was bizarre.

Marcarian was now speaking, with passion, and regularly smashed his fist into the palm of his other hand to reinforce some point. Along with the Livingstones, Marcarian and Mabuse, there were 10 or so people watching him, nodding approvingly, and uttering single word approvals. He kept at it, his head scanning his audience, meeting their gaze, the pitch of his voice raising to match the passion of his speech.

At this point he pointed to a large, bearded man at the front of the group. Harlan couldn't hear his name, but Marcarian was clapping him and welcoming him, and gesturing him to step to the front of the small audience.

Harlan watched as Mabuse moved silently among the crowd. No one paid him any attention.

Then it dawned on him. They weren't greeting, or taking any notice of Mabuse, almost as if...*they couldn't see him.* To Harlan, he was there as plain as day. Harlan stared at Mabuse, only pulling his eyes off him to watch the tall, barrel-chested man, who everyone was now watching. He stood up in front of them. Marcarian called out, energy and passion in his voice, "Do it... DO IT!!"

The large, bearded man stood in front of them all, and his hand slipped under his brown suitcoat, under his shirt, touching his chest underneath. Harlan studied him... *was he activating a spell?* Then he saw a blue grey shimmer flickered over his body. It was familiar...and Harlan realised it was like the same blue grey shimmer he saw when his own body changed. *Shapeshifting magic.*

The man shimmered, his body size expanding as it shed a vague blue light, which reflected off various things in the room. The men sitting at the table exclaimed, and hurriedly shuffled their seats back. A few of them immediately got out of their chairs, and moved to the back of the room, clearly concerned if not outright scared.

Marcarian stood their confidently, with a smile on his face. He had clearly seen this before, or otherwise was not bothered by it. His smile turned to laughter, clearly, he was happy about all this.

Harlan watched from his spot as the man changed, his head grew bigger, his chest expanded outwards, he expanded taller and outwards. His colour changed from a white skinned, dark-haired man, to dark all over, till he was the darkest brown, almost black.

His head was slowly taking the shape of a bull's head, as his body morphed into a huge half man, half bull. A huge sauntering minotaur. It eyes red, baring its teeth at the crowd. Shiny purple black skin, reflecting the various points of light in the room.

Tables scratched the floor, chairs pushed against each other, and fell over. Harlan noticed the Livingstones pushing back, away from the minotaur. A couple stifled surprised cries, emotion in their voices.

The man stood in front of them was frightening, but almost impressively beautiful.

"This is my true form," he said in a deep voice. "This is the form of my people. There are few of us, but soon there will be more. We will supress the mages here, declare magic illegal. I will use magic to assist you. Then no more."

The minotaur spoke in a booming deep voice. Just his voice sent shivers into Harlan's bones. The men seemed to regain their composure but were standing at the back of the room.

Marcarian was waving to them to come back, but they didn't want to go anywhere near him.

Marcarian then looked at them, "Prepare yourself."

Harlan had seen a man turn into a minotaur. *What the hell was going to happen now that needed preparation for?*

The people backed away a bit more. The Minotaur this time put his hands in front of him, his hands moving slowly through a series of forms. He then uttered some words, and his form began to change once *again.*

This time, his form grew bigger. His teeth grew bigger, his horns stretched longer and twisted. His skin went a dark black and his tail swung around, looking longer and more threatening. He had turned himself into some sort of devil.

Now *all* of the attendees, except for Mabuse, had moved back up against the back of the wall. Mabuse watched it all, impassively. The rest were scared, mumbling, some of them openly screaming. Harlan looked at the creature in fear. It looked a little like the demons that summoners would bring forth to the world. Horrific looking things that cast fear into mortals that could not understand their nature.

Marcarian looked at the Demon. "Revert. Revert."

The demon cast the spell again and reverted to his former minotaur self.

The men moved back to their seats.

At this point, Mabuse stood up and left, carefully walking between them. As before, no one reacted to him at all.

The man slowly regressed back to the form of the large, bearded man. He seemed small compared to the creatures he had previously become... but even so, Harlan realised he was still a large man, with a huge barrel chest and huge arms.

The men all sat back down. The large, bearded man pulled out a black shirt from his bag and put it on.

Marcarian stood up once more.

"The people vote on Sunday, only five days away. We need to do this one more time before it votes. The public will be so against magic, the politicians will go with them. This... this is how we strike fear into the hearts of people."

The men started clapping, then started talking excitedly, the odd laugh. They all slapped Marcarian on the back numerous times, and the men crowded around him. Harlan heard them talk on for a while but couldn't make out anything else noteworthy. They eventually started talking about leaving, and then, in twos and threes, shuffled out the door. He sat there grimacing, his long legs squashed into a confined space before it was all quiet. He peeked out, and confirmed the room was now empty.

Harlan heard the crackling of the PA. "WHITE." Was it something to do with Mabuse? Some sort of hypnotic command?

He left quietly the same way he came in, this time feeling very unsettled and wondering what exactly it was he had seen.

When he returned to the group, Sophie ran up and grabbed his arm, then gave him a big hug.

"I was so worried. Are you okay? Did you see anything?"

Harlan put on his helmet. "Let's go. I got photos. I'll tell you when we are gone from here." Harlan drove for some time, driving ahead of the others, not speaking. He eventually stopped at a night Kafe, and they went inside for a coffee to help them with the long drive back to Bamberg.

*****

"He turned into the demon?" Raffaella said, stone-faced. "Cool." She drank the coffee, and shook her head, disappointed at the taste.

"Mabuse is watching the surveillance network in Bamberg?" Sophie stated. This put a new perspective on things. They would really have to start avoiding the cameras.

"...and Mabuse walked among them like they couldn't see him. It was the most bizarre thing I have ever seen. And no, it wasn't cool. Not at all." Sophie could see Harlan expression was quite dour, unusual for him to be quite as serious at this. "It was horrific. There were a bunch of serious, butt ugly, big men, in there, and *they* were scared by all of it. They were practically running up the walls."

Sophie realised Harlan was clearly still processing the whole thing. It was probably a lot to take in. Maybe he was in shock, she wasn't sure.

Tomoko scanned each of them in turn, then Harlan. "So, they are trying to stage these demon attacks?"

Harlan nodded. "These guys are trying to stop magic. They are supposed to be people that hate mages. But they have a huge minotaur there casting magic and doing spells. They've allied with the Livingstone's, who are mages... to effectively stop all Magic users and get what they want."

"Get what they want..." Sophie said. "Apparently, they want the removal of magic here in Bamberg, but while magic remains unaffected in England, where the Livingstones are.

Sophie nodded. "It makes a perverse sense. Well except for Livingstone."

"Maybe they see us as mage rivals? It's completely feasible, though not very sisterly," Tomoko said. "...and un unfortunately formidable alliance," Tomoko said.

Sophie realised Tomoko had picked up what was probably the most alarming fact. That there were so many people working together.

"Oh, yeah. Mabuse and Adeline. That guy scares the crap out of me," Harlan said.

"Not to mention a transmuting Minotaur." Sophie spoke slowly, her thoughts processing the events as she spoke. She looked at her watch. She saw the time and she got a dropping feeling in her stomach. It was 1.15 am, and they still had to drive back to Bamberg.

"Werner's Rule: Never break into someone's house if there is someone there." He muttered it, a tone in his voice Sophie didn't normally hear.

"Hang on. How does that get to be a rule. It's just obvious, isn't it?" Sophie said.

"Let's go home, get some sleep. I'm too tired to think," he said.

31. School and a Discussion

The next day was yet another cold Tuesday morning in Bamberg, and they went to school together. They parked their scooters at a rendezvous point, and then started sending out the photos Harlan took. The first thing was to send off the photos with a carefully worded email to the major newspapers and TV channels. They all sat together, writing the text in a way that highlighted the dangers, and showed the New Nation's part to play in the whole affair.

Finally, they sent them anonymously. They all breathed a sigh of relief that they were gone. Sophie hoped they would treat the photos seriously.

Harlan suggested they take the bus so they could sleep on it, and promptly fell asleep on Sophie's shoulder. Sophie looked out the window, and started thinking through the previous night's events, and then started thinking about the consequences of a ban on magic.

She knew the Livingstones and possibly the London Illusionists were working with the New Nation to ban magic in Bavaria. They could only suppose the Livingstone's were doing it as some sort of mage rivalry... somehow it strengthened their position. Were they using the transmuting Minotaur demon to create a fuss that would turn the public against magic?

They managed to stay awake through the first morning period. Sophie knew the vote was four days away, and she thought about what could happen in those four days. Had they swung the vote in their favour? Could they do more? Exhausted they laid under a tree next to an old red brick chemistry classroom at lunch, except for Raphaella, who had gone to teach a longsword class. Sophie always wondered how Raffaella could focus enough to run one her classes with everything going on…but that was Raffaella. And she wasn't a mage.

The grass gave a little under her body, it was soft. Nature's Mattress, she thought, and smiled to herself. It was like an odd observation Johannes would make. Harlan's long legs as a headrest. The next thing she knew she had fallen asleep, and Raffaella was prodding them all awake with her foot, except for Harlan. She bent over and grabbed his shoulder, gripping it and shaking him roughly. He woke up, looking at her and smiled at her stony expression.

As he woke, Harlan smacked his lips and glanced at the three. "Guys, Soph… Okay, I need to talk about this, what does it all mean? What I saw?"

Sophie shook her head. "From what you have described, I have no idea."

"How about we trying to get the demon to work with us. Maybe he can help us out with jobs," Raffaella said.

"Well… he was a minotaur," Harlan said.

"You said he was a demon?" Raffaella said staring at Harlan inquisitively.

"Well… he was a human first. He said his true form was a minotaur type creature."

Tomoko frowned in thought. "Minotaur… oh the tall monster with the one eye?"

"Cyclops." Raffaella shook her head. "Minotaur is half man, half bull."

Tomoko frowned. "A man's torso and a bull's body? Strange?"

"No, the other way around…" Sophie said.

"A bull's body, with a man's head and four human legs?" Tomoko asked. She looked at Harlan, "What sort of clothes could it wear?"

"Okay…enough with the *monster anatomy questions,*" Sophie stated, hearing the exasperation in her own voice.

"Yeah, I have no idea why they are doing all this…" Harlan said. "…Hey how did Hans know to warn us?"

"They had some sort of spell, maybe? They must have some sort of trace," Sophie thought.

She tried to think of all the spells that could do that. "Tomoko, is there any spell you know can do that?"

She shook her head slowly, thinking, "No. Maybe they have an artefact? Magic item?"

Raffaella nodded. "Oh, maybe a crystal ball. That's cool. We should try to buy it off them."

"Are crystal balls actually real?" Harlan seemed a little incredulous.

"Not in Japan. I thought they were here." Tomoko said, brushing her hair, which had gone a bit wonky from sleeping on it.

"Only in movies," Sophie said.

"Oh," Tomoko said, frowning.

"Well, however they did it, let's meet them and work out what the hell is going on," Sophie noted.

Sophie felt droplets of rain sprinkle on her skin, looking down at the tiny droplets glistening on her jacket. The sky had quickly gone grey, and it had started to rain. They gathered their things and sprinted inside.

There was a vacant chair near the heating unit, and Sophie plopped down on it. She could see the rain gathering in puddles on the concrete path outside the window outside, but the school cafeteria was warm, if not a little mildewy. Sophie was looking at the Spaghetti and meatballs. She decided that Italian food was probably best left to being cooked by Italians, reminiscing of the few times she had been to Raphaella's house, in particular the last time where Mrs Cuppertino had cooked Lasagne for all of them. Tomoko in particular was impressed.

Tomoko, Raffaella and Harlan appeared together, and took the remaining three chairs, Raffaella rubbing her hands together near the heater.

Tomoko shook her head. "I need to…" She paused for second to think of the phrase. "Clear my thoughts. We have so much going on." She took a mouthful of noodles, slurping as she did.

Harlan was chomping down on his sandwiches. As always hungry, and not caring about what he ate as long as it wasn't actually horrifically bad or extremely expensive. He stopped to chew and stared through the table, thinking.

Sophie was also trying to gather her thoughts. It was a little while before she realised her phone was ringing. It was Rupert.

"Hi, Soph, old girl, how the dickens are you?" Rupert said.

Rupert used a range of expressions that were sometimes cute and sort of charming in an old-world sort of way, but many of them Sophie wasn't exactly sure what they meant.

"Oh, hi, Rupert. We are well, I'm glad you rang, it would be good to ask you advice on something…"

"Oh, good to hear, old girl. I'm spiffy at the moment. Listen, I wanted to talk to you, this is more important than you may realise."

Sophie had only thought about herself and Bavaria.

"Basically, the world is watching what happens in Bavaria. If the laws get through there it *will* continue. But if they stop here in Bamberg, and a big enough defence is made… other countries will see it as too hard. I do hope so. It may even mean the countries who still have anti-magic laws may roll them back."

Sophie had only thought about herself and Bavaria. Of course, Rupert was right, the rest of the German states would follow suit, and then possibly the rest of Europe and the world. A sinking feeling hit her stomach, as she realised how much depended on all this. It was enormous.

Sophie nodded, then realised Rupert couldn't see her nodding on the phone. "Yes. I agree."

"Rupert, we actually spied on the New Nation Office, they have a minotaur. He was there casting spells."

Sophie listened on the phone, and it was quiet for a second.

"A minotaur? Like a half bull, half man sort of chap?" Rupert said.

"It doesn't have the man's legs," Tomoko called out to him.

"Yes, you know, like one of the myth folk, but it's real. And from what Harlan said, it's completely terrifying." Sophie noticed everyone was looking at her.

Rupert sounded a bit more serious, "Okay, yes perhaps its best you don't get too more involved in it, I'm still working on things. Let me know if you hear anymore. We'll chat later, Sophie old girl."

"What did he say, Soph?" Harlan looked at her.

"He sounded surprised. I had to describe what a minotaur was. I guess he wasn't expecting one to be around.

"Are they powerful?" Tomoko asked.

Raffaella piped up, "They are normally very strong and evil. Formidable. Pantera does a great song about a Greek warrior fighting a Minotaur. Would make a great tattoo."

Sophie thought for a second. "They don't normally cast magic though." Raffaella nodded.

"Where did it come from?" Harlan asked.

"Probably Adeline. Or the Illusionists. Or the Fae."

"Hey. My people wouldn't do that."

Sophie peered at him. *So, it was "my people" now.* She smiled at the fact that it wasn't that long ago he was refusing to admit he was half, (or even any part!) Fae.

Harlan glanced over at Sophie. "So, what's next?" Sophie scanned their faces, Harlan was staring back at her expectantly.

"Well Rupert said not to do anything and don't get involved."

"Are we going to do that?" Harlan said, before taking a huge mouthful of sandwich.

"No." Sophie smiled.

***

Sophie had told her papa she was having a sleepover. Tomoko tossed out several blankets and doonas out on to the little lounge-room. It wasn't comfortable, but Sophie barely remembered laying down and putting her head on a grey pillow before she went to sleep.

They woke up in the morning.

She was making a huge number of dishes.

Sophie sat down at the little table, on the veranda, overlooking the medieval market square.

It was a beautiful little visage. Tomoko placed a green tea on the table, and Sophie picked it up, automatically, sipping it. It was charcoalish, but always made her feel refreshed.

Something struck Sophie. *How did Three Bells Incorporated know that Harlan was in the New Nation building?* As far as she knew, they were back in Bamberg.

"Tomoko, how did Three Bells know that Harlan was in the New Nation building?"

"Yes, I was trying to think what spell could do that." Tomoko said. "I have thought through all the spells, I can't think of anything."

Sophie woke up both Raffaella and Harlan. "You two. When Three Bells contacted me about Harlan being in the New Nation Offices, what spell would they have used?"

Raffaella shrugged. Harlan, still groggy mumbled as he slowly opened his eyes. "No idea, why don't you ask them."

Sophie was loathe to talk to Three Bells, particularly after she found out they only turned up to look for her, after being offered money. She checked the time, and realised the time for the vote was close.

Sophie only had Ying's number. She pulled out her phone selected Ying's number and called it, her heart in her mouth. Time was counting down.

Ying answered, "Sophie? Hi."

"YING." Sophie was relieved. "Can I ask you something? It's important. The vote on the Anti Magic laws is on Sunday. Just four days away. I need to know something; how did you know that Harlan was in the New Nation office? When Hans rang me to warn me?"

"I can't tell you," Ying said, sounding firm.

"YING! You use magic the same as me. I need to know what spell. What do you know about New Nation? Is there anything you can do that you…or Hans, or any of Three Bells could do to help?" Sophie said, sounding a bit desperate.

Ying hesitated for ten seconds. "Okay, Hans and I have been thinking, all last night. Let's meet at Jeff's."

Sophie looked at her watch. "I'll see you there in five minutes."

Ying called out to someone with her. "Five minutes!... Yes, we can be there, see you then."

Sophie slammed the phone down. "We need to go, Jeff's at five minutes."

Sophie threw her scooter keys to Raphaella, which she caught and stared at, bleary eyed.

32. Missing Mages and Magic Bans

As the scooter engines roared loudly down the street, Sophie looked back at Raphaella. She had only just woken up, and Sophie was scared that she would fall off. She was driving a bit wobbly.

As they pulled up to Jeff's, Sophie's heart almost stopped. They all stopped their scooters.

Out the front were 4 police officers.

Sophie noticed that Jeff's red fiat 500 was parked next to them; Jeff was inside. They were late, and she had told Ying to meet them in the Kafe.

There was a text message on her phone.

We are inside. Push through them. They won't do anything-Ying.

Sophie and the others pulled their scooters up and put them on their stands. As they went to go in, the four Bavarian police stood in front of them, and held their hands up.

"Bitte." A gruff younger police officer looked at the four of them, and then spoke in English,

"We have reason to believe…"

At that point, Jeff appeared. "You have reason to believe…what officer? Because if you are going to bring up the activities of mages, I will remind you that the Kingdom of Bavaria has not yet drafted or made the Bavarian Anti Magic draft legislation. You have no power to do anything about magic."

"Sir." The officer turned. "We believe these four people are doing anti-social activity."

"These four 16-year-olds are coming here to study before their exams. They are all hoping to get into the Bamberg University. There is nothing illegal about that."

Sophie's body shook with nerves, and she felt sweaty. She hadn't seen Jeff quite like this before but wasn't surprised he would be this way. He seemed older than his years, and always came across as wise and a bit sage like. A bit like a slightly hippyish version of Rupert, without the magic. Sophie wondered if they were safe at Jeff's, after the previous visit by Mabuse.

The police officer, studied Jeff momentarily, peeked at his watch, and then gazed at the others.

They police all stepped aside, without a word.

The four rushed up the stairs, Jeff behind. "They're up there already." He called out from behind them, pointing up the stairs.

As they went upstairs, they saw Hans and Ying sitting there, both with oversized cups of coffee. The two of them were staring into their coffees, not speaking.

"Where are the others?" Tomoko asked.

Both stared at each other. Ying clenched her teeth and issued a low audible growl.

"Did you just growl?" Tomoko moved back away from Ying.

"What do you want?" Ying almost raised her voice. Sophie wasn't sure what was going on.

"Ying… is there something wrong? Are you angry with us?" Sophie said. Ying and Hans were sometimes pretty serious, but this wasn't normal.

"Oskar is gone," Ying said, though gritted teeth. The anger was clear in her voice, and a twinge of sadness. Sophie realised even though Oskar had quit Three Bells Inc, Ying was clearly emotional.

"His shop was broken into. He was there by himself. We think. We don't know where he is," Hans said.

Sophie felt a wave of empathy for them. Apart from her own crew, Oskar was the nicest of all the dreamcasters. He had put himself on the line, trying to improve the way Mages were seen by making a very public effort to heal the townsfolk. Plus, he'd helped her papa, and had been her pretend boyfriend for two minutes.

247

"Oskar is such a nice boy. I hope they find him," Tomoko said. Harlan just stood shaking his head; he looked shocked.

As they sat down, Jeff brought them donuts, oblivious to the news of Oskar. Harlan started eating. Sophie peered at him accusingly, the seriousness of a situation never impeded his appetite.

Ying's hand hovered over the centre of the table, then she dramatically opened her palm and placed a small shiny cylinder there. She smiled.

Tomoko studied it, her head askew. "What's this?"

"It's a camera, we have them all through the New Nation office. We were asked to plant them as a job, and hacked access to the feed ourselves. But David knew there was a meeting when he heard about it at the London Illusionists headquarters."

"Ah, I forgot he heard that as well," Harlan said.

"That is not legal!" Tomoko said, pausing to glance at Ying.

Ying ignored the comment, grabbed her laptop. Sophie watched the cursor flick across the screen and activate a video file. Ying angled the laptop screen so they could see it.

They all looked on. Harlan's jaw dropped, while they watched the video.

It was video footage of the large man turning into a minotaur at the New Nation offices, that Harlan had witnessed. All of the people's faces were clear.

"Ying – can you send us this clip? If we get this footage out, it will probably ruin this party. It may turn everyone against the New Law. We've sent photos… but this footage is amazing."

"Yes, you can. For a price. Three Bells doesn't work for free."

"YING. IF THEY MAKE THIS LAW REAL…" Sophie stopped speaking, realising she had raised her voice. Everyone was looking at her in surprise. It was all getting to her; they were now so close to the referendum.

She took a deep breath. "If this law goes through it will stop us all from doing magic. You and Hans included. Plus, the New Nation may be the ones who have Oskar."

Hans looked at them all. "Don't bring Oskar into the negotiation. This footage is worth a lot of money. We can't send it out to all of them. I can sell this to one TV station, and if I promise for them to have it for exclusive rights, I…we…. can earn a lot of money from it!"

Tomoko stared at Hans, moving her chair forward to be closer to him, speaking calmly. "No. If one TV station gets it, they may not release it, or may release it too late. It needs to be sent to all TV stations, with permission to use, and put up on the internet."

Ying and Hans looked at them all. Sophie looked directly at Ying. She was clearly torn, then a flicker of anger crossed her face. She put her computer on the table and started typing into it, her fingers pounding the keyboard harshly.

She dramatically pressed the last key and spun the laptop around so all could see it.

"It's now on YouTube. It will be with the TV stations at the newspapers in the next few minutes. Sophie, I've sent you a copy."

"Oh, damn, I need to get a copy to that email Mr. M gave me." She pulled out her phone, and quickly sent it on to the address, with the message URGENT in the subject line.

After five minutes Ying had spammed the video footage everywhere.

They sat watching the views slowly take off. It was getting hits.

Raffaella, as always, was monitoring the news. She had software set up that told her if keywords appeared in newspapers.

"I'm getting alert notifications on all the major keywords I've setup. Magic. Mage. Law changes. Anti-magic… all these alerts are going off."

Sophie finally felt that something they had done was working. They'd sent the most powerful piece of evidence they could find into the hands of the public, hoping it would stop the anti-magic law. She knew it would make an impact, but was there enough time? And would it be enough to swing the vote their way?

Were they too late?

Bernard M Lyons

33. White Vans in Bamberg

Sophie's scooter flitted along the ancient cobblestoned alleyways of the older district of Bamberg, on her way home from School.

Her mind raced through her current challenges. The referendum was coming up, and it looked like she and other mages would be forced out of the Kingdom. If she wanted to be a mage openly, she would have to tell her father, and he would go crazy if he knew she was a mage. The New Nation Party were in some kind of alliance with the Hansa. The Hansa seemed to be getting control of Bamberg, while surveillance was ruining people's lives. Mabuse and therefore probably Adeline was involved in it all… and they were working with a Minotaur that morphed into a demon.

It all seemed overwhelming.

She tried to put it out of her mind; she was riding and needed to concentrate. The road was getting wet and slippery as it rained. It was a slight drizzle, the wet glistening off the cobbled stone streets, the irregular pattern giving the streets a complex look.

Sophie listened to the clumpy sound of the tyres bumping over the cobbled streets. She had gotten used to the odd noise, but listening to it now, as she drove it sounded obvious when concentrating on it.

The meeting at Jeff's had been good. It was interesting what had been said. As she drove, a van pulled in front of her. She was used to it, people were impatient with scooters which they saw as slow, and often wanted to get past. Fact was her scooter was fast.

She muttered under her breath, as the lights changed, and she had to gear down to stop behind it in time. They had both now missed the lights as they had gone red. Sophie cursed.

Sophie looked at the van, in front of her, waiting for it to move off. It was not moving. The engine was still running. She couldn't see inside.

Stupid old slow vans.

It was too far over the left side of the street, so she went up the right-hand side, accelerating to get past it and get home. As she accelerated past it, her eye caught someone opening the driver's door. Directly in front of her.

She thudded into it; she felt the jolt of her head as she smashed against the door.

And everything went black.

***

Waking up, Sophie found herself in the back of the truck. It looked like someone had been using it as a moving van; bits of strapping and padding that would be used for transporting furniture were strewn about the floor

Despite this, someone had roughly tossed her scooter in the van with her, lying on its side. Sophie had her hands tied and taped, clearly so she couldn't cast spells. Someone had taped her fingers together, then taped her hands. They had also put tape around her mouth. They weren't taking chances, and they knew exactly what they were doing.

Like Raffaella, she had a tiny sword 3 centimetre long. It was taped into the back of her belt buckle, one of the ones they had found in Johannes's buried box. It was there for emergencies, like this. She could make it normal size using *vergrößern* as a command word. But with her hands bound, she couldn't get the tiny sword, or speak, or cast spells, so it was useless… not that she was any good at using a sword anyway.

Then she realized her phone was still in her pocket.

She got on her feet and started jumping up, to get it to fall out. It was a scratched, rough interior, clearly regularly used for transporting things. She couldn't see the driver through the metal wall between her and the passenger compartment.

She was effectively in a metal box. There was a crunch sound and a sudden sharp pain as she hit her head on the top of the van. She sat down, grimacing. Bad idea. She waited till the pain subsided, and then used her elbow to try to push her mobile phone through her black jeans.

The phone came on. She hit it randomly. She wasn't even sure what she was doing. She heard beeping sounds; she had activated an app. It wasn't coming out of her pocket, and there was no way she could call someone *through* her pants.

She listened to noises outside. Should she try to figure out where it was going? How many turns the van took? Should she try to count the time, to guess how far they had driven? What should you do when someone kidnaps you? She tried the door, but it was locked tight.

Then she tried to think who was behind this. No doubt it was Adeline, and the people that were using her, or working with her, whatever it was they were doing. Circle 66 had destroyed her plan to move into the Faehome, this could be their revenge.

But there were the New Nation people active in the town. There was the London Illusionists. There was the Mage hating Hanseatic League.

Thinking about it left her with a sickening feeling in her stomach; it could be anyone that wanted to capture a mage and force them to do spells for them. Lots of people would want that. Or people that hated mages.

She put her back against the flattest part of the van wall and tried to get comfortable. Tried to remain calm, breathing in deep breaths, and holding them, like she had been told to deal with anxiety. She remembered the calm Tomoko said you can bring upon yourself through breathing and emptying your mind.

The truck twisted and turned, and it was dark, but her stomach told her they were going up an incline.

The mountains?

The truck proceeded now slower and stopped.

She could hear voices outside.

The back of the door opened. Three men stood there, two of them, both with short black hair, and wearing black T-shirts, one with a beard and one without. They stood to either side of the open door and a larger man moved into view and stood behind them, with his arms crossed. He was tall and an obviously big man. Even though the two bald men were big, he was a whole other level bigger.

As they opened the door, he lifted the scooter out with two hands, lifting it into the air completely out of the van, without the wheels touching the ground. He put it down, on its side (Sophie thought Raffaella would kill him if she saw this). He looked at it and grunted.

He then lifted Sophie straight out, putting her straight on her feet. He was strong, lifting her for him seemed effortless.

"Take her to the cells. Do *not* take off her hand restraints or let her use her mouth. She'll spell cast your sorry selves into oblivion. *Get it?*" He spoke in a deep voice and seemed very serious.

"Ja, ja," they both said and grabbed Sophie and took her into the old house.

Clearly, they were in the mountainside, turned off the mountain road next to Bamberg. They must have turned off the main Schweinfurt Mountain road, the one that wound scarily up the sides.

As they walked her along, Sophie tried to think of something to do. Calming herself, she went through her options, logically. It would calm her, but also make sure she had missed nothing.

She couldn't use magic.

She couldn't run.

She couldn't call.

She couldn't retrieve the miniature sword.

The men guided her through the corridors, left and right. White walls closed wooden doors, she lost track where she was, it was all very similar. They physically tossed her in a room, and she landed on the floor. They closed the door.

There was someone else sitting in the room. A short person, sitting on the bed, who also had their hands tied and had also been gagged.

Sophie glanced over at the person, and if her mouth hadn't been taped, it would have dropped.

There, sitting opposite her, was Adeline.

34. Adeline

Sophie jumped back, but then noticed tape across Adeline's mouth and hands, the same as herself. Adeline sat, staring at her blankly, relaxed. As always, she was unnerving. It made Sophie realise there wasn't any sense in expending energy now, for naught. It was best to conserve it until the right opportunity.

Then Sophie thought…. this could be some kind of trick, like she'd seen in movies?

Adeline would sit there, pretending to be captured as well, builds up confidence in Sophie, then she gets Sophie's trust and learns all about her.

It made perfect sense. The most forbidden practice, for a mage, is stealing spells from other mages, from other paths. Sophie would never do this, as she had been told by Johannes, it was strictly something you didn't do. *You must not give your spells to other paths, and of course, you must not take or learn theirs.*

To say it was a weird experience, was understating what was currently happening in their room, wooden floors, white walls, and two little beds. A quaint little prison cell. Sophie sat facing her enemy, who was also sitting on the floor. The pair sat, both looking at each other. Neither of them able to talk, threaten each other, or even move their hands.

But if Adeline was genuinely captured… then who captured her?

Sophie stared at Adeline.

Adeline stared at Sophie.

It was the first time she had really got a chance to look at her, close. She had blonde hair, blue eyes, light skin, and looked to be about twelve. She was clearly young, but something about her, the expression, her eyes, that you saw in an older adult. Weary, deathly serious, humourless. Sophie realized she had never seen a more serious child, probably in her life. She was weird, and it was a little unnerving.

Sophie quickly glanced around their cell. It was a brick building, old bricks, the bricks wet with moisture. Little tufts of green moss sticking out here and there.

Adeline pivoted her head suddenly. There was noise. Footsteps, someone... their captor was coming back to the cell.

Heavy footsteps, coming, a man who was talking, but she couldn't make out the words. He came into the room, and now that she could see him close up... he was familiar. She had seen him before, but she couldn't quite place him. Then she remembered. He was a man Sophie had seen before.

It was the man that had stood out the front of the door, with the boy, when they chased the demon back at the *Krampussfesten*. *He had now grown a beard, but it was the same man. She squinted at him, and then she realized. He was also the large man that turned into the demon in Harlan's video. She had only watched it twice, but she was sure it was him.*

So, the demon had changed into a man in the laneway, using a transmutation spell. He must have had a child waiting there? That's why the demon had appeared to of simply disappeared. He unlocked the gate and took Adeline out. He was tall, and had a hulking frame, he loomed over them both. Adeline pushed at him, but she merely bounced off him while he didn't move, she grunted, frustrated. He grabbed her and easily pushed her back into line. He then grabbed Sophie as well but didn't utter a word.

Pushing them in front of him, they went up some stairs, and then out through the mountain entrance, out into the open, and into the back of an old house, sitting amongst the Pine trees. They were then led into the lounge room of a house.

There sitting on a couch, was another figure, his big frame and curly hair making him all to easily recognisable.

It was Oskar.

Oskar was also tied up and gagged, as a healer, he wasn't much of a threat, but to many of the average Bavarians; all mages were dangerous.

Sophie felt a little chirp of delight as soon as she saw him. He was alive and unharmed. Oskar was a nice guy, and she felt he really understood the situation at hand. It made sense he had been taken, his little shop was obvious he was healing people and great publicity for the mages. He had no magic he could use to defend himself, he was a clear accessible target.

Oskar nodded to Sophie, but then looked unusually at Adeline. Sophie realised he probably had no idea who she was.

Sophie looked at the room, and the rest of the house.

The residence was a big German country house. Looking out the window, part of the view was blocked by a big tree, its leaves rustling and waving in the wind. It seemed to be almost beckoning Sophie to come towards it, to leave her present circumstance. She certainly wished she could. Past it she could see a view of the country, some paddocks, bright green. Pine tree covered mountains in the background.

So far, the large, bearded man hadn't shown his intentions. He hadn't harmed them. He obviously had captured three mages for a reason. He hated mages, and was going to harm them, or somehow wanted something from them. Sophie stayed calm and tried to calm the rising fear in her body. She looked for reasons why it would be the later, rather than the former.

It was starting to sink in, that Adeline *wasn't* pretending to be a captive. Adeline and she were two of the best mages in Bamberg, which was why they were here together.

He took the three of them out into the field next to the house, and here Sophie saw two goatkin, waiting. She hadn't seen them up close for a while, the torso of a man, the head of a goat, but with goat legs. One had ginger fur, and a long goat beard, the other was grey. Both had rather magnificent but frightening curled horns, and the strange yellow goat eyes with the horizontal black iris. Sophie had always found goat's eyes unnerving, but they certainly were more so on the face of a 6-foot-tall *goat man*.

"Lutz." One of the goatkin said, to the man, when they first saw him. *The man was called Lutz.*

They wore jeans and T shirts, which sat on them awkwardly. They were obviously made for humans, they were oversized ones, and didn't fit their goat bodies very well.

One of them grabbed Sophie, and another grabbed Adeline and Oskar. Sophie could smell them, it was a pungent animal smell, she instantly turned up her nose, and she tried to turn her head away from them.

Lutz spoke to Sophie.

"You know what I'm trying to do. I need you to watch what I am doing. If I get this right, you can go free. If not, you will help."

Adeline stared at him under her brow and said nothing.

Lutz stood and started spellcasting. Sophie didn't recognize the spell, or even the language. It wasn't something from her path.

He was casting a spell at a pile of things on the ground. It appeared to be a pile of loose detritus. But it was the common ingredients for cooking some arcane magicks that she had heard of but not seen. Bones, rags, bits of branch, in the middle was a medallion. She listened to the words coming from his mouth, chanting…but they made no sense to her. She shivered slightly, shaking her back. He began walking around it, while still casting.

The goatkin stood back, putting space between themselves and the ritual. He was still calling out the spell. Sophie knew big spells used a lot of energy, *Mana*.

Lutz walked around the pile of things. It seemed odd, and it wasn't the type of magic Sophie was used to; seemed he was trying to create *something*.

While observing the big man, she noticed Adeline was studying the pile on the ground. Oskar also studied it, curiously.

There was smoke coming out of it. Or in front of it. It became hazy, so she couldn't quite see it. Then a rough body of haze appeared and became bigger and larger, taking on a roughly human form.

It grew to man height and kept growing.

As its form solidified, she could see that it was tall. It grew taller and then started taking solid shape.

Suddenly, standing in front of her, was a huge minotaur. She could see most of it was solid, while other parts were still amorphous, forming out of the smoke. It completed solidifying and then took its final form.

Lutz gazed at it and beamed.

"Welcome!" He held out his arms to it, he seemed ecstatic, and laughed to himself. The Goatkin seemed in awe of the whole event.

The minotaur stood still, then shook its head.

The goatkin were clearly worried, they moved back, and dragged Adeline, Oskar, and Sophie with them, away from it.

The huge minotaur bellowed, and then screamed, holding its head.

Sophie tried to call out, but realized her mouth was still shut. *It's in pain.*

Lutz put out his hand to it, and then touched the left of his chest above his heart. He chanted something. Sophie realized he was using some sort of spell. It was a shape changing spell.

The man himself changed into a minotaur, not quite the size of this one, but big.

Sophie suddenly realized what was going on.

Lutz was a minotaur, trying to create his own kind. He was trying to break one of the four fundamental laws of magic; she had been told by Johannes. Can't create precious objects, can't create your own kind, can't create space, can't create spells with another spell. *It's impossible to use magick to bring life to a creature of your own ilk. Sophie knew human mages could make Goatkin, and Minotaurs, but no one could use magic to create their own.*

The newly created minotaur held its head and screamed. It ran off around in circles, its hands clutched to its huge brow.

It was clearly in a lot of suffering. It dropped to the ground in a heap and lay there, quivering. Moving a little bit, it would stand up, and then sit down. It seemed bewildered, lost. Like it had arrived somewhere and couldn't see or understand where it was.

Lutz bowed his head. Sophie thought, whatever he was trying to do, it appeared he had failed. Two new goatkin appeared from behind the house and took the suffering minotaur away, its groaning and whimpering cries lingered in the air for some time.

"Adeline. I can't do it. You showed me how to do this, but... it simply can't be done. I need you to show me."

Adeline shook her head, mumbling beneath the gag.

"You *will* show me." He stepped forward to her, threateningly.

She peered at the Minotaur and nodded.

Sophie glanced over at Adeline, she seemed to play with her hands. Clearly, she couldn't get them out of the tape, but she continued fidgeting. The man checked her, fidgeting, examined her binding, reassured himself that she couldn't get her hands out to cast a spell, bent over and took the tape off. Without her hands free, she couldn't make a glyph to command.

Sophie noticed that Adeline was smiling. Then she glanced down at her hands. They were still secure, but she could see that Adeline had loosened them so part of her finger could touch a ring she was wearing.

Sophie immediately realised it wasn't a normal ring. It was a relic. Adeline's thumb reached over and touched her ring. She then muttered a word, just loud enough so Sophie could hear it.

"*Etrupha.*"

A look of confusion came across Lutz's face. He glanced down, then backed off and moved quickly out of the room, down to the farmhouse. Sophie watched him leave, then looked at Adeline, unsure what to do.

Adeline was looking around, trying to find something they could break their bonds with. Meantime, the mud from the ground continued to form up into a monstrous form. A mud golem, an ugly, blocky, half formed creature, brought to life by magic.

It started forming into a large creature, about 7 feet tall.

Sophie could see Lutz anxiously staring at Adeline and pointing. The minotaur that the two goatkin had put in there came out and started moving towards Adeline. It was still holding its head, and roaring, twisting around. There was now no one guarding her, so Sophie knew it was best to leave, and quickly. Oskar was standing there, staring at the minotaur.

"Oskar, run!" she called out.

Oskar snapped to attention, coming back to his senses. "Yes, let's go, before he comes back."

But the next thing Sophie saw, chilled her to the bone. She had started to run, but as she did, she glanced back and stopped, trying to see what was happening at the farmhouse. Sophie squinted, it was hard to see from the distance, but the door opened more.

There was more movement. There was something else in the big   farmhouse. She could see the glint of eyes, in the dark of the interior, the blur of movement.

Another minotaur appeared, and another. They were all screaming, waving their arms.

The sight, the piercing moans, chilled her to the bone. The noise they made was halfway between a moan and a cry of pain. Loud and inhuman, like the noise of an animal being tormented.

Sophie decided not to hang around, she backed off and then started running in the opposite direction, through the forest. Running to escape the noise, the tortured creatures. She tried to see if Oskar was around, looking for his white T-shirt in the green forest, but he was gone. She glanced back over her shoulder, and saw there were now two golems, standing protectively in front of Adeline like a pair of statues, seemingly waiting for the minotaurs to come, as if up for the challenge.

Sophie sprinted. Panic started to set in, but she breathed deeply and tried to calm herself. She was out of sight, and no one was paying attention to her.

She found a snapped tree branch, the sharp part of the broken limb, white and freshly broken, sticking up into the air. She put her hands on either side of it and shoved the sharp part of the branch into her bonds. She wriggled it around loosening her bonds, and then slipped her thing hands out. She reached for her phone, her heart beating fast, as she thought of the monsters not far from her. She didn't know exactly where they were, or what was going on, the thought that dominated her mind was to get away as fast as possible, and to call for help.

She continued running through the forest for a couple of minutes, then stopped to look at the phone. Harlan's name was the first to come to her mind... Harlan answered immediately.

"Sophie! WHERE ARE YOU!" Harlan sounded alarmed.

"I don't know. Near a farmhouse, in the forest?"

"Are you okay?"

"Yes, for the moment."

"You're on the edge of Bamberg near the river. We're coming for you," Harlan called.

"How do you know where I am?"

"You always forget to change your privacy settings. I've told you so many times. You took a photo on Facebook of your pocket, and it we can see the coordinates of where you took it. We are close by. Stay there Sophie. Look for a landmark."

Sophie kept running, keeping the phone to her head. She came across a road. There was a gas station.

"I'm near a Europol service station. Come quick. That man, the minotaur you saw? His name is Lutz apparently, had me and Oskar and Adeline captured. He was trying to use some creation spell, but it was turning out all wrong…you should have seen the minotaurs, all broken."

Sophie could hear Tomoko's voice calling out, she sounded distant. "Okay. I see it on Google Maps. We'll be there in five minutes, hide and keep safe."

Sophie out of the forest, and then sprinted across the road to the Gas station. There was a man inside at the counter. She didn't have time to stop, so ran past him and jumped down behind a metal drum with a big kerosene dispenser on it, staying quiet.

After 20 seconds, the man appeared.

"Frau. Ve gaits? Vas is das?"

Sophie shook her head. "Bitte."

The man stared at her puzzled, he then looked back at the road, screamed, and scurried into the forest. Sophie peeked around the edge of the metal drum. There was a minotaur standing in the middle of the gas station, scanning the forest and its immediate surroundings. It stared at where the man had gone, curiously.

Suddenly, Harlan's voice came over the phone, "Sophie, we can see you."

Sophies eyes widened, it was loud. She saw the minotaur's head turn, and stare directly at her.

Sophie thought about fighting, but decided it was better to run and hide. She ran behind the back of the service station, as fast as she could, then sprinted across the road and, as she did, she saw the three scooters bearing down on her. Harlan, Tomoko and Raffaella were there in the middle of the road.

Raffaella the devils horn's sign with her hand, two middle fingers down, and the two outer fingers up.

"The trusty steed, scared of the devil. Runs like the wind, and the herd will follow." Raffaella chanted. Sophie had no idea what it meant but was happy to see her and the others.

"Sophie, where have you been, we've got all sorts of people out looking for you. Is Oskar here?" Harlan sounded distressed.

Sophie screamed, "Don't stop your engines we need to go. No idea about Oskar."

Sophie hopped on the back of Raphaella's scooter which was the fastest, putting on her helmet, her fingers fumbling for the chin strap to reassuringly pull it tight on her head. As she did the minotaur appeared from the back of the service station.

"What the hell is that?" Harlan screamed.

"Cool!" Raffaella called.

Tomoko screamed, "RIDE' and put her scooter into gear, taking off down the road first.

Sophie got on the back of the scooter, with Raffaella revving the   gears. However, the Minotaur was running fast and had long legs. Sophie looked behind her, she could have taken her hands off Raffaella to cast a spell, but she might have fallen off.

Raffaella was looking in her rear vision mirrors as she sped up. "It's getting close." She screamed, the engine revved, and Sophie felt herself shift back from the force. A wave of relief hit Sophie as she could see that she was gradually increasing the distance, and the minotaur was falling back.

Raffaella called back to Sophie. "Why are we running from it? We can take it."

Sophie called out through her helmet, loud so Raffaella could hear. "That's not what we are running from!"

As they drove down the old road. Sophie looked behind to see what was going on.

Raphaella's souped-up scooter was going the fastest down the old road, followed by Harlan's and then Tomoko's. Sophie was relieved to see all were far enough ahead, but the minotaur still lumbered on, and it didn't seem to be tiring.

However, from the side of the forest, Sophie noticed another Minotaur lumbered out of the forest, clawing wildly at the tree branches as it pushed its way through the thick green foliage. It stepped out onto the road, and then picked up speed, giving chase. And then another appeared, following the others.

The three scooters powered down the road. Suddenly, a minotaur appeared in front of them, crunching through branches to appear out of the forest. It had its back to them; it hadn't seen them. Harlan yelled out, and swerved around it, the others followed.

Raffaella pulled out her sword and hit it on the arm as she drove past. It turned, screamed, and started following them.

The three scooters roared down the asphalt. Raffaella put the sword back in the scabbard, which was on her back, held on by a belt.

Sophie noticed a sign up ahead *Bamberg 1 kilometre*. She looked behind her, the minotaurs were still coming, though a fair way back. But now, there were more of them. She quickly counted ten.

They came onto a straight piece of road, and suddenly, an old stone bridge.

"STOP!" Sophie screamed.

Harlan, Tomoko and Raffaella stopped.

Sophie got off the scooter and stood there. They were on the other side of the bridge.

"Bamberg's only a kilometre away. There are other farmhouses here. We need to hold this bridge." Sophie said.

Tomoko appeared anxious. "What? What do you mean hold?"

Sophie pointed towards Bamberg. "We can't let them past, if they get past here, they will go down to Bamberg and I don't know what will happen."

Without saying anything, Raffaella parked her scooter to the side, and went over to the bridge, with her sword drawn.

Harlan was glancing around and pulled out his phone. "We'll get help, we had other people out searching for you, they're around here."

Tomoko studied Sophie, clearly worried. "Can't we go back down and get help. There's so many of them."

"There's no time. If we go down to get help, the minotaurs will get to those houses before we get back." Sophie walked over to where Raffaella was on the bridge.

Harlan shook his head, hands on hips. "There's so many." She could hear a waiver in his voice. "Sophie...we can't, we can't hold them."

Raffaella was simply staring at the Minotaurs, concentrating, like she was trying to see some fault in them, or work out some plan.

"Tomoko. Harlan. Raphaella. *We* are the ones here. *Here* we make our stand." Sophie said, keeping her voice even and blocking out the fear. She took a deep breath. Sophie took a deep breath, filling her lungs, and planting her feet firmly on the ground.

Harlan turned and saw that the minotaurs had now got close. He put the phone in his pocket, and pulled out some throwing knives, and took off his jacket. Sophie stared at him. He was as brave as Raphaella, he basically had no weapons, the small throwing knives would probably be useless against the minotaurs. But he was going to help.

Sophie thrust out her hands in front of her. She started chanting a sleep spell, and her hands glowed blue.

There's more of them than us. We need to channel them. Tomoko pushed two scooters onto the bridge as obstacles, but it didn't really do anything.

Sophie called out, "Can we destroy the bridge? She peered over at Tomoko, for a hopeful signal there was something she could cast. Tomoko expression was doubtful, she shook her head slightly. Sophie had a range of spells, but nothing that could destroy a bridge, even her fireball spell, the most destructive spell she had, wouldn't burn through a stone.

The first minotaur was now about 20 metres away, about where the spell would work. Sophie's hand flicked the glyph for the sleep spell, through the air, and cast it towards him. The minotaur stopped momentarily, then kept coming. She focused directly on him, urged the mana to build up in her hands, watched as they glowed blue, then looked defiantly in his eyes, making the connection.

She cast the spell again. This time she felt the connection, as the energy of the spell left her hands and hit him square in the chest. She saw him shudder, and then collapse backward onto the bridge. She heard a cheer from the others and allowed herself a smirk.

The other minotaurs didn't notice their fallen comrade, or stop, or even slow down. There was something definitely wrong with these minotaurs. Another one came and she concentrated, did the same spell, however he moved to the left suddenly. The spell missed and hit the ground. As he did, a purple mass of energy ploughed into him.

Tomoko's ice spell hit him, right on the shoulder and left side. Wherever she was aiming, it worked. His leg and arm froze, and he crumpled down, hitting the ground hard.

They were still coming. A third Minotaur crossed the bridge stepping over two. Raffaella screamed loudly and jumped in front of Tomoko and Sophie. She then rolled down and underneath it, and swung up, hitting its arm. It swung at her with the other arm, and she crouched down low and as it swung a fist past her, she thrust into its leg.

Another appeared on her right, lunging at her. Harlan threw his throwing knives at it, and it threw up its arms to block them, distracting it in time. Raffaella lunged at its stomach, sticking into it, and then quickly tried to pull out her sword.

It took a huge swing at her, and she had to let go of the sword. Without a sword, she ducked under the minotaurs second swing, and ran back towards the others.

Harlan continued frantically throwing knives, which distracted them and made them angry, but did little else. Three minotaurs were down now, and one coming towards them, with Raphaella's sword stuck in its stomach. There was an electric surge type sound, then a thump and another ice spell hit the minotaur. It collapsed to the ground.

Another scream, and Raffaella screamed past them, now with another sword she had got from her scooter. This sword was bigger, and she wielded it frantically.

Sophie looked at the bridge. The minotaurs were started to get past them. They realised they needed the bridge. The combat was happening all over. There were now 5 minotaurs on the bridge.

"Circle 66! Hold the line...THEY CANNOT CROSS!"

Raffaella was trying to fight three at once, lunging at one, pulling back, and lunging at another, but giving ground as she did. Sophie glanced at Tomoko, she looked exhausted, her face drained and in pain, trying to summon the mana to cast another spell.

Sophie was feeling weak. She had not cast so many spells since the battle of the Faehome, she was stronger than them, but she was putting so much energy into the spells, her body, her shoulder, her arms were feeling drained. Her body felt like she had run a marathon. She felt she had one last spell in her, and all she could think of was the fireball spell. But they were too close. The fire would get the minotaurs, but at this range, it would roll back and burn them as well. She had no choice but to use the most devastating spell she knew. If she didn't place it at the right spot, it could destroy her... and everything.

"FIREBALL... EVERYONE RUN!!!!"

At that point, they heard a car behind them. Sophie turned to see a little red Fiat flying down the road towards the bridge. It stopped and Jeff got out, with a shovel, Ying immediately hopped out of the car and cast a long bold of lightning which hit one of the minotaurs and knocked it down. Heloisa got out and ran over to the battle, holding a rapier and a red blanket in her hand. Hans got out of the car, running, and cast a spell on Raphaella, and now there appeared to be three of her fighting the Minotaurs. *Gunther's Limited mirror image...* Raffaella momentarily stopped, looking confused, before resuming combat with her two projections by her side.

Ying massaged her hands in front of her, making a yellow orange ball of light... the heat was so great, Sophie could feel the heat coming off it. With a scream, the incandescent ball flew, hitting one of the minotaurs on its head. It held its head, screaming, and toppled over the bridge, its screams trailing off as it fell out of sight.

Heloise, darted amongst the minotaurs. She stepped out at one, slashing at it strategically, rolling out of the way then back on her feet and moving out of range. Sophie watched as the red blanket, or was it a cloak? Swirled around in the air with her as she did, making it hard to see exactly where her rapier was. She then took an acrobatic leap, making it look effortless, and landed on the shoulder of the Minotaur Raffaella was fighting. Her red cloak blinded it momentarily, she slashed at it with her thin point sword, the other hand holding a smaller dagger.

All the spells Tomoko had casted had taken their toll, she had used all her mana. She looked like she had had all the energy drained from her. She had taken her big Japanese longbow and was firing arrows at the minotaurs. The arrows sliced through the air and stuck into their arms. They screamed in pain, flailing at them uselessly.

Hans picked up his sword, and attacked, swinging it left and right, and joined Raphaella. Even Jeff had joined the combat, swinging a shovel at the minotaur that Hans was attacking, though being careful to shepherd behind Hans.

With the flurry of spells, and the hacking and slashing of swords, the minotaurs were driven back across the bridge.

Harlan screamed out, "There's more, more coming from the forest."

Sophie looked across, some more creatures were coming out of the forest. Her heart

sank a little bit. She wasn't sure how much longer they could last.

35. The Forest

Sophie could hear the crush of tree branches, the rustle of leaves that indicated large creatures moving through the forest, towards them. Her heart thumped, more minotaurs coming from the woods? They couldn't handle so many; the bridge would fall and there would be minotaurs down in the houses of Bamberg. She readied herself with another spell, but it faltered before she could speak. A moving mass of dirt and debris lumbered on two massive legs out of the forest. Adeline's golem! Sophie nearly shouted out loud in relief.

The mud creature leaned into the closest pine tree, knocking it over effortlessly. It pushed the tree horizontal, down to the ground, its roots ripping out of the ground, flailing, throwing wet dirty clumps into the air. Its hands reached down, picked up the tree, and tossed it. It sailed through the air, landing amongst the group of minotaurs.

Another two mud golems appeared, moving quickly to join the fray, attacking the minotaurs. The minotaurs, now being attacked from both sides, turned to face them. They struck out at the mud golems, which threw wild punches at them in return, sheer strength, and little finesse. Off to the side, Sophie could see the continuous flash of Ying and Han's spellcasting, small blasts of coloured light, fresh to the melee as they fired off spells in machine gun fashion.

The mud golems smashed at the minotaurs with their big fists. The minotaurs tried to fight back, one of them lowering its broad head, trying to gore the golem with his horns, but the blows seemed to be absorbed into the solid mud mass with little actual affect. From experience Sophie knew you could fight mud golems, but you needed to know how, and the minotaurs certainly didn't.

There were three golems circled around one lone minotaur, pounding it relentlessly. It collapsed as they pounded it down to the ground. Then they stood there, peered at it without emotion for a few seconds, and then peeked back into a spot in the bushes.

Out of the bushes, Sophie noticed a figure. She was a way off, but it was unmistakably Adeline, her bright yellow hair atop her slight frame. She stood impassively, away from the combat, arms at her side, watching her golems do their work.

Sophie witnessed the last minotaur collapse on the bridge and watched the three golems stride off into the forest. As they lumbered off, Sophie quickly surveyed the scene. The combat had covered the bridge in bodies, but to her relief, none were her friends. She could see most of the members of Three Bells Inc lying on the ground, exhausted, trying to catch their breath. Tomoko dropped to the ground, sitting hunched over, breathing rapidly.

"Sophie, everyone. Kentaro texted me. The tracking spell... Mabuse's car is around here."

"Okay. Everyone, okay, keep an eye out for Mabuse," Sophie called out.

Sophie peered up, and her gaze immediately met Adeline's. Adeline turned briefly to look behind here, and there appeared two tall, well-built men, in red tracksuits. Large men, each with their variation of the three allowed typical Hansa haircut.

The Hansa.

Adeline studied Sophie's group. Now that the minotaurs were all down, she was facing her directly. Sophie wasn't sure what to do. Lutz had captured Adeline with her, and they had defeated him. As strange as it seemed, Sophie had a feeling of having a shared experience. Sophie didn't want to attack her.

Adeline had a blue glyph powered up in her hand, floating there, shimmering, waiting to be sent through the air. Sophie could make out, it was three vertical ragged lines, with a horizontal line between them. Lightning bolt... *blitz bolzen.*

But Adeline…was waiting. Was she going to cast it? She stood there. *Did she want to leave?*

There was some peripheral movement out of the corner of her eye, and Sophie turned her head to see Ying, standing there, looking at them both. A car approached and stopped. Sophie, flicking her head back quickly, could see a large red 4-door expensive looking car. A man got out, wearing a suit, and moved into the fringe of the combat. Not wanting to break her concentration on Adeline, she didn't dare to turn to see the man properly. Sophie turned her body back to face Adeline, and now, Ying.

"Ying, leave her. I think she wants to leave. She's powerful, and she seems like she has all her mana."

Ying glanced at Sophie, and with a flick of her fingers, a glowing orange symbol appeared in her hand.

"Stand back Sophie. I'm here to take her." Her voice was low and determined.

Adeline's gaze flicked between both. Sophie could see she was poised and ready, standing on the balls of her feet, probably ready to cast or to move, if need be.

Sophie shot Ying a sideways glance, "What do you mean, *take her?*"

"She's, our job. We must capture her. For our client."

"What… the guy… that just arrived?"

"Yes."

Sophie glanced back, quickly. A man in a suit. Sophie got a glimpse of him but still couldn't look away from Ying and Adeline. Any man in a suit ended up being bad news. Even though it was Adeline, people in suits capturing mages were wrong. Adeline was being used as a sort of magic casting puppet by Mabuse and was now going to be given to someone else, like a possession. *Was this the fate of herself, or Tomoko?*

"Ying, you can't fight her. She's a higher ranked mage than you."

Ying powered up another spell and turned her guard to Sophie. Sophie realised suddenly; they were in a three-way stand-off. Ying was moving the glyph in the air between them.

"Back off Sophie. She's mine."

Adeline stood there. She was poised to jump, or run, Sophie could see she'd moved her weight on to the front of her feet.

The three stood there looking at each other. Sophie could feel the tension in the air. Anyone that moved an inch would trigger a furious cascade of spells.

Sophie focussed on both of them, putting all distraction out of her mind. She could see Ying's chest moving, as she caught her breath. Adeline's expression was pure concentration. Sophie focussed on the two mages in front of her, and everything else dimmed.

Now there was a chance to take down Adeline, or at least remove her from Mabuse's control somehow while he wasn't around. But Sophie didn't want Ying capturing her to be used as someone's personal mage. She would fight Ying rather than let that happen. She knew she needed to capture Adeline first, then deal with Ying after.

Then an obvious sudden movement broke the tense standoff. One of the Hansa men in the tracksuits behind Adeline slipped his hand into his jacket and pulled out what Sophie realised was... a pistol. Sophie reacted instantly and threw up a shield spell.

"Ying. Shield!"

The man started firing at Sophie first, which was lucky for Ying, as she had no shield spell up.

He fired all his bullets into Sophie. The shield spell spatially moved them from the point of impact on the shield spell in front of Sophie, to just behind her, where they flew off into the forest behind her harmlessly. Luckily, there was no one there.

He fired all his bullets, and kept clicking the now empty gun in disbelief, the confusion on his face clear. He stopped, looking at her, eyes wide, waiting for her to fall, not understanding why she didn't.

The other man behind the tiny blonde mage grabbed her by the wrist, she turned with them, and the three of them ran into the forest.

Ying sprinted after them, with Sophie immediately behind. Sophie looked behind them. The man in the suit was following, as was some people from the two crews. She caught a quick glimpse of Harlan's tall frame dodging low branches, moving between the trees.

As they ran, Adeline dropped to her feet and cast lightning bolt spells back at them, but she wasn't stopping to aim, and they flew wildly, smashing into the trees. Sophie dodged a tree as it split in half and part of it came crashing to the ground, Ying cast a spell at Adeline, but it went above her head.

They sprinted through the forest. She could hear the sharp crack of Adeline's Hanseatic guards shooting their pistols, Sophie saw the odd branch explode from a bullet, but most of the shots were wild. Sophie knew she was running into danger, but they had spent so long dealing with Adeline, scared of her, she knew this was the chance to do something about her. Despite being wary of Ying, she knew if she let Ying and the Three bells face Adeline alone, it could end up bad for them. If Adeline couldn't be defeated or dealt with here, there was plenty of cover, she would try to get everyone to get back into the forest. Plus, the Hansa people here, somehow woke up something emotive in her. The Hanseatic leagues hatred of Mages, and their presence here, and the attack on the Café made her feel like she wanted to teach them a lesson. And numbers were on her side.

She could hear people running behind them. Up ahead, she could see the multi shaded green of the forest give way to the grey road. Two cars were parked there with two more guards; they looked like Hansa.

And there, in the middle of the Hansa guards, was Mabuse.

He motioned to the two guards next to him, who pulled out pistols.

"Ying. Sheild!" Sophie screamed, and dodged to the side, running to the right of Mabuse.

Ying threw up a shield spell. Once again, the bullets went through it, and came out the other side, luckily into the forest behind her.

Sophie dove into the bushes, trying to work her way around them. She threw herself to the ground.

Mabuse.

It hit her. The last time she had seen him, he had frozen everyone in the room. The image of everyone frozen in their chairs, herself not being able to move, completely dominated her.

She tried to put it out of her mind. She felt a whole unease, like a queasy feeling in her stomach. The sight of him completely threw her.

She lay, her cheek in the dirt, and for twenty seconds considered not moving, staying there. She could hear shouting, spells flying off, screaming.

She used every ounce of will, to push up off the ground and move low through the undergrowth, and immediately found herself near Adeline. The glyph for lightning, bright blue, was hovering in front of her hand, ready to be cast at its target. Sophie crept up to her, keeping down below Adeline's sight in the brush. The guards continued to fire at Ying's shield spell, and generally into at the voices in the forest. Both crews were calling out from the forest, but wisely not revealing themselves to the armed hansa guards.

She heard running, and Harlan appeared running straight out of the forest on the road, a throwing knife in his hand. He threw the knife at Mabuse, and rolled, landing back on his feet. One of the guards stepped in the way, and was struck in the shoulder, he screamed.

The other guard turned, swinging his gun.

"HARLAN!!!" Sophie screamed.

There was a loud *crack* and Harlan went down on the road.

Sophie turned. Adeline was looking right at her, a look of surprise on her face only a couple of metres away. Her hand flicked and the lightning spell glyph dissipated, and she started tracing the symbol for another glyph.

Sophie didn't have time to cast her own spell, but she was close to Adeline. She leapt at her, grabbed her hands, and as the spell was being cast, she pushed Adeline's hands away from herself, back towards Adeline. If it went off, it would go high.

The spell went off, but it went off close to Adeline's face. She screamed, holding her eyes.

Adeline spun around, her hands over her face, screaming. It looked like she was blinded.

"I can't see!" she screamed out in pain.

Sophie looked over at the two cars. Suddenly one of the guards moved back and looked in surprise. He had an arrow sticking out of his shoulder. He looked down at it, shocked. She looked to Harlan, but he was lying prone on the road. She felt tears welling up in her eyes.

Mabuse was the cause of all this. Feeling of anger to him, and frustrations fuelled her thoughts and actions. She felt her teeth gritting and grinding, as anger coursing through her veins. She started to power up a lightning spell.

Mabuse looked at Adeline, shook his head with a look of disgust, and told the guards to get in the car. Both cars started off. Sophie was shocked. He could easily have grabbed her and put her in the car, but he was simply leaving her in the forest, like he no longer had interest in her.

More members of the two crews appeared out of the forest. Sophie felt the rage inside her.

"Mabuse, you scumbag!" she screamed, running out on to the road. She flicked the symbol in the air, for lightning and powered it up, spitting out the command word with vehemence, *blitzschlag*.

The bolt sailed through the air, not quite straight, but in an arc. It missed the first car but came down on the roof of the second car, which caught fire. However, it kept driving and both cars took a bend in the road and were out of sight. Sophie quickly scanned around them, she needed to chase down Mabuse and capture him, but she wouldn't catch him on foot, and the cars and scooters were back through the forest, at the bridge. They were gone.

People were now gathered around Harlan. She ran over to him, tears welling up in her eyes. As she got to him, she could see Raffaella leaning over him, holding his head. His eyes were open, he was gritting his teeth through the pain. He was alive, he held his stomach, blood seeping from the wound, out through his fingers.

"Can someone help him? Someone, call an ambulance!" Sophie screamed.

Raffaella held his hand, and Sophie reached down to hold his other. Tomoko came over and knelt down, her hand on Sophie's shoulder compassionately. Raffaella glanced up at Sophie. It surprised Sophie to see tears streaming down Raphaella's face.

36. A Blind Mage

Someone pushed through the crowd, and rushed to Harlan, pushing Sophie to the side roughly so she almost fell over.

Her immediate reaction was to turn her head to yell at them, then saw who it was.

It was Oskar. Sophie felt instant relief, he was a welcome sight.

"Oh, thank you." Tomoko touched him on the arm, to show her appreciation.

"Please help him." Raffaella said firmly, almost pleading.

Oskar smiled, "Of course, it's ok, I'll take care of him. It's a stomach wound." A look of concentration came across his face, he rubbed his hands together, and they glowed pink. He then applied them to Harlan's stomach.

"Oh wait!" Raffaella said. She reached down to her belt and pulled out a sword. Sophie was momentarily alarmed, but Raffaella turned it around pommel end, and pushed it to Harlan, putting his hand around the grip, and pressing her hand on his hands. She looked eagerly on.

Something was happening. There was a pink glow.

"Can you feel that?" Raffaella said.

He nodded, slowly, weakly. "Healing."

"The sword you got from Berthold's…" Sophie said.

I have been thinking about this for about a week. The man in the dreamscape had held it and didn't seem to suffer wounds. I realise it healed him.

Oskar looked at it, nodding. "It's a copy of *Jethro's Sword of Rejuvenation*. Impressive!" Without looking away, he spoke to no one in particular, "I think you need to look at Adeline."

Adeline's eyes were closed, her face screwed up in pain, burn marks to the top part of her face. She had an orange spell glyph in her hand, a glowing symbol Sophie didn't recognise. She was still dangerous, even if she couldn't see, though now a number of people had grouped around her.

She winced, screaming, and shook out the symbol, to hold her eyes with both hands. She knelt. Sophie couldn't help but feel sorry for her. As they had seen at the battle of the Faehome, she had evidently been controlled to the point where she had killed her own mother.

Sophie noticed the man in the suit appear. He approached Adeline cautiously. Ying moved in on her from a different direction.

"Who are you? Stay away from her!" Sophie screamed at the man in the suit. There was pain in her voice. Adeline was still very dangerous.

"Mabuse…help me!" Adeline called out. But Mabuse was gone.

Adeline stood up, spinning around, now holding her eyes with one hand, and a flashing glyph in another. Ying and David, the thief crew were circling around as the man in the suit approached from the front, all in different directions. Sophie didn't like Adeline, but she was starting to feel sorry for her. Adeline was her enemy, but they had one thing in common, they were both mages in a world where being a mage was often dangerous.

"Listen to my voice. Adeline. Listen to my voice. Mabuse is gone. He doesn't control you." The man in the suit said to her, in a low controlled tone. The emotions in his voice, he was trying to reach her, almost pleading. His words carried compassion.

"Your voice." Adeline was quiet for a minute and seemed to be standing still.

"Yes, this voice," The man said.

"…papa?" Adeline said, quietly.

Everyone standing around went quiet, watching.

Sophie immediately realised what was going on. She looked at the man in the suit. It was the man they had rescued from

Adeline's *Unter Kathedrale*. He had been a shocking sight, when they found him, dirty, muck through his hair, a gibbering mess. At the time, he didn't say anything that made sense, and they had no idea who he was. But he had obviously been captured and held there with Adeline and her mother, by Mabuse.

Professor Marcus had taken the man away to look after him. Now, cleaned up, in a suit, his hair cut shorter and two shades lighter, he looked nothing like the mistreated traumatised prisoner they had rescued. He seemed entirely healthy now. That man was Adeline's father all along.

He ran to her and grabbed her, hugging her tight. Sophie held her breath, the glyph still glowed in her hand. Adeline paused, and then hesitantly her hand and the glyph dropped. Her other hand reached up and slowly hugged him back, the expression on her face an intense frown. Sophie realised, they had spent all this time fighting against Adeline, but clearly, Mabuse was their true enemy.

Her papa hugged her, and they locked together like statues. He started quietly sobbing.

Sophie couldn't help feeling guilty about blinding her. She knew Adeline had in fact been about to cast it on her, so she had prevented someone else from being hurt. She couldn't imagine what was going through poor Adeline's father's head. But he was hugging her tight, emotional, but clearly glad to have her back. It seemed; he was getting his daughter back from the control of Mabuse. They had witnessed Adeline's mother's death, so there was only the two of them now.

Oskar came over, put his hands over her eyes, trying to heal her, but shook his head.

"Dudes, I've used most of my mana on Harlan." He had a backpack and pulled white rolls of bandages out of it and started wrapping bandages around her eyes. "She's been *blinded*, not sure... If I can heal her anyway." There was a sadness in his voice.

Sophie took a step back, her hand went involuntarily up, touching her jaw.

Tomoko came over, looked at her and then, like she was realising something important, let out a loud, "OH!" and spun on her foot, going over to Harlan. Sophie could see Tomoko and Harlan talking, animatedly.

"NO," Harlan yelled. "I NEED THEM. You can't," Harlan called out, still weak.

Tomoko walked back over, and Sophie looked down. Tomoko had Harlan's glasses of true sight with her. She put her hand on Adeline's head, keeping it still, and then placed the glasses gently on face, moving them up the bridge of her nose.

"Adeline, please do tell me if you can see anything." Tomoko helped her with them, placing Adeline's hands on them so she could put them over her eyes properly. Tomoko nodded reassuringly to Adeline's father, who nodded back.

There was an instant reaction from Adeline, her eyes were bandaged, the glasses were over the bandages, but her head was swivelling this way and that.

"Papa. I can see now. Papa. I can see." Her hand came up to the glasses, adjusting them on to her face, and she moved the bandages up the bridge of her nose, still covering her eyes, but so she could breathe better through her nose. She raised the glasses, and then lowered them a number of times.

"I can see with these glasses."

"You use them until you can see again. It's the least we can do," Tomoko said.

Harlan walked over, helped by Raphaella. "My glasses of true sight…"

"She's blind without them. Harlan," Sophie said. She rubbed him on the arm, consoling. She knew the glasses meant a lot to him.

"But… they…" And he was quiet. Sophie realised the sacrifice he was making. As a thief, they were the only bit of magic he had, apart from being able to change his appearance.

***

Oskar spent some time with Harlan. It was clear from Harlan's face, the red pinking glow emanating from Oskar's healing hands was providing instant relief. Sophie looked on as he then healed a lighter wound on Harlan's leg.

Raffaella had wiped the tears from her eyes, even with Harlan better or their victory. She was now her impassive self again, with a hint of tranquillity about her. She knelt next to Harlan, not leaving his side.

They all started walking back from the forest road to the bridge, Raffaella and Sophie helping Harlan. Harlan groaned, and looked over to Sophie, "Yeah, uhm, when are we getting our own healer?"

Sophie looked at her clothes, checking for wounds. "Future human resource re-alignment project."

"They are refreshingly convenient. I vote too for a Circle 66 party healer. Wherever…they come from." Tomoko.

"I know a slightly dodgy geezer who may hook you up with one. Leave it to me." Jeff adjusted his sunglasses and gave them all a thumbs up. Sophie noted Jeff seemed pretty cheery about the whole thing.

***

Tomoko was walking among the minotaurs, pulling her arrows out, which required two hands and a bit of back work. Harlan was limping around, retrieving his throwing knives, trying not to step on messy dead minotaur, or break Tomoko's arrows sticking out of them.

"Yeah, err, Tomoko…Erhh…. I would write those off if I were you. Not sure they're fit to be used again."

Tomoko kept pulling them out, examining them, a grimace on her face. "They are expensive." She held it up in Harlan's direction so he could see, and he glanced at it. She examined another one, snarling in disgust as she pulled it and shook off the Minotaur goop, then laughed as it flew through the air. "I can fix most of them. I think."

Part of the group was sitting on the ground, trying to catch their breath, staring at the mess around them. Sophie noticed there were some smiles shared between the two groups, and some friendly banter. Seeing them get on, finally, made it feel like an extra success. Sophie walked over to Ying and Hans, who were leaning on Jeff's little Fiat car, staring out across the bridge, into the distance.

"You two. I wanted to say thank you for coming to look for me…and saving us all."

Hans looked a bit awkward, "Well you know. You're a mage like us. We need to stick together."

Ying smiled. "Yeah, the least we can do."

Harlan called out from where he was on the bridge. "Sophie. Don't thank them. I paid them 5000 gold."

"HE PAID YOU!" Sophie's head shook, frowning at Ying and Hans. *Is money all these guys think about?*

Hans and Ying Shrugged. "Well… we gave Harlan a 20% discount. Because we like you."

Sophie rolled her eyes, her hands on her hips. "Thanks…"

Harlan, Raffaella and Tomoko all walked over to Sophie, Harlan still limping. They both paused.

"I can tell something is up with you two. You've been talking about something together' Sophie said.

"You are highly observant, Sophie," Tomoko said.

"Okay, what's up?"

"We want to ask Oskar to join our group. To join Circle 66."

Sophie thought about it. It was logical to have a healer in a group that did what they did. Clearly everyone else was keen. Sophie could think of no reason not too, Oskar was a super nice guy and really had a good attitude to things. She'd love to have him around.

"You realise this means we split five ways."

Sophie could see Harlan involuntarily wince, but he said nothing. They all nodded.

Looking around, they could see Oskar talking to Ying and Hans (who was holding an injured arm), from the smiles on the faces, it was a friendly conversation, and from the mimicked blows and spell throwing, it was a re-enactment of the battle's heroics. Heloise had apparently already got bored and put her headphones on, vaguely dancing while pretending to listen.

As they walked over, they all turned.

Oskar in particular beamed at them, smiling from ear to ear.

"Okay. Oskar, we have something to ask you. Do you want to join Circle 66? We need a healer, and you are a fantastic fit." Ying's face grew cold.

"Oh nice, good to see a professional rivalry blossoming." He rolled his eyes, crossing his arms.

"Err, sorry, Ying. Hans." she shook her head.

Oskar's head jerked back in surprise, a quick frown turned to a half smile, then his hands went to his hips as he regarded the four. He paused, considering his answer.

"Actually." His hand went to the back of his neck, as he rubbed it, glancing between the two groups. "I was going to form my own crew; with someone you guys don't know and someone you do."

"Oh?" Sophie said.

"Yes." He waved at Heloisa; she came over to stand next to him.

"HELOISA?" Ying screamed. Her eyes widened in horror as she realised her fighter was being poached.

"You know Ying, if you weren't so obsessed with money, you wouldn't be losing so many people and..." Sophie started calling out to Ying, Harlan put his hand over Sophie's mouth, as Ying launched a torrid stream of objection at Oskar, who started shrugging and shaking his head. Heloisa put her headphones back on and started dancing, twirling around, oblivious to the abuse that thickly filled the air.

Harlan, Raphaella, Tomoko, and Sophie all backed away carefully, leaving them to it.

***

Jeff shook the icky remains of Minotaur off his shovel, then put it into the boot of his little car, it fitting with difficulty. He then turned to address everyone, running his hands through his hair, "Kids, I think it may be time to go you know. Before a whole lot of people start turning up and asking about magic."

"What happened to Lutz? You said he was Lutz, the minotaur shapeshifter?" Tomoko said.

"Yes, Lutz. I don't know, last I saw him he was at the farmhouse. I think just leave him; we need to focus on the vote now," Sophie said.

Harlan surveyed the mess, broken corpses, arrows, the large tree a golem had effortlessly tossed into the melee, now lying on its side on the bridge, part of its roots reaching oddly towards the sky. He tried to help Raffaella fix her scooter, but she shook her head, batting away his hand.

"Can everyone ride?" Sophie asked.

Raffaella glanced around. "Yes, thanks to Oskar. Scooter is damaged, but she is working."

Tomoko scanned the prone bodies of the minotaurs spread about the bridge. "What about all this?"

Sophie put her Helmet on and then her goggles and pulled her scarf up over the bottom part of her face. "The People from Bamberg can clean this up. They'd be dealing with worse if we hadn't been here."

The four got on their scooters. They watched Adeline's papa scoop her up and put her in his car, and drive away, not saying anything to anyone. She wasn't sure if he was ungrateful or still in shock at all that had happened. They then followed Jeff, Hans, Ying, and the others into town. The wind came in out of the valley, twisting and playing with the tops of the pine trees, and made Sophie's scarf flutter, almost like a little victory flag.

All four were smiling.

It was a good day for Circle 66, Three Bells Incorporated... and Jeff with his shovel.

37. Jeff's Debriefing and Donuts

In what was left of the week they urgently waited for the new poll information, surveying the changes for all the items of the referendum, including the most important one, the magic ban.

Saturday came soon. They had put a lot on releasing Ying's footage of the meeting widely to the press. It was the culmination of all their work. They had sent it to everyone and thrown it on YouTube. It should have showed that the process of the vote was being managed by outside forces, and the main party behind it was under control of a foreign political party and criminals. It should have been completely incriminating.

It was, but it seemed not enough.

The polling percentages had come down, but were now at 58% *for* the magic ban, to 42% against.

Everyone was worried.

At this point, there was no time left. The people of Bavaria would be heading out to vote on Sunday. Tomorrow.

Sophie realised how stressed she had been about everything, and the events at the bridge. She slept till 3pm.

Hisako and her Papa had rapped on the door many times, for breakfast then lunch.

She mumbled something about coming out soon… and didn't.

Finally waking up, she checked her phone, there was about ten messages from the Circle 66 crew.

They all said they were meeting at Jeff's for a debrief, and to work out what they could do with the imminent vote.

Sophie was all out of ideas.

She checked her phone, to look at the news. The news reported the polling, where the media asked people how they thought they would vote. It was closer than before, but it looked like it wasn't enough.

It was too late. May be a final last group brainstorm effort at Jeff's, someone may think of something. But Sophie had a dark feeling she was looking at a Bamberg where magic was banned, and they would force her to leave. She looked sadly at the bags on top of her cupboard. The bags she used to drag around with her papa when he switched jobs every year. The bags she had put away, assuming she would not be packing them to switch cities or countries ever again.

She felt the moistness of tears welling up in her eyes. She wiped them away with the back of her hand. Crying wouldn't help.

***

Getting to Jeff's was easy, there weren't any people around.

The Police were there out the front as per usual; two brawny, slightly bored guys who seemed to be the ones most often standing out the front of Jeff's regularly, stood there. She went around the back door and looked at it.

No *glyph of warding*, there was only one on the front door. The problem of learning magic via the dreamcast, there were sometimes little things you forgot to ask in session, and by the next dreamcast session, you would forget to ask them. Of course, she realised now, this was how Mabuse got in. She didn't exactly know how they functioned, she never seen them affect anyone, all she knew was that Johannes said they would reject anyone with ill intent. Mabuse had to enter through the back door, so they must have worked.

Her hands quickly traced the glyph in the air and put it above the door. Too late now, but anyway. Both doors to Jeff's covered, she felt a bit more secure.

She walked in and took the stairs. She was excited to see the crew after their defeat of the minotaurs and dealing with Adeline. But still dreading the vote. She thought of moving, leaving her school, friends. Her father finding out. It was a disastrous scenario.

But the minotaurs. It was important to celebrate small victories.

She sat down with Harlan, Raphaella, and Tomoko, and started chatting, there was a scream from downstairs, and a broken window. Sophie's sense stood on edge. The sound of breaking glass, and a scream was never good.

"I've only just got here, now what?" Sophie said. At least she felt revived after sleeping most of the day.

"It's the police," she heard Jeff call out from downstairs.

Sophie skipped every second stair as she sprinted down them, getting to the bottom level first to see what was happening. She looked out the window.

"Yeah, okay, what? The police are lying on the ground." Sophie initially couldn't see, but as Harlan said, the Four police that had previously been standing out the front of the café, were now lying prone on the ground. Not moving.

She heard the noise of footsteps come down the stairs, and Tomoko and Raffaella appeared next to her.

"Are they okay?" Tomoko said.

"Dead, probably. Without honour," Raffaella said.

Sophie was silent. She didn't know if they were unconscious, or dead. She tried to peer out the window but couldn't see what had done this. There were no people out on the street.

She moved into the window frame, so she get a better view of the street. There was a sharp intake of air from Tomoko, and she felt Tomoko grab her arm. Sophie glanced up, and to the right.

Standing out the front of Jeff's, was the two and a half metre tall demon. It was breathing heavily. It stared straight at her as she looked at it.

Like it recognised her.

38. The Battle for Jeff's.

Sophie stepped back from the window in shock, but as she moved back, she felt someone brush past her. Raffaella had pulled her hoody up, was putting her goggles on and raced over to the kitchen.

Sophie took a second to realise she would have to do magic, and there couldn't be witnesses or video of her doing it. So, she pulled the scarf she normally wore while riding up over the bottom of her face. She realised she almost feared the premise of the world finding out she was a mage, more than a demon.

Raffaella looked around. "Swords are in my duffle bag, on my Vespa." She stood on the head of a broom, wrenched the head off quickly, and picked up the biggest pot she could find.

Harlan looked around, "I don't have any of my knives here." He ran to the kitchen and Sophie could hear the clink of steel as he grabbed whatever knives he could find.

Jeff stopped him. "Hey those are Swiss made. Too expensive. Take these ones."

"We have to use magic," Sophie called. "Is this going to work? Can we take him?"

"Let's take it down," Raffaella cried.

The three went slowly out of the front of Jeff's. Harlan ran out the back to climb the roof. Jeff stayed inside, trying to get in a good spot to record what was going on with his phone.

As soon as they appeared, the demon roared and charged straight for them.

Raffaella ducked and hit it with the pot, then smacked it with the broomstick. It barely seemed to phase it and gave her a backswing. She flew and hit the wall, then slid down it prone.

Sophie peered at her worryingly. Raffaella laid there, not moving.

Sophie's hand quickly drew the glyph for sleep and commanded the spell. The blue pulse hammered into the demon, it shook its head momentarily and kept walking forward.

"My turn." Tomoko ran straight at it, her hands raised above her, powering up a glyph.

The demon took a step forward and grabbed both her hands at the wrist. Sophie watched as Tomoko's expression turn to frustration and then horror, as she realised, she couldn't cast the spell.

Sophie was horrified as the demon tossed Tomoko through the air and she knocked over a scooter.

There was a sharp clink of metal on the ground, then a slight thud as something hit the demon. It clawed at its own head, pulling out what looked like a long metal object. As it took it out, another stuck in.

Sophie couldn't make sense of what was going on, until she peered up at the building.

Harlan was on the roof, throwing knives. She felt vague chagrin he was in a safe spot, but it was distracting the demon. It started moving around, and the knives kept coming, mostly missing.

Suddenly, there was a loud yelling sound. Sophie glanced over and could see Raphaella, now standing on her feet, looking down at Tomoko lying on top of a slightly dented scooter.

"MY SCOOTER!!!"

In what seemed like a motion too fast for a normal human, in one practiced movement, Raffaella lowered her arm and scooped up two things off the ground. She spun around, lowering her body, and as she did, she hefted the object in her hand and threw it.

The sword flung through the air, majestically, and stopped with a shudder, sticking into the shoulder of the demon.

The demon screamed, its head roaring back, holding its arm.

Raffaella picked up one of her swords from the ground, and in three long steps and a final jump, Raffaella landed on two feet, went to her knees, and swung at its leg. It went down on one knee, but swung its claws out at Raphaella, who dodged to the left and then to the right.

In a moment of clarity, in all the confusion, Sophie realised this was her chance. It was looking at Raphaella, and she was close.

She cast the lightning bolt spell, with both hands above her head, and rammed her hands, with the spell straight at its face at point blank range.

The spell exploded, the demon held his face screaming, trying to stand.

Sophie could see Raffaella moving in for a final attack. "Raph, NOOO!!!"

But it was too late. Raffaella swung her sword up from the ground, low, then lunged forward low to the ground. She pushed the sword up from her low position, plunging it straight up into its stomach.

The creature stood in shock, staring at Raphaella. Raffaella gritted her teeth and pushed the sword up even more. There was a huge shriek from the creature. It clawed at the sword, as if trying to pull it away.

Raphaella, let go of the sword, tumbled backwards expertly, flipping back up onto her feet out of range of the demon. She stood poised on the balls of her feet, ready to move, but looking intently at the demon.

"Lutz!" Sophie called out to it. She didn't know why she did. She knew it was him. But it was all too late.

The demon moved around again, stumbling. Sophie winced and stepped back, as it let out a blood curdling scream. It fell to one knee, then another knee, then toppled forward, collapsing on the cobblestoned street out the front of the café. They all stood there breathing, gazing at it as it lay prone, now lifeless.

Raffaella turned to Sophie. "You said *no*, did you not want me to…"

Sophie shook her head, she was relieved, but there was an element of sadness to it all. She was sure the demon was a transmuted Lutz, who she knew was possibly not in a right frame of mind. He was seemingly obsessed with some desperate bid to create more of his own kind.

But it was done.

"Never mind. You did the right thing, Raph."

Jeff ran out holding his shovel, stared at the body, screamed, and went back inside. Sophie scanned the chaos around her. The police were starting to stir, two of them getting to their feet despite their attitude to mages, she felt a feeling of relief as they rose Then she remembered Tomoko. With a gasp of horror, she ran over to her, hand over mouth. However, Tomoko was already getting up holding her head, an expression of slight confusion.

"Tomoko, you okay?" Sophie gave her a hug.

Raphaella, came over, checked Tomoko's body for damage, and then went to care for her scooter. Harland appeared too, immediately running to Raphaella. She turned to him, and he hugged her, relief evident on his face.

"I'm glad you are okay," he said to her. Sophie felt the honest emotion in his voice.

"I am...not... a... hugger." Sophie could hear her Raffaella say quietly, but she could see the thinnest of smiles on her face.

There were gasps from the crowd. Some of the policemen were standing up, Jeff and the two big Bambergian ladies and people from the neighbouring buildings were clumped around the demon, its large, misshapen form still prone on the ground.

It started to blur. Its shape shifted. They all went over to see.

"Dayum, that's freaky," Harlan said, stepping back a bit. The entire crowd took his cue and stepped back a step or two.

The body lie prone, but the shimmering almost made it appear to be like it was moving, shaking...alive. It shifted, a flow of form, until the Demon shape changed, and then it morphed into the shape of a large man. Sophie peered down at his face. As she expected, it was Lutz, the man that had been at the New Nation headquarters, and the same man that had been in the alleyway, with the child, when they had chased the demon from the Krampus Nacht festival. The man that had captured her.

"Lutz" Sophie said. She glanced over at Harlan, who looked back at her, nodding in confirmation.

As it changed, there were gasps of horror from the crowd. Even the police looked shocked.

But it still shimmered and was starting to change again.

This time the shimmer went dark, the body enlarged, shiny purple-black skin, the head enlarged, two horns appeared.

It was a minotaur. The change to another monster frightened the crowd, and they all took another step back.

Sirens wailed in the background, and there was the screech of brakes.

A policeman, who had been lying on the ground, came over to them. He had a nasty bruise along his jawline, going up the side of his face. He put his cap on, instantly looking more official.

He peered at Sophie, then Raphaella, pointing at them. Thoughts of jail ran through Sophie's mind.

"You two…" He paused and took in a deep breath. "Thank you." He nodded at both of them and went to help one of his men get into the ambulance.

"Oh no. Oh." Tomoko was pointing at something up on the wall.

Harlan too stopped to gaze at it. "Err. Yeah, not good."

Sophie turned to see what they were staring at. There on the wall, apparently recently installed, because Sophie had never seen it before, was a red camera. Facing directly at where they had been standing. Directly at her, with her face in full view.

"Hell. I'm in so much trouble." Sophie put her hands in her pockets.

39 A Referendum in Bamberg

It was Sunday. The day of the referendum vote.

Sophie leant against a table, trying to relax, but if felt impossible. They packed the Greek Cypriot Monarchist's café with about 50 cervitaurs to watch the broadcast of the vote together. For the first time she noticed a number of Fae there, and a few humans who could dreamscape.

The mood amongst *Circle 66* was odd. There was relief that Adeline was now away from Mabuse, and with her Papa...though Harlan was still sore about the loss of his glasses of

true sight.

The only way he could see magic.

There was also a sense of relief that they had dealt with the demon-turned-Minotaur. But Sophie herself felt an odd sadness about the death of the minotaur, who's only real motivation was to use magic to conjure up more of his own. She still didn't understand how it all worked, and he had sent all the Minotaurs towards Bamberg so clearly, he was bad. But to be the only one, or the last remaining of your people? She wondered if they could have helped him somehow? But that wasn't how it turned out.

Sophie so far had managed to avoid being on the red cameras, as far as she knew. But now she had a certain feeling the cameras had recorded her. And a video file was probably going to find its way to her father.

The vibe in the room was sombre as well. The cervitaurs, were all glued to a big TV screen on the wall. Sophie hadn't seen so many of them in one spot since the big battle which saw the defeat of Adeline, a year ago now. Sophie was trying not to let her anxiety get the best of her. Thoughts of what would happen if magic were banned, and a future of her not doing magic, or fleeing Bamberg kept creeping into her mind. She chased them out. She needed to remain calm for the moment.

There was the odd comment from the crowd here and there, but mostly they were quiet, as they tried to listen to the TV. The Cervitaur barista, with a slightly dirty white apron and big brown horns, pointed the remote at the screen, and the volume was turned up to nearly full so the whole room could hear.

Normally the referendums were mundane, but this one was a major deal, there was huge buzz in Bamberg, and the whole town was probably watching. Given the publicity of the events at the bridge, the demon at Jeff's, the vote on the ban on magic, and all sneaky fearmongering promotion and activity the Hansa had done, it was the biggest referendum there had been for a long time.

The newscaster's tone of voice changed, and he switched from the more mundane chit chat to a more neutral, professional tone, signalling he had got the results of the referendum in his hand. Sophie desperately studied his expression, trying to read whether his expression was one of surprise or disappointment, but he was stony faced. What few Cervitaurs were still talking were shushed into quiet.

Sophie felt Harlan's hand softly on her shoulder, then another hand touching her arm, the grip tight. She glanced over and saw Tomoko's hand on her arm. Tomoko glanced at her, then back at the screen, a brave veneer on her face, clearly covering fear beneath. Raphaella's arm was draped over Harlan's shoulder, and his other arm over hers.

"All the polling stations from throughout Bavaria are now in. I will now read out the results from this year's referendum. First result, Taxis in Bavaria will now all be mandated by law to be painted the colour yellow."

There was a roar of exasperation from the crowd, with a few odd laughs.

"What? Who cares about the stupid taxis?" Harlan said.

A big cervitaur next to him grumbled. "Hey. I drive a Taxi. I like yellow." Another Cervitaur next them in a red vest shushed them and both turned back to the screen.

"The installation of public toilets that play classical music, with heated toilet seats and doors that open automatically after three minutes has also passed. The third referendum item, Bavaria has voted for has also passed. Tax collection is to continue in June, instead of July."

The frustration of hearing these other items was driving Sophie crazy. She felt her head warm, the feeling she gets when she was about to break into a sweat. Her neck started to get hot, she wanted the TV host to get to the point. She tried to focus, but her anxiety was getting the better of her. She felt the waves of anxiety bubbling up inside her like boiling water. She tried to calm herself, thinking good thoughts of calm oceans.

She peered over at Tomoko. Tomoko glanced back at her quietly.

"Gambatte," she said. *Good Luck.*

The newsreader continued. Sophie noticed how he didn't seem phased by it all. Most probably *his life* wasn't affected by any of these things. Sophie wished she could be as oblivious and unaffected by it all as he was.

"And now for probably the most important item for *Bavaria Votes* today. The introduction of new anti-magic laws...." He read the information to himself and smiled.

"Without further delay, here are the results." He paused.

"It's very close. 51% to 49%. *Magic in Bamberg will be banned.*"

The words took a while to sink in.

Banned.

Sophie felt her knees feel weak and she looked for a chair to sit in. She slumped down into it. She felt a hand on her shoulder. It was Tomoko, who promptly burst into tears. Sophie reached out and held her hand.

"They can't do this!" Harlan came over. The room was full of people calling out, Jeering. Angry. The occasional scream.

Raffaella came over and put her arm around Tomoko. Harlan being taller than both, leaned over and gave them both a hug. Tomoko started sobbing into Harlan's shoulder.

Sophie noticed a figure looming over her in her peripheral vision, to her left. She was expecting to see a Cervitaur, but it was Rupert.

"Rupert, where did you come from?" Sophie realised she was relieved to see Rupert. She needed someone there to support, to hopefully say it will be okay. It was all too awful.

"Sophie, it looks bad, but there may be hope." Rupert pointed to the screen.

The newscaster kept reading. "And now for the final item, the Bamberg specific item."

The narrator sounded almost bored. For a second, Sophie noticed a look of surprise on his face, he took a few seconds to regain his composure. It surprised her to see him break, even momentarily. With some angry shushing and calls for quiet, the whole of the room went silent again.

"Well, this is…a surprise. The long running referendum item on Bamberg reverting to a Prince Bishopric has… *passed*. 65% to 45%." The newscaster was quiet, like he almost didn't believe it. He shook his head. "Ladies and gentlemen, this referendum item has been raised six times in the last 50 years and has never got more than 30% of the vote."

His hand went up to his earpiece. "I believe we will be crossing to Sebastian von Wittelsbach the…Errrh, Prince Bishop of Bamberg."

There was a momentary confused feed of a camera pointing to a wall, before the camera was repositioned, and there on the screen appeared Prince Sebastian. He seemed completely oblivious to the camera and was standing looking at his phone. Through all the bleakness of the events, Sophie chuckled at him. Another camera appeared. He still hadn't noticed.

"Is he playing *Gopher Fortress* on his phone?" Harlan said.

"Yes. Stupid game," Raffaella said.

Exactly at that point, a man in a suit moved into camera view and whispered something in Sebastian's ear, and he looked up in surprise, noticing the cameras, and confused.

The Prince-Bishop turned to the man and screamed, "What?"

The man leant in and spoke to him again. The look on Sebastian's face was even more surprised.

As Sophie watched the screen, a reporter moved into shot. Sebastian stood up, adjusting his jacket, and pulling down a sharp vest. He snapped into a proud and noble pose, evidently going into *nobility mode*. Immediately a microphone was shoved into his face, and others jutted forward, aimed at his face.

"Ahh, well this is a bit of a surprise, but I am of course happy that Bamberg is returning to its traditional status as an independent Prince-Bishopric. It's been *okay* being part of Bavaria, but we Bambergians deserve more than mediocrity."

"Oh...dang, nice burn," Harlan said, before he was shushed by everyone around him.

"Prince Bishop Sebastian...unh your majesty...if I could..."

"Sebastian is fine," he quickly retorted.

"Oh, Sebastian, if I could ask, what are your comments on the rest of the referendum."

There was a strange sort of quiet, that came across the room. It was like all the people around him froze for a second, waiting to hear what he would say.

Sebastian smiled, "Well, it is not for me to comment. Those changes are for Bavarians. We are no longer part of Bavaria. We won't be adopting them."

Sophie glanced over at Tomoko.

The whole room erupted.

People were cheering, things were thrown in the air. Sophie saw two Fae get up on tables, screaming in delight. Even Rupert lost his normally refined composure and got up on a table, pumping his fist into the air, grinning from ear to ear.

"No magic bans?" She looked up at Rupert.

He shook his head. "No, old girl...in Bavaria, but not here."

Magic was being banned in Bavaria. But Bamberg was splitting off from Bavaria, going its own way, and it was not banning magic. Sophie felt such a relief. Everyone else was jumping around cheering, but Sophie's knees felt weak. Her body was tense from all the stress, but she felt the anxiety lift from her shoulders. She immediately felt the need to sit down and collapsed into a chair. Tomoko came over, gripped her shoulder, and gave her an orange juice.

Sebastian was still speaking, and people were shushing the room to hear what he had to say.

"Do you have any comments on where the new Prince Bishopric will be heading?"

"The first thing I will do is get rid of those stupid invasive cameras. They stick into everyone's business. We don't need them. The Prince Bishopric will *not* be a police state." A slightly wicked smile appeared on his face, and an adviser stepped forward to whisper something in his ear.

The prince ignored him, continuing, "In fact, I would encourage everyone in Bamberg to go out on the street and smash those cameras! Smash them wherever you see them! It will save us a lot of money taking them down."

The adviser appeared to be waving his hands, and frantically shaking his head at the prince, who blanked him. In any case, it was too late.

There was a collective roar of approval from the room, and a wave of blue shimmers flicked around the room, as the Cervitaurs and Fae changed back into their human form and rushed out the door to get out. Sophie followed the crowd out, as they cheered and ran to the nearest camera, mounted high on a wall. A broom appeared among the crowd, whacking at it ineffectively. Then a chair held by one of the taller people, lashed at it, but it was too tall. A cervitaur climbed on the back of another and managed to reach it. He hung on it until something snapped and it came off. He tossed it into the crowd.

The crowd cheered.

A Cervitaur grabbed it and held it above them, like a trophy. The crowd erupted into another cheer.

They went down further into Bamberg. It wasn't just the cervitaurs. People were piling out of their houses with brooms, shovels, rope, all evidently after watching the prince. Young teenagers seemed to be enjoying themselves, but Sophie noticed all sorts, men, women, a grocer smashing one pointed directly at his shop. Angry camera lynch mobs roamed the streets, looking for their one-eyed electronic overseers.

Sophie noticed the police standing, looking at it all. Some of them were protecting the old dull grey traffic cameras, but people were mainly leaving traffic cameras alone and only attacking the new dark red surveillance cameras. She wondered what the police personally thought, possibly they thought there was too many people. They stopped people from ending up on the road, and warned people about being too aggressive, which people apologised for, but the police weren't stopping anyone destroying the scarlet surveillance systems.

To Sophie, the cameras felt like the Hansa itself, watching them. It was a removal of a layer of Hansa involvement in Bamberg. She was relieved and happy.

As they walked back to the Greek Café, Sophie looked down a deserted laneway and spotted a disguised camera, high covered by a tree branch.

"Wait a bit, guys."

She sprinted down the laneway and looked around to make sure no one was around. Powering up a spell, the mana pulsed in her hands, she flicked the symbol for firebolt in her the air. It flew straight to the camera, hitting it directly. A small explosion, and it fell to the ground.

She picked it up, and ran back to the others, waving it above her head. They all cheered.

At that point, she looked back and could see that Raffaella and Harlan had dropped back and were chatting to each other. They were all friends, but something in her told her not to look, and to give them privacy.

***

Harlan walked along, and obviously noticed Raffaella was slowing down, she seemed to be taking her time walking, she was looking around, people were laughing. They both ducked at a camera that was tossed up in the air, a cable flapping around it frenetically like a dead metal box creature and its tail.

Raffaella was quiet, but he was used to it. He knew he spoke a lot, and she didn't speak much, but he didn't mind.

"Harlan, can I tell you something?"

"Yeah? Sure…errr go ahead."

"I like you."

He shrugged. "I like you too."

"No, I mean…" She stopped and put her hands on his waist. A surprised expression came across his face. For Raffaella, this was odd.

"If I kissed you now, what would you do?"

"Well, I'd…I'm… errr."

Raffaella shook her head in frustration and leaned in and kissed him once on his lips.

He stood, just peering at her. Her hand went up to his long hair, and she ran her fingers through it. Harlan kissed her back. It was wonderful.

There was sudden clapping and loud shrieks. Harlan peeked over the top of Raphaella's long black hair.

In front of them were Tylltyr, Akshay, Sophie, and Tomoko. All of them clapping and cheering.

"Well, that was unexpected," Sophie said.

Tylltyr smiled, shaking her head. "You lot. Harlan, I could tell she liked you a week ago. YOU ARE HOPELESS!"

"I think this is the first dreamscape couple." Sophie nodded, beaming.

"Omedeto!" Tomoko called out, clapping excitedly.

Sophie noticed Rupert up ahead, his face concerned, scanning the crowd. He spotted her, looked relieved and trotted over. Sophie could see he was going to reprimand her, but then bit his tongue and probably thought better of it. Instead, held out his hand. Sophie shook it stiffly and formally, congratulating him.

"Marvellous work, old girl. Spiffy. You, my daughter has a distinctive insight into questionable ways of humankind. And so, we are here." He waved his hands around at the general scene.

They went back into The Cervitaur café, where Cerviaturs were reappearing, the flash of blue magic revealing their true selves.

They grabbed a table and sat at it, Akshay had told them to have whatever they wanted, free. The decapitated security camera sat in the middle of the little round table, a proud hunting trophy. Cervitaurs constantly came over to take selfies with them, and asked if they could head butt the camera, which progressively became more damaged as the night went on. There was a steady flow of pastries and coffees, purchased by Cervitaurs, even though they were free anyway. Soon they couldn't eat any more.

Sophie finally headed home, and her head hit the pillow,

grinning ear to ear.

41 Visit to a Prince

After three days, Thursday came around and things had died down. School had finished and it was time to pick up the last payment from the prince. Sophie checked in on her papa and Hisako who in the frenzied activity of the last two days, she'd barely seen. Her papa was unhappy the magic law wasn't passed, but Hisako gave Sophie a sneaky smile.

She thought about the prince on the way to see him. She wondered if he would be different now; he would be overseeing the greater Principality of Bamberg.

Overall, it seemed like with him in charge, things would be better, and Rupert had said as much. The prince liked them, and Sophie like him because, most of all, he saw mages as normal real people, and wasn't afraid of them.

Now that he appeared to be *the* actual ruling Prince of Bamberg as an independent principality, Sophie was wondering if he had time to see them. She assumed he would have been super busy with his new role, but he had arranged to meet them at his office at the university.

They parked their scooters, and as they got off, Sophie realised there was no impending need for mages to leave Bamberg, which meant Tomoko could stay. But she had been offered to go to Japan with her Sensei. Sophie immediately had a pang of concern, as far as she knew, Tomoko was still going. She knew it was selfish, but she didn't want her to.

"Tomoko?"

"Yes, Sophie."

"Are you still going to Japan?"

Tomoko studied Sophie's face and could see the concern. She responded with a big smile.

"Sophie, I was never going to Japan. I told Sensei the day after he offered."

Sophie glanced over at her, confused. "Why?"

"Because of you," she addressed Sophie, and then the others. "You... all. It's hard to find good friends. Well, hard for me."

Harlan gave her a hug, and Raffaella gave her a consoling pat on the shoulder.

"Anyway, sensei told me he can train me over the Internet, from Japan." Tomoko said.

"You... you can do that?" Sophie was surprised.

Tomoko shrugged. "Apparently. Sensei is pretty good at technology, for a 182-year-old Samurai."

As they headed to the grand old Hohenstall history faculty building, Sophie's phone rang. It was a phone number she didn't recognise. She hesitated but picked it up.

"Err Hello, who is this?" she cautiously asked.

"My name is Zha Aznovo, we met at the Grand Magistry Meeting... the European Mages Meeting."

It was Zha, Sophie thought. Her memory of his blond anime character hair instantly came to mind. She was immediately hesitant, but overall, she was in a good mood as most of the threats had gone. There didn't seem any harm in talking to him.

"I need to thank you for that job you did. I offered it to Mr. M, and he gave it to you."

The penny dropped. Zha was the man behind the mysterious email.

"Did you...?" Sophie started before he interrupted.

"I knew Mr. M wouldn't be able to do it, and I shaped the job and offered the right amount so he would probably give it to you. Most of all, I needed photos of the meeting from a neutral party, not connected to me or the Illusionists."

She was unsure about him, but she was curious. "Why?"

"I showed the photos were from you and sent them on to the important mages in the London Illusionists. When they saw the Livingstones were working with the Hansa to get Magic banned, and then those videos came out, they removed him from his office, and he has been banned from the Illusionist community."

None of Circle 66 liked the Livingstones so hearing this was good news, though Sophie didn't quite understand. "So, the Livingstones were working with the Hansa, to get rid of other mages?"

"Evidently, they were putting their own pride in front of their loyalty to mages. They saw the weakening of mages on the continent, giving them move power as they weren't likely to be affected. He seemed to dislike the dreamcast mages, as your spell knowledge was better than his," Zha explained.

`Sophie realised how this affected Zha. "Ah, and as you were Archmage, his number two... *you* are running the London Illusionists now?"

"Ah. Coincidentally, yes," Zha said, no particular emotion in his voice. Sophie realised it was clearly *not* a coincidence. He continued, "In any case, a quick thank you. Oh, also the smoke alarms."

"Hang on, Harlan told me about those," Sophie said.

"Yes, they are actually normal smoke alarms, there's nothing special about them. They were the method of getting either of the two thieves from either crew in the building, at the same time as I was discussing the plan, so one of them would overhear it. As it was, *both* overheard it. You would then hear of it, and know to go there and see the meeting, witness Livingstone there, and hopefully word would get out about it."

"Errr." It took Sophie a few seconds to work out what the whole plan had been. Zha had orchestrated the Livingstones to get involved with the plot, and then made sure Harlan or David would be a witness. And because the evidence about Livingstones involvement with the Hansa was from Circle 66, it came from an outside party, not him."

Sophie knew illusionists dealt with influence and politics, but a plan like this was a bit frightening. But, in this case, both they and Zha benefited.

"Anyway, thank you," he said.

"Auf Weider Sen, Zha. And thank you." She added less assuredly, "I think."

Sophie got off the phone, a little bit stunned. Raphaella, Harlan, and Tomoko, all looked at her curiously, only having heard half of the conversation. She filled them in on the rest as they walked to the prince's office. Essentially, it seemed like it could be the demise of the Livingstone's, and the apparent rise of Zha. No one was quite sure what to make of him, but he seemed a better option than the previous Grand Archmage.

When they got to the old Hohenstall, there were even more of the prince's traditional green jacketed crossbow guards, Sophie counted 20 of them. Most of them had lined their halberds and crossbows along the wall and were carrying some boxes of things out of his office and putting them in a van.

Sophie and Harlan tried to get in, but this time one who was not carrying boxes stood in their way, dropping a halberd to shoulder height in front of them.

"Oh, let them in Heinrich. It's my mages and their friends," the prince called out.

"Yeah, Soph, your mother is here," Harlan said, glancing at Sophie, and nodding at the room.

Sitting down on a couch was Rupert, Sophie had almost not noticed him.

"What are you doing here?" Sophie said, surprised.

"Oh, Royal household business. And yes. Hello, old girl, Harlan, Raffaella, and of course, the charming Tomoko."

"Charming?" Tomoko laughed unusually, Sophie not sure of whether she was pleased at the comment or not.

"Sit down, I believe I owe you something."

"Yes, 10,000 Goldmarks," Harlan said.

Sophie shuddered at his exacting confirmation of the amount. The prince reached under the table and plopped it in front of them. Harlan went to count it. Sophie, realising it would be bad form in front of a prince, shook her head at him subtly.

"So, Sebastian, how is it all going now with the new responsibilities?" Sophie asked.

"Well finishing up here and moving into the Prince Bishops *Alte Hofhaltung*. The old palace. The new one was turned into a library and tossing books out of windows and turfing librarians out on to the street is not a good way to start things." He smiled. "The old residence has definite charm. In any case, Bamberg will be a place where people are free to do what they want, no more surveillance cameras, and the Hansa have been told they can bugger off back home."

He pointed at Tomoko and Sophie. "And mages will be free to spell cast to their hearts content. Just don't burn any buildings…" He paused, considering. "…or people."

"We won't," Tomoko said, beaming.

The prince turned to Sophie. Sophie instantly sensed something important was coming.

"Sophie Wolf, so it seems, now that I have a court, I'm in need of a court mage."

He handed her a box. Sophie opened it. It was a box of business cards, she frowned, pulling out one to read it. She took a double take, they were cards printed with her name on them, and the prince had titled her *Royal Court Mage…* the same role as Rupert.

"How do you feel about this?" Rupert leaned forward. It was a strange question to ask, since he had already got the cards printed. Sophie read the card, turning it over. She did now know what the pay was, what it entailed, but she knew it was a step up and an opportunity to help.

"Oh, thanks…uhhm…yes?" Sophie beamed.

She handed a card to her friends, and the last one to Rupert. The recollection of when all this started a year ago, at the start of the dreamcasting, she remembered another Rupert had handed her his Royal Court Mage business card. So much had happened, she thought of herself back then, it was like she was thinking of a different person.

As she now handed her card to Rupert, it was like things had come full circle.

"Jolly good show, old girl. Seems like Court mages run in the family." Rupert smiled, and Sophie smiled back as well.

"Thanks…" She hesitated before speaking. "…Mamma."

Rupert studied her, quietly for a few seconds, and for once, instead of speaking or offering some sage advice, he said nothing, but grinned.

The End